Praise For Jim Nesk

The Best Lousy Choice: A.. __ __ __.. ~~. ~~ .. ~~~~~

"Ed Earl Burch is a terrific hard-boiled character - a beaten up, beleaguered, boozing ex-cop who also happens to be one helluva detective ... It's a tough world, but Burch is even tougher - an unorthodox lawman with a classic sense of justice who uses both his intelligence and brute force to beat the bad guys time and time again, no matter how badly the odds seemed to be stacked against him."
  – R.G. Belsky, author of the Clare Carlson mystery series

"If you like your mysteries hard-boiled, your characters rough and your dialogue tough (like I do), then not only is this the book for you, but it will have you running back to read the others in this series, and pretty much anything else by Jim Nesbitt."
  – Baron R. Birtcher, *Los Angeles Times* bestselling author of literary thrillers *Fistful of Rain* and *South California Purples*

"Take another plunge with Ed Earl Burch into the badlands of a tough, corrupt West Texas county where violence is a virtue and truth is hard to find ... Nesbitt's flair with believable dialogue and pounding action makes you want to know more — and Ed Earl delivers. A cashiered cop reluctantly turned private eye, Ed Earl knows this trip west of Dallas is no joy ride. This gun-slinging crime thriller plays for keeps. Buckle up, you'll like this."
  – John William Davis, author of *Rainy Street Stories* and *Around the Corner*

"West Texas is a harsh mistress. She'll snake-bite you, shoot you, stampede you. Or-plain-old burn you up inside your own barn. Jim Nesbitt brings these dangers and the beauty of this harsh land to life in *The Best Lousy Choice*, the third book in his series featuring private eye Ed Earl Burch. Burch is the perfect character for mystery readers seeking hardboiled stories, more bad guys than good and unrelenting action... Tough as those he faces, he is as interesting for his nightmares as he is for his sharp mind and sharper tongue when on the job. *The Best Lousy Choice* is a great choice for readers looking for a thriller filled with action, atmosphere and unforgettable characters."

– Rich Zahradnik, author of *Lights Out Summer,* winner of the 2018 Shamus Award for Best Paperback Private Eye Novel

"Ed Earl Burch is former Dallas cop with bad knees, an unhealthy attitude and a seemingly unquenchable thirst for guns, booze and women. If he were on the high seas, he'd be a pirate. But this book isn't about plunder. It's about survival....Will Burch survive another round against enormous odds? Time will tell. For Burch, and for us, *The Best Lousy Choice* is a bracing dose of the West as strong and smooth as a long pull of good whiskey before breakfast."

– Michael Ludden, author of *Alfredo's Luck* and *Tate Drawdy*

What Fellow Authors Say About Jim Nesbitt's *The Last Second Chance* and *The Right Wrong Number*

"If you're looking for gritty, *The Right Wrong Number* is as gritty as Number 36 sandpaper."

- Bill Crider, author of the Sheriff Dan Rhodes mysteries

"If Chandler's noir was a neon sign in the LA sunset, Nesbitt's noir is the Shiner Bock sign buzzing outside the last honky-tonk you'll hit before the long drive to the next one. On the way you'll pass towns with names like Crumley and Portis. Roll down the window; it's a hot night. It's a fast ride."

- James Lileks, author of *The Casablanca Tango*, columnist for the *National Review* and *Star Tribune* of Minneapolis, creator of LILEKS.com

"In *The Right Wrong Number*, Jim Nesbitt writes like an angel about devilish deals, bloody murder and nasty sex. His beat is Dallas — not the glitzy spires of J.R. Ewing, but the back alley bars and brothels of Jack Ruby and Candy Barr. His PI, Ed Earl Burch, is steeped in Coke-chased bourbon; cured in the smoke of Zippo-lit Luckies; and longing for hard-bitten girls who got away. Nesbitt channels the lyricism of James Crumley, the twisted kick of Jim Thompson and the cold, dark heart of Mickey Spillane."

- Jayne Loader, author of *Between Pictures* and *Wild America*, director of *The Atomic Café*

"In *The Last Second Chance*, Jim Nesbitt gives readers a splendid first opportunity to meet Ed Earl Burch, as flawed a Luckies-smoking, whiskey-drinking, serial-married hero as ever walked the scarred earth of Dirty Texas.... In Burch, Nesbitt has created a more angst-ridden and bad-ass version of Michael Connelly's Harry Bosch and a Tex-Mex landscape much meaner than the streets of L.A. Add hate-worthy lowlifes and a diminutive dame, Carla Sue Cantrell, who cracks wiser than the guys, and you've got a book with gumption."

- Bob Morris, Edgar finalist, author of *Baja Florida* and *A Deadly Silver Sea*

"If you like to read, if you appreciate words and the people who run them brilliantly through their paces, give Jim Nesbitt's *The Last Second Chance* a read. And his next one, and the one after that. You'll be enthralled, like I was."

- Cheryl Pellerin, author of *Trips: How Hallucinogens Work in Your Brain*

"Jim Nesbitt's latest hard-boiled Texas thriller is another masterpiece. *The Right Wrong Number* has everything to keep the reader turning the page — vivid characters, stark Texas landscape, non-stop action and a classic American anti-hero in Ed Earl Burch, Nesbitt's battered but dogged Dallas PI. Buckle up and brace yourself for another wild ride."

- Paul Finebaum, ESPN college football analyst, author, host of *The Paul Finebaum Show*

"Cowboy noir for the cartel era ... *The Last Second Chance* is a gripping read with a cathartic ending, and it takes you places you've likely never been."

- Jeannette Cooperman, author of *A Circumstance of Blood*

THE BEST
LOUSY CHOICE

An Ed Earl Burch Novel

Jim Nesbitt

Spotted Mule Press

THE BEST LOUSY CHOICE
An Ed Earl Burch Novel

Copyright © 2019 By Jim Nesbitt
Published by SPOTTED MULE PRESS

Paperback
ISBN 10: 0-9983294-2-8
ISBN 13: 978-0-9983294-2-0
E-Book
ISBN 10: 0-9983294-3-6
ISBN 13: 978-0-9983294-3-7

Cover photograph by Joel Ruiz Salcido
Used with exclusive permission.
Author photograph by Bill Swindell
Used with exclusive permission.
Cover design by SelfPubBookCovers.com/Island
Interior formatting and proofreading by Polgarus Studio

Jim Nesbitt Web site: https://jimnesbittbooks.com

Author's Note

I spent a lot of time knocking around the border between Texas and Mexico in the late 1980s and early 1990s, chasing stories as a roving correspondent for various news outfits and falling in love with the harsh, stark beauty of that land. What I heard, saw, smelled and felt forms the backbone of all three of my Ed Earl Burch novels — partly because I'm a firm believer in creating a keen sense of place, but mostly because the land is so evocative that it becomes a character unto itself. And while there is no Faver, Texas and Cuervo County is also a figment of my imagination, my descriptions of those fictitious places are rooted in what I saw in real towns like Sanderson, Marathon, Marfa, Alpine, Valentine and Fort Davis.

Writing a novel is both a lonely road and a collaborative effort and I'd like to thank the people who helped keep me on track, gave wise counsel, kicked me in the butt when needed and helped shape and polish the finished product. Special thanks to my editor, Cheryl Pellerin, a damn good writer in her own right who kept dogging me to publish my first two novels, and my old border running buddy, photographer Joel Ruiz Salcido, whose marvelous photo graces the cover.

Thanks and a tip o' the Resistol to my semi-irregular cadre of reviewers, fellow writers, beta readers and smart-ass buddies who didn't sugarcoat their opinions. The crew includes writers Dick Belsky,

Baron R. Birtcher, Rich Zahradnik, Kathryn Lane, John Davis, Carmen Amato, Mike Ludden, Robert Crawford and Owen Parr; and my nephew, Patrick Lee. Thanks also to Texas ace reviewer Kevin Tipple; my old friend, Richard Beene, the Czar of Bakersfield, who hosts a great radio talk show; North Carolina political operative Ray Martin, who is a graphics, marketing and social media wizard; and fellow whisky-slinger and history buff Stanley Hitchens, who ceaselessly touts my work to our high school pals.

Most of all, many thanks and much love to my wife, Pam, who believes in me even when I don't.

For Pam and The Panther

One

The rider felt a stab of pain somewhere deep above his left kidney, arcing like electrical current over his buttock and down the hamstring of his leg, causing his calf muscle to spasm against the top of a well-worn leather boot.

He gave a grunt that caused his breath to puff an icy cloud into the clear night cold as he shifted in the saddle to take the weight off his left leg and ease the searing sensation that held the threat of a full-blown cramp.

The horse was a thick-muscled claybank gelding, a long-legged ranch mount well trained in the subtle cues of a rider's commands with rein, leg and seat. Surprised by the sudden shift, the gelding pricked up his ears and lifted his head with a startled snort, jetting twin plumes of frozen breath from his nostrils, moving away from the pressure of the man's right knee and butt cheek.

The rider felt the horse rise underneath him in a crow hop toward the rocky edge of the trail, a barely seen boundary with nothing beyond but a free-fall into a black void. He checked the hop, gritting his teeth as he closed the door on the wayward move by pressing his left leg into the horse's flank while cueing him to move forward, not sideways, with reins and body.

He listened as stones kicked up by steel-shod hooves clattered over the steep slope below.

"Damn, Jughead — you almost took us over the high side. Woulda been the end of the both of us, old-timer."

He stroked the gelding's neck as he spoke and felt rather than saw the horse's ears pivot and turn, nervously searching for a sound or sign out there in the frozen night air. He kept speaking to the horse in low, soft tones, stroking the neck until he felt the ears quit turning and the body underneath him relax. He ignored the spasms that rippled across his left calf muscle and the bright blade of pain buried in his back.

He kept his hands and legs still as he shifted his gaze skyward to look at the pure wonder of stars glittering across a pitch-black dome, his lungs drinking in the cold night air as he felt the sweat caused by fear grow icy on his face. The spasms faded and the back pain dulled.

Slow and deliberate, he unzipped his tin-cloth overcoat and fished out a pack of Chesterfields, thumbing an unfiltered nail to his lip. He dug out a box of kitchen matches, picking out a single lucifer to light with a calloused thumb. His hands were shaky as he tried to cup the flame and a gust of night wind snuffed it out. He was steadier with a second match, leaning in to fire up the tobacco and get a dose of calming nicotine.

After a drag or two, he heard the gelding snuffle, picking up the scent of cigarette smoke, a familiar smell that signaled a rest stop on the trail. With the reins loose in his left hand, he eased back in the slick fork saddle, resting his right hand behind him on the high cantle as he slowly scanned the night, his eyes taking in more than the spectacular sky above, the stars unchallenged by moonlight or anything generated by the hand of man.

He looked at the black nothing of the valley below where he knew his pickup and horse trailer sat in deep darkness. Well away from the rough, caliche ranch road. Hidden in a thicket of brush, shin oak and ocotillo about a quarter mile from the bottom of the trail he and the gelding started climbing an hour after sunset. Hunting reflexes. He never liked to let anyone find out by chance where he was stalking muleys and antelope.

That went double on this night — he was hunting two-legged game. Hadn't done that since he was a young man at war. Had to now. No choice, even if it meant sticking his nose into a man-killer's business. Didn't know for certain, but he was riding up this ridge to find out, pushing himself to learn whether the rumors were true — blood kin doing a dirty deal on land that had been in his family for more than a century.

Damned stupid of him to forget the pouch of Levi Garrett in his coat pocket and light up a nail. Nothing he could do about it now except not repeat the mistake. He cussed himself, wanting to blame the slip on the sudden stab of pain in his back and nerves from the near wreck. Pain, nerves and old age.

But those weren't the real reasons. The truth: he was afraid of what he might find out. And angry at himself for being scared. For too long, he had ignored the outlaw side of his family, content to live a lie and tell himself that he wasn't tainted by their blood or their actions. Even though their money helped the family keep a strong grip on the land they loved.

No more. There might be men out there in the dark who would kill him if they knew he was up here, but he had to know. It was his land, his family. Damn if he'd let kin risk losing it all. He'd kill a cousin or two for that.

He eyed the jagged teeth of the ridgeline above, a gray-black line of sharp, bare rock, backlit by the stars. Those teeth gave the ridge its name — *Espinazo del Diablo.* The Devil's Backbone — it ran northeast to southwest for about fifteen miles, petering out to become a ragged jumble of arroyos and small hills about five miles north of the Rio Grande. Rider and horse were on the last, steep section of the long switchback trail that zigzagged up the western wall of the ridge, roughly 150 feet from the top.

He pulled back the sleeve of his overcoat to check the time, flipping his hand to reveal the luminous dial of a timeworn Hamilton strapped to the underside of his wrist. The watch was a part of him, worn since he was stamped a ninety-day wonder at Parris Island in 1943, handed a shavetail's single gold bar of rank and assigned to a rifle company in the Fourth Marine Division.

His time in hell had been short — two weeks in the fierce fighting on Saipan, wounded in the legs, back and chest by Jap shrapnel when his outfit was surrounded at Tanapag village during the largest *banzai* charge of the war, a last-ditch counterattack that battered but didn't break the American lines. His back still carried some of the jagged metal the sawbones couldn't dig out because it was too close to his spine — likely the cause of the pain that almost carried him and Jughead to their final reward.

Midnight. His eyes traced the steep grade of the trail ahead. Another half mile to the top, he guessed. He wanted to be on that ridgeline and tucked into a rocky vantage point in the next hour. He thought of a prime spot in the rocks above that offered a wide-angle view of the valley below and would keep him hidden from prying eyes.

With the reins still loose in his left hand, he trailed his right arm down and touched the stock of a Winchester 1886 lever-action in .45-70 Government, the bluing of the long octagonal barrel worn away by years in a saddle scabbard. Underneath his overcoat, a Colt Peacemaker rode his right hip, a single-action nestled in a double-loop Mexican holster. Handy for snakes and up-close varmints, four legs or two. Stranger or kin.

These were his grandfather's guns. On horseback at night in the backcountry, they gave him a steely comfort. Next best thing to having the old man riding the trail with him. Following the old ways and the old codes eased his mind and steadied him for the long and risky vigil ahead.

Thirty more minutes of slow climbing brought horse and rider to the top of the ridge. He dismounted with a grunt as he felt another stab of pain in his back. That sliver of Jap steel made him a picaresque if ancient Marine instead of just another old and worn-out rancher. But it bought him no freedom from being one of a rapidly dying breed.

Well, we'll see about that, by God. Plenty of livin' left to do. And plenty of watching to do through the dark, small hours of a new morning. Maybe some killin' at the end of this trail.

He led Jughead north along the ridgeline, careful to stay a few yards down the reverse slope so they wouldn't silhouette themselves against the star-splashed night sky. He found the vantage point he was looking for — a rock ledge halfway up one of the toothy peaks. At the base of the peak was a cupped and rocky alcove of flat, hard ground that offered concealment and shelter from the knife-sharp wind.

He guided the claybank into this windbreak, dropped the reins and pulled hobbles from the near saddlebag to wrap around the forelegs. A short snack of molasses-covered oats was partial payment for the tough climb. A long lead rope clipped to the halter and tied to a clump of mesquite brush bought a bit of extra insurance for the hobbles.

He stroked the gelding's neck and smoothed his mane, talking low and slow as he loosened the latigo strap on the girth a notch or two.

"We been through some times, you and me, ain't we, old-timer? Rock solid is what you are, boy. Damn near bomb proof. Need you to stay that way right here for an hour or three. Need to see what we can see. Then we can get our sorry old asses back to the ranch. Hay and oats laced with molasses for you, boy. Bourbon and a big, thick steak for me. How's that sound?"

The gelding turned his head toward the sound of the man's voice and nickered once. The man chuckled. Running his left hand along Jughead's left flank and over his butt, he eased around to the other side, slipping the thong that held the Winchester secure and easing the rifle out of the leather scabbard.

He walked toward the rock-strewn slope leading to the ledge where he'd keep a lone watch, turning around once to mark the gelding's position in his mind's eye, lining it up with a rock outcropping that jutted into the sky. His horse's coat, a blurry and dull yellow with faint orange tint in the naked light of day, was light gray in the starlight.

Should have ridden Sue Bee or Chester up here. Both were sorrels with darker red coats better for staying masked in the night but neither was as bombproof as Jughead. Damn good thing the moon was down.

He turned again and resumed climbing the slope, his head down to keep both eyes on the uneven ground, his ears cocked for the angry burr of a rattlesnake. That was a constant worry in this harsh and unforgiving country, one of the many eternal verities of West Texas that could maim or kill you.

When he reached a crevice in the rocks that led to the ledge above, he side-armed stones into the black space, listening for that telltale snake sound. Nothing. He squeezed through the rocks and reached the ledge.

More tossed stones sent skittering across the flat stone bench. Nothing again. He placed the Winchester on the ledge then muscled himself up and over, using a rock for a stepping stone. He was rewarded with another stab of pain in his back. Have to get that sumbitch checked out in town. He looked for the best place to set up his vigil.

Near the far end was an overhang that cast a deep shadow. Damn near idyllic.

He edged into the shadow and sat cross-legged with his grandfather's rifle across his thighs. He pushed the brim of his hat upward to clear room for his field glasses, another Parris Island heirloom. The hat was a ratty Resistol 6X that started life with a pinch-front crease, a come-and-go brim and dark brown felt.

Sun-bleached and stained with sweat, grease, blood and cow patties, it was now a hat only he and Jimmy Stewart could love. Hardly the proper cover for a Marine, it was the perfect lid for an old rancher out on a hunt.

His name — Bartholomew Jackson Hulett. Friends, family and strangers called him Bart. At his insistence. He was the proud scion of a West Texas ranching family, a direct descendant of two brothers who helped take this land from the Comanche and the Lipan Apache.

He was also a decorated World War II veteran, an avid hunter, a graduate of the University of Texas law school and a former county judge and state legislator. He was also a saddle-bound cattleman who still insisted on riding and roping with the cowboys who mounted up for his brand, the Bar Double H.

Stocky and long-legged with a ruddy complexion and thick, iron gray hair swept back from a high forehead, he believed in the old-school ways of ranching and wouldn't be caught dead herding cattle with a helicopter.

The valley Hulett was watching ran along the ridgeline's western flank, the drainage for a creek that was dry most of the year, swollen only by the winter rains that caused the creosote brush to turn a shiny olive green and waft the scent of old railroad ties and telephone poles. He glassed the black empty below, relying on his peripheral vision to catch any shape or movement.

He switched back and forth between scans with the naked eye and magnified glass, careful not to strain and focus on the center, letting his eyes get used to the endless darkness below, mindful to let his breathing and heartbeat slow to a level akin to a car engine barely kicking over at idle.

He marked the time by chewing coffee beans, an old trick his grandfather taught him about keeping a cold camp, and stuffing stringy tobacco into his cheek. He refused to look at his watch. He checked his anger and fear. He kept up the rhythm of his vigil, his head slowly turning or nodding as he scanned each segment of the valley, south to north, then north to south. Binoculars then naked eyes.

At the midpoint of a southward scan, Hulett detected movement in his peripheral vision. He halted the scan and waited, field glasses centered on where he thought he saw something in motion, forcing himself to relax and let whatever was on the valley floor move again.

More movement in the lower left corner of his vision. The same something or something else? He shifted the twin lenses slightly to the left and down, hoping he still had the first flicker of something in sight. He was about eight hundred feet above the valley floor. At this range and with this light, it would have to be something larger than a muley, steer or antelope to catch his eye. Something man-made.

He kept his breathing slow and waited. There it was again, something moving in the first spot that caught his eye. Got us two somethings down there.

Faintly, like a ghost whispering in his ear, he heard the sound of an engine. He put the binoculars down and listened, letting his ears take over for his eyes. More engine noise, clearer now. Sounded like a truck in very low gear, muscling over rough ground that made four-wheel drive mandatory.

He heard a second engine rev up then flatten out, the sound of a driver slowly letting the clutch engage. Now that he knew where to look, he could pick up two boxy shapes slowly moving westward across the valley floor — black rectangles slightly darker than the ground they traveled.

He heard a third sound different from the first two. Sputtering and irregular, like a balky engine being coaxed to life. An eternity passed in just seconds. The sputtering was replaced by the unmistakable and throaty roar of a diesel. A generator, maybe. More eternities passed. He scanned the floor with the field glasses, searching for more movement.

A fool's errand. Pinpoints of light popped up on the valley floor, outlining a narrow strip on the western edge. He gauged the length of the strip to be about a quarter of a mile. Maybe a half. He heard another engine sound, this one above him and distantly familiar. He took off his hat and started scanning the sky, shocked to see a red beacon light on one of the toothy spires rising above the far north end of the ridgeline.

Hulett kept searching the sky for the source of that engine sound. Make that twin engines, an airplane for sure, dodging between the ragged peaks that scarred this land. He couldn't spot the plane but could hear that it was below him now, the pilot dragging it toward the strip on the back side of the power curve, flaps fully extended.

He finally spotted the plane, low and slow against the valley floor, when the pilot flipped on the landing lights just before touching down between the marker lights outlining the strip. He could hear the pilot reverse the props to slow down before running out of landing space, stopping with a few hundred feet to spare.

The aircraft turned slowly, then taxied back to a spot where a brace of floodlights suddenly flared. As the plane entered the light, he could see it was painted matte black and had twin tails and radial engines. Its lines looked like something out of the 1930s, a Lockheed Lodestar or a Beech Model 18, but this bird wasn't a tail-dragger. It had tricycle landing gear. A conversion. He watched as jacked-up trucks rolled into the light and men the size of plastic toy soldiers scurried to unload the plane's cargo.

Hulett didn't need to guess about the cargo — cocaine or heroin. Maybe both. He knew who owned these goods — Malo Garza, the big *narco* along this stretch of the border — and he knew who owned this land — one of his own, blood kin from the dark side of his family.

He watched for another ten minutes until the plane was emptied and the trucks pulled away. The floodlights died a quick death, leaving only the runway markers for light. The pilot taxied back down the dirt strip and turned the plane's nose into the wind.

The engines revved up to a roar he remembered well from the war — nothing like the powerful song of an American radial. The memory didn't make him smile. He watched the plane roll down the strip and heard rather than saw it claw a path into the sky. The marker lights died. So did the red beacon, leaving only the cold, black dark.

Hulett stood slowly, waiting for the blood to bring the feeling back to his deadened legs. He stretched until the pain in his back shrunk to the size of a penknife. He tugged the brim of his hat to the cowboy correct angle and stared at the valley floor, gripping his grandfather's rifle tightly in his right hand and clenching his left into a sinewy fist.

His anger started to build, causing his blood pressure to rise and roar in his ears and his vision to mist over. His breathing became

9

ragged, his lungs bellowing to drag in more cold air.

Bart Hulett was a man who was always certain that his way was the right way, even if the Bible and the law books said different. After this night, he was filled with the anger and rage of a new and shameful certainty, a blood lust he hadn't felt since the war.

He was certain he needed to kill his oldest cousin and put an end to the devil's deal the Huletts had lived by for generations — before it put an end to him.

Two

The knife blade gleamed in the darkness above Burch, flashing silvery gray and held by an unseen hand. He couldn't tear his eyes away from its terrible light and that sharpened the spike of fear rising in his chest.

Beyond the blade, he could sense rather than see something hovering in the dark, something watching him with an impatient malevolence, something ancient and agelessly evil.

He was bound hand and foot with rough rope that sawed his wrists and ankles, stretched out naked and face up on a stone altar in a cold, damp chamber. He could smell burnt blood and gunpowder, cigar smoke and incense — and the sickening mix of seared flesh and entrails.

Burch heard the low voices of people he couldn't see, their chants overpowered by the whirring of wings and the hiss of a snake, above the blade but growing louder and closer, causing the fear to shake free of his shackles and become a full-blown terror he couldn't control. His eyes stayed fixed on the blade and its cold gleam. He didn't want to see what was descending from the chilled darkness. He felt his bowels loosen.

"Wooo-weee, that's some stink you had up inside you, old man. Messin' yourself like you was still suckin' on yore mama's tit. Where's the tough guy act now, Big Time?"

It was the voice of a dead man — Teddy Roy Bonafacio, narco and stone-cold killer. A vicious psychopath who practiced an unholy blend of voodoo and Aztec heart sacrifice he thought gave him the power of the

11

ancients. T-Roy — wiry and red-haired, he was the son of a Mexican father and oil-field trash mama, tormented by nightmares of a winged serpent bent on devouring him with unhinged jaws.

"You thought I was dead and I was, but I have a power over death. I'm back and I'm going to finish what I started. Fillet you like a fish with this knife. Cut your heart out and eat it. Slice it into strips and dip it in my secret sauce. Just like the Aztecs used to when they cut the hearts out of conquistadores. You sabe, old man?"

Burch couldn't speak. His tongue was frozen by terror, his eyes fixed on the blade and that evil shadow above. T-Roy's nightmare was now his.

"I want you to see something before I carve you up. You got a visitor who's gonna watch you die. She might shed a tear, but I doubt it. Look here and see who's come a callin' you before I punch your ticket."

Burch didn't want to look. His eyes stayed locked on the blade. But he felt his head slowly turn against his will. His eyes left the blade and the shadow above but he could still feel their presence. Something new filled his vision and he felt his heart rise into his throat.

Dirty blonde hair, thick, swept back and shoulder length. Piercing blue eyes that seemed permanently startled. A tiny, crescent-shaped scar on the cheek. A faint smile playing on thin lips. And a voice that was one part North Dallas money and two parts flat, up-holler East Tennessee twang.

"Hello, Big 'Un. Looks like you got your sorry ass in a sling again. You look like a trussed-up hog on that altar. Not a good look for a guy yore age. Saved yore bacon once. Got you over that river high and dry. What was left of you. Cain't do it again. Won't do it — no, sir. You're gonna take the full ride this time, sad to say."

Carla Sue Cantrell, standing there with a Colt 1911 dangling from her right hand. The perfect accessory for a woman like her — short, lithe, curvy and lethal. She raised the Colt until it was pointed at his forehead, her blue eyes glittering behind the slide and big-mouthed barrel.

"You want me to blow T-Roy down just like before, doncha? You want *me to send him back to hell so he won't carve out that heart of yours. Ain't gone to happen, Big 'Un. I did you no favors savin' you before and I'm not gone to repeat that mistake again. You're on your own, bubba."*

She turned and walked out of his vision. T-Roy stepped into sight — rail-thin with ropy muscles, pale as a corpse and smelling like an old and open grave. Six ragged holes pocked his bare chest and his left eye was a jagged and empty socket.

"Guess she gave you the Big Adios and wanted to get gone. It's showtime now, tough guy. Now it's time to make you mine."

Eyes snapped back to the blade, high above him in T-Roy's hand. It plunged downward, the gleam becoming a blur as he felt its sharp point plunge deep in his chest. Burch arched his back and strained against the ropes that bound him as the blade sawed against gristle and bone.

Burch screamed.

Screams bounced off the thin walls of his bedroom, a bear bellowing in pain. His eyes snapped open to the familiar but still frightening — the framed John Wayne photo hanging on the wall, the Colt 1911 and spare magazine on the nightstand, the partial plate in a glass of water, the pack of Luckies and the scarred Zippo, the open bottle of Maker's Mark standing guard over it all.

Burch was sitting bolt upright in his own bed, sheets tangled around his legs, his heart hammering out a blacksmith's beat, his head and chest on fire with pain, his eyes bulging out, his mind still in that dank, black chamber with the gleaming blade.

The bellowing echo died. His mind slowly drifted toward the here and now. He forced himself to breathe deep until his heart rate no longer redlined. The pain in his head and chest remained. A hand touched his arm and he felt an electric jolt of fear that shot straight to his brain. He jerked his arm away and snapped his eyes toward the hand that touched him and the woman in his bed who owned it.

"Baby, you're safe now. You're safe here with me. Lay back down and rest easy. I won't let nothin' get you here."

Burch said nothing. He reached toward the nightstand and jerked open the drawer. He felt for a plastic bottle of Percodan with his left hand. Found it. Pop the cap. Shake out two of those mama's little helpers. Pop both onto the tongue. Grab the Maker's and bubble that bottle until the pills hit his stomach and the ninety-proof burn seared his gullet.

A ragged breath. One more pull for good luck against the night terrors that walked through his dreams. Better sleep through pharmacology and high-test bourbon. Hose down the demons with pills and Bill Samuels' best whisky. Whisky without the 'e.'

He turned toward the woman. She touched him again and he let her. Her hand felt cool on his burning skin, wet with the sweat of another nightmare, the same nightmare. She traced her fingers along his arm and placed her hand on his chest, gently pushing him until he eased himself down.

Eyes the color of bluebonnets looked at him from a broad, high-cheeked face framed by tousled hair the color of Silver Queen corn silk. She had full lips, a button nose and an easy smile in the early-morning light coming from a casement window with cracked glass and old-style cranks for side panes on either flank.

Carol Ann Gunther, courthouse clerk, sometime lover and fellow regular at Louie's, the pride of Dallas and the best saloon on the planet. A few years back, not long after he got bounced from the force and had to hang out a shamus shingle, she picked him up at Louie's with a smooth line slurred by Herradura shots: "I got one rule. If there are two sets of jeans hangin' on my bedpost, mine better have the smaller waistband." Burch fit the bill and they'd get together when one of them had the itch for meaty, sweaty and no-strings sex.

Her cool fingers traced through his chest hairs and over the lines of his face and closely cropped beard, running over the bumps that marked where his jaw had been broken, then wired so the bones could knit and heal. A parting gift from the real T-Roy, not the one in the nightmare he just left, delivered with the slab-sided slide of the Colt sitting on his nightstand, taking out four teeth as a bonus.

Her eyes followed her fingers. She ran a forefinger along the scar that ran from where his vanished hairline used to be to a point midway on the left side of the top of his skull. Another love tap from T-Roy.

She cupped the back of his head and pulled him closer. She kissed him, her tongue searching for his, her mouth tasting like cigarette smoke and last night's bourbon, flavors Burch favored. He slid his tongue deep in her mouth for another taste. His cock started to stir.

She nibbled on his ear and whispered, "Better now, baby?"

He returned the favor and growled, "Not yet, slick. I still got the shakes."

A throaty chuckle in response. Cool fingers wrapping around his cock. Teeth nibbling his ear.

"Let's see if we can chase them scary ghosts away. I think I know just what will slam the closet door on them."

She rose to her knees, her heavy breasts swaying, her dark nipples hardened, her hair cascading over her face. He eyed her body in the rising light. Thick haunches and a meaty, heart-shaped ass. Short, muscular legs bronzed by a poolside tan that colored her arms and face and ended at her cleavage.

She reached across him, breasts dragging across his chest as she fished a condom out of the nightstand drawer. She ripped the foil open, tossed it and rolled the condom over his cock. She swung one leg over and straddled him, tucking his cock into her pussy and slowly rocking it deeper. He rose, propping himself on his elbows to tongue her nipples as she rode him. He looked up and saw her smile, her eyes half closed as their bodies picked up pace.

"Better now?"

"Some better. Need some more of your medicine."

"I got all the cure you can stand."

He chuckled, grabbed her hips and thrust harder. She cried out and threw her head back, hair whipping away from her face. She placed her hands on his chest and leaned forward to kiss him, tongue stabbing his mouth. Her breath was hot as she whispered in his ear.

"We all got our demons, baby. Sometimes, all you can do is just fuck yourself silly until they crawl back to their holes and leave you alone."

The bedsprings squealed as they reached the top of their mountain, their cries breathless with pleasure. They looked at each other and laughed, then kissed as their bodies slowly descended.

"Big medicine, right baby?"

"You bet, slick. The best."

He slapped her ass and kissed her hard. He felt the whisky, pills and aftershock of sex take hold, pulling him toward sleep. The demons were hiding in their holes, the ghosts back in their closets with the doors slammed shut. T-Roy and Carla Sue were gone. For now.

Burch slept.

The good thing about Percodan was that it gave Burch happy dreams in Technicolor. Vivid images in rich, rippling hues. Grass so green you could taste it. Skies so bright and blue it hurt the eyes. Frost that glittered like diamonds on the cold, hard ground of a winter morning.

He dreamed of his boyhood and teens. Riding his copper-colored Schwinn with a red Bee or Aviator playing card clipping through the spokes. Always red, never blue, from a fresh deck filched from his dad's poker table.

Paddling a canoe on Lake Texoma while camping with his 4-H club. Hunting muleys with his dad and uncle up in the Panhandle in the frozen aftermath of a late fall blue norther. Copping his first feel from Jo Beth Studdard, her warm, pink nipples rising against his calloused fingertips.

Best of all — instant replays of football Friday nights during that magical run his junior year, the first season he started at left tackle and the 1965 Coppell High Rattlers took the Texas AAA regional then won the state championship by a touchdown, beating Lubbock Central. Burch pancaked their defensive end, springing Lonnie Waddell to step into the land of sixes to break the tie. Instant Lone Star immortality.

Colors weren't the only drug-induced enhancement. Sound, smell and taste were also amped-up and straight-edge sharp. The blood in his mouth from a forearm shiver. The grunts and primal cries from bodies thudding together in full-speed collision. The rich, moist scent of spike-torn turf, the stench of sweat both rancid and rotten sweet.

God, how he loved these Percodan dreams. He was young, strong and fast. He had a full head of hair, a clean-shaven face and a stomach so flat and taut you could bounce silver dollars off of it. His knees weren't zippered with the surgeon's scars.

In these dreams, he wasn't bald and big-bellied and his liver was sound. He wasn't a defrocked homicide detective forced to give up his gold shield and work his trade as a private eye. He didn't carry the guilt of a dead partner and a murdered ex-wife. He wasn't tormented by nightmares of dead *narcos*, winged serpents and a killer blonde with a taste for crystal meth, muscle cars and the high-wire double-cross.

In his Percodan dreams, the ghosts and demons were nowhere in sight and the guilt was locked up in a jail cell so far away it couldn't call collect.

But that was also the bad thing about the drug. The dreams were so rich, real and inviting that Burch wanted to leap inside each image and live it all over again. Far better than the life he was living now.

In the textured tapestry of narcotic sleep, he would stretch and reach and will the body in his bed to join the younger self he saw in his mind's eye. He yearned to be the Ed Earl Burch of drugged dreams and young memories. That feeling became so powerful it overwhelmed the dreams and drove them away. He woke up still reaching and yearning, frustrated that the images were gone and the joy he felt while sleeping was shattered.

Same beige walls with the black scuff marks. Same framed photo of

John Wayne on the wall, a still from *Rio Bravo* with the Duke wearing a battered hat with a pushed-up brim, hefting a Winchester with a loop-ring lever and smiling with a deadly gleam in his eye. Same Colt, spare mag, Luckies and Zippo on the nightstand with the bottle of Maker's standing guard with barely three fingers of whisky still left.

He tapped a Lucky out of the pack and flamed it with the Zippo. He sucked the smoke deep for the day's first hit of nicotine and took inventory. The two Percodans left him groggy and made him feel like his eyes were looking at the room through a triple pane of wavy, antique glass.

A thin blade of pain lanced the middle of his forehead. Sinus or slight hangover? Six to five and pick 'em. His mouth felt like a family of boll weevils were camping inside. He fished his partial plate out of a rocks glass half full of water and gunned the liquid down in one gulp. He eyed the remainder of the Maker's. Not yet.

Carol Ann was gone and the rumpled bedsheets reeked of sex, night sweats, stale cigarette smoke and the lingering scent of Opium perfume. A note was tented like a miniature A-frame on her vacant pillow. "Call me if the demons come back. I've got the cure. — C.A."

All the cure he could stand. He chuckled and had a quick frozen flash of her riding his cock, Silver Queen corn silk hair flying. She knew exactly what he needed last night. A hot shot of carnal salvation. Because pills and whisky without the 'e' didn't have enough juju to conquer those demons.

He took one last drag, then stabbed the Lucky into an ashtray to die a soldier's death. He stood to head to the bathroom to take a morning piss. The room tilted sideways with a vertigo lurch. He staggered and crashed backwards into bed. He looked up and felt the room spin. The demons came rushing out of their holes, the ghosts banged open the doors of their closets. T-Roy with his jagged eye socket and slug-pocked chest. Carla Sue with her glittering eyes and the big-mouthed Colt.

The winged serpent descending in the dark. The gleaming blade.

The sharp pain in his chest. The sound of metal sawing on gristle and bone.

He propped himself up on an elbow and reached in the nightstand drawer for the Percodan. Pop the cap. Shake out two capsules and slap them on the tongue. Grab the bottle of Maker's and drain it dry.

Then ride out a daylight nightmare until the drug sweeps you under and those sweet Percodan dreams return.

Three

Chuy Reynaldo and Arturo Herrera passed a needle-thin joint and a bottle of Dos Reales tequila back and forth as they leaned back to look at the sweep of stars above them. They were sitting side-by-side on the dropped tailgate of Herrera's primer gray '61 Chevy Apache, boots dangling as they talked about cars, money, American football and the Mexican obsession — *fútbol*.

And pussy. *Chucha. Culo. Chocha. Panocha. Araña.* They didn't talk about the business both had chosen.

"You look tired, *mi carnal*. You still fucking that Angelina? What does your wife say about that, *guey*?"

"She don't say nothin' 'cause she don't know. Wearin' out *el pene* havin' to ride both of those mules. And I just got my hands on another one, a downriver *chica* I met on one of my scouting runs. She's married to some Anglo guy in Eagle Pass who don't fuck her nearly enough. She likes a little *chaca chaca*, likes it *empinado*."

Arturo grabbed his crotch and grinned. He took another hit, coughing as he handed the joint to Chuy.

"Don't choke on that *mota*. Here — wash down that smoke with a drink. There's no hope for you, *guey*. If you don't fuck yourself to death, somebody's husband is going to shoot you dead."

Chuy faked another hit and eyed Arturo bubbling tequila down his throat to chase the smoke. A slim, muscular guy with dark and flashing eyes, a trim moustache and a thick mane of jet-black hair that begged for a hay rake to keep it tame, Arturo fancied himself a ladies' man and dressed the part. His mahogany lizard-skin boots were needle-toed with silver caps tacked over the tips. He wore tight Guess jeans and a brown aviator jacket in leather chemically distressed enough to look stylishly well worn.

Arturo was everything Chuy was not — a good-looking *macho* with flash backed by a subtle swagger. Chuy was short and fat, a dumpy guy with stumpy legs, thin and stringy black hair and a moon face with the permanent who-me expression of the terminally clueless. His scraggly beard, baggy jeans and scuffed boots marked him as a man you looked at once and immediately forgot, a sad sack who had to pay for any woman he got.

That made Chuy very easy to underestimate. Few saw the sharp and lethal cunning lurking underneath the surface camouflage. Or the eyes and ears that never missed a trick or tell. Until it was too late.

The two men had known each other since boyhood, growing up on the wrong side of the Southern Pacific tracks that ran through Faver, a West Texas town on life support now that SP had closed down a yard for boxcar refurbishment, consolidating maintenance operations further east in Sanderson. A tannery and copper smelter had also locked their gates, making the air less lethal to breathe but a dollar far harder to come by.

The only things keeping Faver from going tits up were its status as the seat of Cuervo County government and its prime location as an isolated but useful hub for anything illegal flowing north from the Rio Grande — drugs and people — or south into Mexico — guns and stolen cars. A student of history would say Cuervo County was returning to its roots since smuggling, cattle rustling and gun-running had always been economic mainstays, a subterranean stream of money running underneath the legal outlets of commerce that were now drying up faster than water poured on the desert rocks.

The town was named for Milton Faver, said to be a Virginian who fled to Mexico in the 1830s, believing he had killed a man in a duel in Missouri. He made his way as a freighter, plying the old Chihuahua and Santa Fe trails between Presidio del Norte and Ojinaga, fierce country known as *La Junta de los Rios,* the junction of the Rio Conchos and Rio Grande. It was hazardous duty that left him badly wounded after an Apache ambush.

Faver was a contemporary of Ben Leaton, a notorious trader who once held a banquet for Comanche leaders at the fortified post he built in what is now Presidio, Texas. After his guests were sated and drunk, Leaton and his men slaughtered them with cannon and rifle fire for stealing his mules, horses and cattle. Leaton then collected the bounty on their scalps from the Mexican government.

By the 1840s, Faver's freighting business was going so well he left it in the hands of trusted employees and moved his Mexican wife and family to Ojinaga. By 1857, he had enough money to buy three tracts of land in the rugged and desolate Chianti Mountains of Presidio County, where he built three strongholds and became the premier cattle baron of the Big Bend Country, growing rich selling beef to Yankee soldiers stationed at Fort Davis and driving herds to New Orleans and the cowtown railheads of Kansas.

Faver was a man shrouded in mystery, the mists swirling about his legend tinted in the darker shades brushed on ruthless men who made their own rules in a lawless land. There is no record he was a smuggler or cattle rustler, but both were common sidelines for freighters and frontier ranchers aiming to quickly augment a herd raised from the thousands of wild cattle roaming this merciless country.

And there is little doubt Faver was bold enough to do whatever it took to seize his main chance and make it big. He was a man who trusted nobody outside his family and his loyal band of *vaqueros,* shepherds and farmhands, and he always insisted on being paid in hard silver or gold coin.

When you bought cattle from Milton Faver, you paid him steer by steer, cow by cow, dropping a coin in his money bag as each one passed. Yankee or Mexican, it didn't matter. As long as it wasn't script and it jangled in that bag.

Parked on a mesa fifteen miles southwest of Faver, Chuy and Arturo didn't know the legend of Milton Faver and couldn't care less about a man dead for nearly a century. They would have shrugged at the notion of walking in the same illegal footsteps as *comancheros*, scalp-hunters, rustlers and gunrunners. But they would have immediately grasped the main motivation of their predecessors — in a hard, unforgiving country, a man did anything he could to grab a dollar and get ahead.

Anything.

The two men worked for Esteban "Malo" Garza, a *narcotraficante* who owned a 75,000-acre *rancho* that bordered the Mexican banks of the Rio Grande about thirty miles south of the mesa. *Los Tres Picos.* Garza's family had owned this land for centuries, fending off Apaches, bandits, Pancho Villa and *federales* with a brutal ruthlessness that made a warrior beg for mercy and a land-grabbing bureaucrat turn away in search of far easier prey.

Arturo was one of Garza's transport wizards, gifted with a mind for logistics and an eye for the soft spots in the front-line defenses America threw up to fight the War on Drugs. He knew the border guards and deputies who would take a bribe and let a shipment roll through. He knew the landowners willing to turn a blind eye to a tunnel or a midnight flight to a rough-hewn strip on a remote piece of land. He knew the bent businessmen who would open up a warehouse to stage a shipment, ship cars with heroin and cocaine tucked behind body panels or haul a trailer with a hidden compartment loaded with product.

Chuy was an enforcer, a remorseless killer whose benign and unlikely appearance made it easy for him to get in close for a swift, clean hit. He also ran security for Garza on the Texas side of the river. His weapon of choice was a Colt Python, a .357 with a four-inch barrel and glossy, midnight bluing. He liked the tight lock-up of the Colt's cylinder and barrel and the balanced feel of the pistol in his hand. But it really didn't matter to Chuy whether he did his wet work with a knife, a shotgun, a pickaxe or his bare hands. As long as he got in close and got out quick.

The two men were meeting on the mesa to outline transport and security details for Garza's next big shipment. They were under heavy pressure to make this one airtight because the last shipment had been a bloody clusterfuck — eight trucks headed toward four different border crossings ambushed on the Mexican side of the border by shooters wearing *federale* uniforms.

Nine of Garza's men were killed, including one of Chuy's cousins, Raymundo Estrella. But the Garza gunmen wasted most of the attackers, saving seven of the bullet-scarred trucks but losing the eighth — a million dollar hit for Garza. Burned-out Suburban hulks and the charred bodies of the ambushers and Garza gunmen were the roadside markers for a battlefield that stretched from Ojinaga to Piedras Negras, providing mute testimony to the deadly efficiency of a rocket-propelled grenade and automatic weapons that could piss high-velocity lead.

Garza knew who was responsible — a downriver rival named Emiliano Flores. Payback was planned, but business had to roll on. The added pressure made both men reluctant to talk about what brought them to the mesa. Both were loathe to leave the easy, raunchy banter of old friends and the familiar role both played in these exchanges — Chuy the stern and chiding older brother, Arturo the younger sibling and incorrigible cockhound. For Chuy, the reluctance had a darker weight. Made him want to linger with the tequila and *mota* a bit more.

"Seriously, *guey*. If Carlota catches you with that Angelina or this new one, you won't have to worry about being sore from fucking — she'll chop off *el chile* and snip off your *huevos*."

Arturo shrugged and spread his arms toward the diamond flash of stars scattered against the deep and velvet black of a clear, cold night.

"I'm blessed with a gift from God, my friend. Who am I to deny it to women who want it? It's my sworn duty to share my blessing with any and all. All women, that is. Homey is no *maricón. El pene* is only for *las chicas.*"

Arturo raised his head and kissed the tips of his fingers and flicked them apart, watching the imaginary gesture fly into the night air. He laughed. Chuy didn't.

"You blessed alright. Blessed with the gift of solid gold bullshit. *El chile* isn't the only thing you wearing out with these women. You giving your wallet a good workout, too. You got Angelina stashed away in a house you pay for and bought her that Camaro. And I know Carlota hasn't forgotten how to spend your money. The money Malo pays us is damn good, but *ay, guey*, you stretchin' it, no?"

"Plenty of *la lana* from *El Patrón* to go around. More where that came from. We do good work for him and he knows it. And pays us for it. You know, this is the only way for two border *chuchos* like us to make money and live *la vida grande*. Once you get a whiff of it, you want more, no? Like a whiff of Angelina's *chocha.*"

"Like sniffing *el chemo*, huffin' all that *panocha*. Rots out your brain. Makes you stupid. Makes you piss away your money like you got a bellyful of *mezcal.*"

"It's my penance. Bless me father, for I have sinned. Take my money so I can sin some more."

Arturo made the sign of the cross and bowed his head.

"No, *mi carnal*. This is your penance."

The Python was in Chuy's right hand, its barrel inches away as Arturo raised his head, his eyes widened by the sudden knowledge that death was about to claim him. Chuy pulled the Colt's glassy, double-action trigger five times, a rapid string of deafening blasts and yellow-orange flashes that turned Arturo's head into a mist of blood and bone shards. The body slammed against the side rail of the pickup, then collapsed into the diamond-patterned steel bed.

Chuy hopped off the tailgate and walked around to the side of the truck where his dead friend fell. He peered over the rail and saw there was little left of Arturo's face and head but a mouth opened wide by a cry of terror that died with its maker, silenced by high-velocity hollow-points.

With his left hand, Chuy jammed the barrel of the Python into his friend's mouth and pulled the trigger one more time. A dark blue '71 Impala rolled up on the mesa and stopped beside Arturo's truck.

One of Chuy's crew hopped out of the front passenger seat and popped the trunk, opening a body bag resting on a sheet of heavy-gauged black plastic. He shouldered Arturo's body, dropped it in the bag and zipped it closed then crossed himself. A second man popped out of the Impala's back seat — Chuy tossed him the keys to his dark green '70 Olds Delta 88.

Chuy wiped down the Python with a black bandana, then tucked the pistol into a slide holster riding above his right kidney. He hopped into Arturo's truck and drove off the mesa, headed to a friend's house deep in the rocky desert outback where a shovel, a brush, a bucket and a bottle of bleach were waiting.

It was his duty to kill his boyhood friend. It was also his duty to make sure his friend was buried deep and proper, with a small measure of respect, a nod to that friendship. Even if it was an unmarked grave hidden by the desert rocks.

"It's done."

"Any problems?"

"No. He never saw it coming. Kept talking about pussy and money right up to the end."

"*Chingado* motherfucker. Arturo got greedy and then he got stupid and careless. He thought he was smart. He thought no one would find out that he was taking Flores' money. And mine. He forgot I have eyes and ears everywhere. I see and hear everything. Everything."

Chuy knew the story but said nothing. That *chica* Arturo was banging in Eagle Pass was the wife of a Maverick County sheriff's deputy who belonged to Flores. Arturo had been dumb enough to brag to her about being a smart guy who could outwit both Flores and Garza while taking their money.

Pillow talk of the fatal kind. She was a cousin to one of Chuy's crew and sang her song to him. He sang to Chuy. Chuy told the story to Garza cold and flat. No music, no song. No chirping. Arturo got dead.

Chuy listened as the voice at the other end of the line vented his anger. More than likely, he was also bleeding off frustration that his finger wasn't the one that pulled the trigger on Arturo. Malo Garza liked to deliver his payback personally with an ivory-gripped Browning Hi-Power but Chuy had insisted on killing Arturo himself.

It was the right thing to do. It was also the only thing to do if he didn't want to wind up as dead as Arturo, dumped in a desert hole like a deer carcass.

"Any remorse? You two have been friends for a very long time."

"No, he betrayed us, got my cousin iced and needed killing."

"You sound like one of those Anglos talking about the West Texas self-defense plea."

"Your honor, he needed killin'?"

"That's the one. Been watching John Wayne movies again?"

"*True Grit.* A man needs to study the habits of his enemy."

A soft chuckle on the other side of the line.

"That's what makes you so valuable to me. You were born in Faver and know the ways of the Anglo and our people. It's natural and allows you to easily go everywhere I need you to be."

Chuy said nothing. He knew what the flattery meant.

"I have another job for you."

"*Sí, patrón?*"

"We think someone was up on the ridgeline the night we flew that load to our friend's land. You know the ridge I'm talking about? Don't say it. Just say if you know it."

"*Sí, patrón.* I know it. One of Flores' people?"

"That would be my bet, but we don't know. Could be another player. We need to find out. Fast. Get your crew working on that. One of your *vaquero* buddies who knows the backcountry."

"I know just the man. He can read the ground for sign like you read a book."

"*Bueno.* Might mean more work for your Python, but not just yet. I want to know who was up there. Find out for me. Then we'll figure out what to do about it."

"*Sí, patrón.* A done deal."

Another chuckle then the line clicked dead. Chuy hung up and stepped out of the phone booth and walked into a dimly lit bar. He ordered a double shot of Dos Reales and a Carta Blanca. He gunned the shot and grimaced, then lifted the glass in a silent toast to Arturo Herrera.

Four

It was deep dark by the time Burch woke up. The street outside his apartment was carless and quiet. Cool night air filtered through the screens of the casement window's open side panels, lightly puffing the curtains like a whispered secret from a corpse.

He flipped on the nightstand light with the battered parchment shade, staggered into the bathroom and took a long piss, sighing with relief as his bladder emptied. Most of his piss streamed into the toilet bowl. Some didn't.

He padded back to the bedroom, stepping slow and careful like a palsied geezer on an icy sidewalk, fearful of that fatal slip. Burch was wary of another sudden vertigo assault, dreading the banshee rush of demons and ghosts that followed the loss of physical and mental balance.

He was surprised to make it back to the bedroom with his power to stay vertical still intact. He felt groggy and glassy-eyed from the Percodan, his innards drained and hollowed by bourbon, pills, sex and nightmares. Nothing another drink couldn't cure. The empty bottle of Maker's mocked him.

Couple of Pearl longnecks in the fridge. They'd have to do. Surprised he remembered them. Must mean he was approaching semi-normal, ready to venture into the deeper waters of his living room. He pulled on a pair of dark gray sweatpants, picked up the Colt, the Luckies and the Zippo and plowed a course straight into the doorjamb, banging his head and right shoulder.

"Dammit to hell. Fuckin' clumsy-assed bastard."

The living room was dark and colder. He was bare-chested. He tucked the Luckies under his chin, reached around the treacherous doorjamb and felt for the wall switch with his left hand, balancing the Colt and Zippo with his right.

A burgundy-hued La-Z-Boy beckoned, its leather worn with alligator cracks on the armrests. Beer first. He plunked the Colt and Luckies on a foldout wooden TV tray stand that served as an end table — a Wal-Mart special so precious he bought two.

He limped into the galley kitchen and fetched two Pearl longnecks out of the fridge, using the edge of the blood-red laminated countertop to slap off the tops with the heel of his hand. That added fresh and toothy marks that made it look like a rat with a taste for plastic and particleboard had gnawed along the edge. Kiss that $250 deposit goodbye if he ever moved from this Marquita Street brownstone.

Feeling light-headed, he slumped into the recliner and draped a heavy, rough-napped Navajo blanket with a red and black thunderbird pattern over his shoulders. He took a long pull of Pearl, then stuck a Lucky on his lip and fired it up, taking a deep drag then watching the smoke curl from the business end of the nail.

"Damn, this is gettin' old."

Nobody answered. Not even the voice in his head, the one that delivered the nonstop monologues about his past sins and guilt, his screwups and his fears. Hard to get that bastard to shut up without hosing him down with a few slugs of Maker's. Burch welcomed the inner and outer silence, sucking in smoke and tasting the sharp, bittersweet Pearl as it rolled over his tongue.

Time to take stock. A year and a few months change had passed since he was on the run with the crazed and lethal Carla Sue, framed for the murder of T-Roy's mistress and hunted by a mystic half-breed Houston homicide detective named Cider Jones and T-Roy's maximum muscle, a psycho force of nature with a bad toupee and a high-pitched voice named Willie "Badhair" Stonecipher.

On their fugitive run, they were the hunted but also the hunters. Both wanted T-Roy dead — revenge for the death of his partner and her uncle. They tracked T-Roy to his Mexican ranch, but were betrayed by a double-dealing guide and captured. T-Roy had Burch trussed up like a hog, ready to carve out his heart, before Carla Sue gunned him down. He could still see T-Roy's remaining eye, staring and still murderous, like a shark or marlin that had a predatory gleam even in death.

The nightmares began when he returned to Dallas. He still had his apartment on Marquita and his ratty office on Mockingbird — his landlord for both was the sister of his shyster, Fat Willie Nofzinger, who spotted him the rent during his absence. Fat Willie liked to keep Burch on a short leash of debt. Made it harder to say no when the shyster wanted him to dig up dirt on a witness dropping dime on one of his scumbag clients or the cop who made the collar.

The dead drove the lesser terrors of his nightmares, wearing the look of their last living moment while parading past. His murdered ex-wife, her blouse torn and bloody. His partner, chest blown open by a shotgun blast. The hooker who gave him a mercy fuck when his first ex left him — wearing the bloody dress she had on when she was found stabbed to death in a downtown Dallas parking lot. The son of a rich Dallas art dealer who was found garroted in his bathtub — he was naked, his eyes and tongue bulging out and the wire still biting deeply into his neck.

The characters changed, but the end game didn't. They blamed him and wanted him dead. The worst was that cold, stone slab and T-Roy with the gleaming blade and the jagged eye socket. The winged serpent. And in a late-breaking twist, Carla Sue, refusing to save him, turning away as the blade plunged toward his chest.

At first, the dreams of fear and terror were constant. He had them at night and in the middle of the day. Sometimes, a dream image would flash through his mind when he was wide awake. When that happened, he felt the vertigo rush and feared he was losing his mind.

Burch didn't eat much. He lost weight. He couldn't work. He went to see a VA shrink who listened to his tale, told him he was getting rocked by a rude mix of middle-age crazy and post-traumatic stress and wrote him prescriptions for Valium and Oleptro.

He never got them filled, opting to self-medicate with Maker's and Percodan cadged from an East Dallas doctor with a bad gambling habit who owed him for divorce work — black-and-white glossies of the doc's wife getting fucked doggie style by one guy while sucking another guy's cock.

That saved the doc from a hefty alimony payment, but didn't cure his addiction to dice, cards, NFL over/unders and ponies with long-shot odds.

As time passed, the pace of the nightmares slowed. Once a week instead of every day and night. Twice a month. Twice in one week, then nada for the next three.

Burch started to work out again. Slow jogging in spite of his ruined knees, followed by ice bags, aspirin, a big glass of ice water, a Lucky and a Maker's. Long sessions in the gym, pumping iron, grunting through leg presses and whirring the rowing machine to keep a hard layer of muscle under the fat and bolster his wrecked getaway sticks.

He knew it was a semi-pitiful ploy to stave off middle age and flip a middle finger at what was evident to all — he was an ex-jock gone to seed and no amount of huffing, puffing and pumping would change that. But returning to this old athletic ritual was a balm to his wounded soul. It also washed some of the alcohol and pharmaceuticals out of his system.

He also started to work again, cranking up his niche specialty of tracking down fugitives from the savings and loan crash that ravaged Dallas after the oil bust of the mid-80s, wrecking the Texas economy, spreading its shock waves through the Dallas real estate market and making Texas banks easy pickings for financial marauders from North

Carolina and elsewhere. He made a nice chunk of change from folks who wanted him to find a partner who left them holding the bag or ferret out the hidden assets of a guy who filed for bankruptcy and claimed he was penniless.

Most days, he felt like a vulture feeding off roadkill. On other days, he smiled while depositing a five-figure check into his bank account that allowed him to pay down the debt Fat Willie held over him.

On those fat money days, he'd put on a clean, crisp, bone-white rancher's shirt with fake pearl speed snaps, a string tie with a silver-and-onyx slide, his best snakeskin boots with the name of a South American river species he could never remember or pronounce, a sports jacket with Western piping and get a fresh beard trim and haircut that cleaned up the ragged edges around his bald pate.

Then he'd head to the Hoffbrau and order up several deep bourbons and a big porterhouse. He might even fire up a spicy Partagas Churchill with a double maduro wrapper for dessert. Sometimes, he'd treat Carol Ann to dinner, which always led to fierce carnal frolic. He'd feel almost normal until another round of night sweats and terror struck.

Burch was a walking contradiction. Steady and relentless when working, shaky and terror-stricken when idle, afraid he was losing all of his marbles and plunging into dark madness.

This was an extension of the biggest paradox of all. The fugitive tour with Carla Sue gave him back something he thought was gone forever — the sure knowledge that in the clutch, he still had the bone-deep and ornery toughness, smarts and easily outraged sense of right and wrong to rise to the challenge. He thought he'd lost all that in the long slide between his partner's murder and getting his gold shield yanked and was living the life of the terminal burnout — one drink at a time.

But running that harrowing gauntlet across Texas and down to T-Roy's *rancho* of Mexican horrors also carried a heavy price tag, a psychological butcher's bill that cracked open the armor Burch wrapped around the pain, guilt, shame and drunken craziness of a defrocked ex-cop who had seen too much already.

He started out just to keep one step ahead of the lawdogs and T-Roy's ultimate enforcer. When the Badhair killed his ex-wife, Burch became a blowtorch bent on revenge. What he wound up with was a rough-hewn form of redemption with a side order of terror and madness.

The last case Burch handled brought in enough gelt to take a breather. Which he did, only to get T-boned by this latest attack of the vertigo terrors. He was tired, but knew he needed to get back to work. What he longed for was a nice, juicy homicide, a case to get lost in, a case that engaged all of his gears and left the nightmares behind.

Burch was so focused on the key to keeping his madness at bay that he forgot a cardinal rule of life. Be careful what you wish for. You just might get it. And a whole lot of hurt you don't really want. Or need.

Five

Bart Hulett nursed his third cup of black, chicory-laced coffee on the front porch of his adobe-walled house, his low-topped ropers propped up on the thick wooden top rail, his aching butt cushioned by a pillow slapped on the seat of his grandfather's favorite rocking chair.

The porch was made of oak planks, hand-hewn from logs shipped by river and rail from Louisiana then soaked in creosote and pegged into place on a frame that wrapped around the northern corner of the house. A tin roof covered the porch, shading a broad and comfortable vantage for watching a sunrise from the northeast side or a sunset from the northwest.

Hulett was facing the sun as it rose over the low range of jagged hills that traced the eastern border of the ranch, eyeing its slow ascent over the rim of his mug, watching the searing light rip the darkness off the land below like a flame burning through a moth-eaten blanket.

He savored the coffee — strong enough to float a mule shoe, cut only by a dollop of blackstrap molasses he spooned into every serving. He kept his mind focused on the rising light that brought cattle, rocky slopes, brushy flats and the thin water ribbon of Seco Creek into sharp focus, resting from the chores just finished as the sweat dried from his clothes and avoiding the worry of the day ahead and the cold dread of blood ties he knew he had to sever.

He had climbed out of bed two hours before dawn, stretching to ease the soreness from his legs, butt and hips that still nagged him two days after the long night ride on the Devil's Backbone, rubbing the spot above his left kidney that was only a needle of pain instead of a knife blade.

Slipping on jeans, a flannel shirt, ropers and a lined denim jacket to ward off the chill of a dark early morning, he ambled into the kitchen, grabbing a handful of coffee beans to munch on and plucking his hat from the pegs in the mudroom leading to the back door. He stuffed a chaw of Levi Garrett in his cheek as he headed toward the barn to feed Jughead, Sue Bee and Chester and muck out their stalls.

The lights that lined the low-slung roof of the long pole barn were already lit. He nodded to Juan and Roberto, two of his wranglers, as they muscled bales of hay to stalls that housed twelve other hungry horses. Jughead, Sue Bee and Chester were his to tend — always had been, always would be.

The two geldings, Jughead the claybank and Chester the sorrel, were his favorite mounts. Thick-muscled and long-legged, both had the cow sense of a well-bred quarterhorse boosted by thoroughbred blood that made them tall, rangy and ready to cover a lot of ground.

Sue Bee was all short-coupled quarterhorse, a deep-chested sorrel with three white stockings. Sharp of eye and as quick as an angel dancing on a moonbeam, she was born to cut calves from their mamas come branding time. The mare had been a Christmas gift to his wife, Mary Nell, dead from ovarian cancer and buried on a mesa overlooking the ranch ten years ago. All the Huletts from his side of the family were buried there. A plot beside Mary Nell was waiting for him.

Let it wait. Let it all wait — death, the day ahead and those blood ties, rank with the stench of decades of lies and hypocrisy that made the Hulett family name as false as the main street façade of a Hollywood cow town.

He sipped more coffee as the sun continued to climb, letting his memory roll a film of Mary Nell on Sue Bee. Cutting calves for the hands ready with branding irons and worming medicine. Drawing whoops and hollers as she and the mare flowed as one. Quick and sure and dancing in the sun that haloed the sorrel's reddish-brown flanks and Mary Nell's blonde hair.

That memory lingered in his mind's eye — sweet, painful and hard to let go. She was a decade younger than him and gave him two children, a boy and a girl, grown now and living their own lives. He loved them both, but neither measured up to her. Both had a dark wildness inherited from the other side of the Hulett family, the cousins living on the west side of the Devil's Backbone — part of this ranch and bloodline, but apart and angrily estranged from him. Mary Nell was his shining pride and he wanted to watch her cut one more calf while he sipped coffee.

The phone jangled loud and sharp from its perch on a hallway wall, echoing through the open front door. The memory faded to black. The day and the dread rushed in. Bart Hulett dropped his boots to the porch planks, ran his fingers through his dark gray hair and stood up to face them down.

"Mister Hulett? Lucius Schoenfeldt with the Bryte Brothers Group out of Houston. I hope I'm not disturbing you."

"No, just my morning coffee."

Silence on the other side of the line. Hulett glanced into his mug and saw he had only a few gulps left, wishing he had been smart enough to grab a refill before picking up the phone.

"My apologies. I didn't mean to disturb you before you had your coffee."

"Mister Schoenfeldt, what can I do for you that can't wait until I finish my coffee? Daylight's burnin' and I got chores to do before I head into town."

"I'll get right to it, then. We were wondering if you had a chance to review our offer."

"You mean the low-ball bid to buy this place and turn it into a dude ranch?"

"Well, what we would ultimately do with your land has not been settled. And we believe our offer is more than fair at $250 million."

"Only if I sell you half and keep pumpin' the water right from under what I sell you. That's where the real value is for land in this country — the water underneath it. You control the water, you control a helluva lot more land than where that water is. You're going to have to sweeten that offer considerable to even get my attention, much less listen close."

"Does that mean you're open to negotiation?"

"Not hardly. It means I know what our land is worth. And I also know you want to make it a dude ranch with riding stables, trails, a spa, a pool, a bunch of adobe guesthouses and an 18-hole golf course. Very pricey for those who can afford to indulge their True West fantasies."

Silence again. Hulett polished off the last of his coffee and waited.

"You seem to know a lot about our plans."

"I still have friends. In Austin — and Houston. New York, for that matter."

"So it seems. Have your friends told you the cattle market hasn't hit bottom yet? Might be a smart time to cash in on a good offer."

"Mister Schoenfeldt, we Huletts are old West Texas money. Been out here since the 1850s. Killed Comanche and Apache to claim our land. Made a pile of money on cows and lost our fair share. But cows and the Bar Double H ain't the only things our money is in. We're diversified — a little banking, a little oil and gas, a little commercial real estate, a little what have you. Even own a piece of an outfit that makes bass and pontoon boats. But I imagine you already have a pretty good idea about all that."

"We've done our homework."

"Maybe not. Have you talked to my cousin, Gyp Hulett, yet?"

"We're not interested in his land. Too rough and rocky. Too remote.

THE BEST LOUSY CHOICE

Yours, though, is prime property."

That comment gave Hulett a chilly jolt. It made him wonder if the Bryte Brothers front man knew about the secret deal between his father and Gyp's that split ownership of the Bar Double H between the two wings of the family shortly after World War I. That contract made formal what had been informal and had never been filed in the Cuervo County courthouse.

But seventy years was a long time for a secret to stay that way, and the Bryte Brothers had enough money and muscle to dig deep and drag what was hidden into the harsh light of a hostile land grab. Or, Schoenfeldt didn't know shit and was bluffing.

Either way, doubling down on tough and ornery was the only play. Hulett dealt another card from his hand, pressing Schoenfeldt and steering the conversation away from the secret deal.

"The Bar Double H has been prime for cattle for four generations of Huletts, and I'm not of a mind to flush all that down the crapper for a dude ranch and that airstrip you want to build on the south end so your guests can fly themselves in. What did that little bird tell me? About five thousand foot with some hangars and a pilots' lounge, right?"

Silence again. Hulett placed his coffee mug on the floor and fished a pouch of Levi Garrett from the back pocket of his jeans, stuffing a stringy chaw into his cheek.

"Mister Hulett, you've made it clear that you've done your homework and that you know we've done ours. And our homework tells us you're not so diversified that a plummet in cattle prices doesn't cause your bankers to squirm a little."

"Sounds like you been talking to Dud Satterfield over at West Texas National. I heard Dud was getting the drizzles about a couple of notes he was carrying on us so I paid his sorry ass off. Pulled out a goodly amount of our money, too. Damn shame since my grandfather put up some of the capital to start that bank back in aught four. Dud might just get his ass fired over this. Yessir, a damn shame."

"Can't say that I've made Mister Satterfield's acquaintance. No sir, but he sounds like several other folks I have talked to who are nervous about the financial health of your diversified business empire. To hear them tell it, you're about to get squeezed hard and sharp when cattle prices keep dropping. And drop they will."

"Heard them tell it or is that the story you told them? Been hearing from good banker friends that someone is makin' the rounds telling scary stories about my finances. Heard that from a bank examiner, too. And a county judge you'll need on your side to turn your little pipe dream into reality. All of them wonder why you're trying to piss off a man who owns land you want."

"Again, Mister Hulett — we've made you a fair offer and your pockets aren't as deep as your bluster."

"You're a piss poor salesman, Mister Schoenfeldt, and I've seen hookers and nuns put the muscle on somebody better than you. You really haven't done much homework at all if you don't realize how deep our pockets truly are and don't know that if you talk to me, you've got to talk to my cousin Gyp. We're kinda like Siamese twins — one doesn't make a move without the other."

"What the hell's that supposed to mean?"

"It means that if you keep messin' with me, you get Gyp. And he ain't near as nice and tolerant as me. But I imagine that you're going to be too busy explaining some things to your masters here in a bit. That bank examiner has some sudden interest in the loans you guys are using to buy out some of my neighbors. Finds it far too speculative for a little state-chartered outfit like Bank of Cuervo. The county surveyor isn't too happy with how the property lines are plotted on some of that land you're buying. And I imagine my attorney can get a deposition or three from some of those bankers you've badmouthed me to. It's about to get real messy for you real fast."

Silence on the other end of the line. Hulett tossed the front man a final hunk of gristle to chew on.

"Let me tell you one last thing, Mister Schoenfeldt. Blood's thicker than both water and a banker's drizzles. Study on that a while."

Hulett slammed the phone onto its hook, picked up his coffee mug and stalked into the kitchen for another refill. Instead of blackstrap molasses, he laced the coffee with a long pour of Evan Williams bourbon pulled from a cupboard above the sink.

Whiskey before breakfast. Whiskey with an 'e.'

Helluva time to get loaded. Still hadn't eaten breakfast. Still had some chores to do, then a lunch meeting in Faver with a couple of wildcatters flying their Beech Baron in from Midland to try and rope him in on some oil and gas leases that had their blood up. Good guys with a history of bringing him damn sweet deals.

He was half tempted to blow it all off, plunk his sore butt back in his grandfather's rocker and continue some deep drinking and dark brooding. Plenty to brood about because Schoenfeldt was right about cattle prices in West Texas — they were dropping fast.

Cattle on ranches east of the Bar Double H were dying off from hard yellow liver disease, thought to be caused by a toxic plant or fungus that popped up during unusually wet weather. And last fall and winter had been very wet for West Texas. This winter was also a wet one, although not lately. Still moist enough to keep that thin ribbon running through the normally dry bed of Seco Creek.

The disease wrecked the liver of a cow quicker than a barfly's lifetime of rotgut booze. It forced ranchers to sell stock for beef before they got too far gone instead of keeping them for breeding, flooding the local market and causing prices to plummet.

None of his cattle showed signs of the wasting disease. So far. Didn't mean they wouldn't.

Didn't change the flattened price for cattle either. That meant two things. He was denied the easiest way to raise a quick injection of cash — selling off a hunk of his herd. And he was keeping more cows than his land could carry under the normally brutal and arid climate of West Texas. Back-to-back wet winters helped, but they also carried the threat of that unknown toxic plant or fungus that could kill his cattle.

Hulett needed cash. Pronto.

Boxing in the Bryte Brothers had cost him plenty to grease the palms of the county surveyor, a state senator and a couple of legislators, a Railroad Commission member, a county judge, that friendly state bank examiner and those nervous bankers. Of course, he bought the politicians with campaign contributions from straw donors that masked his identity and maintained a façade of propriety. The others he bribed outright. Throw in attorneys' fees and the bills from two private investigators, one in Marfa, the other in Houston. Call it $750,000 in ice-box cold and rounded numbers.

Another brace of pricey moves slammed his cash reserves like a sledgehammer smacking into sheetrock. First up — the quiet purchase of key tracts of land the Bryte Brothers wanted for their rancho deluxe plans. Using a couple of out-of-town attorneys and real estate agents, he had swooped in and trumped their bids, paying way too much but gaining acreage that gave him control over the most coveted prize in arid country — water. Something a dude ranch golf course just had to have.

In West Texas, that mostly meant groundwater, crucial in a state where water laws gave a landowner an unfettered right to use any of the water underneath his land. This legal doctrine was often referred to as "the law of the biggest pump" because it allowed a landowner to suck up all the water he wanted to, leaving wells on neighboring property dry and his neighbors with no legal recourse. One of the tracts he picked up had a spring on it. He also snapped up surface water permits on two drainages east of Seco Creek.

All this gave Hulett a handy wrecking ball to swing at the Bryte Brothers' plan. It also gave him a bigger bulwark protecting the northern and eastern flanks of the Bar Double H from hoggish water marauders. The price tag — $3.5 million. With the added bonus of terminally pissing off the Bryte Brothers once all these moves were filed and made public.

Hulett had one other ace up his sleeve, a card that came from his knowledge that the bright line of the family would probably die out with his death. He never remarried after Mary Nell died. There had been dalliances with grass widows living in the towns and ranches surrounding the Bar Double H, most of them short-lived flings to scratch a mutual itch and warm an empty bed — his or hers.

A fling with a rich divorcee in Alpine flared into a longer affair that left him severely singed and gun shy. She was a Tejana who burned through lovers and husbands at a furious pace and wanted to add him to her parade of broken men who poured their money into her bank accounts. He bowed out before she wrecked him.

She still called, even though she was married, and dropped by unannounced one summer afternoon to fuck him cross-eyed and remind him of what he was missing. She said she had her eye on him — a chilling thought that made him feel like a muley in a hunter's crosshairs. He heard she was getting set to ditch *Esposo Numero Cinco* and dreaded the carnal onslaught to follow.

He sure didn't want to be *Esposo Numero Seis*. And by his lights, there were few things more sorry-ass than the sight of an older man marrying a much younger woman to sire more children in a pitiful attempt to deny death. That left him stuck with a son and daughter who both had that dark Hulett wild streak that regularly led to shouting matches, harsh words and slamming door departures that cut him deeper than he cared to admit. Knowing they were more like Gyp than he or his dead wife didn't just feed his anger — it stoked his loneliness and a rising need for salvation and redemption.

He wasn't much of a churchgoer anymore, but salvation and redemption were twin motivations powerful enough to make him pick up the phone a few months back and start talking to some sharpies from a tree-hugging outfit called The Range Conservation Trust about signing over his part of the ranch to them. It was a dangerous move that would freeze out his own children and earn him the hatred of ranchers across the state. It was also a deadly card that might just get him killed — by Gyp or some of his nasty friends, like Malo Garza.

He didn't mention any of these land deals to Schoenfeldt on the phone and stayed silent about that lethal ace. That bastard had been bluffing about his knowledge of the inner workings of the Bar Double H. He'd find out soon enough how badly he'd been fucked by a severely underestimated West Texas rancher who wasn't nearly as toothless and broken down as a city slicker assumed.

The Bryte Brothers would strike back. That was a dead, solid certainty. In court, in the legislature and in other more underhanded ways. They had a nasty reputation for turning their opponents into flaming financial wrecks. You didn't build a shipping, trucking and ranching conglomerate by being nice. No win-win for these boys. They aimed to conquer and leave your house a smoking hulk. There was talk some of the folks who crossed them wound up dead.

Some of those rumors were not so ancient history from the 1890s, when the brothers started buying up ranches in Texas, Montana and Wyoming to try their hand at the cattle game. A couple of smaller ranchers who got in their way either disappeared or wound up shot dead in cases that never saw the dim light of a courtroom.

The Bryte Brothers still owned a big ranch in the Panhandle — the Four Nines. But their forays into the Big Bend country had been rebuffed by the Gage and Holland families. And the Huletts.

Fast-forward ninety years and some change. Their descendants were trying another run at his family's rocky slice of heaven. With plans for a dude ranch instead of a cattle outfit. Could get grim because not all of the lethal rumors swirling around the Bryte Brothers were ancient. Time to lock and load. And dial up a few nasty friends of his own.

His cousin Gyp was first on the list. Up on that ridgeline, Hulett wanted to kill Gyp. Now he needed to tap his cousin's money and his other more unsavory virtues. Gyp had some rank and unpleasant acquaintances. On both sides of the border. Turning to Gyp felt like plunging a knife into his guts and ripping them open. Seppuku with the seven-inch blade of the Ka-Bar he carried on Saipan. Perfect.

As he walked into the hallway to dial up his cousin, he felt the cold and remorseless gaze of ghostly eyes and the dark pull of blood and kinship stronger than the Good Book's call for virtue and righteousness. Easy enough to figure the specters looking over his shoulder — Judson and Malachi Hulett, the Louisiana brothers who fled to Texas in the 1850s after killing a riverboat gambler for dealing seconds from a stacked deck.

Judson spotted the cheat. Malachi fatally folded the gambler's hand with a pepperbox, a .36-caliber Allen & Thurber he had stuffed in his boot. Judson was blond and righteous — Bart Hulett was his great-grandson. Malachi was dark and violent — Gyp Hulett was his descendant.

They started out as freighters, lugging goods both above-board and illegal up the treacherous Chihuahua and Santa Fe trails, following in the footsteps of Milton Faver. They scraped together enough money to start the Bar Double H, claiming the rugged land split by the Devil's Backbone, rounding up the wild cattle to start their herd, rustling Mexican cattle to flesh it out, fighting off Comanche and Apache, killing raiders, rustlers and land swindlers with no more remorse than that shown when butchering a steer for the smokehouse.

They split the ranch into two parts — Malachi taking the more rugged part of their claim west of the Devil's Backbone, Judson settling the eastern half, each building a fortified campo that protected family and the hands they hired. They ran the ranch like two separate fiefdoms, but the brothers remained bonded by more than blood. Springs on the north end of the ridge fed both Seco Creek and the Dead Wolf Creek drainage that ran through the land Malachi staked as his domain.

Each brother followed his own star, one bright, the other dark. Judson volunteered for the Confederacy and fought with Henry Sibley at Valverde and Glorieta Pass, then returned home and drove herds east to the ever-dwindling part of Texas still under Confederate control. Malachi swore allegiance to nobody but his brother, selling beef to the Yankees at Fort Davis, rustling Mexican cattle to rebuild his herds, running guns to the Confederacy and the Comanche, earning the Bar Double H a measure of immunity from Yankees, Confederates and the feared Lords of the Plain.

Through the years, the pattern of dark and light continued, with Judson's descendants appearing to walk the straight and narrow of ranchers, businessmen and civic leaders while Malachi's worked the subterranean currents that flowed beneath the surface of legitimate West Texas commerce.

Judson's grandson — Bart Hulett's grandfather — fought with Roosevelt at Kettle and San Juan hills. Malachi's grandson — Gyp Hulett's grandfather — sat out the Spanish-American War, rustled Mexican cattle every chance he got and later ran guns to Pancho Villa and any other Mexican warlord who could cross his palms with gold.

In 1887, both teamed up with neighboring ranchers, the owner of the copper smelter and other Faver businessmen to carve off a hunk of Presidio County to form Cuervo County. During an early meeting at the Cattlemen's Hotel in Faver, a squat, three-story limestone and brick box that was still the tallest building in town, Rulon Carl Hulett, Bart's grandfather, wrapped their secession plan in noble words drawn from the Declaration of Independence, Sam Houston and Robert E. Lee.

"We ship our pound of flesh to Presidio but get little in return other than empty words and promises. We demand fair representation, but get the gerrymander that keeps us under Presidio's thumb. Our interests are vastly different than Presidio's and it's high time we free ourselves from their heavy yoke and hew our own independent path."

Jackson Herbert "Black Jack" Hulett, Gyp's grandfather, was a bit more piquant.

"We're gettin' cornholed by them crooked sumbitches down in Presidio who take our money but won't stay bought. We got us two choices — saddle up and ride down there to kill all them bastards or buy us our own county where the crooks are owned by us."

They raised a war chest of a million dollars in gold coin to line the pockets of state and federal politicians, a pot that mixed rustling and gunrunning money with clean, cold cash from copper and cattle.

The deal got done. Rulon Carl Hulett, Bart's grandfather, was elected the first county judge. Cuervo County was bought and paid for — cheap at twice the price.

Bart's daddy served with the Big Red One in the Great War, leading a platoon at Cantigny and losing the pinkie and ring finger of his left hand as he raised it to wave his men forward, a permanent mark of patriotism that served him well when he asked voters to send him back to Austin as their state senator. Which they did — time and time again — even though he voted with the drys.

Gyp's daddy kept rustling Mexican cattle to sell to Army training camps then ran bootleg liquor across the Rio Grande during Prohibition, using the old La Brava crossing favored by smugglers well before Judson and Malachi's day.

Bart joined the Marines to fight at Saipan where he got a Purple Heart and a Bronze Star; Gyp was 4F with a punctured eardrum earned in an Ojinaga whorehouse brawl. No Purple Heart for Gyp.

The Huletts knew the truth about each other and weren't afraid to talk frankly about it. But only to family. To outsiders, there were the bad Huletts living on the rough and rowdy side of the Devil's Backbone and the good Huletts living on Seco Creek and attending services at the First Baptist Church of Faver every Sunday.

The sharp contrast between good and bad, light and dark fascinated the loose-tongued gossips of Cuervo County and beyond, fueling speculation about whether the virtues of the good Huletts were fatally tainted by the sins of the bad.

To those of the hard-shell Baptist persuasion, drawing a distinction between the family's good works and outlaw enterprises was biblically unsound — Old Testament hellfire and damnation awaited every generation of Huletts with no chance of New Testament redemption.

But while outsiders might whisper about the Huletts and debate their final reward, they learned quick never to let somebody from one side of the Hulett family hear any badmouthing about the other.

A bootlegging crony of Gyp's daddy found that out the hard way when he started cussing out Bart's daddy for being a dry as they muscled a truck full of liquor across the La Brava crossing. Gyp's daddy shot the man dead with a short-barreled Colt thumb-buster, kicked the body out of the truck cab and let it float downstream.

A Baptist preacher from Fort Worth who was a big wheel in the Anti-Saloon League questioned the commitment of Bart's daddy to the temperance cause, wondering aloud in an Austin restaurant how the cousin of a bootlegger could be trusted to stand firm against the evils of alcohol. Bart's daddy used his good right hand to punch the man's lights out.

Blood was thicker than water, wild West Texas gossip and a banker's drizzles. When the Great Depression wiped out the savings and investments of Bart's daddy, bootlegging money and gold coins cached in a backcountry bat cave saved the day. When Mexican cattle infected with brucellosis forced Gyp to quarantine and kill off his herd, money from Bart's oil and gas leases paid the bill to restock Gyp's land.

For the generations that followed Judson and Malachi Hulett, there had always been a distance between the rustling, bootlegging and gunrunning of Malachi's descendants and the above-board actions, businesses and politicking of Judson's line. That made it easy for Judson's descendants to live a lie, strike a righteous public pose and deny the truth about the family's darker side.

But running rustled Mexican cattle on Hulett land was one thing. Nobody on the north side of the Rio Grande gave much of a damn about that. Allowing a drug-laden aircraft to land and off-load its cargo was sin of a different color — reckless beyond belief, an act that shattered any measure of hypocritical Hulett deniability. Nobody but a *narcotraficante* lawyer would even try to excuse that.

Not in this hard-edged era of the War on Drugs. Not when the high and mighty sheriff of Cuervo County was turning himself into a poster child for that war on the state and national stage. Not when law enforcement needed little excuse to slap any and all assets into forfeiture and use the power of the RICO Act to punish the entire Hulett clan.

Not when Bart Hulett's newest enemies were circling like sharks, looking for an opening to rush in and devour him whole.

As he dialed Gyp's number, he told himself:

Swallow that Ka-Bar blade, son. Suck up the pain and tamp down the pride. Cool the jets of that flaming bloodlust for killing Gyp you felt up on that ridgeline. Can the false virtue and self-righteous anger. Time for another bite of that rotten and worm-infested apple of Hulett hypocrisy and duplicity.

Because this was still West Texas, an ageless and unforgiving land of stark and barren beauty, harsh choices and sudden violence both ancient and modern. To make it here, you still had to have the internal iron of a Milton Faver or a Judson and Malachi Hulett. A willingness to do anything to survive and thrive.

Anything.

Six

Burch felt as rancid and hollowed out as a month-old Halloween pumpkin, his stomach empty and sour from the steady diet of Maker's and Percodan, his head unmoored from reality and rational thought, his mind just a stutter-step ahead of the rattlesnake fear he felt was ready to strike his soul one more time.

In the cool, neon-tinged gloom of Louie's bar, he tried to read a copy of the *Dallas Times Herald* by the early afternoon light that glared through the glass door behind him like a Baptist deacon shocked by the sin of a day drinker with the nightmare shakes.

The words of the bold-faced headlines eluded Burch, their letters pouring off the page and dropping to the floor like loose change. He pretended they made sense and flipped to the next page, shaking the paper smooth again and taking a bite of Maker's served neat, chasing that with a sip of Coke on ice in a juice glass. He shrugged his shoulders and adjusted his glasses — a reader settling in for another hit of news. Smoke from a lit Lucky ribboned above the ashtray that flanked his drink.

Pure fraudulence. His best imitation of a man bracing himself to read the rest of the story. No Academy Award here. It was an act that wouldn't even pass muster in a hicktown dinner theater, but might fool a bored bartender studying the weekend betting line.

Little Hutch was the bartender, a hulking lad with unruly black curls that fell across a deceptively innocent face. He took pity on Burch, let him in well before the opening bell, fixed him a smoked turkey sandwich and poured his drink. Then left him alone.

The bar's portable phone rang just about the time the Maker's calmed his nerves enough for him to make sense of the headlines. Near as Burch could tell, George and Barbara Bush still lived in the White House and were trying to figure out who to tell America to hate now that the Cold War was over. Any Arab would do in Burch's book.

Another headline snapped into sharp focus — the Cowboys were still having a train-wreck of a 1989 season. Tom Landry, Tony Dorsett and Dammit Danny White were long gone. Taking their place was a patchwork roster of raw rookies and veterans well past their prime.

It was a damn shame. A once-proud franchise was getting run into the ground by a new owner, a loud-mouthed asshole named Jerry Jones, and his best Razorback buddy, Jimmie Johnson. Burch couldn't stand that strutting bantam of a first-year coach with his helmet of lacquered hair. He did take grim comfort in the fact that Johnson was finding out damn quick that college boy national titles didn't mean much in the pros.

Burch watched as Little Hutch listened to the voice on the other end of the line, murmured into the mouthpiece then punched the hold button.

"You here or not?"

"Never can tell. Depends on whether I can get you to pour me another drink."

Little Hutch shot him a middle digit salute. Burch laughed and killed off his whisky.

"Quit fuckin' around, Double E. Got the man on hold and he don't sound happy."

"Fuck him, then. Hang up on his sorry ass and get me another Maker's."

Little Hutch punched the call off hold and started warbling the well-practiced lyrics of that barkeep classic: *He's Not Here.* He barely got through the first bar when Burch heard loud cussing explode from the phone's earpiece from halfway down the bar.

"You tell that miserable cocksucker to take my call or I'm going to jerk his note and throw his fat ass out on the street...."

Little Hutch held up the phone and shrugged. The cussing continued, calling the legitimacy of his lineage into question and kicking severe dents in already battered virtues like sobriety, sexual prowess and fiscal stewardship.

Burch frowned, signaled for the phone with a weary wave, pointed an index finger at his empty glass and flashed four fingers — a regular's semaphore for how much Maker's he wanted poured. Dealing with his shyster, Fat Willie Nofzinger, always required another round of powerful medication.

"Gimme the goddam phone. Willie, you really need to quit cussin' in front of impressionable children like Little Hutch. He's a very sensitive lad. And you really need to quit bothering me when I'm trying to read the paper and enjoy a quiet lunch with friends."

"You're an asshole, Burch. You don't got any goddam friends...."

"Got it on the first guess, Willie. And they say you can't find your needledick with a pair of tweezers."

Burch killed the call and placed the phone on the bar. Little Hutch poured four fingers of Maker's into his glass.

"He'll call back. He wants me to do something for him, something I probably won't like. Cockroaches and shysters — they're the only ones that'll survive the nuclear winter."

"Why put up with that guy? Just give me the phone and I'll tell him you blew out of here. Then you can enjoy that drink in peace."

"Can't do that, Hutch. Got to dance to the man's tune. His sister is the landlord of my office and apartment. And Fat Willie holds the note on my business. Doesn't mean I can't fuck with him first before we start the two-step."

Little Hutch shook his head and walked back to the middle of the bar and his racing form.

The phone rang again. Burch took a sip of Maker's then picked up the phone and punched the talk button.

"What kind of goddam goat ropin' do you want to throw me into this time, Willie?"

"You're a piece of shit, Burch. I still haven't seen dime one from that last job you wrapped up and here you are yankin' my chain when I'm trying to send more business your way. I don't know why I don't just pull the plug on your note and throw you out on the street."

"Easy answers, Willie. I know where all your bodies are buried and I'm the only guy you can get in Dallas smart enough, mean enough and in hock enough to you to do your dirty work. I don't pay you on time because I don't like you. Not a little bit. I like your sister-in-law, though. Her I always pay the first of the month. Like a clock."

"Are you done pissin' in my ear, cockbite? Christ amighty, dealin' with you is worse than shittin' day-old chili with a bad case of the piles."

"It's a gift, Willie. Part of my legendary charm. Just ask my exes, my bookie and my bartender. They'll tell you Ed Earl Burch is well-liked and beloved in this town."

"Wasted on me, fuckhead. Can the fandango and let me lay out this job for you. I'll even tell you about a sweet'ner that ought to make you happy I called."

"Jesus, must be a real clusterfuck if you're already talking about sweet'ners. Tell me the bad news first so I can tell you to go fuck yourself and get back to my lunch."

"Not before you listen to what I have to say. It's a divorce case out in West Texas."

"Hell no, Willie. You know I don't do divorce work. And the last time I was in West Texas, a crazy man tried to carve out my heart and eat it. The only thing I need to do about West Texas is a whole lot of leavin' it alone."

"Don't you think you need to get back up on that bronc and ride it?"

"I ain't no cowboy, Willie. When a horse throws me, I shoot it and walk away."

"*Thought you was a John Wayne fan. The Duke wouldn't shoot his horse 'less it had a broken leg.*"

"That's for the tourists and the bubba dumbasses who worship the Duke and the rugged independence of the Texas myth. You're starting to bore shit out of me, Willie. Let's get to talkin' about that sweet'ner you mentioned. And that nasty turd you're hiding behind your back that you haven't mentioned."

"*Okay. First the sugar. This is divorce work you hate, but it couldn't be easier. Client is named Nita Rodriguez Wyatt. She was married to one of Sid Richardson's heirs. One of the Wyatts. Kept his name and a shitpot full of that oil money after they split up. Lives out in Alpine and cavorts with all those artists and musicians livin' out there.*"

"Cavorts? Hell, Willie — you want to go easy on them fancy words. Give yourself a brain aneurism if you're not careful."

"*Shit, son — I'll keep it dirt simple so even a dumbass like you can understand it. What's the old Will Rogers line — never met a man he didn't like? That's our girl. But she's also the marrying kind. Tends to play house with artists, musicians and drugstore cowboy types. Gets bored with them and gives them the chop. Usually after finding someone like you to dig up some dirt so she can be the aggrieved wife. Makes it easier to execute or scrap the pre-nup and give them a less golden kiss-off.*"

"So how come she's not using one of those high-dollar divorce firms out of Dallas or Houston? Woman with her kind of money wouldn't get caught dead dealin' with a cheap-o like you. Or me, for that matter."

"*Here's where it gets real inner'estin, son. Seems like a little bird whispered your name in her ear. Also mentioned the best way to get you was to talk to me.*"

"Who in the hell would be stupid enough to do that?"

"*Buddy of yours. Makes guitars out there. Does a little cowboyin' too.*"

"Damn. Gotta be Spider Throckmorton. Haven't seen that ol' boy since he left Austin."

"*Bingo.*"

"Well, I'll have to give that man a call and renew the acquaintance. And tell him 'hell, no' right personal."

"Lookit, Burch. Lemme tell you why you won't do that. And lemme tell you why you'll take this job and like it. First off, it's easy money for about five days of work — maybe less. Five grand and expenses. The husband shacks up in a no-tell motel with this little cowgirl from a town or two over about twice a week. They're none too quiet or subtle about it, either. So, it's an easy mark — all you do is show up, stake 'em out, get some snaps and get gone."

"If it's that easy, why not get a local to do it or one of the investigators from those Dallas and Houston firms?"

"The woman wants you and knows I'm the one to get you. Your buddy has built you up big. Said you saved his ass. Has you pegged as some kinda cross between Sam Spade, the Duke and Sonny Liston."

"All I did was beat the hell out of some guys trying to muscle in on his business. Had to shoot one of them. Got ruled self-defense. As in, 'Yore honor, he needed killin'.'"

"You made an impression."

"Still haven't talked about that sweet'ner. Or that turd."

"Okay. The sweet'ner is, you take this gig and I'll chop ten grand off that note I'm carryin'."

"Shit — must mean you're getting something big out of this. Lemme guess — an ongoing business relationship with the aggrieved wife and her regular lawyers."

"You got it. Truth is, they're tired of dealing with her little marital adventures and would like to farm out that part of her business while keeping the more lucrative parts — tending the oil and gas leases she got from one of Sid's whelps."

"So tell me about the turd behind your back."

"Oh, that's almost a no nevermind. Lookit, word's gettin' 'round that you're real shaky right now. Do okay when you're working. Go off the rails when you're not. Them fellas that have been givin' you steady work chasin' down partners that skip town and hidden assets of guys who

declare bankruptcy? They're gettin' real nervous about you and have asked me to step in. You want more of that work, you gotta deal with me. You want their jobs, you gotta do this one for me."

"So, what you're tellin' me is this is the best lousy choice I've got."

"No, son — what I'm tellin' you is you got no choice at all. You need to work to stay sane. You need money. You need to deal with me and do this job."

"I'll think about it."

"Think fast, bubba. The clock is tickin' and time's about to run out on your sorry ass."

The line clicked dead. Burch took a drag from his Lucky and crushed it out. Then gunned the rest of the four fingers of Maker's in one gulp.

It didn't help.

Seven

"Bite my nipples, baby...yessssssssssss, yessssssss...uhhhhhhh-huh, uhhhhhh-huh. Harder, dammit. Harder. Bite them hard and keep fuckin' me."

Jason Powell, fast-fingered guitar slinger and wayward husband, did his damnedest to oblige, clamping his teeth on one nipple, then the other while he gripped the thin hips of his young blonde lover and plunged his cock into her pussy at a pace meant to punish rather than pleasure.

She liked it that way — fast, raw and rough. Bent over the hood of a car. Riding him in the front seat of his pickup. Making the bedsprings squall in a no-tell motel on the outskirts of Marfa, Sanderson, Fort Davis or Faver. Wrecking the sheets in the plush and well-cushioned bed he shared with his wife in Alpine.

His goddam wife. The Hellbitch. Nita Rodriguez Wyatt. Rich and ten years older and probably out fucking somebody else while he balled his lover. Thinking of his wife made him spin the blonde girl onto her hands and knees, his cock still inside her, taking her from behind as he roughly gripped her hips and pulled her back to meet his slamming cock.

Sweat dripped from his face and chest, mingling with the slick, moist sheen of her back and ass. She shook her thick, dark-blonde mane, looking over her shoulder, her eyes half-shut, her mouth open and making a silent ohhhhh as her tongue darted between her teeth to lick her lips. Then her eyes popped open with an angry flash.

"Where the hell you at, lover man? You fallin' asleep back there? You need to wake up and give it to me harder than you are right now. Don't make me call in the hired help. I want to be fucked not cuddled."

"Baby, I fuck you much harder I'll break my cock off."

"You ain't fuckin' me near hard enough for that. You know how I love it *empinado y rapido*. Give it to me."

He snarled and gave her a savage thrust. She gasped and her head pitched forward, her thick, sweat-streaked hair whipping over her face.

"Yes, baby. Yesssssssssss. Uh-huhhhhh. Un-huhhhh. Uh-huhhhh. Don't stop. Don't stop. Don't stop."

"No stoppin' now, baby. Damn, I'm gettin' close."

A banshee wail from her as she drummed her palms on the twisted sheets. The sharp sound of flesh slapping sweaty flesh. A deep, guttural growl from him.

She spasmed, her cunt gripping his cock tighter as the wail turned into a shriek. His growl became a strangled cry for mercy as he came deep inside her, then fell forward, wrapping his arms around this wild rancher's daughter and stabbing her mouth with his tongue.

The thump and rattle of the room's ancient air conditioner jolted him awake, his eyes wide open, his heart lurching in his chest. He felt her taut, cowgirl body curled into his and it chilled him right down.

Stella Rae Hulett was sleeping in his arms, snoring lightly, her sinewy shoulders and back pressed into his chest and belly, the curve of her muscular ass pushed against his groin. He buried his face in her damp, tangled hair and breathed deep, his fingers tapping and tracing her nipples, his cock starting to stir.

Stretching like a cat, she turned toward him and flashed a smile that showed ghostly white in the no-tell gloom. Her hand circled his cock, then cupped his balls.

"My, my — what have we here?"

"My pride and joy. You and him should be pretty good friends by now."

"You bet. And I know how greedy he can be. Won't let a girl get her beauty rest and recover after fucking her to a frazzle."

"He cain't help it. He ain't got no table manners. Ain't been housebroke. Got no faith or religion, neither."

"You make a piss poor hick. Don't know how to talk country worth a damn, do you, city boy?"

"True. I only know how to do two things. Pick a little guitar and this..."

He slipped a finger into her, sliding easy and deep into her wet sex. She let out a breathy moan and bit his left nipple, drawing a sharp yelp of pain.

She looked up at him and laughed, then started sliding down his body, her tongue tracing a path down his chest and belly, her hair spilling across his thighs.

"Let's see if a little mouth worship will restore his faith."

Sex as holy sacrament. No wafer or wine. No church or chapel. Just a naked cowgirl as his wicked high priestess in a no-tell on the outskirts of Faver.

Call him a true believer and his cock a faithful follower.

They shared a cigarette, trading puffs on a Salem Light while resting easy and close in the languid afterglow, stretched out and facing each other and talking softly about whatever came to mind. Anything but the dreaded L-word and the fact that he was a married man.

This was their time. They were crazy for each other and both knew how the other felt without talking it to death. They focused on the here

JIM NESBITT

and now, on Stella Rae and Jase, jealously guarding these moments against the hard realities of a domineering father, the powerful *patrón* of the Bar Double H, and a rich bitch of a wife who kept him wrapped up in the best velvet chains her wealth could buy.

That included a pre-nup with a $250,000 payout and a five-year fidelity clause. He signed it with a shrug before the wedding, figuring it was just paper a lawyer used to keep his ass well covered in the name of serving his client. Didn't matter to him because he loved his wife, not her money.

He loved her slashing wit and unbridled energy that made her the center of attention as soon as she walked into a room. He loved to watch her in motion, a powerful Latina with black curls framing a broad, high-cheeked face. Long-legged with the bountiful curves and unstoppable carnal drive of a mature woman who knew what she wanted — in the bedroom and everywhere else.

And for the first two years, she loved him back, dazzled by the soul-searing notes he could squeeze from a guitar and the raucous sex that left him bruised, sore and sated and her always ready for another round. To Nita Rodriguez Wyatt, Jason Powell was a prized possession, a guitar-slinging studhoss who gave her authentic entry into the inner chamber of that magic clan of musicians that her money could never buy.

The catch? Nita got bored with every possession she ever bought, from husbands to last year's sleek party dress. That left Powell tied to a loveless marriage while she had her one-night-stands and short-lived affairs with the same crowd of artists, musicians and writers that was once his domain. Men mostly, but sometimes women. When Nita was on the carnal prowl, gender didn't matter.

Most of his Alpine crowd were Austin ex-pats like himself, folks who fled the town once the weird and the funky started dying out, killed off by the high-tech suits and their corporate office parks. They were refugees out for a slice of West Texas realism. Just as long as it didn't get too rattlesnake real.

He moved to Alpine after a dozen years on the Austin music scene as the front man for a handful of mid-level bands that headlined the smaller clubs but were only good enough to be the opening act at the larger joints like Antone's, the Continental Club and Armadillo World Headquarters.

Back then, he went by a stage name he hated, hung on him by a manager who never met a gimmick he didn't like — Speedy Powell. As in Speedy Powell and the Nighthawks, Speedy Powell and the Midnight Riders, Speedy Powell and the Lonesome Range Boys.

With a tall, lean frame, coal black hair swept back from a widow's peak, a hawk nose and glittering green eyes, he was a natural front man because of both looks and talent, the common denominator for bands that covered the musical waterfront — blues, R&B, country rock and Western swing. He also did session work in Austin and Nashville, his slick guitar work appearing on records by Willie Nelson, Jerry Jeff Walker, Marcia Ball, Rosie Flores and Asleep at the Wheel.

He was still in demand as a session player and could drive to Austin or jet to Nashville for a few days or a couple of weeks, then return to Alpine and sit in with a couple of local bands, no longer feeling the need to be the front man sporting a stage name he never liked. When times were good, Nita would join him on these jaunts. When the marriage went south, he did them alone.

Stella Rae barged into his life on a late summer Friday night when he joined some musician buddies who agreed to help a friend launch a bar in Faver called Sharp's Last Call Lounge. Calling themselves The Rank Strangers, they were the opening night house band, playing the gig for beer and gas money as a favor to the owner, a ponytailed stoner and small-time promoter named Billy Dean Sharp, another Austin refugee.

Powell had played worse places in his early years, but he really couldn't remember ever picking guitar in an abandoned grocery store before. With a makeshift bar made from packing crates joined by rough pine planks, backlit by the florescent glow of refrigerated display cases that used to hold ice cream and frozen pizza but now kept the bottled beer ice cold. And a dance floor that still showed the bolt holes that anchored the four aisles of long gone food shelves. Overhead signs that hawked the selections of each aisle still dangled from the ceiling — Bread, Canned Vegetables, Canned Meat, Condiments.

They kept it West Texas simple that night — Waylon, Willie, Guy Clark, Gary P. Nunn, Townes Van Zandt, Rusty Weir, Ernest Tubb and Bob Wills, even though they didn't have a fiddler in the band. The crowd was raucous and whistled and stomped their approval through all three sets. They two-stepped and line-danced and waltzed to the slow ones, then shook it to the faster numbers. They bellowed out the chorus of "London Homesick Blues" and wouldn't let them finish the show without playing "Waltz Across Texas" and "Faded Love" one last time, back-to-back.

He saw her out on the dance floor with a revolving door of cowboy studhosses vying for her attention. Hard to miss in a white tank top stretched to the limit by full, unfettered breasts, dark blonde hair spilling shoulder length from underneath a battered straw hat with a rancher's dip and tight jeans that showed off flared hips and the lean muscles of a horsewoman. A tooled leather belt and tall, black boots with red floral cutouts and underslung riding heels spelled cowgirl wild in neon letters even a dead man could see.

She danced with all the one-night-stand suitors, but when each number ended, she wound up back on a lone barstool close to the stage, her eyes on him, watching as he opened the next song, ran through a solo then picked filler notes and chords when the band's other picker took the lead.

During the second break, he walked over and stood near her while flagging the bartender for a freebie bottle of Pearl. She looked him up and down with a wicked smile and eyes that telegraphed the challenge of a line that blew right past the predictable banter of bar-rail mating rituals.

"You're a damn good picker. Do you fuck as good as you play?"

He damn near choked on a mouthful of Pearl, but managed to swallow and pull off a cool, appraising gaze while he lowered the bottle from his lips.

"Only one way to find out, little sister."

Then he turned and walked back to the stage for the third and final set.

When the music died, last call was over and the gear was packed, he strolled to the back end of the emptied-out gravel lot where his black Chevy Silverado was parked. He walked around to the passenger side, keys out, ready to heft the case that held his sunburst-bodied Les Paul inside the cab.

He almost had a heart attack when the passenger door opened as if a ghost was working the handle and the cabin light popped on. Stella Rae Hulett sat on the front seat facing the open door, naked except for that battered straw hat. Her breasts bounced as she started to laugh, the cab light playing across her dark, hard nipples. Her eyes and smile still held that carnal challenge.

"You said there was only one way to find out."

"I damn sure did."

"Put that guitar away and get in here and prove it."

"Take off that goddam hat and I will."

He unbuckled his belt, shucked his boots and jeans in the gravel and climbed into the cab. She was twenty-four, hard to handle, but impossible to deny. He was thirty-five and in bad need of everything she had to offer — wildness, youth and unquenchable lust. What they both got was an unexpected side order of love that was rapidly becoming the main course.

"Where you at, lover man? Thinking about that damn wife of yours?"

He jetted smoke toward the motel room ceiling, reached over her to crush the cigarette in a glass ashtray on the nightstand, then turned on his side to look at her. The nightstand light was on and played over her skin, highlighting the rose-tinted olive hue that hinted of Cajun or

Spanish blood and the strands of gold in her thick, dark blonde hair that spoke of the Anglo. Her hazel eyes searched his face for an answer to her question.

"No baby, the Hellbitch wasn't on my mind. I was thinking about the first night we met."

She laughed, then punched him lightly in the chest.

"Fuckin' in your truck. Some first date, huh?"

"Sure as hell hooked me. You damaged the lock on my rig when you jimmied it."

"You didn't seem to give a damn at the time."

"Still don't. Worth every penny."

She frowned and shifted gears on him. Hard and fast.

"You know, baby, it's high time for you to cut yourself loose from that round-heel wife of yours and be with me. It's been fun slippin' around and grabbin' love on the run, but we're way past a casual fling on this deal."

"Sure as hell are. We've gone somewhere neither one of us expected this to go — gone from true lust to true love. Cain't get enough of each other and don't want to quit. Cain't quit."

"Don't want nobody but you, so why don't you leave her now and be with me?"

"Cain't just yet. And I speculate it's for the same reason you won't leave that ranch even though you and your daddy fight like a couple of junkyard dogs every chance you get."

"What's that got to do with leavin' her?"

"Just this — I didn't sign that pre-nup agreement for the money. Not back before I married Nita. But I damn sure want that dough now. Feel like I earned it and want to get paid. Got six more months till payday. And you don't like to admit it, but I think you feel the same way about that ranch — you've earned a piece of it and you want your daddy to pay up."

He saw the anger flash in her eyes, turning them into hazel lasers aimed straight at him.

"It's more than money to me — that ranch is in my blood. I'm a Hulett, goddammit, and the Bar Double H is as much as part of me as my ass or tits. More so."

"I know, sugar. That's why you go back there and patch things up with the old hard-ass and go on those backcountry rides with him and cover yourself up with all the ropin' and ridin' and sho'nuff all-round cowgirl chores you can stand. And that buys a truce between you two. Until the next blowup hits."

"Who the hell died and made you the god a'mighty expert on the inner workings of the Hulett clan?"

He ignored the question and the double-laser death stare, reaching across her cool, naked skin to grab another Salem Light off the nightstand. He fired it up with a cheap Bic knockoff, took a deep drag then placed the filter on her full, red lips and held it there as she took a puff.

"Here's what I see. I know it ain't money you want your daddy to give you. It's more than that — you're looking for recognition, validation, acknowledgment. A simple goddam blessing. A nod from him that you're his flesh and blood. That you're a Hulett and you're as much a part of that fuckin' ranch as he is. But he keeps holdin' back, holdin' you at arm's length, makin' you prove up again and again. And it pisses you off and pretty quick, there goes another blowup."

Stella Rae was quiet and seemed a million miles away as he spoke. She took a deep drag, then reached up with her other hand to caress his face, her eyes filled with sadness instead of anger.

"You're pretty damn smart for a city boy guitar picker."

"Nobody ever accused me of that before. Smarts ain't exactly my long suit."

"I didn't call you an Einstein, baby. What you say hits damn close to the mark, but it doesn't tell you *why* my own lovin' daddy won't give me that blessing, why he keeps his own daughter at a distance. To know the why of this you need to know a whole lot more about us Huletts and the great, dirty secret we've got and the lie we been livin' for generations."

Her words had an angry edge. The fire came back into her eyes. Neither were aimed at him.

"Lemme tell you about us Huletts, baby. My side of the family, we're supposed to be a bunch of goody-two-shoes, upright citizens and straight shooters — one calloused hand on the Good Book and the other passing on God's blessings to the good people of Cuervo County. Just take a look at my daddy — war hero, rancher and businessman, county judge. Just like his daddy and his daddy before that.

"My Uncle Gyp's side of the family — well, Gyp's really my second or third cousin, I think. Don't matter. His side of the family are all outlaws — gunrunners, smugglers, bootleggers, rustlers. Every crooked way they is to make a dollar, they've done it and are doin' it still. Wouldn't surprise me a damn bit if Gyp wasn't runnin' drugs, workin' with the biggest Mex drug lord along this section of the border. Yeah, don't know it for certain, but would bet cash money that Gyp's in bed with ol' Malo Garza his ownsef.

"So, there's supposed to be Good Huletts and Bad Huletts, right? Wrong. We're all dirty as coal-black sin, baby. We're all one outlaw band, with the Good Huletts putting on that saintly act, weatherin' the tribulations heaped upon them by the Bad Huletts like a family of latter-day Jobs, putting up a good front.

"What happy horseshit. The truth is we all live off that blood money. The Bar Double H couldn't exist without it. Yeah, we Good Huletts have made a ton of nice, clean cash on cattle, oil and other business deals. But we'll tap that blood money every time we need it and will bribe a politician or two to buy protection for the whole family, outlaws and all.

"That's why my daddy won't give me that blessing. He cain't live the lie no more and it's eatin' him up. He looks at me and knows I know the truth and won't live that lie. Same with my brother, but Jimmy Carl is gutless and no-account and Daddy wrote him off a long time ago.

"Daddy looks at me and knows I'm more like Gyp than I am him. Well, no fuckin' foolin'. I ain't a hypocrite. And I ain't gutless like Jimmy

Carl. I'm a Hulett through and through, good and bad, dark and light. Daddy sees that and hates himself all the more for it."

The anger left her voice. The fire in her eyes dimmed. She turned toward him and hugged him fiercely, her body wracked with a strangled cry muffled by lips pressed against his chest.

The embrace only lasted a moment. Like the sudden silence that follows a jailhouse door slammed after midnight, the crying and trembling stopped. She pushed him away and she raised her head.

"You know, there are times when I think this world would be a helluva lot better off with my daddy dead."

Her voice was sharp and cold. Her eyes held a glow that chilled his spine with a glimpse of the steely hate inside Stella Rae Hulett. Hate that had the power to make those words a lethal reality.

Cowgirl wild with a killer lurking inside. Maybe so.

Eight

Burch sipped watery, lukewarm coffee and shifted his legs so the steering wheel of the gutless rental car he was forced to drive wouldn't gouge a groove in his thighs. A goddam three-year-old Plymouth Reliant with a four-banger engine, peeling light blue paint and all the roomy comfort a midget or contortion artist could ask for.

He was parked in the deep shadows of a rock outcropping looming over the highway on the northern outskirts of Faver, the car angled so he could watch the door of Room 35 of The Cactus Blossom Motel. Last room on the right on the second deck of a concrete block building with a sagging balcony and sun-faded coral and yellow paint streaked by the rusty condensation from the air conditioners hanging from the window of every room.

Thirty-five rooms were testimony to the optimism of the motel owners. Only five cars and two pickups were parked in slots that fronted each door. And this was late fall, the season when the dry, punishing heat dialed itself down to tolerable levels and the desert rats who loved this harsh, rocky country started showing up to hike or ride horseback on steep, stony trails.

Only one of the pickups was hitched to a horse trailer. The other was a shiny, black '82 Silverado with a short, fleetside box, chrome wheels and dual-exhaust tips and a Texas vanity plate that read PICKR52. Truth in advertising that included a birth year and made

Jason Powell's rig dead easy to spot and trail. Just a shade more difficult to track than the cherry red Z28 Camaro with CWGRL vanity plates.

More truth in advertising — the Camaro was registered to one Stella Rae Hulett, daughter of a rich rancher with a spread southwest of Faver and just a little north of the Rio Grande. Those nuggets of background weren't the result of his superior sleuthing powers. A Faver lawyer named Boelcke, part of the expanding network of legal eagles serving the needs of Nita Rodriguez Wyatt, filled him in after he had a cop buddy run the Camaro's plates that gave him her name.

Boelcke, a local boy who done good in the big city but flew home to roost for reasons he never mentioned, also gave him a list of no-tell motels in Faver, Alpine, Fort Davis, Marfa and Van Horn. Good to know in case he lost track of Powell's pickup on a tail. The lawyer, who also had an office in Alpine, even cleared his stalking and stakeouts with the law dogs in Cuervo and Brewster counties.

Playback of meeting Boelcke in his office that first day in Faver, eyes on the door to Room 35 as the memory tape rolled and the lawyer gave him a long-winded briefing about the big dog of Cuervo County, Tyrus Lamar "Blue" Willingham.

"Look, Blue Willingham is too damn busy burnishing his image as a drug-busting crusader to give two shits about a guy like you tailing a hippie Alpine guitar picker to a motel love nest. Particularly since he knows you're working for me and that my client is Nita and she's donated some heavy coin to his campaign fund. Might be a little different if he knew lover girl was Bart Hulett's daughter, but he doesn't."

"Sounds like a man with a mighty high opinion of himself. Also sounds like a man with his eye on a bigger prize."

"That's our Blue. Thinks he's the second coming of John Wayne, Jack Hays and Frank Hamer all rolled into one. And you're right — Blue firmly believes he's God's gift to democracy and that every voter in Texas should get the opportunity to cast a ballot for him. Not just the good people of Cuervo County."

"Believe I met him once when I was still a cop in Dallas. Made a name for himself as a Ranger, right?"

"Sure did. Solved that Gonzalez double-killing and kidnapping case about fifteen years back down in Uvalde. Rich Tejano couple with an only daughter about eleven at the time — Carmen. The snatch went bad when daddy and momma came home too early. Scumbags cut 'em down with double ought right in front of Carmen. Blue tracked them down to a double-wide outside Carrizo Springs and shot 'em both graveyard dead. Not before they killed Blue's partner, though."

"That's it. Met him not long after that, when he was still a Ranger and still had a hitch in his giddyup from that bullet. I remember that picture, the one with him carryin' the Gonzalez girl with blood runnin' down his leg."

"You bet. Damn near every paper in the country ran that one. He's got that sumbitch blown up bigger than God and hanging on the wall of his office. Right next to the display case with his great-granddaddy's break-top Smith & Wesson, the one he carried when he was a Ranger."

"Best of both worlds for a sheriff needing votes — got him one boot planted in the Anglo camp and the other in the Mex savin' that Gonzalez girl."

"More to it than that. Blue's got a Ranger legacy but he also has some Tejano blood in him. Like just about everybody else around here, including me. That might have been a liability back in the bad old days when Anglos ruled the roost, but it's a card Blue can play these days with La Raza on the rise."

"Does he?"

"Oh, you bet. Blue is pretty fluent in Spanish — he can speak it a damn sight better than the border Spanish most Anglos use around here. He's been pretty smart with his law-and-order tough guy act. That used to mean beating the shit out of wetbacks and keeping Tejanos under your heel. Not with Blue. He doesn't ignore crimes against Tejanos. Got three or four brown deputies and a chief deputy who is brown and black. And the truth is, a lot of Tejanos don't much care for wetbacks if they aren't *family and hate the dealers and drug lords just as much as Anglos do."*

"Smart man. Let's make damn sure the High Sheriff stays in the dark about lover girl. I imagine daddy is also a campaign contributor and draws a lot more water around here than Nita."

"You got it. Just don't step on your dick or shoot anybody and you should be fine. Keep my card handy in case you step in some shit, okay?"

Playback over. Burch sipped more coffee and opened a tin of Copenhagen to slip a pinch between cheek and gum. No Luckies on a stakeout. No Zippo flare. Ruined the night vision and might just get him spotted by his quarry. Old reflexes from his days as a Dallas homicide detective when the quarry would kill you quick if you screwed up.

Nothing deadly about peeping out paramours in a no-tell love shack. Never could tell, though, so he kept the .45 cocked, locked and secure in the shoulder holster hanging below his right armpit. Eight in the mag and one in the pipe. Prudent, but probably unnecessary.

Nothing honorable about what he was doing, either. Not like taking a killer down. With handcuffs or hollow-points, depending on how the bad guy dealt the play. He missed the clarity, sense of purpose and jolting adrenaline rush of those showdowns.

That's why Burch hated divorce work like a Baptist deacon hates Original Sin. Reminded him of the gold shield he could no longer carry and how far down the ladder he had slipped. He also hated admitting his shyster, Fat Willie Nofzinger, was ever right about anything. But so far, Fat Willie had been on the money. This had been dead easy work, no matter how much it left a rank taste in his mouth that whiskey couldn't wash away. With or without the 'e.'

The only hitch had been a blown head gasket on his '75 F-150, a faded red rig he called Ol' Blue that had 187,000 miles on the odometer. And a nickname not to be confused with the local sheriff. The truck made it out to Alpine only to cough up a billow of white, oily smoke in the middle of downtown Faver after he left Boelcke's office his first day in town.

Not the best way to remain inconspicuous. He had Ol' Blue towed to a mechanic Boelcke recommended. Then he shuffled over to a used car lot owned by a fat, brassy and fast-talking Mex named Diego "Dirt Cheap" Bustamante and rented the gutless Reliant, one of those K-cars Lee Iacocca relentlessly hustled to bring Chrysler back from the dead.

While his rig was getting major engine surgery, he let Boelcke stash his Winchester Model 12 riot pump in a locked office closet, cradled in a silicone gun sock and zipped up in a canvas bag. He first carried that pump as a beat cop then a detective. It was in his hands the night he was too slow to keep his partner, Wynn Moore, from getting killed. A bad memory but a damn good gun. Hard to keep it hidden in the back seat of a K-car and useless to keep it locked up in the trunk.

Just another reason to be rankled by the shabby ride he was forced to drive, but the car was good enough to keep him on the trail of Powell and Hulett. Long as he kept the gas pedal floored. Powell led him to Hulett and her cherry red Camaro parked at a Motel 6 outside Van Horn his second day on the job. Good thing he didn't have to trail her.

The two lovers acted like they wanted to get caught, using the same no-tells and often booking the same rooms. The Cactus Blossom was a favorite. He stuffed Boelcke's love shack list in the glove box. Didn't need it. He just tailed Powell out of Alpine as the picker made a beeline for the next honey-pot rendezvous.

It didn't take long for Burch to start piling up photographic evidence with a trusty Olympus OM-1, a small-bodied camera with a sharp zoom lens, loaded with fast, black-and-white film perfect for low-light work. Four days on the hunt and six rolls of film.

He even hit paydirt with a voice-activated mic tucked under the base of a night table lamp in Nita and Jason's bedroom while Nita was out of town. That yielded a 60-minute cassette of moans, cries, passionate profanity and pillow talk where the man's voice was clearly Powell's and the woman's voice sure didn't belong to Nita Rodriguez Wyatt. Another day or two and he'd be headed back to Dallas.

Burch had to admit Fat Willie was also right about the healing grace of slipping back into the harness of a familiar routine. Kept his mind occupied with the hunt, no matter how easy. Kept the nightmare demons in their holes, loosening their hold on him.

He remembered Hemingway wrote about the restorative power of ritual in one of his best short stories, a two-part Nick Adams piece, "Big, Two-Hearted River." In Papa's story, Adams was a scarred veteran of The Great War, fishing alone in Michigan's Upper Peninsula, his mind focused on the details of fishing familiar honey holes he had dreamed of while recovering from his wounds in a hospital near the Italian front.

Burch wasn't a combat veteran, but his years as a cop had left similar physical and psychic scars. Sitting in a beater Plymouth in the cool, desert dusk, he knew he was living the essence of a story he read and liked in high school. On this West Texas jaunt, nobody was trying to shoot him or carve out his heart. Nobody was trying to hang a murder wrap around his neck. Nobody was trying to use him for tiger bait.

Not yet.

And that helped ease his fears about returning to this country, helping him disconnect the place from what happened here and over the river in Mexico. Maybe not forever, but for now. Now would have to do.

The door to Room 35 popped open with a metallic squeal and the rasping sound of metal scraping concrete. Door needed to be rehung, Burch thought as he reached for the Olympus sitting on the seat beside him.

No motor drive on this little baby, which was fine by Burch. As a cop, he once watched a subject spook at the sound of a motor drive before the incriminating money shot could be snapped. Advancing the film with his thumb didn't scare the game.

Stella Rae bloomed into his viewfinder, fuzzy then sharp, up close then farther away, as he adjusted the focal length and focus of the lens. She was a short, hard-bodied woman with a pug nose and full lips on an oval face framed by dark blonde hair and a straw hat pushed back on her head. She was wearing boots, tight jeans and a loose white T-shirt that didn't hide the fact that she wasn't wearing a bra.

She was leaning on the railing in front of the open room door, smoking a cigarette, her face lit by a quartering light beaming down from tin overhang that ran the length of the balcony. Burch snapped three or four shots and noticed a leather bag hanging from her shoulder. Get gone time. He waited for Powell to step out of the room.

Didn't take long. The lanky guitar picker closed the door after one last look inside, swept his long black hair back with his hand, then pressed his body against hers, pulling her hips back and leaning forward to whisper in her ear.

Burch clicked through three money shots.

She raised her head to look back at him with a smile, reaching up to touch his face and arching her back to push her ass firmly against his crotch.

Four more money shots.

Powell turned her around and kissed her deeply. Her hat fell to the balcony floor. The lip lock was in fine, well-lit focus as Burch tripped the shutter on five shots. They broke the kiss but held each other tight, their smiling faces in obliging profile, lit by love and the balcony light as Burch clicked away.

Money in the bank.

Time to deliver the goods to Boelcke, get Ol' Blue out of hock and put Faver and the rest of West Texas in his rearview mirror. The job was over. He wondered when the demons would come calling again.

Nine

Burch sat slumped in a chocolate brown leather wingback with brass studs, his legs stretched out and crossed at the tops of his scuffed Justin boots to ease the pain in both knees, an icy rocks glass of his favorite medication in his right hand — four fingers of ninety proof.

The chair was one of a matched set in the inner sanctum of Boelcke's Alpine law office. Cheap, honey-colored pine paneling. A torn Navajo rug in faded ochers, browns and yellows. A framed University of Texas law degree behind Boelcke's head, flanked by gilt-edged membership certificates from the Alpine Chamber of Commerce and the Sertoma Club.

Burch sipped his medicine, happy to be sprawled in a comfortable chair instead of scrunched up in a rental car. He watched as Boelcke riffled through a stack of numbered, eight-by-ten glossies, pausing to cross reference them to the written report Burch had banged out on a Selectric he commandeered in the lawyer's outer office, scrawling notes on a yellow legal pad.

Boelcke was wearing a starched white cowboy shirt with pearl speed snaps, a bolo with a walnut-sized lump of turquoise on the slide, and round-lensed, horned-rimmed reading glasses that made Burch think of Peter O'Toole as Mister Chips.

The lawyer's surname said German and was spelled the same as the World War I *Luftstreitkräfte* ace whose Dictum Boelcke became the

Bible of fighter pilots everywhere. But his look was pure border Tejano — curly, dark brown hair cropped fairly close and parted on the left side, skin with a slight olive tint and a trim moustache Pedro Infante would have envied. Only his blue eyes betrayed the *Texasdeutsch* heritage common to the Hill Country and beyond.

Burch squinted at the scripted name on the law degree — Santiago Quinones Boelcke. The name on both the chamber of commerce and Sertoma Club certificates was a simpler read — Sam Boelcke. The lawyer as border *menudo* personified.

"This one I really like."

Boelcke tapped one of the last glossies in the pile and slid it across his desk toward Burch. It was the ultimate money shot from the hunt, the result of a chance Burch took during his last stakeout of a no-tell rendezvous between Powell and Hulett at the Desert Air Motel in Sanderson.

From his perch in the Reliant, he saw light leaking from a gap in the curtain of the couple's ground-floor room. It was dark and he crept in close to snap a shot or two through the gap. Pure, ballsy luck brought pure gold — Powell with his head thrown back, thrusting into Hulett, her legs wrapped around his hips, both clearly lit by the overhead light.

"You really earned your pay with this one. The other stuff is really damning and damned good fodder, but this here is the clincher."

Burch grimaced, shook his head and polished off his medicine.

"Gonna need to take a shower with a pressure washer to get shed of all the pigshit I been wallowing in to get you this."

"Sorry you feel that way, but this is damn good work. Slam dunk to get Nita out of paying hubby that pre-nup money."

"Not a damn thing in that pile that I'm proud of. I used to be a homicide detective. Went after badass killers and either smoked 'em or cuffed 'em. This here is a slimy keyhole job that will take me a river of whiskey to forget."

Boelcke gave Burch a dead-eyed stare over the top of his reading glasses, tapping his pen on the legal pad. He broke the stare with a sharp nod of his head.

"Okay, then. You're getting a five grand bonus for this. That ought to buy you some of that whiskey river. And she wants to meet you to hand you the check."

"Who?"

"My client. The happy, soon-to-be-ex-wife of Jason Powell. The lovely and talented and very rich Nita Rodriguez Wyatt. You saved her a chunk of change and she's very grateful. And she's one to express her gratitude directly instead of leaving it up to flunkies like me."

"Where and when is this meeting supposed to take place?"

"Tonight. At the home of Spider and Rhonda Throckmorton. Dinner will be served. Some form of cowflesh would be my bet. Their place is about forty miles south of town, so figure on staying out there overnight."

"Spider's the guy who got me into this goat-ropin' — need to speak sharp to that boy."

"Now, now — be nice. Yeah, he talked you up to Nita like you were the second coming of Sam Spade and Mike Hammer and that put you in play. But you needed the work and you're getting paid handsomely for it. By the way, Nita's picking up the tab on getting your truck fixed and the rental. Just bring me the receipts before you head home. Like I said, she's grateful."

"So you keep tellin' me. Just how grateful is she?"

"You're about to find out."

"You gonna be at Chez Throckmorton, son?"

"Not me. I'm going to be too busy. Have to tell lover boy the bad news about his pre-nup money. Have to draw up some paperwork for that and a quickie divorce in Reno. Give lover boy a peek at the evidence and get him to sign a release. Nita won't leave the boy high and dry. He'll get some kiss-off money, but not near as much as he was counting on."

"Cash to get out of town with his tail tucked between his legs?"

"Might be the smart choice. Or start shacking up with Stella Rae Hulett. His choice."

"Frying pan to the fire if you ask me."

"Probably so. Not our problem, though, right?"

"That's exactly right, son. I best leave you to it and get myself cleaned up for the shindig. Only thing I've got left to do tomorrow is pick up my truck and dump this piece of shit renter. So, unless you need me for anything else, this'll be adios."

Burch stood up to shake Boelcke's hand, wincing as his knees popped. The lawyer smiled, stepped from behind his desk and slapped Burch on the shoulder.

"You done real good on this. Got the goods without steppin' on your dick or shootin' anybody. You're in my Rolodex now for the next time Nita needs to get shed of a husband. And there'll always be a next time with her. Got other work I can throw your way that doesn't involve Nita so it don't need to go through that windbag attorney of yours."

Burch nodded and walked toward the door. He wished he could feel better about this, but he couldn't. The job was over and the nightmares might come calling at any time. All he could think about was getting through a night at Chez Throckmorton and getting long gone.

If those demons climbed out of their holes again, he wanted to be the hell out of West Texas and back on home turf, armed with a fistful of Percodan, a gallon of Maker's Mark and Carol Ann's number on speed dial for some midnight carnal nursing.

Ten

Two phone calls, five men and the nightmare shrieks, squeals and screams of the dying in the dark.

"*Bueno.*"

"My man did some tracking. Found a single set of hoof prints going up the trail and back. One rider. Boot prints on the top of the ridgeline. Oats on the ground near a rock ledge overlook with a view of somethin' we don't want seen. Coffee beans on the ledge."

"*Coffee beans? Did this gabacho brew up a pot of coffee while watching us?*"

"No fire. Man might have chewed on beans to stay awake."

"*We know for sure it was a man watching us, my friend?*"

"Pretty sure. Also pretty sure we know who it is. My man has worked and gone hunting with someone who chews coffee beans to stay awake."

"*Who?*"

"You're not going to like it."

"*I already don't like it. Not knowing who it is makes me hate it even more. Who? Dame su nombre.*"

"*El Patrón* Hulett. The cousin of our friend."

"*No chingues! This is very bad, my friend. Bad enough to have a spy poking his beak into our business, but this is a matter of family, of blood. Which makes it very difficult to deal with. You're sure it's who you say it is? Not the pinche DEA or one of Flores' people?"*

"Pretty damn sure, *patrón.* My man found a place down below the ridge where somebody parked a rig. Tried to be clever and parked it off the ranch road running past the ridge. Hid it behind some brush and mesquite. Looks like he didn't want anybody to find it while he was up top, but my man found the spot while tracing the back track off the ridge. Looks like a pickup and horse trailer, he says. Took some Polaroids of the tire tracks."

"Good enough for a match?"

"*Sí.* He's pretty sure already. Says the man's horse trailer has some missing tread on the right rear tire. He'll make sure today when he goes to do some work at the ranch for his cousin."

"Bueno. We need to be damn sure about this."

"What do you want done when we're sure?"

"Nada. Not until we're sure and we talk to our friend. It's his cousin, his blood. He may want to handle it himself. Or he may want us to handle it. Either way, it is a delicate matter that will require some finesse. We just can't shoot the man. He's too important. The last thing we need is a bunch of Anglo lawmen on a murder manhunt. Bad for business. Very bad."

"What do you have in mind?"

"I know this man. His family and mine have been living in this country for a very long time. We've fought the Apache and the Comanche. We've killed bandits and land swindlers. We've rustled each other's cattle. And when we weren't doing that, we've done business together — some of it legal, much of it not. We've been rivals and we've been allies. For many, many years."

"This will not be an easy thing to do. I understand that."

"I know you do, my friend. The truth is, I like this man far better than I do his cousin. We do business with the cousin because of mutual benefit. It's simple pragmatism and we must protect him to protect those mutual interests. But he is not a man I want to have to my house because I would not be honored to be his host. The man we are talking about is a man of

honor, a war hero, a fair-minded man who has been a leader of the people, including our people, not just the Anglos."

"I know this man and like him. I know that whatever we have to do, it will grieve me and grieve you."

"Sí, my friend. Whatever we do must look like an accident or something natural. Yes, natural is what we want. And it must be quick and merciful. No cruelty. If we have to kill him, we must do so with a measure of respect. That requires skills I regret to say are beyond your considerable talents. If we must make a move, I know just the man to call upon. A specialist. You will work with him."

"*Sí, patrón.* Whatever you ask. I will get back to you once my man reports to me."

"Bueno. It's sad to think of killing a man you respect, but ours is a dirty business without much honor."

The line went dead.

Chuy Reynaldo hung up the handset and squeezed his baggy bulk out of the narrow phone booth at the rear of Maria's Café, a clean, well-lit greasy spoon on the south end of Faver. The café was a small jewel among the jumble of body shops, *mercados, taquerias* and *tiendas de ropa* that served as a commercial district for the barrio that sprawled across both sides of Main Street.

It was his favorite place to eat and he was hungry. Hungry and upset. He didn't like what his boss had in mind. And he didn't like playing second fiddle to outside talent.

He bellied up to the counter with a sigh and ordered up a plate of *huevos rancheros* and a cup of coffee to ease his troubled mind. He nodded when the waitress reached under the counter and pulled up a bottle of El Presidente brandy.

She filled a juice glass nearly to the rim and set it beside his coffee cup. He drank it dry in one pull and held the glass up for a refill.

"That sumbitch has fucked us from hell to breakfast. Got bank examiners looking at our loans. Outbid us on tracts of land we need and thought we had sewed up. Got county judges and state legislators calling us up and blessing us out. And the bastard knows every move we're about to make just about as quick as we decide to make it. We've got a leak in our organization somewhere."

"Calm down, son. Don't get rattled and don't get paranoid. Next thing you know, Bart Hulett'll have you peeking underneath the bed for the boogeyman."

"That old man has double-fucked us and left our little project dead in the water."

"Don't mix your metaphors, son. This is just a little setback, a bump in the road. And all it's cost us is time and a little more money — a helluva lot less than it's cost Bart Hulett to try and stop us. Ain't nobody he's bought that we can't buy back. And we can tie up those land deals in court and bleed ol' Bart white with lawyer fees."

"Nice to see you're taking the long view on this, but I believe we need to rethink our approach to Hulett. We've underestimated him."

"Naw, son. You've underestimated him. I haven't. I figured he was too proud to go down without a fight. And he's done just about what I expected he'd do. But I believe our good friend Bart has about shot his bolt."

"Not so sure he doesn't have another ace or two up his sleeve. He kept talkin' about his cousin Gyp, about how if we kept pushin' him, we'd wind up with Gyp comin' after us. Words to that effect. Also said him and Gyp were joined at the hip like Siamese twins and that Gyp ain't as nice and sociable as him. Don't know what the hell that means but it sounded like a threat."

"It was. But you let me worry about ol' Gyp. He's mean as hell and will kill you just as soon as look at you, but he's a businessman. Crooked as your granny's backbone, but a businessman. And I believe he'd be delighted to not have to truck with Bart no more and be able to do his business without having to kowtow to the Hulett name and his holier-than-thou cousin."

"Okay, what's our next move?"

"We're going to fire a little message pitch at Bart Hulett. Yessir, a little chin-high fastball to make him dive into the dirt and show him we don't much care for him crowdin' the plate."

"Can the sports metaphor, Deke. What have you got in mind?"

"Best you don't know, son, 'cause the wheels are already in motion. But it's something that hits that old man right where he lives. And where he lives is that ranch and those cows and horses he loves so much. We're giving him something that will make him realize the error of his ways and do business with us."

"What if he doesn't get the message?"

"Simple, son. We escalate. Nobody gets to live forever. Not you, not me and most of all — not Bart Hulett. That's the gospel truth, son."

Lucius Schoenfeldt, Bryte Brothers front man, shook his head and hung up the phone. He reached for a bottle of Macallan fifteen-year-old and poured five fingers into a rocks glass. Single-malt Scotch. No ice. He gunned it in one gulp and poured himself another five fingers.

Gospel my pimply white ass, he thought. Sounded more like an eye-for-an-eye Old Testament jeremiad to him, pimped up with tough-guy baseball patter. Also sounded like someone whistlin' through the graveyard of a broken business deal.

The flash of gunfire lit the ragged American line, stabbing into the dark island night, tearing bloody hunks out of the seething wall of flesh charging toward Hulett and his dug-in Marine platoon, screaming the banzai battle cry of the Jap soldier.

One of his Marines stood up and yelled "Eat shit, Tojo!" as he emptied the eight-round clip of his M-1 Garand. Hulett was close enough to hear the distinctive piinnnggg of the clip being ejected when the final round was fired, quickly followed by the triple thwaaaack of slugs cutting down the Marine.

The crump of a grenade shot shrapnel into his back and legs, staggering him with searing pain he grimaced against to stay focused and direct his men. He sensed rather than saw the Japs punch through just beyond his left and right flanks. He bent the ends of his line back to face the new threat, placing his men in makeshift positions, and pulled a rifle squad with two BAR men and had them face the rear and fan out.

A stray thought entered his head, ringing clear above the roar of gunfire and the high-pitched screams and guttural yells of men fighting and dying: So this is how Custer felt at the Little Big Horn.

The stench of spent gunpowder filled his nostrils. The salty brass taste of blood filled his mouth. Shellfire ripped the rear of the Jap ranks, the salvos adding deep bass notes to the crash, clang and chatter of battle, but doing little to check the floodtide rush through gaps in the American line.

Shrieks, squeals and screams pierced the din. From the mangled and the dying. Shrieks, squeals and screams. Jacking up the fear and dread of his combat nightmare. Dredging up another night terror just beyond the reach of recall.

Shrieks, squeals and screams, double familiar from the war and a time well before that. A horror from his boyhood. A barn fire on the ranch. The screams of horses trapped by the flames.

Death screams in the fiery night. Horses.

His eyes snapped open. He gasped for breath like a drowning man bursting through the water's surface. His skin was slick with sweat. The nightmare visions of battle and boyhood juddered and dissolved, like film from a projector snapped off in mid-reel, leaving him alone in his bedroom with the sputtering afterimages. But the screams still filled his ears.

They weren't just a nightmare. They were real. So was the flickering light flashing through the open bedroom door. Horses. His horses. And fire.

He clambered out of bed, shaken, unsteady and alone, his ranch hands granted two days off to attend a fiesta on the Mexican side of the river. He slipped on his jeans and boots, then grabbed a Remington 870 twelve-gauge pump propped up in the corner nearest his bed. He was bare-chested as he hustled toward the mudroom and side door leading outside, pausing to jam on his hat, slap on a barn coat and pocket a flashlight.

He jacked a round into the shotgun and stepped through the door. The outside cold was cut by sharp waves of heat radiating from the barn. Flames bright orange and wavering lit up the night, casting a harsh light on the house, the railed paddocks and the bare dirt lot leading to the barn.

The barn was a blazing beacon, a funeral pyre. Smoke roiled from the hayloft, the tin roof already buckled and collapsed. At ground level, tongues of fire licked upward from the open bale doors that marked each stall, feeding on the weathered wood panels of the outer walls.

The screams of his horses filled the night, punctuated by the boom of hooves slamming against stall doors and stout walls. He ran toward the double barn door and saw a padlocked chain tightly wrapped through the iron outer handles. *Bastards were barnburners and horse killers.*

Two rounds of double ought shattered the padlock and severed the chain. He grabbed the chain to yank it free from the door handles, crying out as the hot metal burned his palm. He used the tail of his barn coat to buffer his grip on the handle of the right-hand door, grunting as he slid open the heavy-framed wood panel, careful to keep low and shielded from flame he knew would roar through the gap. *Jesus, Jesus, Jesus — move faster, old man. Stay small.*

Heat seared him as a jet of fire shot over his head, sucking up the oxygen of the cold night air. He ducked under the blast and sidestepped to his left, toward a pocket free from flame and smoke. He propped the shotgun against the tack room door and tied a bandana around his nose and mouth.

He pulled out the flashlight and flicked its beam down the broad center aisle that ran between the fourteen stalls, seven on each side.

The beam danced across a roiling wall of flame-lit smoke that barricaded the back end of the barn and all but the four stalls nearest him, two on each side of the aisle.

No squeals, shrieks and screams from beyond that wall. His heart lurched. Sue Bee's stall was behind the smoke. No more living link to his dead wife, Mary Nell. *Gonna track these bastards down and kill every last mother's son of them.*

The shrieks and thudding hooves came only from the stalls nearest him. He crossed the aisle to the first two, ripping open one door, then the other, throwing himself against the narrow dividing wall to avoid being crushed by a quarter ton of terror-crazed gelding exploding toward the safety of the night outside.

Chester and Jughead safe. A buckskin gelding named Jingles was next, the favorite mount of his wrangler, Ramon Cifuentes. Last was a bay mare named Little Bit, his daughter's horse. He wasn't quick enough to get out of her way. The mare slammed him to the dirt as she rushed past, busting his ribs with her shoulder and stomping on his right leg. He heard his femur snap and screamed.

The flames and smoke rolled closer, drawn by the draft from the open barn door. He started crawling, dragging his body through the dirt with his arms and left leg, half blinded by smoke and white-hot pain from his busted femur. He could feel the night air on his face and willed his body to keep moving toward its soothing grace.

Grace was denied by the rasping, metallic sound of the barn door being closed from the outside. Chain links rattled through the door handles. He kept crawling away from the flames, toward his shotgun and the closed door. *Had to blast my way in. Gotta blast my way out.*

He heard a crack and a boom above him. It was the last sound Bart Hulett ever heard as the flaming hulk of a main rafter hurtled down and snuffed out his life.

Eleven

Burch was hurting in an old and too familiar way. Hungover from too much tequila bubbled straight from the bottle, empty and aching from being rode hard and put up wet by a client who wanted to show her gratitude with more than a fat bonus check from a bottomless bank account.

He was sitting on a metal folding chair in the cinder block office of the used car lot owned by Diego "Dirt Cheap" Bustamante, shifting his weight to ease the pain in his butt from the hard seating surface. He was waiting for the short, fat, bug-eyed owner with the bald dome and thin moustache to wrap up hustling a cowboy eyeing a dark green Dodge pickup in the gravel lot.

Burch kept his smoky gray prescription Ray-Bans on to protect his bloodshot eyes from the blinding, mid-afternoon glare firing through the office front window. His chair was in a shadowed corner, out of the sun's harshest rays, but he still had a good view of the lot.

A sharp spike of hangover pain nailed his forebrain despite the four sleeves of BC Powder he poured into his mouth while standing in a convenience store, chasing them with an ice-cold Big Red, the strawberry-and-bubble-gum flavored soda of choice for true Texans.

Hangover sweat soaked through a denim shirt with faux-pearl speed snaps. He wore a black windbreaker despite the heat and alcohol residue pouring from his body to cover the Colt tucked under his right armpit, butt forward in a leather shoulder rig, two extra mags dangling under his left. A green nylon gear bag with a tan canvas bottom sat on the floor next to the chair, home for his clothes, shaving kit, camera, sap and spare ammo boxes for the Colt.

The clock was ticking on his frayed nerves. He marked the seconds with the metal tap on his right boot toe. Dull, flat clicks against a bare plywood floor. An impatient rhythm. All he wanted to do was grab the rental receipt for the gutless Reliant, drop it at Boelcke's office, fire up Ol' Blue and its overhauled engine then get gone.

To reel himself in with mindless routine, Burch sipped sour coffee left too long on the burner from a small Styrofoam cup, listening to the window unit air conditioner wheeze slightly chilled air into the room.

On the wall to his right was a glossy poster that featured an air-brushed image of Bustamante, leaning toward the camera with a maniacal grin. Speed freak eyes that looked ready to pop out of his skull on coiled springs and a pointing finger. Bright red letters spelling out his "Dirt Cheap" tagline. A solid side door flanked the poster.

Burch looked outside as the real Bustamante hustled the cowboy in the lot, banging his hand on the hood of the Dodge to emphasize the price he was offering. Dirt cheap, no doubt, with a skinful of pharmaceutical energy.

The pickup was flanked by a ragged line of tired automotive metal. Hulking and rust-streaked American gas guzzlers from the '70s — an Electra 225, a Caprice, a Gran Prix, a Delta 88. F-100s, C-10s, C-20s and D Series for the pickup crowd, most dented and swaybacked from rough use. Dished-in tin boxes from Japan with all the get-go of a lawn mower, a couple of Datsun 210s, some Toyota Corollas.

Burch winced, put the coffee cup on Bustamante's desk and fished a pack of Luckies out of a damp shirt pocket. Zippo fire to the end of the nail. Smoke sucked deep into his lungs. Freeze-frame images from the night before rolled across half-closed eyelids.

Nita Rodriguez Wyatt strolled into his bedroom at Spider and Rhonda Throckmorton's ranch house just as he was shucking his boots after a long night of grilled steaks the size of hubcaps, a Rio Conchos of red wine, loud music of the Texas kind and raucous banter and laughter that lit up the dining room.

His last Lucky of the day curled smoke from a shallow clay ashtray on the nightstand. A small table lamp made of tarnished brass sat next to the ashtray, providing the bedroom's only light. His Colt and shoulder rig hung from the headboard nob nearest the table.

Her right hip brushed his left shoulder as she stepped past him and plunked a ribbed bottle of Dos Reales Tequila Añejo on the nightstand. The light from the table lamp flashed gold through the aged amber spirit.

She turned to face him as he sat on the bed, a tall, full-figured woman with a smile flashing dimly in the dark above, the lamplight catching the dull gleam of coin-grade silver linked across wide hips sheathed in a pleated, calf-length skirt of black gabardine. A matching necklace dipped toward deep cleavage framed by an open-necked, white silk blouse.

Long, bloodred fingernails combed through the chest hair peeking through his unsnapped shirt. She leaned forward, placing her free hand on his shoulder as her nails raked down toward his belly, the silver necklace swinging forward as she gave him an up-close view of flesh straining against silk.

"You know, I don't think I've ever fucked a detective before. A cop, maybe, but not a private dick."

"What makes you think you're going to fuck one now? You need to call my office and make an appointment. But not on Wednesdays — that's my poker night."

She cocked her head, arched an eyebrow then laughed. They had been sparring like that all night over drinks and dinner — her not-so-subtle advances, his not-so-subtle putdowns, Rhonda and Spider ringside, laughing at them both, enjoying the semi-witty prelude to the inevitable.

"I don't need an appointment — I'm already a client."

"Not anymore. Job's done and you've already paid me off. Handsomely. Gave me a big bonus. Even got my truck out of hock. Many thanks."

"Maybe I've got a new case for you. Maybe I want to sign you to a personal service contract."

"Lady, I don't do well as a kept man. Or husband. I pee on the carpet, talk rude to my elders and bust up all the fine china. I'm not a trick pony. And I don't do novelty fucks."

She slapped him — hard enough to sting, but soft enough not to leave a red mark underneath his beard. He grabbed her wrist on the back swing for another love tap. She wagged a finger at him with her free hand and laughed again.

Ribbed tequila bottle to her lips. Bubbles in the amber. A hard kiss. A warm jet of tequila into his mouth. A burning swallow. Tongues and suction.

He broke the kiss and grabbed the bottle out of her hand. He bubbled it back and held the swig as he unbuttoned her blouse, watching her heavy breasts tumble free. He bathed both dark red nipples in tequila, nibbling one then the other. A sharp hiss from her and a love bite on his left ear.

Tequila as foreplay. Tequila gulped as she rode his cock, pitching forward to share the well-aged amber burn from her mouth. Tequila splashed down the valley of her cleavage and lapped up. Tequila as interlude, shared straight from the bottle as their bodies cooled then fired again for another round.

One more shared sip before a languid, farewell kiss, the bottle almost down to the dregs.

One tequila too many. A steep understatement. Otherwise known as a lie. Better make that too many a baker's dozen.

The windowed front door banged open, startling Burch as Bustamante hustled in, sweat marking the armpits of a tan Mexican wedding shirt that bulged over his belly and dark brown slacks and giving his bald head a sheen that reflected the harsh glare of the fluorescent overhead lights.

The fat man's eyes were red-rimmed, the pupils pinned. If Burch had still been a vice cop, he would have rousted the man to pat him down for pills or white powder in a glassine envelope.

"Damn Anglo redneck — no offense, buddy — hell, he wouldn't know a good deal if it bit him on his scrawny left butt cheek. He'll stay out there another hour in the hot sun, kickin' tires, moonin' over that goddam Dodge and pretendin' he ain't interested."

"How much you askin'?"

Bustamante's eyes lit up. He ran a palm over his mouth and lowered his head to hide the greed.

"Hell, you interested, *señor*? It's a '79 D Series. Got a rebuilt 318 with a three-speed stick with overdrive and a brand new clutch. Stepside box and a fresh spray job. New rubber and a retread spare. Got fewer miles than that Ford you blew up when you got here. Man like you coverin' ground in Texas needs a truck with a V-8 instead of that pissant six banger you got — 'specially since you had to have the top end of that six overhauled."

"How much you askin'?"

The fat man rubbed a palm over his mouth again, his face a picture of false contemplation about the great mysteries of life. Burch contemplated the strange mix of the man's patter — a border *estofado* that was part twangy West Texas bubba, part sing-song Mexican.

"We talkin' trade?"

"Straight sale."

"I can tell you one thing, *señor*. I'll make you the best deal on the border for that little Dodge or my name ain't Dirt Cheap Bustamante."

"Quit stallin' and name a price."

"Don't rush me. Anybody mention you act just like a cop?"

"Been brought to my attention a time or two. Now, what's the price?"

"I can wrap a bow around that rig for two."

"Hunnert or thousand?"

"I may be Dirt Cheap Bustamante, but I got mouths to feed, *señor*."

"Two large on a truck that's likely got axle grease and sawdust in the crankcase and probably won't get me to Abilene? Shit, son — no sale. I'll just dance with what brung me here. Let's get the paperwork done on that cracker box you rented me so I can get on up the road."

Bustamante looked like a man who had been slapped. He stared as Burch ignored him and took another drag off his Lucky.

"Got the mileage?"

"Car's parked right outside your door. Go get the odometer digits and let's wrap this up."

Burch could feel the anger rolling his way, but didn't give a damn. He looked up, sliding his Ray-Bans forward on his nose to lock Bustamante in a naked-eye stare. Dirt Cheap broke first, grabbed a pen and notepad off his desk and rushed through the front door in a huff.

He watched the fat man open the driver's door on the Reliant and lean in to read the odometer, his backside facing Burch, the dust-covered Plymouth angled toward the front door as if reluctant to rejoin the other tired iron on the lot.

Two men entered the far side of the lot, one tall and lean, the other short and muscular, both Mexican, both wearing dark blue windbreakers despite the heat. They ignored the line of cars and walked toward the office. When Bustamante stood straight, the short man nodded and the two men split apart, each focused on the fat man.

Burch was at the side door, Colt in his left hand, doorknob in his right. His mind didn't register his movement from chair to door. He was on autopilot, looking through the window to his left, eyeing the angles between Bustamante, who was already spinning up his hustler's rap, and the two men, eyes locked on their target.

Time slowed.

Twist of the doorknob. Side door swinging inward. One-eyed peep through the cracked opening. Shooters and Bustamante out of view. Slow steps through the door. Back flat against the side of the double-wide office. Cover to the front corner. Voices from the lot. Shuffle slide steps to the corner, Colt level, unlocked and leading his movement.

At the corner. No voices. Awkward spot for a lefty. Hard to keep the body covered to take a look. Gotta risk it. Quick peek around the corner. Freeze frame of Bustamante, one foot stepping back, hands up, the two men reaching behind for guns Burch couldn't see but knew were already in hand.

No choice. One step to clear the corner. Combat stance, Colt on the closest target on the left. Freeze frame — the target's gun hand filled with a black semi-automatic and swinging toward Bustamante. Three shots from the Colt — 200-grain Corbon hollow-points down range. Flying Ashtrays. Two shots smacking the target's chest, slamming him into the grill of a gray Electra, a third whanging a groove into the stained, white vinyl rooftop of a blue Impala.

Two snap shots at the second man, a blurred target with his hands filled with something bigger than a pistol. A dozen short, choppy steps toward Bustamante. A horse-collar tackle. A loud grunt as the fat man bit the gravel.

The stuttering snort of an automatic weapon.

Rounds zipping through the thin sides of the Reliant, thunking into seats, splintering the dashboard, shattering glass into geysers of powder and shards that rained down on Burch and Bustamante as they hugged the gravel.

Rounds snapping clean through the car — angry bee sounds inches from Burch's head. Down to three shots. Drop the mag from the Colt. Slap in a fresh load of Flying Ashtrays.

Sudden stop to the bullet rush. Ringing echo of gunfire. Curses in Spanish from the other side of the bullet-pocked Reliant. A flashing thought. A jam or an empty mag. Gut instinct that could get him killed if he was wrong.

Scrabble toward the front of the car like a wounded crab. Engine as poor man's armor. Now or never last stand before the jam gets cleared or a fresh mag is slapped in place. Right hand pushing him up, gravel cutting his palm.

Loud grunt as belly and chest flatten across the Reliant's hood. Colt steady in his left hand, arm stretching toward the shooter slapping the bolt closed on a short-barreled CAR-15.

Deep booms from the Colt. Four Flying Ashtrays downrange. Shooter jerking sideways from hollow-point hits aimed at center mass. Trigger finger reflex from a dead man falling. Lead spray from the shooter's CAR-15, lethal only to old American iron. Sudden silence as the shooter hits the ground.

Time snapped back to normal speed. Burch pushed himself upright from the hood of the Reliant, keeping his Colt pointed toward the two downed shooters, his ears ringing. He scanned the rest of the lot, looking for movement, then stepped around the front of the Reliant to check the shooters. He kicked a Beretta 92S away from the first and leaned down to press his fingers into the man's neck. *Nada.*

He walked over to the second shooter and saw one of his shots had ripped away the man's lower jaw. No need for fingers to the neck. *Nada y nada.* He picked up the CAR-15, flicked the safety on and walked back to the Reliant.

His stomach lurched and Burch leaned forward just in time to puke a stream of coffee, Big Red and tequila dregs into the gravel. His hands began to shake. He needed to bubble a bottle of Maker's to steady his nerves but knew that wasn't in the cards.

Not now. Not with the sound of sirens from two sheriff's cruisers slamming around a corner and banging into the gravel lot from opposite flanks. He put his Colt and the CAR-15 on the Reliant's hood and raised both hands, stepping away from the scarred and gutless beater and facing deputies with their guns pointed at him.

Bustamante was still hugging the gravel, yowling like a dog getting kicked by its master then growling guttural Spanish that Burch with his gunfire deafness couldn't make out. The fat man's right arm was bent back, his hand pressed into a fleshy buttock, blood leaking through his fingers.

A stray bullet in the ass. Still Dirt Cheap, no doubt, but still alive.

Hot breath soured by coffee and cigarettes struck Burch like a slap in the face as a tall, barrel-chested man in a gray Stetson and a dark green shirt with a gold star pinned over the left pocket loomed over him and bellowed.

"Just who in the fuck are you? And why the hell are you trying to turn my town into a shooting gallery?"

Burch was seated in another hard metal chair that made his butt hurt, this one welded to the floor of a small interrogation room in the Cuervo County Sheriff's Office. His handcuffed hands were in his lap, a heavy chain looped between the cuffs and pulled tight through a D-ring bolted into the floor.

He eyed the nameplate of the big man. Willingham. As in Sheriff Tyrus Lamar "Blue" Willingham. His ownself. Burch stayed silent.

"Answer my goddam question, you needledick bastard."

Burch raised his manacled hands as far as they would go and rattled the D-ring chain at the big man.

"Let's start by telling you who the hell I ain't — I ain't John Dillinger and I ain't Clyde Barrow. You got my wallet and my ID, so you know who I am and what I am. Lawyer named Boelcke told you why I was here."

"Yeah, I know who you're supposed to be — a Dallas peeper by the name of Ed Earl Burch. And I know Boelcke told me you were snooping after a wayward husband who liked to shack up around here, which I could give two shits about. But son, after the O.K. Corral act you just pulled in the middle of my goddam town, I'm of a mind that Sam Boelcke's story was just a bunch of horseshit."

"It wasn't. Get Boelcke down here and ask him."

Willingham took off the Stetson and raked his fingers through thick, blue-black hair shot through with gray the shade of iron filings. He leaned close to Burch and blasted more sour breath.

"Why don't you tell me what the fuck you're really doing here and who the fuck you're really working for?"

"Call Boelcke. I work for him and he's my attorney."

"You a gun for hire, Burch? Down here to do a little wet work for Malo Garza? Maybe a little extra security muscle for ol' Malo?"

"Same answer, Sheriff. You know, you might thank me for keeping one of your upstanding citizens from getting his ass shot off."

"Upstanding my ass. Bustamante is Malo Garza's cousin. Awful convenient you being at his office and so handy with that Colt just when ol' Dirt Cheap needed protection."

"Might be helpful if I knew who Malo Garza is."

Willingham snorted a laugh and grabbed Burch by the shoulders, leaning in eyeball close.

"Don't fuck with me, boy. Malo Garza's the big dog along this part of the border — *Narcotraficante Numero Uno*. Got a ranch just over the river. Acts like a spic grandee whose shit don't stink. You just saved his cousin's sorry ass and your lawyer buddy is sleeping with Malo's daughter. So don't tell me you're here just to chase some husband who can't keep his dick holstered."

Burch shook his head. Caught in the West Texas spider web. Again. Mex *narcos* and blood ties stitched across both sides of the river. An Anglo sheriff with a hard-on for him and a reputation to protect. He looked up at Willingham and smiled.

"What's so goddam funny, asshole?"

"Got to appreciate the little ironies in life, Sheriff, and the curse of poor timing. I was trying to leave your fine little town when those guys showed up to waste Bustamante. They show up ten minutes later and I'd be on the road to Dallas and Dirt Cheap would be dead."

"Didn't happen that way."

"No, it didn't. But those two shooters weren't there because Dirt Cheap sold them a lemon. Bet there's more to this than Dirt Cheap being Malo's cousin. Bet he's more of a player than that. And playing right here under your nose."

"You talk too much."

"Thought you wanted me to talk. I'll shut up and you can get Boelcke down here."

"No, go right ahead. Spin your tall tale. I like to see a man build a big pile of bullshit I can bury him under."

"I'd prefer to call it an educated guess. Your buddy Bustamante moves used cars. Where's he get 'em — over the river? Real interesting possibilities there. Might be he's moving more than just cars. And now you got a shootout with two Mex gunsels out to clip Dirt Cheap right here on the streets of your little town."

Burch paused and saw the color rise in Willingham's face and the anger in his blue eyes.

"You run the ID on those shooters I blew away? Bet they're either freelance talent or connected to some other drug lord slimeball. Looks like you got a little turf war going on. Or maybe Dirt Cheap crossed his cousin. Just guesses on my part. But either way, it ain't a good look for an anti-drug crusader like you, Sheriff."

Burch looked at Willingham. The anger that colored his face and flashed in his eyes was gone. He wore the stone mask of a poker player and his voice was a husky whisper as he asked a quiet question.

"You a barnburner, son?"

Burch was flummoxed. No smartass quips, no barbed conjecture. All he had as a comeback was the brass to meet the sheriff's stare head-on and not flinch.

"Let me put it to you this way — are you a man who could set another man's barn on fire, burn up his horses, burn up the man himself? Are you that kind of murderin' sumbitch, a fire worshiper, a man-burner?"

"Jesus, Sheriff — you need to make up your mind what you want to frame me for. First you have me as a gun for hire workin' for this Malo Garza fella, now you got me as the second coming of Ben Quick's daddy in *The Long Hot Summer.* I'm way too ugly for any frame job that needs me to look like Paul Newman."

"Ugly will do, my friend, if I find out you did the crime."

Willingham held up four fingers.

"Let me lay it out for you. One, I got a dead rancher killed in a barn fire somebody may or may not have set..."

Index finger only, pointed at Burch.

"...Two, I got a body found in a hole out in the backcountry with the back of his skull blown open..."

Index and middle finger forked at Burch.

"...Three, I got you blowin' away those two shooters and me not buyin' your story about bein' some accidental hero..."

A three-finger trident aimed at Burch.

"...And, four, I got you runnin' loose all over my county with nobody to account for your whereabouts except a lawyer who sleeps with Malo Garza's daughter and has some of his lowlife friends for clients."

Four fingers held high, then balled into a fist.

"And here I thought you were a badass Texas lawman. Guess it's one thing to gun down those scumbag meth freaks who kidnapped that Mex gal and shotgunned her parents. Hell, those idiots left a blood trail so wide even Barney Fife could've tracked 'em down. Guess it's another to do some real police work on that rancher and that body. No photo ops on grunt work, though, right Sheriff?"

Burch had a nanosecond to roll with the roundhouse right Willingham slammed into his jaw, sending his glasses flying and knocking him sideways, stopped from falling out of the chair by the tight chain looped through his handcuffs and the D-ring bolted to the floor.

He pulled himself back into the chair with the chain, spat blood on the floor and locked eyes with Willingham.

"You punch like a pussy-starved seventh grader whose balls haven't dropped."

"Shut this asshole up and throw his ass in a cell until we get some things sorted out 'round here."

A rail-thin deputy with a handlebar moustache and a ruddy complexion stepped into the edge of Burch's vision. Burch heard a swishing sound just before a flash of white pain exploded in his brain.

Lights out.

Twelve

Blue Willingham cupped his big, calloused hands under the faucet of the sink in his office bathroom and let the cold water fill the rough-skinned pocket before leaning his head forward and splashing his face. He did it twice more before raising his head and raking his wet fingers through his thick hair.

He toweled his face dry and picked up a long barber's comb to sweep his locks back from his broad forehead and tuck loose strands behind his ears. He eyed himself in the mirror, his fingers tugging at the hint of the jowls starting to sag the flesh below his long jawline. Thick and gnarled from calf roping and fist fights, they traced his chiseled chin and the crooked hawk's beak nose broken in gridiron contests as a second-team All-Southwestern Conference defensive end up at Texas Tech, and barroom brawls and rowdy arrests when he was climbing the law enforcement ladder as a sheriff's deputy in Presidio County and a Texas Ranger.

The eyes staring back at him from the mirror were still a piercing blue, but puffy bags underscored them, marring a face that was tanned and otherwise unwrinkled, the skin colored by a faint olive cast that hinted at the Mexican deep in his bloodline.

The automatic actions of combing his hair and taking a middle-aged man's physical inventory kept his mind off the violent events of the past few days. Blue saw these as unexpected and unwelcome threats to his meticulously mapped plans to turn his political ambitions into reality, to parlay his well-burnished image as a Texas sheriff with a rightful claim to all that high-noon imagery taking the righteous fight to the prime threat of modern times — the drug dealer.

Commissioner Willingham, Governor Willingham. Senator Willingham. Had a nice ring to it. And why the hell shouldn't he climb that ladder? He had the looks, smarts, track record and savvy to make the voters swoon and the donors fork over bales of money. But in his darker moments, Blue Willingham saw his plans begin to unravel.

Better to shift his mind into neutral and let the memories and ambitious dreams drift on by. Back in his early days as a Presidio deputy, not long after getting cut at his third pro training camp and hanging up the spikes on his NFL dreams, a drunk road contractor he arrested in a bar for beating his wife spit in his face and started cussing him out.

"Motherfuckin' big shot football player, think yore sumthin' doncha? You ain't nothin' but a taco bender and a goat fuckin' wetback."

Blue broke the man's jaw with one punch, punctuating the shot with a *chinga tu madre, pendejo* that was natural and fluent — not the broken border Spanish most Anglos used. That was a small reminder of his mixed border heritage. His great-great grandmother was Josefina Huerta, the fifth daughter of a sheep herder, married at fifteen to his great-great grandfather, Big Jack Willingham, a Ranger who hailed from San Angelo.

Willingham's grandfather was also a Ranger, Franklin Albert "Bad Eye" Willingham, who lost his left eye in a knife fight with a Mexican rustler but was still a crack shot with the break-top Smith & Wesson .44 hanging from his hip, and the .351 Winchester Model 1907 self-loading rifle he carried in a custom-made saddle scabbard that accommodated the gun's 10-round magazine.

Willingham's father, Yancey, was born nearsighted, with one leg shorter than the other. That ruled out wearing a badge but he was a pretty good horseman and heeler come branding time. And a wizard bookkeeper who served businesses in Presidio and Cuervo and the big ranches like the Holland-Gage and the Paisano, where Blue learned to rope and ride working summers as a hired hand.

Like his father before him, Yancey Willingham married an Anglo woman and raised his family as Anglos, but made sure they met and knew their distant Mexican cousins and learned to speak fluent Spanish. He also taught his children to respect Mexicans and whipped them good if he caught them calling somebody a wetback or beaner.

That put the Willinghams in a cultural no-man's-land, a tough spot in the years when Anglos still ruled the West Texas roost and kept a boot heel on any Mex's neck. Anglos in Presidio and then Cuervo, where Willingham's father moved the family when he was five to be closer to the big ranches he served, kept them at arm's length.

What passed for polite society — the church-going Baptists and Methodists — talked behind the family's back, whispering about the Mex blood that tainted the Willinghams. Ranch hands and roughnecks weren't so subtle, calling his great-great grandmother a Mexican whore to his face and calling him a greaser. Blue had to keep busting his knuckles in schoolyard and back alley scrapes until he got too big to cross.

Mexicans also kept their distance. Most were polite, some noted the family as *muy simpatico* — for Anglos. Others viewed them as condescending and hypocritical pretenders. More than once, Blue got into a fight with a Mexican kid pissed off about the family that enjoyed the Anglo advantages while still trying to claim a piece of *La Gente.*

The face in the mirror looked angry now, the blue eyes flashing with the memory of fights caused by his family's split allegiance — another distraction from what was really troubling him.

"*Chinga tu madre, pendejo.* Right up the old *culo*, needledick motherfucker."

That was Blue's growling answer to the flashbacks, the growing sense of losing control and the face in the mirror with its telltale signs that a half-century milestone was just around the corner.

Half a hunnert, as that shitbird Barry Switzer, the jackass coach of the dog-ass Oklahoma Sooners, liked to say. As in, "Let's go out and hang half a hunnert on some Longhorn ass." As in, God, his Ownsef, was getting set to hang half a hunnert on Blue Willingham's ass.

The bags below his eyes were just another sign of God-as-Barry-Switzer's intent, another tell of advancing middle age and the extra flesh layering his six-foot-four-inch frame, making his playing weight of 245 pounds a long-gone memory, buried under 25 extra pounds of lard.

Still narrow at the hip and long-legged, he carried the extra weight in his face, shoulders and beer-barrel chest. And a thickening middle that was still hard muscle underneath. Hair that was once raven black was now dulled by dark gray.

What Blue saw in the mirror was a rude reminder that time was relentlessly ticking away and he needed to keep moving fast to make that leap into the arena of statewide politics. That made Blue Willingham a man in a hurry, willing to cut corners to get where he wanted to go, looking to grab the limelight and the next rung up the political ladder.

Willing to cut a deal with the Devil, trading his soul like Robert Johnson at the crossroads — for money and power, not lightning fingers on a blues guitar. And in Blue's case, El Diablo was the devil he knew very well, and he didn't have horns, a forked tail or scaly red skin.

Blue's personal devil lived just across the river in a big hacienda, surrounded by thousands of acres of land owned by his blood kin for almost two centuries. Estaban "Malo" Garza, *patrón* of *Los Tres Picos* rancho, home of the family-run cattle, drugs and guns enterprise that straddled the rugged borderlands of Chihuahua and Cohuila states — a *narco* territory that stretched from Ojinaga to Cuidad Acuña.

When he was a Ranger, Blue had a burning ambition to take down a *narco* like Malo Garza and add another chapter to the Ranger legend. When he was elected sheriff of Cuervo County, he started hammering low-level Garza operatives and seizing the occasional shipments of heroin and cocaine, donning a bulletproof vest and leading the raids himself, kicking down doors with a Winchester twelve-gauge riot pump at the ready.

One night in an *arroyo* thirty miles south of Faver, it all went sideways for Blue and five deputies when a tip about a Garza load turned into a trap. Muzzle flashes from the thickets on either side of the cut lit up the night, riding the deafening boom of shotgun blasts and the unmistakable automatic chatter of AKs.

Two of his deputies went down, their screams adding to the din. Blue and the three remaining lawmen charged up one side of the cut, blasting the brush with buckshot and killing two shooters. The other shooters disappeared into the night. One of the wounded deputies died — Bert Samuels, an ex-San Antonio cop who took a cut in pay to get away from a train-wreck divorce and live a quieter life in the dry heat of Cuervo County.

Blue realized an awful truth that night — he wasn't a bulletproof avenging angel; he was like a fly gnawing on a horse's ass. Annoying and sometimes painful, but one hollow-point swat could make him very dead while the horse would be very much alive. And Blue wanted very much to stay as alive as that horse and chase his dream of higher political office.

They call politics the art of the possible, greased by mutual compromise that gives both parties something they want. Not the whole loaf, but an acceptable hunk. Blue wanted higher office based on the image of a tough, uncompromising sheriff waging a one-man war on drugs. Garza wanted to be left alone and knew that killing a Texas sheriff and third-generation Ranger would be very bad for business.

Garza called Blue and asked for a sit-down. At an after-midnight meeting at *Los Tres Picos*, the two men reached *El Alojamiento* — The Accommodation. Garza could run drugs, guns and whatever else he wanted to smuggle *through* Cuervo County as long as he didn't sell his wares *in* Cuervo County.

In return, Blue could bust all the low-level dealers and Garza rivals he could get his hands on, parlaying these arrests into hard state time served at the Cuervo County jail and hard work on county road crews. Garza would even feed him tips on shipments by rivals, border crossings by *coyotes* muling marijuana on the backs of dirt-poor Mexicans they were leading to the promised land and meth labs popping up in the backcountry, run by freelancers with no allegiances.

There was also the whispery electronic transfer of regular payments to an offshore account in the Turks and Caicos as part of a blind trust controlled by a Dallas lawyer.

This freed Blue to chase his dream. Now in the middle of his third four-year term as Cuervo County Sheriff, Blue was the walking, talking face of an anti-drug campaign called Texas Tough, fronted by the Sheriffs' Association of Texas.

His face was splashed on highway billboards across the state and he was the glowering punctuation mark at the end of a TV ad, eyes shadowed by a Stetson as he pointed at the camera and growled: "We're Texas Tough on drugs."

He gave speeches all across Texas and lobbied the legislature for stiffer penalties on drug crimes and bigger bucks for training, automatic weapons, surveillance equipment and more officers and deputies for smaller towns and rural counties.

His phone number was on the Rolodexes of print and television reporters in Texas and beyond. They dialed him up because he was always willing to give a colorful quote about being on the front line of America's War on Drugs. He'd been interviewed by Ted Koppel on *Nightline*, Charlie Rose on PBS and Larry King on CNN.

King asked him whether a sheriff was a throwback to a bygone era, out-manned and out-gunned by drug gangs.

Blue, speaking from a local television studio in El Paso, growled: *"We don't string 'em up from the closest tree anymore like cattle rustlers and horse thieves, but I tell you what, Mister King — I'll make a man graveyard dead if he tries to sell his poison in my county or turn my town into a shootin' gallery. That's a promise."*

On the studio monitor, Blue saw the famous black-and-white photo fill the screen, the one that captured him carrying Carmen Gonzalez down the steps of that double-wide with blood from a bullet wound showing wet and dark down his pants leg.

"That's you, Sheriff, rescuing Carmen Gonzalez after tracking down the kidnappers who killed her parents."

"That's right, Larry — back when I was a Ranger. My partner, Charley Bowness, and I tracked them down to a double-wide outside Carrizo Springs. Charley got killed, but we saved that little girl. She's married now and living in San Antonio with her husband and her own little girl. I get to have dinner with them every month or so and bounce that little girl on my knee. I get to see the good Charley and I did for Carmen and her family."

Pure gold. Blue even managed to tear up on cue with the camera zooming in for a close-up that led right into the next commercial break that skipped Larry's usual "We'll be right back."

Women of a certain age still saw him as ruggedly handsome — grass widows, divorcees and badge groupies, mostly. And the bored wives of Chamber of Commerce types he met on the rubber-chicken-soggy-salad-and-sweet-tea circuit he was riding these days to spread the gospel of Blue Willingham's worthiness for higher political office.

He hoped to bed one down tonight after he gave a speech in Fort Davis to a local gathering of the Texas and Southwestern Cattle Raisers' Association — a divorcee named Rebecca Jo Harnett. She was a rangy redhead with the taut body of a horsewoman, a ranch outside town her husband deeded over when they split the blanket and a wicked smile that crossed her face and lit up her green eyes every time she wrapped her hand around his cock.

Women like Rebecca Jo made up for the lack of interest shown by his wife, Darlene, a busty blonde Texas Tech cheerleader he married his senior year in a fit of peppery passion that confused lust for love.

She was the mother of his two sons and his daughter. These days, sex with Darlene was brief, perfunctory and could be scheduled with a Mayan calendar. Dull as grits without the cheese or salt — and forget all about that *lujuria picante* of youth.

Plenty of pepper with Rebecca Jo. An hour or two of her carnal spice would wake him up for the long drive home. First, he'd give his standard speech, some righteous thunder about standing tall against marauding drug traffickers and the rising wave of crime and violence they fostered, tailoring his words to warn about the link between drugs and the theft of expensive tractors and ranch equipment and the modern-day rustler who used a tractor-trailer rig instead of a horse.

He'd top it off with a nod to the Association's special Rangers who focused on crimes against ranchers and stock, pointing to an old Ranger *compadre* he knew would be in the audience and now wore a badge for the TSCRA, Joaquin Bartlett.

In his mind's eye, he could see himself standing at the podium in a white uniform shirt, a pearl-gray Stetson and a gleaming, hand-tooled gun belt riding over whipcord tan slacks, the holster filled with a Smith & Wesson Model 29 .44 magnum, blue-black with a six-inch barrel and staghorn grip.

Every inch the Texas sheriff and ex-Ranger, with ranchers eating out of the palm of his hand. He could hear himself charm them with his words and his presence.

"I rode with Joaquin when I was a Ranger and can tell you true there's no tougher or more determined lawman in this state — none better to have protecting your ranches, your stock and your equipment."

He'd wait for them to spot Joaquin and start clapping their hands.

"With Joaquin riding the range, sheriffs like your very own Jim Ben Taggart can keep their focus on the pushers and dealers and drug lords who want to turn our children into addicts and our streets into shooting galleries. Talk about a double shot of Texas tough — I pity the rustler stupid enough to cross Joaquin and the dealer dumb enough to do business in Jim Ben's county."

Pure showmanship. And pure bullshit, truth be told, because Joaquin was way past his prime and Jim Ben spent all his time pickling his liver and chasing Mexican whores. Wouldn't stop Blue from serving up just the right dollops of false humble long used by carney barkers, evangelists, con artists and politicians to slap a glaze of sincerity on their silvered, lying patter.

The man in the mirror gave him a smile as he splashed Old Spice on his face, neck and chest. *Lord help me, but I dearly love to get in front of a room full of people and make 'em dance.*

The smile disappeared as he felt a throbbing pain across the knuckles of his right hand, the fist that rocked that smartass Dallas peeper. That brought the dark worries back.

Had to give it to that boy — he could take a punch and still crack a cutting remark. He looked at the swelling puffing up his right hand and scowled. Thoughts of charming a roomful of ranchers and driving deep into Rebecca Jo vanished like gun smoke caught in a desert crosswind.

"Goddamit, gotta get some ice on this hand."

He plugged the sink and ran cold water to fill it, yelling for his secretary, Shirley Jean Holmes, spinster, Sunday school teacher at the First Baptist Church of Faver and lightning rod for every bolt of gossip in the county. If Shirley Jean hadn't heard it, it wasn't worth hearing.

"Hey, Shirley Jean — bring me a couple of trays of ice out of the freezer, if you would please, m'am. And bring me that white uniform shirt hangin' on the hat tree."

"Now, Tyrus Lamar Willingham — you're a full-grown man and sheriff of this county. Seems to me you could fetch your own ice and uniform shirt."

The banter did little to lighten his mood. Instead of looking forward to the evening ahead, he slipped into more dark brooding about the gunfight at Bustamante's car lot, the dead body found in a desert hole, the death of Bart Hulett. And a Dallas peeper named Ed Earl Burch.

Awful convenient for that Burch fella to be Johnny-on-the-spot when two Mex gunmen showed up to cancel Dirt Cheap's check.

Helluva move for Burch to dust both shooters without getting a scratch on him — more like the work of a gun for hire than a peeper chasing a wayward husband for Lawyer Boelcke.

The lawyer's client was that hot britches Wyatt woman, one of his big campaign contributors and a gal who went through husbands like they were made of Kleenex. She was enough of a bona fide for Blue to buy Boelcke's initial explanation about Burch working in his county. But not now, not after Burch's O.K. Corral act.

Burch didn't seem like a flat-natural killer. Glasses, beard, thinning hair and a paunch gave him the look of every Bubba in Texas, even if he didn't wear a gimme cap from the local feed and seed.

A big man with a gimpy gait that made you think of a broken-down ranch hand. A slow drawl that made you think the man was semi-dumb. But that drawl came from a smart mouth that didn't know when to quit. There was also the hint of a mean streak, some muscle under the flab and the instincts and unblinking eyes of a cop.

More to this Ed Earl Burch than showed at first glance. Blue needed to know all there was to know — right now. He had one of his deputies, Needle Burnet, running a background check on Burch with some of Blue's Dallas contacts. Burnet was the same deputy who sapped Burch into dreamland in the interrogation room.

He could tell ol' Needle took an instant dislike to Burch and truly enjoyed getting the chance to smack him down. Should make him extra motivated to dig up the dirt on the man, find out what kind of a fall from grace plunged a cop into the purgatory of peeper hell.

Burnet was a bad *hombre* to have on your trail, particularly if he was already primed to hate you a lot. His given name was Ricky Don, which was not shorthand for Richard Donald. His parents took a shortcut, giving their son a first and middle name straight out of the Bubba Hall of Fame.

Nobody but family called him Ricky Don. To the people of Cuervo County, he was Needle Burnet, rail-thin and mean as a snake, traits hidden by an easy smile and that brushy red handlebar moustache with the well-waxed tips.

Needle got his nickname in Vietnam, where he served as a Marine scout-sniper. He racked up forty-five confirmed kills, with an unofficial tally topping 100. Kept a black leather notebook wrapped in oilskin where he detailed each kill, confirmed or unofficial. At first, his nickname was a nod to his skinny physique, but as his body count rose, it took on a more lethal meaning.

As in: *Those bastards are kicking the shit out of us, sic the Needle on 'em...The Needle goes in and the gooks go bye-bye...Needle makes 'em all good gooks...*

There was another reason for the nickname — he had a taste for the heroin spike. China White in Vietnam. Mexican Brown in Cuervo County. More of a skin popper than a mainliner, Needle kept his smack habit under control — a functioning addict with a badge. And he still knew how to make people go bye-bye — from long range or up close and personal.

Needle goes in and a problem disappears. Tossed into a hole in the rocky desert and quickly forgotten.

Nice and nasty talent to have on a leash, a tie Blue had to keep tight because Needle didn't get along with his chief deputy, Elroy Jesus "Sudden" Doggett, an Army vet who served as an MP.

Doggett was also a former Professional Rodeo Cowboys' Association calf roper who earned his nickname by being so slick and fast it seemed like the calf was running free one second and roped and tied the next. Until he broke his left leg in three places, ending his rodeo days and leaving him with a metal rod in the bum wheel.

Blue hired him in the first year of his first term, partly out of empathy for a man who also had a foot in two cultures, not fully at home in either. Doggett had Mexican blood, but no Anglo. His great-grandfather, Elias Doggett, was born a slave in Mississippi in the late 1850s and brought to Texas by his master, Tom Lamond, who staked his fortune on cattle ranching.

The elder Doggett learned to rope and ride. But what gave him near mythical status was his way with horses — his unique ability to think like them and become part of the herd. The transformation was subtle but magical and the ex-slave became a local legend as a man who could round up a herd of wild mustangs by himself.

Sudden Doggett had his share of scrapes as a youngster, called out by Anglos, Mexicans and the occasional black kid. But he also inherited his great-grandfather's calm and subtle way with horses, a gift that carried over to the way he related to people. He spoke fluent Spanish and looked like a *moreno*, a Mexican with dark brown skin. He kept his curly hair closely cropped, a habit from his Army days. He had large brown eyes that usually looked sad but took on a deadly glitter when he got angry.

Doggett was Blue's ambassador, a man respected and liked by most of the law-abiding folks living in Cuervo County. He made it easy for Blue to be the sheriff for all the people, not just the muscle for Anglo *patróns.* Needle Burnet was Blue's enforcer, the man he sent when a firm word and a flash of the badge just weren't the best weapons of choice.

Only Burnet knew about *El Alojamiento* with Garza. Only Burnet got a slice of hush money doled directly from Blue's pocket. Others might guess, including Doggett, but they weren't on the inside of a deal he kept compartmentalized and humming along.

Running smooth, like a well-tuned, small-block V-8. Until now.

The gunfight in the heart of his hometown — the dead shooters weren't locals, a sign that a rival's challenge to Garza was spilling over the river. The body of one of Garza's lieutenants, Arturo Herrera, found in a hole in the outback of his county, the face blown away by high-velocity lead — could be part of the turf war between Garza and a rival, might be something else.

And at the top of Blue's worry list was the grisly item that gave him the most pain — the death of Bart Hulett, which may or may not have been an accident.

Blue knew he had to dive deep into Bart's death, but was wary about what he might find. Hulett was a prominent citizen from one of the founding families of Cuervo County. He was also a friend who convinced Blue to run for sheriff, seeing a hard-nosed Ranger as exactly the kind of tough lawman needed to tame the county's outlaw elements.

Blue respected Bart Hulett and loved to sit on his front porch, deep whiskeys in hand, and talk about politics, horses, women, old guns, the brutal land they loved and the violence both men had seen. Those were mighty fine moments that almost let Blue forget about his betrayal of Bart Hulett's trust.

He knew about Hulett's land battles with the Bryte Brothers and knew about their nasty and long-standing habit of getting even in a terminal kind of way. He also heard vague rumblings about a falling out between Bart and his cousin, Gyp, a crooked bastard Blue had to ignore because of his connections to Garza. While that might be more of the idle tongue-wagging about the Good Huletts and the Bad Huletts that had fascinated generations of Cuervo County gossip mongers, Blue couldn't shrug it off.

Bart Hulett died before he found out just how wrong he was about Blue, which relieved Blue of his occasional pangs of guilt about his chosen path. But Blue still owed a debt to Hulett, one that wouldn't let him sweep his death under the rug if it was murderous payback for crossing the Bryte Brothers. He wasn't in bed with those bastards and could fuck them hard if he found out they killed his friend and mentor. But if Garza was involved ... Blue let that thought dangle.

So far, the tracks pointed toward an accidental death — Bart Hulett crushed and burned while trying to save his horses from the flames. An investigator from the state fire marshal's office hadn't found any obvious telltales of arson — no traces of accelerants, no re-routed wires spliced or jumpered to cause a junction box to overheat and spark.

But there were lingering suspicions. The blaze started on the ground floor, near the barn's rear entrance where an old Massey-

Ferguson 135 tractor with a front-end loader was parked close to a stack of hay used for fresh stall bedding, raising the possibility of a hot exhaust pipe as the ignition source.

Ranch hands said the tractor was left there after being used to haul horse dung and piss-soaked bedding out to a compost heap. The fire left the old machine a charred hulk sitting on seared metal wheels, its tires gobbled up by the hungry flames.

Nothing ruled out an artful barnburner using that tractor to start the blaze. Just enough fuel carefully pooled around the mouth of an uncapped tank, just enough hay piled around the exhaust pipe and trailed over to that stack. Light 'em up with a kitchen match and trust the flames to cover your tracks.

Blue felt a small spike of fear stab his guts and a touch of vertigo that made him take a step to regain his balance. That small-block eight driving his political dreams was knocking and missing now. Yessir. Yew bet.

Might throw a rod before too much longer. Might just put his favorite candidate — himself — in deep peril. Had to get a handle on all of this. *Muy pronto.* Had to reach out to Garza and Gyp Hulett. Had to get a line on those Bryte Brothers shits.

And that caused his thoughts to turn to that Dallas peeper. If he could rule out Burch being a barnburner or gun hand for the Garzas, maybe Blue could turn the peeper into a useful tool. A stalking horse, maybe. Or a patsy.

Maybe both. Use him then lose him. That would make Needle Burnet a very happy man.

Blue felt a tad bit better, a touch more under control and in command, like a rider almost dumped from the saddle who pulls himself upright and regains the reins. He slid his bruised right hand out of the ice and water and toweled it dry.

He slipped on the starched white ranch shirt and pinned on the gold star and brass nameplate. He buckled on his gun belt, settling the thick leather on his hips before holstering the .44 magnum wheelgun.

Ready to roll on up to Fort Davis, make that speech and plant a high, hard one in Rebecca Jo Harnett. Maybe stay the night and go for a two-fer. Plenty of time to make a couple of pay phone calls along the way.

One to his Garza contact, a cutout who would set up a face-to-face meet. One to Gyp Hulett — direct, no middleman.

Thirteen

"Well, at least you waited until you got paid before you stepped on your dick and started shooting people."

"Perfect timing is one of my many virtues, Counselor."

"So's getting whacked on by Cuervo County jailers, looks like. Nasty shiner you got there. And that knot on the back of your noggin' looks like a hard-boiled ostrich egg."

"Wasn't no jailer who dotted my eye, son. That was from your boy, the High Sheriff of this here county. The right and righteous fist of Blue Willingham, his ownsef. Yessir, when I step in it, the proud and the mighty take notice and give me their personal attention."

"Blue give you that knot, too?"

"Naw, that was a lovely parting gift from one of his step-and-fetch-its. Skinny little red-haired runt with a handlebar moustache that makes him look like a whorehouse piano player. Fucker buffaloed me with a sap and I owe his sorry ass some payback."

"Might be an IOU you don't want to try and collect. That was Needle Burnet who whacked you. He's twelve kinds of mean and a killer. He doesn't look it, but he's Blue's enforcer. You don't cross him and expect to live."

Burch snorted, then hawked a loogie up from the back of his throat and spat it on the floor of his cell. He was seated on the lower pipe-framed bunk, leaning forward, his elbows on his knees. The top bunk, hinged to the wall and braced by chains, was vacant. He looked up at Boelcke for the first time, noticing how the bars cast straight-line shadows across the lawyer's smooth and olive-toned face.

"You got a goddam cigarette?"

"Yes, but not your brand."

"Yours will do."

Boelcke pulled a red pack of Pall Malls from his inside jacket pocket, shook some nails loose and snaked his arm through the bars. Burch plucked one from the pack, then leaned forward as the lawyer ran his other arm through the bars and snicked fire out of a gold Ronson Varaflame.

Burch took a deep drag, jetted smoke from his nostrils and examined the long, thin unfiltered cigarette. He looked at Boelcke and smiled. He cupped a hand to his ear and dropped his voice into a deeper baritone.

"OUTSTANDING — and they are MILD!"

"What the hell are you talking about?"

"You're just a youngster. You don't remember the tagline in the Pall Mall commercials? I liked the Lucky tagline better — 'It's Toasted.' Like you were going to slap butter and strawberry jam on the damn thing and eat it for breakfast."

"I think that whack on the head shook some screws loose. Quit babbling about cigarette slogans. And quit talking in that fake voice — you sound like a used car dealer on 'ludes."

"Well, hell, Counselor — I was going for the Gary Owen effect."

"Who the hell is that?"

"Right, you're too young. Remember *Laugh-In*? The announcer with the really deep, syrupy voice who always talked with a hand cupped to his ear?"

Boelcke just stared at Burch like a man cornered in a bar by a chatty drunk. Burch shook his head and waggled his hand through the air to part the smoke.

"Never-damn-mind, Counselor. You here to throw my bail and spring me?"

"No charge, no bail."

"You're fuckin' kiddin' me, right? When your boy, the High Sheriff, wasn't trying to punch my lights out, he was sizing me up as prime suspect for a killin' and a barn burning. Toss in charges for those two Mex shooters I nailed and wrap me up for the jury to convict me as Public Enemy Number One."

"The High Sheriff changed his mind."

"That a fact? He seemed convinced I was a gun hand for the local drug lord — Garza? Seemed pissed at you for selling him a song and dance about doing a divorce job as cover for me being a one-man crime wave."

"You talk too damn much. Let's get you the hell out of here. Get you cleaned up and fed. Get you a pair of cheap sunglasses to cover up that shiner."

"Like Lana Turner after she got smacked around by Johnny Stompanato?"

"Yeah, just like that, but you don't have the tits to swell Lana's sweater. We'll get you breakfast and shades. Then we'll have a long talk at my office. Got to get you caught up on some things."

Burch took a drag and arched the eyebrow over his un-blackened eye. Boelcke shook his head and gave him the cutoff sign across his throat.

"Fine by me, Counselor. But we won't need the cheap sunglasses for the Lana Turner look. Got some Ray-Bans we'll reclaim with the rest of my things unless some scumbag trusty has light-fingered them. They're prescription shades, so he'll get a headache after he puts them on."

"Yeah, yeah."

"I could use about a gallon of coffee, a big greasy plate of *huevos con chorizo* and refried beans and a dessert shot of Maker's Mark. After we pick up my Colt, my wallet, my keys and those Ray-Bans. And any folding money and pocket change these bastards haven't swiped."

"Jesus, give it a rest. Let's get you out of here before they decide to give you another knot on that hard head of yours."

"By all means, Counselor. Tell 'em to open sesame and lead me to the promised land of good breakfast grease. You're buying, by the way."

Boelcke waved for a jailer to open Burch's cell. Burch ground the cigarette out with his boot heel, grabbed his windbreaker and ambled through the swinging door, whistling a nameless tune like a man walking his dog around the block. He nodded at the prisoners in the other cells.

"Always smoke a Lucky Strike, boys. It's TOASTED!"

Boelcke rolled his eyes toward the ceiling, searching for a god of sanity who wasn't there.

Burch cut loose a long, loud belch as he and Boelcke walked into the lawyer's inner office, then made a beeline for the liquor cabinet and poured himself four fingers of Very Old Barton in a rocks glass — neat. Whiskey with an 'e.' No Maker's Mark.

He pointed the bottle at Boelcke. The lawyer shook him off. Burch shrugged, then settled into a deep nail-head leather chair, crossing his boots at the ankle, fishing a Lucky out of his pocket and using the Zippo to fire it up with one very practiced hand. Boelcke, perched on the front edge of his desk, watched and waited for the ritual to end, smoothing his thin moustache and running a comb through his curly dark hair.

"You comfortable?"

Burch smiled and held up the whiskey glass in his left hand and the cigarette scissored between the first two fingers of his right.

"Dessert after a mighty fine breakfast. It's the most important meal of the day."

"Jesus, will you quit clowning around? I need to talk serious business with you, catch you up on some shit that's gone down while you were on that little overnight vacation at Sheriff Blue's House of Delight."

"Defense mechanism, Counselor. I'm acting the fool to stave off this serious talk you want to have with me because I've got a strong feeling you want to throw me into a shitstorm that I'd be better off leavin' a whole lot of alone in order to get a whole lotta gone."

"Will you at least listen while I run it down for you?"

"You've got until I finish this whiskey and this smoke, then I'm headed east, Counselor. Besides, the High Sheriff already grilled me about a laundry list of bad news — body in the desert, the two Mex shooters I dusted, turf war between this Garza guy and a rival. Has Ol' Blue torqued up something fierce. Only thing I'm out of the loop on is this barn burning shit — somebody's dead, but Blue didn't say who."

"Man name of Bart Hulett. Prominent person in these parts. Rancher, war hero, county judge and what they quaintly call a civic leader. Most times that's a polite word for chicken thief, but in Bart's case, it was meant out of respect. His family helped found this county and he was a damn good man."

"Was the fire an accident or arson? The way the High Sheriff grilled me, I'd bet the latter."

"They don't know for sure. My guy says they didn't find any obvious signs of arson, but that doesn't mean much. And there's a lot of talk Bart was in a dogfight with some nasty developers who wanted to buy his part of the ranch. Bart made some moves that jammed these guys up pretty bad and they're known not to play nice."

Burch arched an eyebrow and took another sip of Barton. Not a bad substitute for Maker's. There was another shoe to drop and silence instead of a question was the best way to get Boelcke to let it go. He watched the lawyer fidget with his moustache — an obvious tell of nerves. He took a drag from the Lucky and kept his eyes level on the lawyer.

Boelcke quit fidgeting, took a deep breath and looked Burch in the eye.

"This is the delicate and speculative part. There's talk of a falling out between Bart and his cousin Gyp, who controls the other part of the Bar Double H. Now, you've heard me run through all of Bart's virtues. Let's just say Gyp has none of those and is Bart's polar opposite. He's one of a long line of Hulett outlaws — smugglers, rustlers, gunrunners, bootleggers and worse. He and Bart are what folks around here mean when they talk about the Good Huletts and the Bad Huletts."

"And Gyp does business with Garza, right? And Garza looks to be in the middle of a turf war with a rival, right? So far, Counselor, you've just given me a lot of reasons for shuttin' down this little chat and headin' back to Dallas right now."

"Let me counter with this — I've got two clients who want to find out whether Bart Hulett was murdered and who did it. One of them you already know quite well — you just wrapped up a job for her. She was quite fond of Bart."

"Horizontally fond?"

"You know Nita."

"Who's the other client with an unhealthy dose of curiosity?"

A deep voice boomed from the open office door.

"That would be me, son."

Burch turned to look over his shoulder. Leaning in the doorframe was a tall man in black jeans, a gray canvas vest and a battered black hat with a Gus crease and salt streaks from dried sweat.

The hat covered coarse and shaggy white hair above a weathered, pock-marked face, bushy eyebrows and coal-black eyes of the kind that froze a man's heart. Eyes a man didn't want to see staring down the sights of a gun aimed at him.

Gyp Hulett, his ownsef.

Hulett walked to the cabinet where Boelcke cached his liquor with the bow-legged gait of a man who'd spent decades in the saddle. As he passed, Burch noticed the grip and cocked hammer of a Browning Hi-Power riding in a slide holster just behind Hulett's right hip.

The tail of his canvas vest did little to cover the pistol, but Hulett didn't look like he gave a half a damn whether the whole world knew he was packing heat. He poured himself four fingers of the same bourbon Burch was drinking, didn't offer to top off Burch's glass, then sat down in the vacant twin of the nail-head leather chair Burch was sitting in.

Burch eyed Hulett while sipping his own whiskey, letting the silence stretch between them. He wanted the old man to speak first and didn't mind the black, gunsight eyes trying to bore a hole in his battered skull. Boelcke resumed his fidgeting while the two older men played their game of silent stares.

Hulett broke the silence but didn't break the stare.

"Alrighty, then. We've got it settled that we're both pretty tough waddies who like drinkin' breakfast whiskey and don't play well with others. As you heard our learned counsel say, I'm what folks in this town mean when they talk about the Bad Huletts — and mister, believe everything bad you hear about me."

"Haven't been in town long enough to hear much about you beyond what Lawyer Boelcke tells me. You ain't the reason I'm here, you ain't my client and I ain't too sure you ever will be. But if you two have talked about hiring me to look into Bart Hulett's death, I'm guessing you've done a little homework beyond what our lawyer friend here has told you."

"I've still got a friend or two in Dallas."

"Well, I'll flip you the same coin of advice you tossed me — believe everything you hear about me, the good and the bad. I like good whiskey and bad women. I don't take shit off nobody and got tossed off the force for getting my partner killed, smackin' some dirtbags around who deserved it and speaking my mind once too often to the brass. Folks have a bad habit of underestimating me — I'm still standin' and most of them ain't."

"Got any other coins you want to flip my way?"

"Just one — I'm steady when I work, shaky when I don't for reasons that don't have a damn thing to do with the whiskey."

Hulett nodded once, like a man hearing something that matched what he'd already been told, then shifted gears.

"Looks like Blue Willingham gave you a warm welcome to his jail."

"The High Sheriff didn't appreciate me dusting two Mexican shooters in his town. He also wanted to know if I was the one who set the barn fire that killed your cousin."

Hulett snorted, downed a slug of whiskey and shook his head.

"Lort-a-mercy, that's one of the dumber things I've ever heard Blue say. Then again, he always has been more bullshit and bluff than brains."

Burch gunned the last of his whiskey and held his empty glass out to Boelcke.

"Pour the man another goddam drink, Counselor. He's telling us he'll hear me out all the way to the end of my sales pitch."

Boelcke, looking like a man who has just been slapped in the face, hustled the bottle of Very Old Barton from his liquor cabinet and poured four fresh fingers into Burch's glass. He stepped over to Hulett and topped his glass, then resumed his perch on the front edge of his desk.

"Well, I've heard Lawyer Boelcke say what you want me to do, but I haven't heard the why."

"Got a couple of whys for you. First off, I don't think Blue has the brains or the balls to figure this out, especially if he thinks Malo Garza is behind it. Now he's called me up and given me a bold line of talk about getting to the bottom of Bart's death. Mostly, I think he was trying to figure out whether I wanted Bart's death investigated or hushed up. He also asked me about you — which is how you got on my radar screen."

"In my line of work, word-of-mouth always does beat paid advertising. What did he ask about me?"

"Whether you were working for me. When I told him no, he asked whether I thought you were a hired gun workin' for Garza or those shitbird developers. I said 'Blue, I don't know the man from Adam's fuckin' housecat and don't have a goddam clue who he's workin' for.'"

"Got you curious about me, I bet."

"Mister, I figure a man who blows the socks off of two Mex shooters in the middle of town is a man I need to know. Thought you might come in handy. Then I found out you were an ex-cop and knew you would."

"A handyman with a gun to do the thing the High Sheriff won't."

"Thas' right. I think if push comes to shove, Blue will call this thing an accidental death, close the file and forget the whole damn thing while shedding crocodile tears about what a great friend Bart Hulett was to him and Cuervo County."

"That's one why. What are the others?"

"I've got the balls and brains Blue Willingham don't. Bart Hulett was blood kin and if he was murdered, I want to know who did it and why so I can settle the score."

Hulett's voice sounded like gravel poured over a bent panel of corrugated tin. The gunsight eyes bored into the wall — and into somebody who wasn't in the office. Burch took a drag then stuck the needle in.

"Even if Malo Garza ordered it done? That's your business partner we're talking about, right?"

"Malo and I do business, but it'd be a stretch to call him a partner. He runs his show. I run mine."

Burch sipped his whiskey and let that boast pass — for the moment.

"Word is, you and Bart had a falling out. Was it over you doing business with Garza?"

"We had a few words. Got pretty heated, as a matter of fact. Bart got wind of a little business between Garza and me that took place on my part of the Bar Double H and was angry as hell about it. Worried the ranch would get seized. Worried it would bring the whole world crashing down on both our heads — DEA, FBI, Rangers."

"But not the High Sheriff. Everybody else in law enforcement but not Blue Willingham. Seems odd you don't mention a guy who's made a career out of being such a righteous anti-drug crusader, waging a one-man war against desperados like you and Garza."

Hulett chuckled. The gunsight eyes held no laughter.

"You sound like a man who ought to be writing Blue's stump speeches. You also sound like a man who answered his own question about the high and mighty Blue Willingham and his war on drugs."

"Yeah, I get a strong whiff of bullshit when it comes to the High Sheriff as scourge of the *narcotraficante*. He's all hat no cattle on that score, right?"

"Oh, Blue will nail him a meth lab or two and is hell on street dealers — them sorry-ass fuckers deserve what they get. He even lucks out and seizes a load or two passing through Cuervo County. All part of keeping the good folks feeling safe and sound while burnishing Blue's image. But when it comes to the big dogs, let's just say the sheriff has developed a live-and-let-live philosophy long as the contraband is just passin' through."

"Is Blue on the take?"

"I don't pay him nothin' — 'cept for campaign contributions I routed through Bart and some of his cronies. Don't know whether Garza pays him for lookin' the other way."

"Never met a *narco* yet who didn't want to sew up a bent lawman tight with cash."

Hulett smiled, his thin lips stretching over cigarette-stained teeth. It made him look like a wolf licking his chops over a fresh-killed calf.

"You've answered your own question again."

"For that matter, never met a *narco* who didn't eat a partner whole and take over his operation. They like to be vertically integrated and trust only their own people."

"Mister, what can I tell you — I'm still standin' and I think Malo

Garza would find me a fairly tough piece of meat to swallow. He tries to eat me, it'll be that greaser's last goddam supper."

"Let me ask a question I don't know the answer to. That deal your cousin was pissed about — did he hear about it or see it?"

"As angry as Bart was when we had words, I'd say he saw it firsthand. He liked to ride the backcountry and scout for hunting season. Or just get lost for a day or three, camping out — just him and his horse. Take himself back in time, so to speak, and ride the trails like our daddies and granddaddies did, usually with his granddaddy's guns."

"Did anybody else know he saw that deal go down?"

Hulett broke his stare and took a sip of whiskey, then looked Burch in the eye.

"Yes. Some of the crew workin' that deal saw a faint light up on the ridgeline."

"Was that crew your men or Garza's?"

"Some of both. And a few of my men — well, I pay 'em, but they got family over the river. And in this country, blood ties are stronger than cash. Always have been, always will be. So, there's a strong chance Garza knew Bart was stickin' his nose where it didn't belong."

"And you want me to believe you'll go after Garza if I find out he ordered Bart killed? Before you answer, let me ask that question another way — how do I know you didn't have your cousin killed and just want me pokin' around to make it seem like you didn't."

The room got very quiet. The black, gunsight stare bored into Burch's skull again.

"You don't other than me tellin' you plain I didn't because Bart was blood kin. We Huletts may fuss and fight and work up a strong hate for each other, but blood is still the tie that binds. Bart was a Hulett, goddamit, and if he got killed, I want to know who did the killin'."

Burch used the needle again.

"You're preachin' to the choir about blood bein' thicker than water and preachin' that gospel mighty hard. Makes me wonder whether you're trying to cover up another reason for hirin' me."

Gravel across tin, again. With the gunsight stare.

"Mister, I'm about as bad as they come. I've killed men, fucked wives with a rovin' eye, rustled cattle and smuggled just about any form of contraband you care to name across that river, headed north and south. One thing I ain't, though, is a liar. I'd as soon cut my tongue out with a rusty hedge clipper as tell a lie."

"There's a helluva image I won't forget soon. Couple of basic questions. Who found the body?"

"Stella Rae. Bart's daughter. Expect you know what she looks like, with or without clothes. She showed up at the ranch just before daybreak to go on a morning ride with her daddy. Fire was still burnin' but had died down considerable. Door wide open and horses milling 'round in the yard. Burned her hand when she found Bart under some rafters all burned up. Damn hard way to go."

The two men fell silent, looking at each other. Burch had seen plenty of burned bodies. So had Hulett. Both men were shuffling through grisly mental images. Blackened husks that used to be human. Hair, clothes and flesh burned away. Claws that were once hands, reaching for life already gone.

Each man knew what the other was seeing. Their eyes said it all. Boelcke might as well have been sitting in another area code.

"Where'd she come from?"

Hulett didn't blink or look away. Neither did Burch.

"The Cactus Blossom. Expect you know that place rather well. She and that guitar picker stayed the night. Clerk told a deputy he checked them in. Didn't hear 'em leave. Couple of my boys went over and leaned on him a little. Story didn't change."

"Why the hell were they there again? Their cover was blown. They didn't need to hide out anymore."

"Sentimental reasons."

"She didn't strike me as the sentimental type. Anybody else at the ranch that night?"

126

"Nobody but Bart. He gave the hands the night off to go to a fiesta over the river. One of 'em showed up a few minutes after Stella Rae and helped her gather up the horses and get 'em fed and watered. Then she called it in to the sheriff."

"I'm betting them deputies leaned pretty hard on that hand. The perfect patsy if they wanted to pin a rap on somebody quick."

"Oh, you bet. Leaned on all of them. So did we. Couple of my boys were at that fiesta. The stories held up."

"If somebody killed Bart, who do you think did it and why?"

"Bart was a bull-headed, self-righteous prick who thought none of the stink from my side of the family rubbed off on him. But he sure wasn't shy about hitting me up if he needed money. I gave him a cash injection to refill his tank after he swung some of the land deals that jammed a board up the ass of those developers."

"Tell me about them developer dudes."

"Those fellas believe in payback — financial ruin or something more terminal. Garza's in play because Bart stuck his nose where it didn't belong and saw something he was better off not seein'. Bart was in politics a real long time and didn't mind playing rough if he had to. A man makes enemies that way, ones I might not know about."

"Yeah, you always have the chance of a wild card, somebody out of left field that nobody thinks about with a grudge deep enough to kill for."

"Thas' exactly right. You sound like a man ready to ante up."

The wolf smile returned. Burch shook his head.

"I wouldn't be so God-a-mighty sure of that. You still haven't sold me on why I should take this on."

"Thas' sumthin' that sells itself with two easy reasons — money and a man gettin' to do what he does best. I know what that fat-ass shyster in Dallas promised you to get you to take that job for Lawyer Boelcke here. Promised to rip up the note he's carrying on your business. Well, he'll crawdad on you just as sure as I'm sittin' here. But if you take this deal on for me, I'll money whip the shit out of him and make him rip up that note. I'll also toss you ten large on top of that."

"That's the money part. Now tell me what it is you think I do best and why you think I'd ever want to do it again."

"Lawyer Boelcke tells me you done a damn good job chasin' down that guitar picker husband of Nita Wyatt's when he was shacking up Bart's daughter. You also told him that made you feel like you needed a river of whiskey to wash away the stink of divorce work that made you remember the cop you used to be."

Burch polished off his whiskey and threw a hard stare at Boelcke.

"Lawyer Boelcke's got a big goddam mouth for a man who ever wants me to work for him again."

"Now, now — don't go get so hard-assed at Lawyer Boelcke. Besides, you'd be working for me and Nita — well, me mainly. And I'm offering you a sweet deal to go do what you're made to do and haven't been allowed to do in a long time — track down a killer. So, we got a deal here, mister?"

Hulett stuck out his right hand. Burch didn't trust the man, but reached over and gave a firm handshake. His best choice just got a whole lot sweeter, but it was still lousy — lousy with the prospect of high-velocity trouble and blood-soaked pain.

And that made Ed Earl Burch about as happy a man as the demons that haunted his moody soul would ever let him be.

Fourteen

Vicente Roca was spooked by the sound the armchair made when he hurled it across the motel room, shattering the mirror mounted above the rust-stained sink and splintering the wood. To his ears, it was like the booming echo of a freight car door slammed shut in the rail yards after midnight, a sound from his childhood.

Roca crouched in the middle of the room, frozen in double surprise by the sudden rush of anger that caused him to heave the chair and the memories jarred lose by the sound. Long walks with his father at night near the yards bordered by Avenida 16 de Septembre and the old Custom House in Juarez. His father's incessant insomnia and the need for his eldest son's company to stave off his loneliness.

They would pause near the edge of the yards, listening to the clatter and clang of cargo getting loaded onto the cars, of cars being linked together to form the trains for the next day's haul — and, that final boom of doors slammed shut and locked. The sound Roca heard when he hurled that chair.

His father would talk softly to him, pointing out the bobbing lights of lanterns the workers carried and used to signal each other. Sometimes he would speak of Roca's dead mother, taken from the family at too young an age by spinal meningitis, his voice filled with longing and loss.

Other times, his mood was light and playful. He would make jokes about the customers who entered their small *farmacia* on the west side of Avenida Benito Juarez, just south of its intersection with Calle Ignatio Mejia. How Señora Gomez waddled like a duck when she walked in to get her gout medicine. How Señor Castillo looked like Jorge Negrete, impeccably dressed and groomed with a perfect pencil-thin moustache, when he picked up the nitroglycerin tablets for his angina.

Roca stared at the shattered mirror and the pile of padding and splintered wood on the tile floor. Perfect for an indoor bonfire. He shook his head and snorted at the thought of a bonfire and the rush of memories. Why the sound of the chair striking the mirror reminded him of those midnight walks with his father was sweet mystery to him.

Why he hurled the chair was dead easy to explain — $75,000 he was already counting ways to spend was chopped in half with a three-minute phone call. But there was more to it than money lost.

Gaunt and habitually monkish, Vicente Roca had one vice he turned into a virtue — a bloodlust and keen eye for diamonds and other jewelry-grade gemstones. He would hoard his hit money until he had enough to make a run to Monterrey or Mexico City, where he knew several discrete and very private jewelers who required a referral and cash-only transactions. He bought only loose stones and stashed his diamonds, emeralds, sapphires and black opals in large safety deposit boxes at eight banks — six in El Paso, two in Midland.

Roca was also obsessively possessive. When he accepted a contract, he took ownership of not only the job, which he meticulously planned and executed, but the soul of the target, ushering his victim into whatever afterlife awaited with a painless and untraceable death.

His weapons of choice were the chemical compounds he mastered studying pharmaceutical biochemistry at the *Universidad Nacional Autónoma de Mexico* in Mexico City and working in pharmaceutical labs for paltry pay that caused him to seek extracurricular sources of income. He was boyhood friends with a Juarez lawyer, Esteban Alvarez, whose mother, Rosario, was a customer at the Roca family *farmacia*.

Alvarez was a flashy dandy with expensive mistresses, tailored Italian suits and a checkered list of clients that included drug lords, badly bent politicians, sketchy import-export proprietors, *maquiladora* operators and brothel owners. He was a man with easy access to money who always seemed to need more.

Over lunch at a quiet back table in a side-street café, Roca listened as Alvarez doled out details about his latest mistress, the wife of a *maquila* client named Quinones, an older, overweight and overworked executive who had little time for his trophy wife. Those details included her voracious sexual appetite, trumped only by her lust for money and her impatient hunger to get her hands on her husband's million-dollar life insurance policy.

"The man's pushing seventy, has a bad heart and is a diabetic, but doesn't seem to be in any hurry to die. He lives to make money and is rolling in it. That's what keeps him going. She's tried fucking him to death, but his cock doesn't work, so that's out. Ay, mi carnal, *she might wind up fucking me to death, she's so frustrated."*

"Why the rush? Why not just wait for nature to take its course?"

"The stars are aligned right now. She's the beneficiary of his life insurance policy. His will gives her his controlling interest in the maquila. *That might change if his first wife, the mother of his children, makes good on her threat to hire a lawyer and reopen the divorce settlement."*

"Hasn't he taken care of them?"

"Of course. They have the house, tuition at the university, generous living expenses and a big hunk of cash set aside in his will. But the first wife wants more."

"Don't they all."

"True, my friend. Very true."

"Tell me this — does he take insulin injections for his diabetes?"

"Sí, he often lets her do the shots. Between his toes. Like a heroin addict."

"Perhaps I can help you solve your problem."

Alvarez cocked his head like a curious dog and arched his left eyebrow.

Over flan, Roca introduced his lawyer friend to the concept of better murder through chemistry.

Over double espressos and brandy, Roca was well on his way to a new and lucrative career as a hit man.

A hypodermic for hire.

Better murder through chemistry became Roca's sales pitch to clients. An array of compounds could be used to trigger an untraceable death and Roca was master of them all.

His current favorite — a lethal injection of potassium chloride, which causes sudden death from cardiac arrest. Hard even for a suspicious medical examiner to spot because the body produces elevated levels of potassium when muscle tissue is damaged — and the heart is a muscle.

He also used back-to-back shots of calcium gluconate and potassium phosphate, a double whammy that caused severe hypertension and failure of the heart's right ventricle. In a pinch, he even killed by injecting air into a target's vein or artery, causing a fatal blockage. Death from the very source of life.

As part of his careful planning, he liked to know the target's medical history. His clients were usually able to obtain a copy of a doctor's records or a list of medications from a local pharmacy. Helped to know if the target already had a history of heart trouble or had a stable of drugs that included painkillers or sedatives with an overdose hazard.

He preferred to work alone, but his clients often provided him with muscle to watch his back, trick out an alarm system, slip a sedative into a nightcap or strong-arm a target who woke up unwilling to accept one of Roca's lethal injections. Whether he worked alone or had a partner, Roca insisted on delivering the kill shot himself.

His room was in a motel on the outskirts of Marfa, a clean but well-worn single-story building of concrete block and light blue stucco in the shape of an L. The short side held the office entrance and faced U.S. Highway 90, fronted by an arched portico. The long side stretched back into the gloom of the dying dusk. Green neon with random segments of burned-out tubing imperfectly traced the white Oleo Script of the roadside sign — Traveler's Rest.

Roca had just checked in after a three-hour drive from El Paso, taking time to unpack his canvas bag and wash the road grit and dried sweat off his face and neck before placing the call that brought him bad news. Chuy Reynaldo was on the other end of the line.

"*Señor,* my *patrón* has instructed me to tell you that we no longer need your services."

"Why is that?"

"There has been an unforeseen development that removed the problem we called you to resolve."

The target has already been killed by somebody else. Somebody has swooped in and stolen what was mine alone — my target and my money. Roca could feel his anger start to flame. He kept his voice calm and cold.

"Did you bring in another problem solver? If so, I am afraid I must insist on full payment of my fee."

"No, you were the only one we called. In truth, we don't know who removed the problem. We only know the how."

"And that is?"

"It appears to be an accident. More than that I am reluctant to share on the telephone."

"Very wise. However, appearances can be deceiving. You hired me to create a deceptive appearance."

"My *patrón* regrets any inconvenience this has caused you and has authorized payment of half your fee to the account you gave us. He also wishes me to tell you that he is very angry about this turn of events because it is not the way he does business and feels it puts a black mark on his reputation."

"I appreciate your *patrón's* generosity and his concern about conducting business in a professional manner, but I very much doubt his anger is greater than mine."

"*Señor,* with respect, the anger of my *patrón* is limitless."

"I don't wish to argue about whose anger more perfectly matches the fires of hell, but I do want to make one point. When I agree to accept a job, I immediately assume complete responsibility for the problem until it is completely resolved to my satisfaction and yours. In a very real sense, the problem you entrust to me is no longer yours. It is mine. I become the sole proprietor."

"Like a shopkeeper?"

"More like the owner of a fine jewelry store or a dealer in exceedingly rare antiques. Think how you would feel if something precious was stolen from you — a nearly flawless diamond or a priceless artifact. Your problem became my precious jewel the minute I accepted this job and it has been snatched away from me. This pains me greatly and makes me angry. That's how seriously I regard my work."

Silence on the other side of the line. Broken by a short, choking cough.

"I don't know what to say other than on behalf of my *patrón,* I express my sorrow and regret about this turn of events and the very personal loss you feel. He has told me that you are a professional without peer and I can see why he holds you in such high regard."

"Permit me one final question. You say you don't know who removed the problem, but surely you must have suspicions."

"*Sí,* but I'm reluctant to discuss this on the phone."

"I understand your reluctance and your discretion. Very admirable. Tell your *patrón* what I've shared with you. I have the greatest respect for him and this unfortunate circumstance does not tarnish that. Should you have need of my services again, you can leave word with my exchange."

"Certainly. I will tell him what you said. *Suerte, señor.*"

The line went dead with a metallic click, leaving Roca to brood in angry silence. The client expected him to quietly accept his cash kiss-off and return to Juarez. Pride and anger wouldn't let him do that.

He would go to Faver. He would find out who poached his target and kill them. He spent the next three hours on the phone, dialing up cousins in Cuervo County, bent lawyers like Alvarez and other middlemen who had put people in need of his services in contact with him.

His questions were always the same. Was there a contract on his target? Were there strangers in town? Strangers who made people uneasy — killers, not tourists, truckers or saddle tramps.

Near the end of those hours, Alvarez called back and gave him a name and the possibility of a new target. An Anglo named Burch. An ex-cop from Dallas who made a bloody splash in Faver by gunning down two *sicarios* in the middle of town.

Word on the street was Burch was a gun for hire. Word was he was a suspect in the target's death. That didn't fit the accidental appearance of the target's death because a gun is never subtle, but it was all Roca had after three hours on the phone. He would go to Faver to find out more.

Burch. A man he would have to find. A man he would have to get close to. Very close.

Better revenge through chemistry.

Fifteen

She kept her head perfectly still, willing herself to keep her eyes locked on the image staring back at her from the mirror of the antique mahogany dressing table with the braided brass drawer handles, spindly legs and gold-leaf accents.

Those eyes were clear and blue. With wide pupils that gave her the look of a hyperalert cat stalking a fat robin through the tall grass. They took careful inventory of the face staring back from the mirror — the crescent-shaped scar high on her left cheek, the long and flinty jawline, the faint beginnings of laugh lines running from a thin-lipped mouth, the slightly turned-up pug nose and the shoulder-length hair that was tinted from a bottle several shades lighter than a natural color that wasn't quite dishwater blonde.

Her hair was thick and straight. Parted high on the right side of her head, it swept across a tall forehead, brushing over her right eyebrow. She kept those predatory eyes on the mirrored image, refusing to glance down at the blur of her hands engaged in a fast muscle memory of something she practiced every day — field stripping a full-frame 1911 and reassembling it without looking.

By feel. Fingers dancing over the barrel bushing, the slide, the guide rod, the recoil spring, the barrel — and the trickiest part, the slide stop. Seeing the pieces and how they came apart and fit together in her mind's eye. But not the eyes she kept locked on the mirror image.

Sometimes she did this blindfolded. Today, she was naked.

Perched on a velvet cushion plumped on the cowskin seat of a mahogany chair with spindly legs that matched the table, her taut, petite body had the well-muscled calves, thighs and ass of a dancer or horsewoman. She was formally trained to do both. Her breasts were full — more than a mouthful for a man and sometimes a woman, with red, peaked nipples. Her skin had an all-over poolside tan.

Her hands racked the slide of the reassembled pistol, her thumb snicking the slide stop into the notch that locked open the breech. Eyes still on the mirror image, she slapped a magazine packed with eight rounds of .45 ACP hollow-point into the well, then tripped the stop that caused the slide to slam forward and a round to get stripped from the magazine and parked in the chamber. She locked the cocked hammer with the ambidextrous safety.

Breaking the stare at the mirror image, she finally looked down at the object of her muscle memory — a Colt Series 70 with a matte chrome finish, a gift from her Uncle Harlan on her eighteenth birthday. He taught her how to shoot a 1911 at the crude range thrown up behind his log cabin, not much more than twenty-five yards of rocky ground picked clean of stones and rolled smooth in front of the side of the hill, with railroad ties marking the firing line. Rough planks nailed together in a rectangular frame provided a shelf for targets — bottles, paint cans, milk jugs full of water.

"This is the boss gun, girl. You got it and you got them — ever' time."

Harlan lived at the high end of a narrow, nameless mountain hollow in East Tennessee, about twenty-five miles northeast of Newport. His father and grandfather were moonshiners. Harlan kept pace with the times, running a small meth lab even deeper in the mountains, growing high-grade weed and moving loads of cocaine and heroin for big suppliers, relying on a small band of nephews, cousins and other kin to provide safe transport at a sweet price.

She loved Uncle Harlan and loved the gun he gave her — loved its heft, its heavy recoil and the icy power she felt when she shot somebody who needed killing. She used it to blow down a Dallas pimp and drug lord who ordered her uncle killed and to snatch the life out of a protégé who arranged the hit, a border *narco* and full-blown psychopath. She used a twelve-gauge shotgun to kneecap the cousin who actually pulled the trigger on her uncle, then blast his head into a misty blood pulp after he gave her the *narco's* name.

The *narco* was a strange and deadly bird. He had nightmare visions of winged serpents and jaguar-headed Aztec warriors wielding their obsidian-edged wooden swords — the *maquahuitl,* a weapon so strong and sharp, conquistadors said it could chop the head off the horse with one blow.

They called him T-Roy or *El Rojo Loco,* the latter for his psychotic nightmares and rages — and his flame-red hair. She sent him straight to Hell with eight rounds of hollow-point from the birthday present her Uncle Harlan gave her. Or maybe it was the Aztec underworld, Mictlan, where the winged serpents roamed free and Mictlantecuhtli, lord of the dead, ripped the flesh of those he ruled.

That would be fitting given T-Roy's tight relationship with *La Madrina,* an octogenarian *bruja,* and her sons. The *narco* ran his operation from the *rancho* owned by the *bruja* and was under the sway of her unholy hybrid of *Santeria* and the ceremonial and selective cannibalism of those ancient Aztecs — eating the heart of a fresh-killed human offering.

It was *La Madrina* who wanted him dead, a man she loved like a son until the gods she worshipped told her he mocked them by invoking their names when he didn't truly believe. The *bruja* handed her the Colt with a silent nod.

Killing him once wasn't enough. She killed him many times in her dreams. The boom of the big .45. Chunks blown out of his skull and a crater where one eye used to be. Head shots to keep him from plunging the dull, gray gleam of a huge blade into the heart of a friend.

Friend. Could she call him that? Not hardly. Fugitives on the run and hunters who wanted the same man dead, their time together charged by the lethal likelihood that both of them would be killed. An acquaintanceship of desperation. Say that three times fast. A sign she had been hanging out in Mexico far too long — florid and sweeping phrases came to mind and tongue more easily. What would Uncle Harlan say about that?

"Keep it simple, girl. Don't get above your raisin'. And your raisin' is up holler grit. Keep your mind on that gun. Break her down and build her up blind one more time."

Eyes locked on the mirror image again. Fingers poised to start fieldstripping the pistol. She heard the door open and saw a man's reverse likeness enter the image — small, at first, then looming larger as he stepped up behind her, reaching under her arms to cup her bare breasts, leaning forward to nibble on one ear and then the other. She felt his hard cock press into her back, sheathed by the silky fabric of his suit trousers.

"Down, boy. We got business to discuss before you have your dinner with those friends of yours."

"Later, *mi amor*. We'll have time to talk before I have to go. And they're business associates, not friends."

"You'll extend my regrets, of course. Lovely as it might be to meet them, it's way too risky."

"Of course. Now, put that gun down. I have something much more interesting for you to play with."

"You can fuck me later, lover. Right now, you need to listen to me and pay attention. Your buddy Flores is busy lining up some of the smaller outfits on either side of your turf to give him more muscle to move against you."

She watched the image of Esteban "Malo" Garza raise his head from her neck and frown, placing the tip of his right index finger on the edge of his moustache, a full and black chevron riding above thin lips pursed in thought. The lip hair was an inverted counterpoint to the pointed V of his clean-shaven chin and jawline and a widow's peak accentuated by slicked-back and wavy hair.

His nose was aquiline and gave him the air of a patrician or Spanish grandee, a somewhat misleading look given his family's hard-scrabble roots, but fitting for a man who spoke four languages, appreciated modern art and classical music and had an undergrad degree from the *Universidad Nacional Autónoma de México* and a law degree from Texas A&M.

His eyes were large, brown and almond-shaped. They filled with mirth when he laughed and provided an early warning sign of the arc flash of anger that fired a violent rage.

No refinement or culture when his eyes flashed. Count on a killing. Often by his own hand, using his favorite gun, a jet-black Browning Hi-Power with ivory grips and engraved scrollwork on the slide. Malo Garza preferred to deliver gunsmoke vengeance up close and personal to rivals who crossed him and employees who betrayed him.

"Who told you this?"

"*La Madrina.*"

"*La bruja?* When did you speak to her?"

"On that last run to see Flores and cut a deal for my people to run some of his product through the promised land."

"Promised land. *Ay dios mio*, your beloved Tennessee. And you waited until now to tell me?"

She saw a small flame in his eyes, a hint of anger in the stare aimed at her image. She broke the reflected stare, spun around and jabbed a finger into his chest, her eyes locking on his with a cold, blue glare. Direct. No mirror.

"You need to cool your jets, *muy pronto*. I had to check this out and do it in my own way to see if she was right. I got no doubt *La Madrina* and her sons are getting squeezed by Flores to get in line. Probably some nearby outfits, too. But I wanted to see just how far this went or whether this was just more of her cigar smoke and voodoo chants."

"And what did you find out, my little hillbilly lover?"

"That she's right. You got Obregon and Prieta upriver, Moya and Falcon downriver. They're throwing in with Flores. The rest are staying on the sidelines to see how this all shakes out. Right now, Flores has more muscle than you and is getting ready to make his big move."

"That fits. Where did you get this confirmation?"

"From the horse's mouth."

"How?"

She arched an eyebrow at him and swept her right hand down the length of her body.

"Pillow talk. Flores gets right talkative after he fucks."

Garza swept up the vase of dried flowers sitting on the end of her dressing table and hurled it across the room to shatter against the far stone wall.

"*Coño! Voy a cortar el pene de Flores y llenarlo abajo su garganta antes de que le mate!*"

"You do like your trophies, doncha, lover? There'll be plenty of time for slicing off that greaseball's cock and feeding it to him after we figure out how to beat his play. Now, come on over here and show me what you've got that's more fun to play with than my gun."

Garza stared at her for a moment, then laughed, peeling off his jacket as he stepped between her open thighs.

Garza snored lightly, his face burrowed in the pillow beside her, his right arm flung across her upper body. A catnap after sex. Soon she would have to wake him to dress for dinner, an event she was glad to skip. But not quite yet.

Some cat — carnal tiger more like it. She was still buzzed from the orgasms he shook out of her. He was a fierce and long-lasting lover who tongued her until she begged for mercy, then punished her with his cock — payback for fucking Flores, but damn it made her cum like a wide-open faucet.

She was still wet — his semen, her juices — and that made her smile. Good thing she remembered to take her little pill because like most Latin lovers, Garza refused to wear a condom. She slid out from under his arm and grabbed a hand towel from the nightstand, sliding it under her rump as she sat on the edge of the bed and lit a cigarette.

Jetting smoke from both nostrils, she punched her mental rewind button for a replay of their conversation. Something he said bothered her, but she couldn't put her finger on it. Rewind. Play. Puff. Rewind. Play. Puff.

Nada y nada.

She let her mind drift, knowing this was the best way for her subconscious to dredge up what bothered her. Up rose the image of *La Madrina* handing her the Colt. After she killed T-Roy, she cut a deal with *La Madrina* to become the southern end of a transportation network that muled coke, heroin and high-grade weed from smaller *narcos.*

La Madrina's sons and cousins would get the loads across the river, slipstreaming the goods shipped north along the NAFTA trail. At random spots in Arkansas or Louisiana — sometimes, eastern Oklahoma — they'd hand the loads off to her cousins for the long haul to Tennessee and a straight shot to the buzz-hungry big markets — Atlanta, Richmond, DeeCee, Philly or New York. Smaller markets closer to home, too — NashVegas, Knoxville, Memphis or Charlotte.

They kept their cargo small and were careful to stay off the turf of bigger players, catering to a niche market enthusiastic about their high-grade goodies and low-key ways. She cranked up her uncle's old meth labs and added primo crystal to their menu. Everybody made money, but stayed off the cartel radar screens. She should have been happy, but grew bored real quick.

She was a fiend for action. She loved vintage Detroit iron that ripped up the blacktop with the roar of big-block engines and the snort of loud dual exhausts.

At her uncle's spread, she kept a Nocturne Blue '68 Olds 442 with a 455 Rocket engine — biggest block alive, as the song went — a four-barrel Quadrajet carb, oversized pistons, a performance camshaft and a Muncie four-speed gearbox. Disc brakes on all four wheels. Just the thing for running the ridgelines and scaring herself half to death on mountain curves.

Down on the border, she drove a flashy but slightly more sedate boulevard cruiser — a '72 Cutlass Supreme ragtop in Matador Red with white bucket seats and a smaller 350 Rocket engine. Four-barrel Quadrajet, bucket seats and the Muncie gearbox. Perfect for those wide-open highway miles between Texas and Mexico.

No doubt about it, she loved the cars that were Ransom E. Olds' legacy.

But what really turned her crank was pulling off the high-wire double-cross. She lived for finding the soft spot between two rival outlaws, gaining the confidence of both by bedding them down and being sharp enough to help them find a better way to do business. Waiting for the moment when she could score a lot of money by betraying one, the other or both. Leaving bodies in her wake, killed by hollow-points from the gun her uncle gave her.

She was living that jolting electric dream right now, playing Garza and Flores, becoming lover to both, making them want her body and her brains. She was already making money off Flores while undermining his organization from the inside on Garza's behalf.

The play was simple, but dicey — enticing Flores' men to betray him. With money and her body. Then turning them in to Flores. Six holes in the desert marked her success. Three held the bodies of key Flores lieutenants. A necessary evil, she told Flores. A housecleaning for war with Garza. Fat money to buy silence from the widows. Fear annealing the loyalty of those still standing.

The payoff from Garza would take a longer play.

Until then, she had to be ultra-cautious. No flashy red Cutlass run between Flores' turf and Garza's *Los Tres Picos* ranch. Nothing that stupid or direct. Instead, she drove from Piedras Negras to San Antonio under the guise of flying to Knoxville to check on her crew, parking the Cutlass in the garage of a friend's house before taking a cab to the airport.

When she changed planes at DFW, she made sure to wander the concourse, buying food and a magazine, just in case there were watchers. When she got to Atlanta, she ducked into a restroom to don a brown wig and eyeglasses, then switched to a flight to El Paso via Chicago using a fake ID made by a forgery artist and a legit credit card in the same name, Karen Summerall, an accountant from Chattanooga.

The final leg — a bumpy, cross-border hop in a Beech Baron flown by an aerial brigand named Lefty Moore, the brother of the dead partner of that ex-cop she teamed up with to kill T-Roy.

This cross-country subterfuge left her jet-lagged and jittery and cost her $2,000. A necessary evil, part of a careful plan that considered the smallest detail, including picking up a second .45 in matte chrome in a Midland pawn shop for the run to meet Flores and leaving her favorite gun at Garza's.

Cost her another $700 for a Series 80 with the solid bushing and the firing-pin safety that offended Colt purists but didn't bother her at all. Pull the trigger and the gun still went "boom" and blew down someone you wanted to kill with slugs that hit like a runaway dump truck. That's all that mattered to her.

Leaving her favorite gun behind seemed like a small matter, but Garza noticed and was strangely moved, knowing the gun was her uncle's gift. He saw it as a sign of her sincerity that she would leave her favorite gun in his care. Trust and truth. In her game, even honesty could be a con used to forge a bond that would be betrayed.

Flying with Moore reminded her of the ex-cop, the one she called Big 'Un. Bearish guy with bad knees and a wounded gait. Wounded soul, too. She roped him into her revenge run against the old pimp and *narco* once the pimp framed him for the murder of T-Roy's mistress. She didn't need a rope to convince him to help her kill T-Roy, the man he blamed for his partner's death.

Big 'Un. Hard muscle underneath his belly. Made him hard to knock down and easy to underestimate. But she saw the sharp mind underneath the slightly slow demeanor and good ol' boy blather.

Hard innards, too. He didn't flinch when the shooting started. She saw him use his own 1911 to blow down some people who wanted them both dead. Cold eyes, a steady gun hand and no hesitation. Made him even harder to kill.

But she also saw him cry outside the mouth of a bat cave near Mason while looking down at the body of his ex-wife, killed by a hitman T-Roy sent, a big, black psycho with a squeaky voice and a bad toupee. The crying came after Big 'Un gave the hit man a Third Eye with a hollow-point slug to the forehead, straightened out his toupee and left his body in the bat cave for flesh-eating beetles to gnaw on.

Big 'Un. Hard and heartless, then shedding a tear for his ex.

She'd never met a man who could be so ruthless and tough one moment then show grief and vulnerability the next — and not give a damn who saw it or what they thought.

She hadn't seen him since the night *La Madrina's* sons ferried him across the river on a stretcher at Los Ebanos with a busted jaw, broken teeth, deep cuts on his scalp, a separated shoulder and a concussion. They stashed him in a room on the backside of a border motel owned by one of their cousins; a doctor on their payroll wired up his jaw, stitched his scalp and made sure the concussion wasn't a fractured skull.

She called him to say goodbye. He couldn't talk that much — he just grunted a few words. The gist — killing T-Roy didn't even the score for his dead partner and ex-wife. Or her Uncle Harlan. He was right. That's why she kept killing T-Roy in her dreams.

She knew Burch went back to Dallas as soon as he healed up enough to travel, cleared of the murder charge but not his own sense of guilt. He was gone before she came back to cut her deal with *La Madrina* and her sons. Every now and then, he crossed her mind but not enough for her to reach out. Best to leave him be — she'd brought enough blood and pain into his life.

Big 'Un — you need to stay long gone from this country. Nothing but bad craziness and a bullet waiting for you here.

Rewind. Puff. Play. Right to the words she was looking for: *"That fits."* Garza's unguarded reaction to her paydirt on the muscle Flores had lined up, muffled by his question about how she got confirmation.

She turned and shook his shoulder. He muttered and buried his face deeper into the pillow. She punched him on the shoulder and yelled, "Hey!" He turned his face just enough so he could look at her with his right eye.

"Coño! Si jodes a un hombre a muerte, entonces no lo dejará descansar. ¿Tienes hambre de más? Let a man rest between labors."

"You think fuckin' me is a job? Poor baby, did I make you work too hard? Your dick didn't seem to mind that chore. And don't flatter yourself. I've had my fill of you for now. Besides, it's you who almost fucked me to death, but you don't see me napping, do you? You need to get up and get ready for that dinner with your buddies."

Garza groaned and reached for her. She slapped his hand away.

"You also need to answer a question I've got from our earlier conversation. When I told you about Flores lining up more muscle, you didn't seem all that surprised. You said, 'That fits.' What did you mean by that?"

Garza flipped over on his back so he could look at her with both eyes. He sighed, then started talking in the flat tones of a business executive summarizing a quarterly report to the board of directors.

"There have been some developments since you've been gone. Some events that may mean Flores is already making his move. Another shipment was hit. We lost some men, but we recovered the goods and killed more of them than they did us. Two gunmen tried to kill my cousin in broad daylight at his car lot in Faver. A rancher — a prominent Anglo, a man of respect — was killed in a barn fire. He was the cousin of a man we do business with."

"What's the connection?"

"The first two feel like Flores is testing us, testing our defenses to see how we react. The shipment that was hit wasn't very large — a load for our minor buyers. My cousin is also a minor player — we hide smaller loads in the panels of the cars and trucks he brings across the border for his used car lot."

Garza reached for her cigarette. She let him take it from the fingers of her right hand.

"And the rancher?"

"We're pretty sure he saw some business with his cousin he shouldn't have seen. I don't like people poking their nose in our business, no matter how much I respect them. And I respected this man more than the cousin we do business with. But I wanted to learn more before taking any action."

"You were going to take action, right?"

"*Sí*, even though I respected the man. Lead eliminates uncertainty, although we weren't thinking about shooting this man. Something that looked like a natural cause was what we had in mind. I brought in a specialist for that — *un artista de la muerta naturale.*"

"Someone beat you to the punch."

"Or somebody — how do you Anglos say it? — somebody jumped the gun."

"One of your people?"

Garza hesitated. He wasn't a man who liked to admit he wasn't in control — over any situation. He also seemed to be struggling with having respect for this Anglo rancher and ordering him killed.

"Could be someone got overzealous. Could be the man we brought in. More uncertainty. More lead, maybe."

"Your version of *plata o plumo — plumo o plumo.*"

Garza smiled, but it wasn't friendly.

"I suppose so. Sometimes lead is the best answer — the only answer — when you don't know what or who you're buying. Or when circumstances start popping up that you can't explain. I don't believe in coincidences. I believe in lead. It's clean and it's clear."

She thought it was stupid to kill the rancher, no matter how artfully the deed was done. No percentage risking a shitstorm of heat from every letter in the American law enforcement alphabet. But when she saw his eyes grow cold and the Vs of his face freeze into a mask, she kept her mouth shut.

Garza was thinking about lead spitting from his own pistol, his ultimate answer to any question or doubt. The hesitation was gone. So was the telltale of that wrestling match between respect and lethal necessity. She shifted gears.

"Your cousin — he wind up dead?"

He didn't answer at first, lost in lethal thought. Then he looked at her. His eyes were warm and the Vs had softened.

"No. He was saved from certain death by a customer who shot both gunmen dead."

"Damn. Some customer. A gunfight in downtown Faver? Sounds like the O.K. Corral. With cars instead of horses."

Garza handed her the cigarette — not much more than ash and the filter. She stabbed the butt into a cut crystal ashtray on the nightstand and lit two more, handing one to Garza.

"Yes. A gunfight that doesn't make our friend, the sheriff, very happy. And my cousin's savior makes for a very unlikely Wyatt Earp."

"Who is this Good Samaritan? Must be handy with a gun to dust two *sicarios.*"

"*Sí,* but he doesn't look the part. He looks like a truck driver. What the Anglos call 'a good ol' boy.' But looks can be deceiving. He's a private investigator who was hired by a local attorney to handle a divorce case down here. We know the attorney well. Santiago Boelcke. The Anglos call him Sam. He dates my daughter, Valentina, and we sometimes send business his way. Land deals and contracts for the rancho. Nothing heavy. He's not a part of our organization."

Garza frowned, flattening the V of his eyebrows, lost on a side trail of thought.

"Not a very honorable job, peeking through windows, photographing lovers who are just trying to escape the boredom of marriage."

"Jesus, lover — get back on point. A good ol' boy outguns two shooters on a hit. That doesn't sound like your average investigator handling a divorce case."

"No, he's not. Turns out he's an ex-cop from Dallas, a former vice and homicide investigator. Santiago told us he was forced to resign from the force some years back and has apparently fallen on hard times that require him to take on work beneath his former station. But perhaps he's found a more lucrative calling as a gun for hire."

She felt her blood run cold and her body stiffen. Garza noticed.

"Do you know this man?"

"Yes, I do. He doesn't mind shooting somebody, but I doubt he's a gun for hire. His name is Ed Earl Burch."

It was the first time Carla Sue Cantrell ever said his full name.

Sixteen

Burch sat in the cab of his pickup, parked in a small gravel lot behind Lawyer Boelcke's office. Both door windows were rolled down, but did little to offset the rising heat of mid-morning. He looked blankly at the backside of the building — brick painted over in a muted yellow that was darker than flan but lighter than mustard, marred by rust stains bleeding from the drainpipes.

His left elbow rested on the warm sill of the driver's door. With his right hand, he tapped a small, buff-colored envelope on the steering wheel — an uneven staccato fitting for thoughts that were out of synch and unfocused.

As he studied the rust stains and tapped away, he shuffled and reshuffled the cards of the case, cutting the mental deck and dealing himself a solitary hand.

He flipped up two aces. A spade and a diamond. Garza and those land-grabbing Houston boys — Bart Hulett had given both parties plenty of reasons to want him dead. He poked his nose into Garza's business and jammed a board up the ass of those developers.

Next card. The jack of spades. That would be Gyp Hulett. Burch couldn't be sure the old outlaw wasn't stringing him along and knew that certainty could come in the form of a 9mm slug to the brainpan. Bart Hulett had crawled up his cousin's ass about letting Garza use Hulett land for a dope delivery and family feuds could get bloody real quick.

Burn and turn. The joker.

Of course. For that killer nobody was thinking about, fired by a motive nobody knew about. An old lover. A political foe. A loser in a business deal. Bart Hulett had been a successful rancher, businessman and politician with a reputation for not being shy about playing hardball.

Burch quit tapping the unmarked envelope and gave it the stink eye. Another joker. Two in every deck. Inside the envelope was a hand-scrawled note, pencil on lined paper from a steno pad:

Guerrero's

Four corners

8 AM

Tuesday

Boelcke dealt him this second joker in his office. After the heart-to-heart with Gyp Hulett, Burch let the old man leave first — through the front door, big and bold, not giving a damn who saw him or what thoughts they might have about why he was in town.

Gyp's parting shot: "See you at Bart's viewing." Sartell's Funeral Parlor. Seven sharp.

Burch stayed in his nail-head leather chair, planning to slip out the back door to where his rig was parked after giving Hulett ten minutes to clear town. He already felt a twinge of buyer's remorse that tempered the thrill of being a manhunter again.

Too many moving parts to this jackpot. Too many angles. Too many loose ends. Too many ways to get killed. Need information and need it now. He thought of calling his best buddy in Dallas, Krukovitch, the hip and ever-nervous columnist for the weekly alternative rag and a chain-smoking research wizard with contacts all over Texas.

While Burch was still lost in thought, Boelcke splashed two more fingers of Barton in his glass, then poured four fingers for himself. The lawyer slipped a hand inside his jacket and pulled out the envelope to hand to Burch.

"A friend wants to meet you."

"Who?"

"Sudden Doggett would be my guess, but I don't know for sure. A trustee handed it to me when I came to spring you from the graybar motel. Charlie Blanco. He takes care of Doggett's horses when he's not serving thirty days for drunk and disorderly."

"Why the cloak-and-dagger?"

"Sudden don't like the High Sheriff but isn't dumb enough to cross him. Let me rephrase that — he isn't dumb enough to get caught crossing him until he's ready to drop the hammer. If it's him, he wants a face-to-face to size you up."

"And if it's not him, it could be a setup."

Boelcke shrugged, then sipped his bourbon, watching as Burch slipped the envelope into the unsnapped pocket of his denim shirt.

"Didn't know the blood was that bad between them."

"It's not open warfare between him and Blue, but Sudden don't like some of the deals Blue has cut to climb up the political ladder."

"Another way to put that is he thinks Blue's in bed with Malo Garza, right?"

Burch looked at Boelcke with a dead-eyed stare. The lawyer took a sip of whiskey before answering the question.

"Let's just say Sudden is offended that Blue has decided to adopt a live-and-let-live philosophy when it comes to our friend Malo while playing up this image of being a hard-as-nails Texas sheriff waging a one-man war on drugs."

"He hates Blue just for being a hypocrite? Hell, he might as well hate every churchgoing citizen in Cuervo County."

"No, just the Anglo church folks, the ones who thump the Bible on Sunday, but hop Mexican whores on Saturday nights and call us beaners on weekdays. He also hates Blue for getting his pockets lined with Malo's money."

"So he hates Blue for being a rich hypocrite with dirty money. Might as well hate just about ever' bidnessman in the whole state of Texas. Jesus, the man's got a broom handle up his butt, don't he?"

"Not hardly. Sudden isn't a Holy Roller who wants to wage the war on drugs that Blue pretends to fight. He just might decide to be as live-and-let-live as Blue with one major exception — he wouldn't take Malo's money."

"That won't work. Drug lords want to buy their political protection and make sure it stays bought."

Burch started to say more, but Boelcke raised his hand and cut him off.

"Let me finish my thought. Sudden figures he's got a good shot at being the next sheriff and thinks he can bring some honesty and humble back to the office. Maybe he doesn't trust Blue to endorse him. Maybe he just wants to hurry Blue's departure a bit."

"If you follow all them 'maybes' down the line, you'll get to this one: Maybe Doggett thinks Blue had something to do with Bart Hulett's death."

"More like, maybe with you stirrin' the pot, Blue's little deal with Malo might get exposed. Or maybe he just wants to make sure Blue does the right thing by Bart."

"One thing we haven't talked about is whether the High Sheriff will let me poke around. Does he know you jokers have hired me?"

Boelcke killed the rest of his whiskey in one gulp, blew out his breath then looked at Burch.

"I haven't told him and don't plan to, but can't imagine he won't figure it out pretty quick when he sees you're still in town."

"Will he try to stop me?"

"I doubt it. I get the distinct impression he knows all about this and won't block your play. I think Blue wants you to stir the pot just as much as Doggett does. For different reasons, maybe."

"Why the hell would he want that? Most local law hate the idea of a shamus setting foot in an open case."

"You're a convenient cutout, a guy who can ask rude questions of nasty people and keep Blue from getting his hands dirty. If one of those nasty folks pumps you full of lead, Blue won't shed a tear and might have an answer to some of his questions."

"Nice. Seems like everybody has an angle on wanting me to look into this. How the hell did Doggett know I'd even take the case? Hell, I didn't even know when he got that trustee to hand you that note."

Boelcke smiled.

"Hell, we all knew you would. Even if you didn't."

Burch grew tired of the mental card shuffling. He kept hoping it would give him the "aha" moment, a burst of sudden clarity about where to start, sparked by the next flip of a card. It didn't. Doubt still dogged him.

His dead partner and mentor, Wynn Moore, had a simple maxim about doubt: *When the doubts got your brainpan locked up, take action. Don't much matter what action you take, sport model. Just pick a path and go. Shake that ol' shit tree and see what kind of turds drop to the ground. But be ready — one of them turds might take a bad hop and dot you right in the eye.*

Moore's approach to detective work was straight-line basic and he drilled it into Burch like a D.I. breaking down a raw recruit at Parris Island. Not surprising since Moore was a Marine who fought in Korea, same as Burch's G.I. daddy. Leathernecks aren't known for subtle tactics and Moore applied the Marine Way to the never-ending war against Dallas criminals.

Straight up the middle. Fast and brutal. Nothing complex or blueprinted. Hit the streets and rattle the cage of the nearest scumbag. Work your snitches. With knuckles or a sap if need be. Go from Point A to Point B. Keep one eye on the target, the other on the path you followed. Bust 'em or blow 'em down. Keep moving. And don't get yourself dead.

That last part didn't pan out the night he and Moore tracked T-Roy down to a ramshackle East Dallas house with a second-story apartment and an iron staircase tacked on in the back. They were after the once and future *narco* for the murder of a street-level rival named Oscar Moon, a blood whose body they found stuffed into a rusty refrigerator junked on the dry bed of the Trinity River. Moon's pants were missing and his severed cock was stuffed into the empty eye socket T-Roy cut out in an earlier knife fight.

Moore was creeping up the stairs in his socks, his .44 Special Smith & Wesson drawn and cocked, with Burch covering from below with his Winchester Model 12 pump. The door banged open and a naked woman filled Burch's sights, a human shield for a shooter who aimed two twelve-gauge blasts at Moore.

The shooter shoved the woman down the stairs, cutting loose a third blast that ripped into her back and slammed her into Moore. Burch blew the shooter down with two rounds of buckshot. Too late. Moore was dying with a naked dead woman pinning him to the rusty stairs. T-Roy escaped. He didn't pull the trigger that killed Moore, but he was the reason his partner got dead.

In his mind's eye, Moore was sitting across the table from him at Joe Miller's bar in Dallas, smoking a Winston and nursing a Dewar's and water. A short, wiry man with long sideburns, an acne-scarred face and slicked-back black hair, he wore loud plaid jackets, string ties with a simple silver slide and black lizard-skin Nocona boots. He talked fast and called everybody "sport model."

Don't think too much, sport model. Get it in gear and go shake the shit tree. But don't let one of them turds kill you. That would flat piss me off.

Shakin' it, Wynn. Sure thing. Yew bet.

Burch grimaced, then cranked the starter on his pickup. His Model 12 pump was back where it belonged, tucked behind the seat to Ol' Blue. His Colt was where it always was, cocked and locked, nestled under his right armpit.

The nearest scumbag was right down the street. Burch was about to ruin his day.

Dirt Cheap Bustamante was sitting behind his desk with a pillow stuffed under his bullet-scarred ass, working figures in his accounts ledger with the aid of a clattering adding machine when he heard the sound of a fast-moving vehicle crumple the gravel of his used car lot.

A sharp panic spike caused his heart to staccato when he saw the snout of a faded red pickup through the office window and heard the juddering slide of jammed-on brakes. He reached in his desk drawer for a snub-nosed revolver, a cheap Iver Johnson .38 Special, a five-shot with a worn blue finish.

Before he could pull the gun from the drawer, the door banged open and Burch loomed above him, backlit by the sun, his left arm fully extended with a Colt 1911 filling his hand.

"Don't be stupid, Bustamante. It'd be a sorry-ass sin if I had to kill a man I smoked two men to save."

Bustamante froze, his right hand still in the drawer, palm on the pistol, his left hand rising in surrender.

"You can't have it both ways, son. You twitch and I'll plant a hollow-point in your brainpan. Turn it into a bloody canoe. Now, ease your hand out of that drawer nice and slow. I want to talk to you, not kill you."

The voice was hard. The eyes staring at him were dark, wide open and cold, the deadly chill magnified by the lenses of the glasses Burch wore.

"OK, OK! You scared the shit out of me, *compadre*. I thought you were another shooter sent to finish the job you stopped."

"Shut up and get that hand out of the drawer. Nice and easy. If I was another shooter, you'd already be dead."

Bustamante slowly pulled his right hand out of the drawer and raised it to the same level as his left. Burch stepped into the room, hooking the door with his boot and slamming it shut. He shuffled to the side of the desk and fished the revolver out of the drawer with his right hand. The big Colt stayed steady, its bore a tunnel Bustamante didn't want to travel.

Burch pocketed the revolver in his windbreaker, then closed the drawer and leaned on the edge of the desk, crowding Bustamante, forcing the hustler of tired automotive iron to slide his chair to the left to give the big man room.

Sweat popped out on Bustamante's bald head. Burch propped his gun hand on his thigh, keeping the Colt leveled at Bustamante's chest, hidden by his bulk from anybody looking in from the street.

"Got a couple of questions to ask. You answer them to my satisfaction and I'll leave and you can get back to gougin' workin' folks for cheap tin cans with clapped-out motors and retread tires."

"Who the fuck do you think you are, *pendejo?* You can't come in here and strong-arm me. And you can go to hell before I answer any of your questions."

Burch popped Bustamante in the forehead with the heel of his right hand — a short, sharp blow that slammed the back of the man's head into the wall behind him. Bustamante yelped in pain, sounding like a lapdog smacked in the snout with a rolled-up newspaper, then snarled.

"Motherfucker ... *Hijo de puta. Puedo hacer que te maten* ... All I have to do is make one phone call and you're a dead man."

Another pop with the heel of the hand. To the nose not the forehead. Burch heard and felt the snap of broken cartilage. Bustamante howled as blood gushed from his flattened nostrils, leaking past fingers grasping to staunch the flow, droplets dribbling on a yellow Mexican wedding shirt and the pages of his ledger.

Burch flipped the ledger to a blank page, ripped it out and jammed it into Bustamante's face. More howling.

"Bleed on this, asshole. I can bounce your head against that wall all day long. Oh — go ahead and make that fuckin' call to your cousin Malo, buddy. But I think you'll be signin' your own death warrant, not mine."

Bustamante blinked, holding the crushed ledger sheet against his bloody and broken nose.

"Wha' tha' fuck you talkin' 'bout?"

"Just this — you make that call and you remind your cousin you're a liability. Now, he already knows that because of those shooters gunnin' for your ass. He's got a turf war on his hands and needs to shore up his defenses, eliminate weak links."

Burch pointed a finger at Bustamante's forehead and cocked his thumb. The fat man flinched.

"That would mean you — the weakest link he's got. You're a small-timer he keeps on the payroll for sentimental reasons. You're family and he takes care of you. But he can't afford to be soft right now. You make that call and the next shooters coming for you will be Malo's."

Bustamante's eyes widened in fear. Sweat mixed with blood and ran down his fat cheeks as he did a quick tally of the odds and figured out he was a favorite in the daily double down at the county morgue.

"You know I'm right. You know Malo's gonna want you dead. You know you gotta run. So, you got nothin' to lose by answering my two questions. You know the rancher that got burned up in that barn fire, right? Bart Hulett, right?"

Bustamante nodded.

"Did he get dead because he saw something he shouldn't have? Some business of Malo's?"

Bustamante stayed silent and sullen. Burch cocked his right hand.

"Okay, okay. Heard he saw a deal go down up on Gyp Hulett's land. Plane landin' a load at night. Malo didn't like that."

"Did Malo order Bart Hulett killed?"

"Tha' was the plan."

The fat man coughed up blood-laced mucous and spat it on the floor.

"Gonna bring in some outside talent, guy who knows how to make it look like an accident."

"Who told you this?"

"Chuy Reynaldo. Runs security for Malo on this side of the river."

"Malo's got a security honcho with a loose tongue? Shit, that doesn't add up."

"Doesn't have to. You're right about me bein' a small-timer. Malo throws me some crumbs. Hides small loads in the cars I bring up from Mexico. Goes to some of his smaller buyers. Guy comes in, pretends to buy a car from me. I fix him up with tags and title and off he goes with the load. I get paid on the back end."

"Tidy."

"It was until them shooters showed up. And you."

"Why doesn't it have to add up with this Chuy guy?"

Bustamante had his head tilted back, hoping to cap the blood gusher from his nose. The ledger page was soaked. He lifted the page from his nose to speak.

"Hell, it's not like he came in here and gave me the latest Malo gossip. He wasn't even talkin' to me. He was bitchin' to a couple of guys in his crew. He don't like Malo bringing in outside talent for a job he thinks ought to be his. I just happened to be in the room at the time. And those guys don't pay me no mind — I'm like a piece of furniture to them."

"Did the accident ace do his thing?"

"Can't say for certain, *señor*. Las' time I saw Chuy, he looked mighty agitated. Kept mutterin' about Malo bein' pissed about that rancher gettin' dead."

"Thought Malo wanted him dead."

"Thas' right. And he is. But the way Chuy was actin' tells me there was somethin' fucked up about the way he got dead. Sounded like somebody didn't do it the way Malo wanted it done, which was clean and quiet. And that somebody is gonna be sorry he was ever born."

Burch had a different thought. Maybe that somebody wasn't one of Malo's guys. Or maybe the somebody was an eager beaver trying to impress *El Jefe*. Either way, that somebody was a dead man walking.

"What's this Chuy guy look like?"

"Short, dumpy and got a face as round as a pie pan. Clothes that always look like he slept in them. Stringy hair. Scraggly beard. You have to look twice to notice him, but don't let that man get behind you. He's killed ten that I know of."

"Good to know. You say Chuy didn't like bringin' in this accident ace. Would he be dumb enough to jump the gun and kill Hulett himself?"

Bustamante, soaked ledger paper pressed to his nose again, shook his head no.

"How 'bout somebody else in Chuy's crew, somebody lookin' to move up by impressing the boss? Maybe a part-timer looking to make his bones, an *hombre* on the outside looking to get in?"

Bustamante pulled the paper from his nose and sat up straight, ignoring the fresh blood dribbling on his ruined shirt.

"*Sí*, there is one guy begging to get on Chuy's crew, always hanging around. He is the cousin of one of Chuy's guys. Name's Eduardo Lopez. They use him only when they need an extra gun hand. Chuy was bitchin' about him the other day. Said Lopez was chewin' on his pants leg like a dog about being a regular on Chuy's crew instead of a day laborer."

"What else can you tell me about him?"

"Not much more 'cept he's a mean little shit who also does work for the other Hulett — the bad man."

"Lopez works for Gyp Hulett?"

"*Sí*, he sure does. He's hungry to make a move and dumb enough to try to make a big splash."

"Yeah, but is he slick enough to set a barn fire that doesn't look like arson?"

"That I don't know, *señor*. I very much doubt it."

So did Burch. But it wouldn't take much smarts for a punk with ambition to make sure Malo Garza knew Bart Hulett was up on that ridgeline, seeing something he shouldn't have seen. Maybe smart enough to parlay that knowledge into a bigger opportunity. Didn't have to be with Garza. Something to ask Gyp Hulett.

Burch pulled out Bustamante's revolver and broke open the cylinder. He shucked the five slugs and dumped them into his pocket.

"You're gonna need this. It'll be waitin' for you at the bottom of your stairs. Slugs will be in the gravel where my truck is now. And you're gonna need to get gone. *Muy pronto.*"

Burch slid his bulk off the desk and backed his way to the door, gun hand pointed at the fallen used car king of Faver. Bustamante was still whimpering when Burch stepped across the threshold.

The wheedling patter and exaggerated persona of the border sharpie were gone, leaving a fat man with a busted nose, a bloody shirt and a target pinned to his back.

He was Dirt Cheap no more. Out of luck and running out of time.

Seventeen

Burch drove the five short blocks from Bustamante's lot to the courthouse square, looping around a turn-of-the-century, two-story building anchored by huge granite blocks on the four corners of the first floor that must have cost a ton of cattle money to ship in by train. Weathered, reddish-brown brick fronted the other floors, topped by a metal mansard roof with peeling, sun-blasted green paint.

He parked in back of the Cattlemen's Hotel, a squat, flat-topped limestone and brick building on the north side of the square that had one more story than the courthouse, but lacked the crowning glory of the mansard roof. He grabbed his go-bag, walked through the back entrance and checked in, taking a top floor room at the back of the building.

The desk clerk was a thin, sallow-faced man with a sweep of spray-lacquered brown hair that failed to hide a scaly bald patch. A cigarette was glued to his lower lip, curling smoke that caused his eyes to water. He smelled like stale whiskey, Old Spice and a long stretch in a graybar motel he never wanted to see again.

Burch signed the register. The clerk spun it around, read the name, then gave Burch an up-and-down once-over. Burch stared back, his eyes hidden by his Ray-Bans.

"How many nights?"

"Three."

"That'll be seventy-five plus five for the great state of Texas."

"Charge it to the Bar Double H. I'm sure they have an account here."

The clerk's droop-lidded eyes popped open.

"Bart Hulett's place?"

"That's right. On second thought, better make the charge to Sam Boelcke, Mr. Hulett's lawyer. Here's his number. Call him."

Burch slid Boelcke's card across the front desk. The clerk jotted down the number on a plain white pad then ducked into his office to make the call. Burch lit a Lucky and waited. The clerk reappeared with a smile wrapped around the cigarette on his lip. He handed Burch a key with a dark blue plastic fob and a number etched in white.

"You're all set. Room 310. Top floor, back — just like you asked. Got the floor all to yourself. Anything else?"

"Nope. Many thanks."

He pocketed the key and hoisted up his bag, turning the corner leading to the elevator, whistling "Faded Love" as he walked away, certain the clerk was an ex-con who would burn up the phone line to dime him out just as soon as he was out of sight.

Anybody could pick up that ringing phone — a deputy, a *narco*, a bent lawyer, hired muscle for a hardball developer. Anybody who would feed a sawbuck to an ex-con eking out a living as a hotel clerk, selling information on the side.

Burch didn't blame the man making the call. And he didn't care who was on the other end of the line as long as the call was made. He knew he was being watched and wanted to draw them in close. Close enough to spot. Close enough to kill.

The elevator was out of service and his knees didn't appreciate climbing three sets of stairs to get to his room. He was huffing hard by the time he topped the third set, wishing he wasn't addicted to nicotine.

Burch spotted a tarnished brass floor stand with a sand-filled ashtray he lifted out with his free hand, careful to keep it level as he slowly walked toward his room and the window leading to a fire escape at the end of the hall.

He dropped his bag at the door to his room, then carried the ashtray to the window and placed it on the floor. He slid his room key into the worn lock cylinder and found he had to hold his mouth just right to find the sweet spot that would trip the bolt.

His room was spare, but clean. A double bed with varnished *piñon* headboard and footboard and a matching dresser with three drawers and a mirror. A burgundy leatherette club chair in the corner with a walnut-stained writing table that looked like it could do double duty for room service fare. Plaster walls painted a pale yellow and a bathroom that was an add-on made obvious by sheetrock and mud painted a darker yellow that didn't match or blend.

A ceiling fan with a light globe stirred the currents that a window unit air conditioner barely cooled. Burch shifted both into high gear and peeled off his windbreaker and shoulder rig, then shucked his boots, jeans and sweat-stained shirt.

He felt shaky from his session with Bustamante and fished out the bottle of Percodan and a dented nickel flask from his bag. He shook out a pill, broke it in half and popped it on his tongue, washing it down with a long pull of Maker's. It wasn't quite noon but he needed a Percodan cocktail to get rid of the jangles and keep the demons in their holes.

He stood under the fan in his boxers, smoking another Lucky until he felt the half-hit and e-less whisky take hold, then carried the Colt into the bathroom and placed it on the porcelain top of the toilet tank. He reached into the shower stall to turn on the water and wait until it was as hot as he could stand it, then stepped into the scalding spray.

You ain't right, sport model. Poppin' them pills, sluggin' whiskey and it ain't hardly noon yet.

Keeps me sane, Wynn. On track and movin' down the trail instead of curled up in a corner screamin' about demons and snakes with wings.

Turnin' into a goddam junkie and day drinker, you ask me.

I ain't askin'.

Never could talk sense to you, sport model. One more thing, then I'll shut my yap. You fly the black flag on this one. Take that rule book we usta have to work around and chuck it right out the fuckin' window. You sabe?

Rule book already chucked, Wynn. No quarter. No prisoners. No judge and jury.

Good deal, sport model.

Easing out of the shower, he felt smooth and glassy, his mind sharp, his soul unruffled and self-medicated. He put on a fresh shirt — a brick-red Wrangler with speed snaps — clean boxers and socks, then pulled on his jeans and boots. He was running out of fresh clothes but had spotted a *lavandería* near the café where Boelcke took him for breakfast. That would work.

He donned the shoulder rig and windbreaker, then fetched the Colt out of the bathroom, toweling the moisture from the slide and frame before parking it under his right armpit. He'd oil it down later.

He pocketed the flask and pill bottle then pulled out his camera to hang around his neck. He slid out his "pacifier" — a spring-loaded black leather sap, the stitched pocket of the head stuffed with lead shot — and tucked it in the back pocket of his jeans. He zipped up the bag, then stepped out of the room with no intention of returning there to sleep. Not in this lifetime. Or any other.

Burch opened the window to the fire escape and stuck his head out far enough to see over the steel deck and caged stairs and eyeball the wide alley below. Perfect. He pitched his bag over the rail and waited until he heard it land with a dull thud. He ducked back inside and closed the window.

He picked up the ashtray and slowly poured a thin layer of sand on the floor just underneath the windowsill. With a groan, he kneeled down to smooth the sand with his hands. His left knee popped when he straightened up and leaned over the sand to wedge a wooden matchstick between the upper and lower sash of the window. He then spread sand along the sill of the door to his room, wedging another matchstick just under the latch.

Burch studied his handiwork, then gave a satisfied grunt. *Let's see if any midnight creepers come calling. They can knock all they want to, but I won't be home. Not tonight. Or any other night. But I'll know if they stop by. They'll leave me a calling card. Sorry bastards.* No answer from Wynn Moore.

He strolled down the hallway, whistling "Waltz Across Texas," headed for three flights of stairs his knees truly hated. He swore he would only climb them one more time to check for those midnight callers.

"Eduardo Lopez — he one of your boys?"

"Yes and no. He does some work for me when I need an extra hand, but he's kind of a free agent. Does some work for one of Garza's crews. Does some honest work for Bart and the other ranchers."

"Know where he's at?"

"He's out at Bart's place workin' some calves."

"Find him. Hold him there. Need to talk at the boy."

"What for?"

"I'll tell you when I get to Bart's, Gyp. Just find the boy and keep him under wraps."

"You bet."

Burch hung up the pay phone centered in a rectangular metal box bolted to the cinder-block front wall of a *tienda* on the Mex stretch of Main Street. The wall to the small grocery store was painted an electric lime green that hurt his eyes in spite of the Ray-Bans.

He ducked inside and bought a cold Big Red, a narrow concession to Anglo customers outflanked by bottles of Jarritos, Chaparritos, Penafiel and Sidral Mundet, then walked across Main, dodging traffic, to drop off his dirty clothes at the *lavanderia*.

He sauntered into the café and bought four breakfast tacos to go, then walked across Main to fire up Ol' Blue and cut a meandering trail of false starts, random side-street detours and U-turns to check his backtrail before heading out to the Bar Double H.

No tails spotted in the rearview. No suddenly familiar cars or trucks dogging his every move. No nose-dives from a car with a panicky driver surprised by one of his sudden turns. No telltales of parallels and an artful double or triple-team of tails.

He whipped down a side street, rounded a curve and slammed Ol' Blue into the empty driveway of a house that looked like its owner was at work. He waited for twenty minutes, munching on a breakfast taco and washing it down with slugs of Big Red. *Nada y nada.* That didn't ease his mind. Or stop the feeling that unfriendly eyes were on him all the way.

Gut instinct made up his mind. One stop on the outskirts of Faver. One more hip fake. The Cactus Blossom Motel. He parked behind the faded coral and yellow building and asked the clerk for Room 35, the love nest of Bart Hulett's daughter and the guitar picking husband of Nita Rodriguez Wyatt, checking in as Wynn Moore and paying in cash.

You don't mind me using your name, do you, partner?

Go right ahead, sport model. I ain't workin' it none. Hell, I cain't — I'm dead.

The metal door to the room was still out of plumb and squealed as it dragged across the concrete walkway, chasing away the voice of Wynn Moore's ghost. Burch stepped into the room, unsure if he was making an ironic gesture or an act of contrition.

Probably both.

The go-bag was still in the truck. So was the Model 12. He still felt watched by unseen eyes.

Didn't matter. Burch didn't plan on sleeping here, either. He fired up Ol' Blue and pulled out of the motel's gravel lot, heading north and keeping one eye on the rearview mirror as he rounded a curve that caused the Cactus Blossom to slip out of sight.

Once Burch was gone, a short, rail-thin man stepped from the shade covering the backside of an abandoned gas station about fifty yards south of the motel, on the opposite side of the road. He doffed a sharply creased Stetson straw to wipe sweat from the headband, raked his fingers through thinning red hair, then took his time to set the hat back on his head at a jaunty angle.

Squinting in the sunlight, he stared in the direction Burch took, absently twirling the ends of a droopy, handlebar moustache in thought. Shaking his head, he turned toward an unmarked cruiser hidden behind the gas station, muttering to himself.

"There goes a man what needs killin'."

Needle Burnet. Tin star on the take. Gun for hire.

Burch crossed a culvert rerouting a bright, thin rivulet snaking along the bottom of a gravel-banked arroyo, then checked the directions scrawled on the page of a steno pad he kept in the truck to record mileage and road expenses. He eyeballed the odometer.

Four-point-two miles past Seco Creek. Look for a gravel and caliche road on the right. White pipe double gates topped by a rolled metal frame with a crosspiece for a rust-tinged sign with laser-cut letters. Bar Double H. Also in white. Nothing fancy.

The turnoff was about thirty-five miles southwest of Faver. As the crow flies. But Burch had to travel two-lane blacktop with switchbacks and steep grades through a narrow pass in the Sierra Vieja Mountains that played to the torquey strength of Ol' Blue's big six banger. The pass spit him out on the western flank of the range, dropping him down to a broken country of flats, arroyos and orphan ridgelines running downhill to the Rio Grande.

As he made the turn, one of those orphans filled his windshield. Probably the Devil's Backbone, the ridgeline Gyp Hulett told him was the divide between his part of the ranch and Bart Hulett's domain. Probably the perch that gave Bart the view of that midnight flight of Garza dope that put him on the path of the Big Adios.

Maybe. Burch had his doubts after grilling Bustamante.

He didn't doubt Garza wanted the rancher dead. But there was something too loose and uncertain about a barn fire to make it the weapon of choice. Garza would want something subtle, but sure and direct.

Instead, the drug lord got a clusterfuck that Bustamante said made him angry even though it gave him the result he wanted. That suggested another player beat Garza to the punch. All of this was gut instinct — Burch didn't know a damn thing he could take to the bank. He didn't even know if he was looking at the Devil's Backbone.

Didn't stop him from gnawing on the possibilities.

Burch kept Ol' Blue in third gear as he bounced up the rough ranch road, passing the surprising deep green of an irrigated pasture with slick-looking brick red Beefmaster cattle grazing away on his left contrasted by the shin oak and creosote that marked the passage of Seco Creek through scrubby flats on his right. He was five miles from the highway when he had to jam it into second gear to climb a steep switchback carved into the side of a rocky bench.

When he topped out, Burch saw the burnt orange splash of the adobe-walled ranch house with a tin hip roof that gave him a dull silver wink in the sun, hinting of old gun metal rubbed smooth by decades in a leather holster. A wrap-around porch with thick wooden rails and a stout wood deck was shaded by a slash of the same gunmetal tin.

As he drove closer, the charred remains of the collapsed barn came into view, ugly and black, with beams, rafters and boards pointing toward the sky at odd angles — random leftovers of the ravenous flames bearing a silent accusation that made Burch flinch.

In that split second, Bart Hulett's murder — call it what he knew it to be, with or without the evidence to prove it — passed from the abstract black-and-white of a case file and became distinctly real and intensely personal to Burch.

It was an old and familiar transformation, as close as a murder cop gets to being filled with the Holy Spirit. Burch hadn't felt its dark grace in a very long time.

A man died in that pile of flame-blackened wood, metal and ash — another leftover, his body just as withered, black and lifeless. A tough, good man by most accounts, flawed like the rest of God's forsaken creatures, torn between the good and the bad.

A rancher, a war hero, a leader of his people. A man who looked his family's sins in the eye, shouldered the guilt, lived with it and still did right by his particular lights.

A man Burch was sure he would have liked to drink a whiskey with on the wood deck of that porch. Burch couldn't do that now and his innards lit up with an anger that would burn for a long time.

He owned this case now. It was a part of him. He owed Bart Hulett a reckoning, inside or outside the law.

Bust 'em or blow 'em down. Didn't matter.

Shucking his Ray-Bans, Burch stepped into the stale, overheated air of a wooden tool shed and felt the sweat bead up on his forehead and across his back. A single light bulb hung from a cord draped over a rafter, its harsh glare shaped by a simple metal shade and centered on a slumped figure strapped to a chair in the middle of the dirt floor.

The man's long, black hair hung forward, hiding his face, shiny with sweat and *Tres Flores* brilliantine. Burch could smell the strong jasmine and chrysanthemum pomade from ten feet away, reminding him of every Mex *pendejo* he ever busted. Burch hated floral scents and could never smoke enough Luckies to chase away the stench that permeated his cruiser long after he booked a greasy-haired suspect.

Burch peeled off his windbreaker and draped it over a wooden crate. He slipped on his regular glasses and stepped into the tight cone of light. The man looked up, flicking his head to whip the hair out of the flat, sharp reddish-bronze features of an *indio* ruined by the beating he took from the men who strapped him into that chair.

His right eye was swollen shut, both cheeks were puffed with purple-black bruises, two mottled knots the size of hen's eggs rose from his forehead. His nose was flattened and pointing toward the left side of his face. Blood ran from the nostrils, over battered lips and a pointed chin before dripping onto a pale blue cowboy shirt with a paisley pattern and a left sleeve torn at the shoulder.

He looked at Burch with his only good eye and spat a gob of bloody mucous in the dirt. Burch could see the gold filling of a broken tooth centered in the dark red goo. He grinned at Burch like a simpleton hearing the punch line of a knock-knock joke, showing the black gap where a central incisor used to be.

A voice from the gloom, one Burch didn't recognize.

"Had a little jackrabbit in him. Had to chase him down and cool him out."

"And kick the shit out of him. All y'all put the boots to this boy or just one or two?"

Same voice answered. Sounded Anglo. Nasal twang. No singsong Mex lilt. Burch could sense rather than see four or five men perched along the walls of the shed, lurking just outside the light from the single shaded bulb. The voice came from one of the corners.

"A little payback. He kicked Lupe in the balls before we got him hogtied proper. Had to square the deal."

"I'd say you boys are a mite overdrawn on this account."

"Shee-yit."

Burch pulled Luckies from his shirt pocket, shook a nail out of the pack and placed it between the man's swollen lips, careful to pick a spot that wasn't covered in blood. Fire to the tip with a snick of the Zippo.

Eduardo Lopez sucked down the smoke like a Death Row con wolfing his last supper. His lone eye flicked to Burch's face, then away, then back again. Like a whipped dog wary about a friendly scratch between the ears.

"Eduardo, I'm gonna ask you a couple of questions that you best answer true. You play ball with me and I'll see whether you and I can walk out of here together. You don't, I'll leave it to these boys to finish what they started."

"Who the hell are you, *guey*? You a cop? You smell like the *pinche rinches*, but I don't see no fuckin' badge. You an angel sent by *El Señor* to save my soul? Don't see no halo or wings on you, I think you're just another fatass *gabacho* who likes to hear himself talk."

Muffled sniggers from the gloom that Burch ignored. He kept his eyes on Lopez.

"I ain't the law no more, Eduardo. And I ain't nobody's angel. But you're a man who surely needs to be saved. And right now, this fatass *gabacho* is your only ticket out of this jackpot."

"*Chúpame la reata.*"

Guffaws from the gloom. And a voice to his left.

"You're wasting your time with this good cop routine, *cabrón*. Playing the nice guy isn't going to work with this *chingadera*."

Burch took a step back, then turned his head toward the voice.

"Do me a real big favor and shut the fuck up, slick."

"What the hell did you just say?"

The voice was closer, but still in the gloom. Another voice growled a warning. Burch recognized it — Gyp Hulett.

"Benny ..."

Benny stepped into the light, short and swarthy with a handlebar moustache and a grimy gray hat with a pinched crown and a broad floppy brim. His fists were clenched and looked like they were made of rough-hewn granite.

"I want this *pendejo* to look me in the eye when he tells me to go fuck myself."

"Benny ... sit your ass back down."

Burch let Benny take one more step, then slipped the spring-loaded leather sap out of the back pocket of his jeans and launched a left-handed overhead slam that would have made Rod Laver proud. He put his weight behind the swing and caught Benny squarely on the forehead.

The crack of lead shot on skull filled the shed. Benny dropped like a burlap bag of horseshoes, his face in the dirt, his hat at Burch's feet. No twitches or moans from Benny. Just a stunned silence that Gyp Hulett broke.

"You might have killed him."

"Maybe so, but I think I could make a pretty good argument for self-defense. Besides, you warned his sorry ass."

Burch spun on his heels and took a step toward Lopez, aiming a sidewinder swing that slammed the sap into the man's right kneecap. Lopez screamed like a stuck hog headed for a throat cutting. Burch let the man howl, staring him down while wagging the sap back and forth, keeping time.

"Thought a macho like you could stand the pain, Eduardo. Guess I overestimated how tough you really are."

"*Vete a la verga.*" Hissed through clenched teeth.

Burch lightly tapped the head of the sap on Lopez's left kneecap. Lopez flinched and tried to jerk his knee away, halted by the ropes binding him to the chair. Burch leaned inches from Lopez's face, staring into the man's good eye.

"If you want to walk again, Eduardo, you'll talk to me. If you don't want to end up like Benny over there, you'll talk to me. If you want to live, you'll talk to me. I won't turn the boys loose on you. I'll kill you myself."

Burch brushed the sap across Lopez's forehead. The man jerked his head away from the touch of lead shot and leather.

"That was a good guess about me being a cop. Used to be. Up in Dallas. Never was a Ranger. Just a homicide dick. Pretty good one, too. But that was dead and buried a long time ago."

Lopez watched him with his one good eye. Tense and ready to dodge leather and lead — as far as those ropes allowed.

"I ain't playin' by a cop's rules. Naw, on this one, I'm flyin' the black flag. Know what that means, Eduardo? It means I'm a pirate. No quarter asked or given. No mercy. No free pass. You either answer my questions or get dead. Real simple."

Burch waggled the sap in front of Lopez's face.

"Know your history, Eduardo? Ever heard of the *Degüello?*"

Lopez cocked his head like a curious dog.

"That's the tune Santa Anna had his buglers play at the Alamo. Mournful and haunting. Played it over and over again. Meant to tell the Texans that no prisoners would be taken. Meant Santa Anna would kill every man, even if he surrendered. That's what 'no quarter' means. That's what the black flag means."

"This ain't no Alamo, *cabrón.*" The voice was flat and listless.

"That's where you're wrong, Eduardo. In the little deal we've got here, you're all those doomed Texans. You're Davy Crockett and I'm the reincarnation of Santa Anna. Except I might just show you a little mercy."

Lopez's good eye jerked and danced like it was wired to a faulty circuit, dodging Burch's stare. Burch stood straight and started a lazy backswing with the sap.

"What's it going to be, Eduardo?"

Lopez flinched, causing the chair to buck.

"What do you want to know?"

"At the end of the line, I want to know who killed Bart Hulett and why. But let's start at the beginning. Let's start with that midnight dope flight into Gyp's place. You were part of Gyp's crew that night, right?"

"*Sí,* I was a lookout. Kept my eyes on the ridge *con los binoculares.* Made sure the beacon was lit for the plane. Had a transmitter to turn it off when it landed, turn it back on when it took off."

"See anything else up on that ridge?"

"*Un poco de luz.*"

"A little light. Like a flashlight?"

"No. *Una llama.* It flickered then went out. Then flickered again. I was looking right at the spot when it came back. Brighter that time. Then — *desapareció.*"

"Who did you tell?"

"*Mi primo y Chuy Reynaldo.*"

Burch leaned in close, letting Eduardo feel his bulk and the sweaty heat coming off his body, ignoring the sickly-sweet pomade scent.

"Your cousin and Chuy Reynaldo — they work for Malo Garza. Why didn't you tell the man you were working for that night, the man sitting right over there in the dark?"

Burch pointed toward the wedge of gloom that harbored Gyp Hulett's voice, certain that the gunsight eyes were watching every step of this dance with keen and lethal interest. Lopez said nothing.

"Come on, Eduardo. You took the man's money. He's sitting right over there. Why don't you tell him why you went to Garza's men instead of him? I'm sure Señor Hulett would like you to answer that question."

Burch brushed Lopez's face with the sap. The man jerked away from the leather touch, twisting his head and shoulders until stopped by the rough rope binding him to the chair. His good eye was wide with fear, twitching to the beat of that misfiring brain circuit.

Fresh sweat popped across Lopez's bruised forehead and deepened the dark stain of both armpits. Burch could smell the dank musk of fear cutting through the smothering floral intensity of the pomade. Lopez was deathly afraid of Gyp Hulett and didn't want to answer this question.

Burch stepped back and studied the man's ruined face, lighting a Lucky and letting the silent seconds stretch and bend like an endless string straight out of Einstein's elastic theory of time.

Or a murder cop's dog-eared playbook.

The strung-out seconds became long, slow minutes marked by an ember turning tobacco into ash.

"Let me help you over the hump on this one, Eduardo. You went to your cousin and Chuy because you want to be part of Garza's *familia*, right? You been knocking on that door for a while now but they still won't let you in, right? But you're tough and persistent and keep playing that loyalty card every chance you get."

"You talk too much, fat man. Like *una mujer vieja.*"

"An old woman? Maybe so. Let me ask it this way. Why the hell would Malo Garza have anything to do with a piece of shit like you?"

Lopez jerked his head like he'd been slapped. The features of his ruined face flushed deep red. Anger flashed from the only eye he could fix on Burch. The words tumbled out in a hoarse bellow.

"I belong with Malo Garza! I deserve to be with Malo Garza! *Soy más inteligente y más valiente que mi primo.* Smarter and braver than Chuy Reynaldo. It was me who saw the light. It was me who climbed the ridge with that old tracker they brought in. I was the one who found the tracks while he was sleeping in the shade. I was the one who climbed the rocks and found those coffee beans that told us *El Patrón* was watching."

"*El Patrón.* You mean Señor Bart Hulett, right?"

"*Sí. Él era un gran hombre.* Treated me with respect."

"And you repaid that great man's respect by ratting him out to Malo Garza's people."

Lopez started to speak then fell silent, the flush of anger gone, leaving a pale backdrop for the welts, bruises, cuts and blood on his face.

"That was a nice speech you just gave, Eduardo. Lemme ask you this — what did all that get you from Chuy Reynaldo and Malo Garza? Get you a seat at Malo's table? A place on Chuy's crew?"

No answer from Lopez.

"I'll answer my own question. You didn't get the time of day from Chuy and Malo. They still treated you like a dried piece of cow shit. Didn't give you a damn thing after turning all those backflips and selling out a man who treated you like a man. I bet Bart Hulett even served you up a cup of coffee and let you sit a spell in the shade of the big house porch."

Paydirt with a wild guess about a cup of coffee. Lopez's head jerked and the lumps, bruises and blood couldn't hide his shame.

"A great man treats you with respect, brings you up on his front porch and serves you a cup of coffee and you stab him in the back. Make him a target. And the guys you sold him out to rolled you up and threw you away like a used condom. Must be real proud of yourself, Eduardo."

Lopez kept his head down. Wouldn't look at Burch. Burch pressed the sap under his chin and forced Lopez's head to rise.

"I can see you're ashamed of yourself, Eduardo. And scared shitless of that man sittin' in the corner over there. With good reason. Unless I talk him out of it, he'll probably kill you and throw you in a hole in the desert somewhere. Or just chuck you out in the rocks so the coyotes and buzzards can gnaw on your corpse. Unless you answer one more question for me, that's exactly what'll happen."

Lopez met Burch's stare with his good eye. Burch tapped the sap on the man's right knee, drawing another hiss of pain.

"My bet is all this shame and fear you're feeling is a right now thing. You didn't feel any of that when Malo and Chuy told you to fuck off. You got angry and you wanted some payback for getting rejected. You also wanted some money and recognition. Some goddam respect. Am I right?"

"Ask your question, *gabacho.* It's the last one I answer."

"Who else did you tell about Bart Hulett being up on that ridge?"

"*La Aguja.* The one they call 'The Needle.'"

"You talkin' about that sheriff's deputy, Burnet? The skinny runt with the red hair and big moustache?"

"*Sí.* We call him *El Chilito* behind his back. He's pissed off all the time like a *cabrón* with *el pito pequeño* who gets teased by the whores. We laugh at that hair on his lip — must grow it long to make up for having a little dick."

"Why'd you tell him?"

"He likes to know things and pays for information."

"How much did he pay you?"

"*Cien dólares y un trabajo.*"

"Hunnert dollars and a job. Doin' what?"

"Leading a man here in the dark."

"What man?"

"*El incendiario*. The man who makes the fire."

Burch could feel the burn of the gunsight eyes scorching a laser line to Lopez. *Shit, son — not even El Señor can save you now.*

"The barnburner, Eduardo. Gimme a name."

"*Hamburguesa.*"

"Hamburger? That don't make no sense. Quit fuckin' around and gimme a name."

Lopez was done talking. He held his head high, his good eye locked on the dark place where Gyp Hulett lurked, a crooked smile on his busted lips served up for the old outlaw.

One last flash of anger and pride.

The solitary boom from a Browning Hi-Power sounded like a thunderclap. The slug wiped the smile from Lopez's lips and turned the back of his skull into bloody pulp as the bound body and chair tipped backwards and thudded to the dirt floor.

Acrid and sharp, the smell of spent gunpowder cut through the floral scent of the dead man's pomade. Another fragrance rose from the dirt floor — the metallic tang of blood from a fresh kill.

Burch turned his head to spit out the bile that rose from his throat. He pulled a bandana from his back pocket to wipe away the blood and brain bits that spattered his face and glasses.

Gyp Hulett walked into the light, his Hi-Power held loose at his side. Burch snatched up his windbreaker, then crooked his finger for Hulett to follow and headed for the shed door and fresh air.

Tres Flores, gunsmoke and blood. There weren't enough Luckies in the world to kill those smells.

Burch hobbled over to a galvanized horse trough and dipped his bandana into the sun-warmed water. He took off his glasses and cleaned blood spatter off the lenses, then dipped the pair into the wet and put them in his shirt pocket.

He had the shakes again and needed a drink with a half-pill chaser. Liquid salvation awaited in a dented nickel flask. Holy sacrament nestled in an amber pill bottle. Both were in his go-bag. Both would have to wait.

He dunked his head in the trough, then straightened up, dragging the bandana across his eyes and over his forehead and bald pate before scrubbing his face and beard. He wiped down the front of his shirt. He slipped on his Ray-Bans to cut the glare of the late afternoon sun and glanced at Gyp Hulett, who was watching him with the wolf smile on his face.

"We know two things we didn't know before."

"Yessir — I know you like to use that sap and you know I like to use this gun."

Burch snorted a scornful laugh.

"That wasn't hard to figure. And shouldn't surprise you none that an ex-cop is pretty handy with a sap."

"Handy, hell — you might as well've hit ol' Benny with a railroad tie. Never saw a man drop so fast."

"Let's talk about the new things we know, not the shit that's no shock to either of us. We know the barnburner had a tour guide in the late and lamented Eduardo and we know Needle Burnet was the matchmaker."

"Makes for another man what needs killin'."

"Not yet. We don't know who is pulling Burnet's string. You blew Eduardo away before I could ask him more about the barnburner and Burnet. Hell, for all we know, it could be Malo Garza who ordered this up."

"I kindly doubt it."

"So do I since I talked to ol' Dirt Cheap. He said Malo wanted Bart dead, but was real upset about the way it went down. A barn fire ain't clean enough or sure enough for a man like Malo Garza. Dirt Cheap said Garza was bringing in a specialist who could make a killin' seem like an accident but somebody jumped the gun."

"You can cross Blue off your list. The boy may be crooked, but he was close to Bart. Besides, he don't have the heart no more for killin'. Doesn't want to get his hands dirty now that he's got his eye on the governor's mansion."

"You don't know that. Burnet's his attack dog. Push a button. Keep your hands clean while a problem disappears."

Gyp Hulett sighed, then slipped the Hi-Power into the belt slide holster behind his right hip. He pulled out a pouch of Red Man and stuffed three fingers full of stringy tobacco into his jaw. He sighed again.

"Lemme show you somethin'."

Hulett pulled a mangled, brass-cased padlock out of his vest pocket and handed it to Burch.

"Looks like somebody took a sledgehammer to it."

"Look closer."

Burch slid the Ray-Bans forward on his nose to eyeball the lock. One side of the brass case was badly scored and ruptured, the edges of the breach curling inwards, the gouges brighter than the surface.

"Shotgun."

"The boys found that and a length of heavy chain in the brush about a hunnert yards from the barn. Chain was charred. Whoever chucked it there was smart enough to wipe away their tracks."

"But dumb enough to throw it there instead of carry it on out of here. Where's that chain now?"

"Bed of my truck. C'mon."

Burch followed Hulett to a dark green '72 Chevy C-20 fleetside longbed and helped him drop the tailgate. He climbed up into the bed, hearing his right knee pop in protest. He propped his butt on the passenger-side rail to check out the chain, hefting a section and running the heavy links through his hands. The charring on the metal left his palms black.

Didn't fit the story told by Stella Rae and the ranch hand; both said the barn door was wide open. Didn't mean they were lying, but this flame-scorched chain and that shotgun-ruptured lock were new pieces to the puzzle of Bart Hulett's fiery death. Burch aimed to find out how they fit.

"Sure wish I'd known about this before I started asking Eduardo questions. Sure wish you hadn't blown him away."

"Too late to worry 'bout that. We got a viewing to go to."

"Can't go to town with Eduardo's blood all over me."

"Hell, let's go up to the house. Bart's got a bunch of suits and sport coats from back when he was in the legislature. When he was in Austin right regular, he put on some pounds. Got almost as big as you. Bet there's something in there that'll fit."

"Bet there's some whiskey in there too."

"Yup. Let's get you fixed up with some clothes. Then we'll have time for a snort or two."

"Need it now, Gyp."

Burch felt the gunsight eyes on him again.

"You okay, son?"

"Will be in just a minute."

Sweet Jesus — wearing a dead man's clothes while looking for his killer. The thought made him head straight for Ol' Blue and the ninety-proof salvation and narcotic sacrament within.

181

Eighteen

Hunched in the passenger side cab corner of Gyp Hulett's pickup, Burch smoked and listened to the tires whine over the blacktop that snaked and streaked toward Faver, taking care to brush stray ash from the soft, navy fabric of a dead man's blazer.

Not a bad fit. A 54 Long. Roomy enough to cover the Colt and shoulder rig without the telltale outline. The shirt fit, too — a blue oxford with a button-down collar, open at the neck. No tie. No fake pearl speed snaps.

The rancher's khaki slacks were a little snug, pinching him at the waist and forcing his belly fat to flop over his belt buckle. He wore his own boots, scuffed and dark brown Justins with pointy toes and an underslung heel.

Ninety-proof salvation and a half-pill sacrament coursed through his bloodstream, chilling his nerves and driving fresh nails into the lids on those demon holes. He felt cool and calm again, unfazed by the killing of Eduardo Lopez and the spray of blood and brain matter that spattered his face, untroubled by taking a sap to the man to get him to answer questions.

Wearing a dead man's clothes no longer bothered him, although he was surprised they fit so well. Bart Hulett must have dropped a lot of weight when he left the Texas Legislature. The picture Burch saw at Boelcke's office showed a man who looked thirty pounds lighter, his face weathered by the wind and kiln-cured by the sun, framed by a thick shock of granite-gray hair.

Burch glanced at the outside mirror and saw the reverse image of Ol' Blue trailing them, driven by one of Gyp Hulett's crew. He had asked to ride with the old outlaw to grill him in private but hadn't asked the first question, reluctant to break the icy stillness of self-medication and start busting balls again.

Thinking about the fit of Bart Hulett's clothes was just another stall, but it did turn the gears in his brainpan to less tranquil topics. The smell of spent gunpowder and pomade. Blood spatters on his glasses and face. A charred length of chain and a shattered lock. Time to be a detective again and start asking questions.

Gyp Hulett beat him to the punch and broke the ice.

"Pretty quiet over there."

"Thinkin'."

"'Bout what?"

"That chain rattlin' in the bed of this truck. What we don't know 'cause you snuffed Eduardo's candle before we could find out. Makes a man wonder whether you blew him away to shut him up."

Burch felt the gunsight eyes sweep over his face, then center on the road ahead.

"Goddam, but you are a suspicious bastard. Bet the only person you trust is your mother."

"She's dead and I made her cut the cards."

"Shit. I'm gonna tell you this one more time. We got what we needed out of that little greaser. He ratted Bart out to Garza. When that got him nowhere, he peddled his ass to Burnet and led the barnburner to the barn."

"We don't know who the barnburner was workin' for."

"I got a pretty good hunch. Call it gut instinct."

"You want to kill on a guess or a dead-solid certainty?"

"I've killed men with less than both."

"I don't doubt it. But you hired me to find out the truth — or as close as we can get to it. You want to just start killin' folks without knowin' as much as you can, I'll cash my chips and bow out."

Silence in the cab again, anger from Hulett tightening the tension. Burch eased open the right side of his coat with fingertips Hulett couldn't see, freeing a clear path to the Colt. He stopped when he felt the strain ease off.

"Shit and goddam but you're a pisser. Ain't too many who would keep pokin' a stick at me, but I get the point. No more gunplay from me until you get some more solid answers. Satisfied?"

Burch grunted but kept his coat open.

"What else is ailin' you?"

"That chain."

"What about it?"

"Means we got another player in the game. That wild card we haven't thought about."

"I know."

"What's your gut say about that?"

"Not a goddam thing. Yet. You?"

"My gut still tells me somebody close is a lyin' sack of shit."

"So you picked me."

"Had to poke a stick at you to see which way you jumped."

"Did I pass?"

"For now."

The coat stayed open.

Burch slipped through a thick snarl of gawkers, glad-handers, gossips and genuine mourners going nowhere fast in the vestibule of Sartell's Funeral Home, nodding and smiling like the prodigal returned to the paternal table.

To ease his passage toward the chapel where Bart Hulett's charred corpse was surely hidden in a closed casket, he patted the passing shoulder, shook the hand thrust his way and mouthed the "good to see you" to the stranger's face that smiled in mistaken recognition. Baptist reflexes from a long-ago boyhood, handy for the preacher, pol or low-rent peeper — remnants of an endless string of God Box Sundays he'd rather forget.

The chapel was packed and the well-mannered buzz of polite stage whispers filled the room, triggering another Baptist flashback — the hushed sanctuary conversations of the flock anticipating the opening chords of a Sunday service first hymn.

Ten rows of hard-backed dark wooden pews flanked each side of a center aisle leading to a low lacquered plywood platform topped by a glossy Texas pecan wood casket with burnished brass lugs and fixtures. Two blown-up photographs in fluted gilt frames faced the mourners, standing guard at each end of the casket — a colorized, wartime portrait of a young Bart Hulett in Marine dress blues and visored white cover at the foot; a candid of Hulett and his blonde wife on horseback at the head, their smiling faces goldened by the setting sun.

Behind the pews, five rows of equally unforgiving aluminum folding chairs, all sporting the durable silver-gray institutional enamel common to the breed, stood as ready reserve for the overflow of mourners. The pews were filled and a butt claimed every chair — a testament to Bart Hulett's standing as a fallen civic leader and member of one of the founding families of Cuervo County.

No cushions in pew or chair. Comfort wasn't on the dance card in this part of West Texas. The land was too stark, harsh and demanding, intolerant of those seeking a soft life of leisure. And Baptists damned dancing as a sin and kept those pews rock hard so you'd stay wide awake for the preacher's fiery reminder about the brimstone wages of sin.

Dark blue carpet covered what Burch's knees told him was a concrete floor. Flocked, deep-red fabric lined the walls, brightened by a line of wall sconces trimmed in shiny brass that reflected the dimmed light from electric candles. Two brass candelabras hung from the ceiling, bathing the chapel in a warm, yellow glow. Heavy, burgundy velour drapes lined the front wall and flanked the rear entrance and the opening to a sitting room to the left of the casket.

The total effect was meant to be plush, somber and churchly, yet welcoming. *Don't fear death. It comes to us all. Just a part of the great circle of life and God's eternal plan. Let us gather together and celebrate the days on earth of this great man who has left us for his final reward.*

But Burch wasn't buying the undertaker's refried Baptist bill of fare. To his eye, the drapes, the wall covering and the brass light fixtures looked more like the lush trappings of a high-dollar whorehouse than a church, an old-timey sin palace that packaged purchased pleasure in a luxury wrapper. All that was missing was a line of near-naked whores for the choosing and a piano man in a bowler hat and gartered shirt sleeves, tickling the ivories while chomping a cigar.

Nothing more honest than a fifty-dollar blow job from a working girl who knows her trade.

Nothing more bitter than the cynical heresy of a backslidden Baptist sinner.

Nothing more useless than a de-frocked cop still ready to call out the hypocrisy of a church he thought was just a dot in his rearview mirror.

Burch cold-cocked his bitter musings and wiped the smirk off his face. He grabbed a corner at the rear of the room and continued his chapel observations. He tried to settle into the old routine. *Relax. Watch and wait. Keep the eyes moving and let it come to you. Don't force it.*

But the watcher's mantra wasn't working.

Couldn't shake the feeling that eyes had been on him while he juked and doubled back through town earlier in the day and that eyes were on him now. Couldn't blame the demons for this. He was still cool and calm from that special cocktail he served himself before leaving the ranch. That meant the sixth sense was real, not a figment of his nightmares. And he was far too old a dog to ignore it.

Burch took a deep breath and let it out slow, just like he did at the rifle range before squeezing off the next round. His heartbeat slowed. He felt himself relax. The uneasy feeling was still there, but it was a small sliver of edginess. *Do the job. Watch and wait. Keep the eyes moving. Let it come to you.*

From the chapel entrance, a thick line of mourners broke toward the right rear corner of the room and angled along the wall opposite Burch before bending again to crowd the closed casket, leading to a small knot of Hulett family members standing next to the photo of Bart and his dead wife.

Stella Rae was playing the head of household role, reaching across her body to shake hands with her left because her right was burned, bandaged and hanging loose at her side, the white tape and pinkish gauze riding below the rolled-back cuff of a navy cowgirl shirt with white piping and a bright red cactus blossom on each yoke.

She was wearing Wranglers too new to be faded and pointy-toed lizard-skin boots the color of peanut brittle, her dark blonde hair swept back from her oval face and touching her shoulders. The warm light from the candelabras picked up the slight rose tint of her olive skin and the flash of white from her smile.

A beautiful woman putting on a brave front. A woman custom-made to be looked at with lustful intent. Burch didn't need imagination to mentally undress Stella Rae Hulett. He had seen her at her carnal best while staring through the telephoto lens of a camera as she fucked her lover in a dimly lit motel room. He had his own highlight reel of her taut body stored in his brainpan.

But his mind was on the charred chain in the bed of Gyp Hulett's pickup, his eyes locked on the bandaged hand dangling at her side. *How'd you really burn your hand, missy? Where were you when your daddy died?*

Jason Powell stood behind her, looming over her right shoulder, the protective hand of a lover on her upper arm as he nodded to each mourner paying respect as Stella Rae shook their hand. *Gotta give the guitar picker some credit. Looks like he's in it for the long haul.*

To Stella's right stood a young man in jeans, boots and a red brocade vest over a crisp, white shirt and a bolo with a silver and onyx slide. His round face was pale and pockmarked, his hair black and wiry. Burch guessed he was looking at Jimmy Carl Hulett, Bart Hulett's only son.

Jimmy Carl looked like a sawed-off version of his ancient cousin, Gyp, minus the gunsight stare, the wolf smile and the Browning Hi-Power on the hip. Which was another way of saying the boy had more than a few dollops of bad outlaw blood running through his veins, but none of the lethal menace.

The younger Hulett looked uncomfortable shaking the hands of mourners, his eyes shifting but always downcast, his head nodding with a nervous jerk, the overhead glow highlighting a slight sheen of sweat on his forehead. Between handshakes, he wiped his hawk's beak nose with a dark blue bandana.

He looked like a man who needed a drink.

Or a spike of Mexican Brown.

Burch knew the look. Saw it a thousand times as a Dallas street cop. Telltales of a junkie. A loser. A Hulett in name only. A weak link who would sell his soul for his next fix. Or sell out his daddy. *How bad are you hooked, boy? Who has his claws in you besides your dealer? Malo Garza? Needle Burnet? Or another player to be named later?*

Burch tucked these questions into his mental deck and resumed scanning the crowd, ignoring that edgy sliver, keeping a slight smile on his face — just a prodigal looking for old friends and neighbors. Damned tedious work, standing in the corner of a whorehouse chapel, watching and waiting, working a cop's most hackneyed routine — hitting the victim's funeral.

His feet and knees started to ache. Never cut it walking a beat again. He ignored the pain and kept his eyes moving. He wasn't expecting a lightning flash of sudden insight or the appearance of a beady-eyed suspect wearing their guilt like a gaudy neon sign. That only happened on *Murder, She Wrote* and Angela Lansbury didn't fit in with this West Texas crowd.

Burch was looking for smaller stuff. Dribs and drabs. A pattern. A sense of how people caught up in a case fit together — or didn't. A loose thread. An odd moment. A step out of line or time.

A facial tic or look. Like a Hulett with the junkie's sniffles.

A mismatch. Like a beautiful woman with a burned and bandaged right hand.

A shard. Anything that caused his cop instincts to tingle, triggering questions he needed to ask. He found two. Small kernels, granted, but grist for the mill.

He kept his eyes moving, looking for more of something he wouldn't know until he saw it. Minutes dragged by, grinding like a gearbox with sand in it. The line of mourners grew shorter. The pain moved up to the small of his back.

The sliver grew into a sharp stab of warning. Eyes were on him. Felt rather than seen. He shifted his gaze to his right, keeping his head still. Across the center aisle, at the near end of the last row of chairs, a gaunt brown face with thin black hair turned to face the front of the chapel. Before the turn, Burch saw intense, dark eyes studying him — the watcher being watched.

Both knew the other was there so Burch took his time studying the man's profile. Thin, bony nose, hair brushed back dry from a receding widow's peak, black suit with an open-collar white dress shirt. The man quit pretending he hadn't been made, turning to look at Burch with a slight smile and close-set eyes that flashed a predatory interest.

Burch returned the stare with the dead-eyed look of a cop and burned an image for his memory bank.

Who are you, friend? Another Garza hitter? Jesus, Burch, that isn't what the narcos call their gunsels. Get your head out of the 1940s. Sicario — that's it.

What about it, friend? You another of Malo's sicarios? Or are you outside talent? Maybe that specialist Bustamante talked about. Maybe a freelancer working for Malo's competition. Or the Bryte Brothers.

You the eyes I feel watchin' me? Why the sudden interest? Those two shooters I smoked friends of yours?

Movement up front caught Burch's attention. Gyp Hulett, hat in hand and wearing a black frock coat straight out of the 1890s that wasn't in the truck cab during the ride to town, parting the sitting room drapes. The old outlaw walked up to his younger cousins in a bow-legged stride, whispering to each, then beckoning them to follow him as he retraced his steps.

Burch glanced back toward the gaunt Mexican. Gone. A sucker's play if he followed. Burch slid out of his corner perch and along the back row of chairs to get a better look at the sitting room entrance. Gyp parted the drapes to let Stella Rae and Jimmy Carl enter.

Through the opening, Burch could see Boelcke standing next to a tall man with a thick, dark moustache, an inverted V above a stern, downturned mouth, echoed by thick eyebrows. He had ramrod straight posture and was wearing a tailored, dark gray suit, a pearl gray shirt and a black tie. Black hair in a conservative businessman's cut, light brown skin and an aquiline nose gave him the look of a *criollo*, the New World Spaniards who ripped the land of their birth away from the mother country.

Malo Garza, paying his respects in private. Gyp Hulett swept the drapes closed as he ducked into the room. Burch braced himself for the bark of a Browning Hi-Power he hoped he wouldn't hear and marveled at the high hypocrisy of Garza showing up at the funeral of a man he wanted dead.

Took balls and brass to do that. Matched by a restraint Burch didn't know Gyp Hulett had.

"Bet you'd like to be a fly on the wall in that room."

For a split second, Burch thought he was hearing the voice of Wynn Moore's ghost. Then he looked to his right and met the sad, brown eyes of Cuervo County Chief Deputy Elroy Jesus "Sudden" Doggett.

"Wouldn't mind that one bit. Imagine it's quite the show. Lots of polite words of sorrow and respect. Lots of posturing. Lots of restraint. Have to be considerin' one man in there would like to kill the other."

"That would be your client, right? The ever-popular Gyp Hulett, gringo gangster of the Trans-Pecos."

"Can't tell you who I'm working for, Deputy. You know that's confidential."

Doggett's eyes went from sad to flat annoyed and his voice took on a metallic edge.

"That ain't no secret, hoss. Not to me or anybody else who matters around here, including the other big mule in that room. And that man probably wants to kill you."

"Malo Garza? The man don't even know me."

"That's a point in your favor. If he did know you, he'd put you out of your misery right now."

"A big dog like him? He's got more important things to worry about than lil' ol' me."

"You don't know Malo Garza. Anybody pokin' his nose anywhere near his business draws his personal interest. And believe you me, that ain't healthy."

"Ol' Malo might find me a tad hard to kill. I tend to shoot back. If he wants a piece of me, he'll have to get in line."

Doggett paused. His eyes turned sad again. When he spoke, the edge was gone from his voice.

"Listen to us — two guys talkin' about killin' at a great man's funeral. Let's step outside for a smoke and a talk."

"Unless this is the type of talk that follows an arrest, I'd rather stay here and watch the floor show."

Doggett chuckled.

"Don't have that kind of talk in mind right now, although the man I work for just might. This'll be a private chat between you and me."

"Thought we had a meeting tomorrow. You *are* the *hombre* that had that trustee give Lawyer Boelcke that invitation to Guerrero's, right?"

"Right. Things change. Come ahead on. I'll have you back for the next act. It's one you won't want to miss. Star of the show. Blue Willingham, shedding crocodile tears for Bart Hulett. He won't show up until Garza's done paying his respects."

Nothing like dancing the West Texas waltz with bent lawmen, lupine outlaws, patrician drug lords, gaunt killers and Baptist undertakers with bordello tastes.

In three-quarter time.

Nineteen

Sparring with a smartass shamus gave Sudden Doggett a bearded, chain-smoking reminder why he loved horses far more than he liked people.

His four-legged preference was the natural result of a rough Faver childhood that made him feel like a permanent outsider and the gift of bloodline and family lore centered on his legendary great-grandfather, Elias, the man who could out-think the wild mustangs of the Trans-Pecos and get them to do his bidding.

He loved the stories of Elias Doggett's innate understanding of the horse. His ancestor would wrap himself in an old brown blanket of coarse-knapped wool and walk out among a herd, staying with them for days, keeping still and quiet to let them get used to his presence then curious enough to take a closer look.

Gradually, they accepted him as one of them. And just as gradually, Elias Doggett would work his quiet, still magic on the boss stallion until the horse would follow him, trailing the rest of the herd in his wake. Right into a rough-hewn corral thrown up in an arroyo or pocket in a rock formation to become saddle broke, the start of a new life as a ranch *remuda*.

Doggett's great-grandfather rounded up wild horses for ranches all over West Texas, earning enough to buy his own small spread near Carrizo Springs. He raised cattle and horses and married a Mexican woman named Rosalie Sanchez. They had nine children — the fourth eldest was Sudden Doggett's grandfather, who also married a Mexican woman.

Back in the days of the elder Doggett and Milton Faver, people married whoever they fell in love or lust with. Not a lot of thought was given to race or pure bloodlines back then. Not a lot of church folks or civilized society to pass judgment back then.

Racial hatred was far more primal, fueled by the violence and savagery between settlers and the tribes that warred against them — Comanche, Kiowa and Apache. The fiery axis was red on one side; white, brown and sometimes black on the other.

The rise of Jim Crow ushered in Anglo dominance and a pecking order based on bloodline that was a faint echo of the racial obsession seen in Deep South states like Louisiana, where legal definitions of race were parsed by the percentage of black blood in the family, reviving the old French colonial terms for mixed-race people like quadroon and octoroon.

It wasn't that formal in West Texas.

But if you were an Anglo with a dollop of Mexican blood in your family, there were whispers about you in the church pews, the doors to political office were slammed shut in your face and the local banker might not loan you any money.

Doggett's family was even farther down the social ladder, with Mexican and black blood, a mix that earned them a total lockout from Anglos and a lot of hostility and mistrust from the others.

That made Doggett, growing up in the final decades of Jim Crow, fair game for a fistfight in the schoolyard. Or a knife fight in a back alley if you wound up on either side of the tracks. Nobody claimed you; everybody could call you out for a fight. He never ran. He won more than he lost, earning respect with his fists and a want-to that always made him rise after he got his dick knocked in the dirt, no matter how bloody and battered.

He was quick and wiry, long in the legs and strong in the chest, shoulders and arms. Big hands that were fast and sure with a rope. Or a punch. And he inherited his great-grandfather's quiet magic with horses. He knew their ways and preferred their company — their subtle shifts in stance and station as they accepted him into the herd, their curiosity, their spirit, their willingness to do what he asked just by him thinking it and shifting his hands, legs or hips.

He was also a rodeo natural. He could head or heel in team roping, but preferred the solo challenge of calf roping. To onlookers, his runs were a quicksilver blur — the loop arcing out, the calf jerked horizontal, him leaping from the saddle and sprinting down the line.

All at once.

Then the whirr of the piggin' string and Doggett popping up, straddling the trussed-up animal with his hands raised like a Pentecostal preacher leading his flock in prayer, to signal God and the judges he was done.

After one of his lightning runs, a rodeo announcer shouted into his mic: "That boy ain't just quick — he's sudden." Whoops, yells, whistles and stomping in the stands. Sudden was what it was and Sudden became his name as he rode the amateur circuit then turned pro when he was eighteen.

Four years in the Army cut into his prime, most of it spent as an MP in Saigon and Danang. That's where he found out the gift of Elias Doggett worked just as well on drunk or doped-up soldiers, sparing his fists and baton for the hardcases. Didn't change his preference for horses, but taught him he had a hand for coaxing people to move where he wanted.

Back in the world, he picked up his PRCA card and the rodeo rope with a vengeance, hell-bent on making up for lost time. He was blazing a prize-winning trail near the top of the money leaders, headed for the 1977 National Finals Rodeo in Oklahoma City, when he stepped into that chuckhole at Pocatello, breaking his left leg in three pieces and shattering his calf roping dreams.

The metal rod that held his leg together caused it to throb when rain was two days out and set off metal detectors in airports and courthouses. Left him with a limp, but one that wasn't much worse than any other West Texas cowboy. He could still rope and ride and might have stayed on the circuit as a team roper, but his heart wasn't in it.

Heartsick and nearly broke, Doggett came home to Faver and asked Blue Willingham for a job, using his DD-214 as a resume. He was surprised when Blue hired him and shocked when the sheriff made him his chief deputy six years later.

By then, Doggett knew Blue was in bed with Malo Garza, but the sheriff kept a tight lid on his corruption, running off deputies with a handout, letting Doggett run a clean shop and insisting that all the people of Cuervo County be fairly served — white, black and brown.

That was fine by Doggett. Somebody had to play it straight and be the lawman Blue used to be as a Ranger but was no longer. The setup worked because Blue kept a tight leash on his enforcer, Needle Burnet. Good thing — Burnet and Doggett hated each other. But when the bad blood threatened to boil over, Blue brought Burnet to heel.

Doggett saw himself as the real sheriff of Cuervo County, took his job seriously and cultivated the right contacts — Anglo, brown and black. He bided his time while Blue took Garza's money and hit the road aiming for higher office. He was waiting for one of two things to happen — Blue getting busted or Blue getting elected to an office other than the one he held right now.

He kept his private life simple. He lived in an adobe house with a tin roof on a small spread east of town where he kept three horses and two cattle dogs. No wife. Two women who lived in two different towns, neither place named Faver. Neither woman more than a semi-regular roll in the hay. The house fronted a caliche road that ran up a narrow and rocky valley. Last one on the left. His neighbors, few and far between, were all Mexican.

Right now, he was wishing he was home, sitting on his front porch sipping mescal, eyeing the endless sweep of stars splashed across the black desert sky, scratching a dog's head, listening to his horses nicker in their stalls, safe and secure for the night.

Instead, he was standing on the concrete stoop of a side exit to Sartell's Funeral Home, looking at a shambling Dallas shamus he'd just as soon run out of town as look at. The big man lit a cigarette, waiting for him to say the first words of this quiet *tête-à-tête*.

"Got to say you're a man who leaves a trail. Since you hit town, we got bodies piling up in the morgue and people shedding tears over a favorite son in a closed casket."

"You sound like your boss, the High Sheriff, trying to make me out to be a one-man crime wave because I smoked those shooters and saved one of your fine, upstanding citizens."

"I wouldn't break an arm patting yourself on the back. We found that upstanding citizen shot dead in his office right after sunset."

The big man let out a low, long whistle and shook his head.

"That happened a helluva lot sooner than I thought it would. Told him he was a marked man and needed to get gone."

"Was that before or after you slapped him around a bit?"

"After. And after he answered a couple of questions. Didn't know you boys cared enough to put a tail on me."

"We don't. But you tend to draw attention like horseshit draw flies. Somebody used a big gun to blow out Bustamante's candle. A .45. Just like the one you carry."

"So it just had to be me who did the killin.' Shit, slick — this mean I get to sample your jail's luxury accommodations again? If so, think I'll stroll back inside and chat up Lawyer Boelcke."

The big man turned to duck back into the funeral chapel. Doggett stopped him by placing a palm on his chest.

"Relax, Burch. Our man saw you leave Bustamante's and that *gabacho* was still above ground when you did. My guy was supposed to stay put but decided to follow you instead. That opened the door for the killer. A pro, looks like. Two to the chest, one to the head. Used a silencer. Nobody heard a goddam thing."

"Tell your man he's pretty good. I felt him but never spotted him."

"I'll tell him that after he comes back from suspension."

"Your man spot anybody else tailing me? Short, gaunt, light-skinned Mex in a black suit and a white dress shirt, no tie? Looks like a monk or something out of a Goya painting."

"He didn't mention seeing anybody. Would have if he had. Why do you ask?"

"*Hombre* I just described was here tonight and seemed more interested in me than the Huletts or Garza. We stared each other down once I made him. He didn't flinch. Bold as brass. I got distracted then looked back. Gone like a ghost."

"Doesn't sound like one of Malo's crew. Must be outside talent."

"That was my impression. A solo player."

"Told you it wasn't healthy for you in this town. You best have eyes in the back of your head and keep that .45 of yours cocked and locked."

"Always. Got another one for you."

"Shoot."

"You boys got a badass wanderin' around here nicknamed Hamburger or *Hamburguesa?*"

Doggett shook his head and started laughing.

"Sounds like you're looking for Wimpy. Gladly pay you Tuesday for a *hamburguesa* today."

"Maybe so. Wouldn't be surprised if Popeye and Olive Oyl showed up for this goat ropin'. You boys camped out on Bustamante for a reason?"

"No flies on you, Sherlock. Yeah, we were sitting on ol' Dirt Cheap, gathering string to bust him for that little drug shuttle he was running. Pretty slick deal. Buy a piece of shit car and get a little narcotic bonus tucked behind the fenders. Didn't come from the factory that way. Strictly aftermarket."

"Whoever shot Dirt Cheap did you a favor."

"That so?"

"You bet. Garza would never have let him go to trial. Sure as I'm standin' here, you'da had a corpse in your jail with a shiv stickin' out of his back."

"Maybe Garza just decided to get rid of a chink in his armor now that he's in a turf war. Malo's cold-blooded as hell so it wouldn't bother him none to kill a cousin."

"That's what I thought. And that's what I told Bustamante to put the fear of God into him. Spooked hell out of him. Now I'm not so sure. If Garza wanted him dead, that body would be in a hole somewhere in the outback, not left in the office like a calling card."

"You thinkin' whoever sent those shooters you smoked sent somebody else to finish the job?"

"Not much point to sending Garza the same message twice, slick. He got it the first time even though I iced those boys. A big, loud hello from one of his rivals sending shooters to piss lead on Malo's front lawn and kill his cousin. Hard to miss. I'm a little surprised to see Malo here given the circumstances."

"You shouldn't be. Ties between the Garzas and the Huletts go back a long, long way. They've been allies against the Apache and Comanche, rivals who stole each other's cattle and business partners working both sides of the law."

"Tradition, loyalty and respect are fine things, even among scumbag wiseguys and *narcotraficantes*, but it damn sure don't make you bulletproof."

The big man paused to fill his lungs with smoke, jetting it out of his nostrils before speaking again.

"About our ol' pal Dirt Cheap — I think you were in the ballpark the first time when you were trying to make it sound like you thought I did the killin' to see which way I'd jump. I think the killer was trying to jam a stick in my spokes to keep me from nosin' around."

"Got a candidate in mind?"

"If I were you, I'd be looking at somebody close to home."

"Playin' them close to the vest, eh? Do me a favor and drop one of those cards with a name on it."

"Needle Burnet. A little birdie told me he helped the guy who burned down Bart Hulett's barn. Lined up some local talent to guide the guy to Bart's place and watch his back while he did his thing."

"Sumbitch, we can't even prove a firebug lit up that barn. State arson investigator says it's suspect, but that's just his gut. No proof. Yet. Bringin' in the feds with all their Star Wars gear to take another look. You got any proof on what you're saying about Burnet?"

"Not the kind you need. Then again, the folks I'm working for ain't too big on the rules of evidence. They just want me to shake the shit tree and see what kind of turds fall out."

"What about that little birdie?"

"You don't want to know."

"So why tell me this when you know I can't do a damn thing with it?"

The big man sighed, slipped a metal flask out of his jacket pocket and took his time unscrewing the cap. He took a long pull then blew out a breath heavy with the sweet, burning scent of ninety-proof corn distillate.

"I'll give you a couple of reasons why. I've worked up a pretty strong hatred for that scrawny little sumbitch. Same as you. Burnet's so crooked he has to use a screwdriver to get his jeans on in the morning. Just like your boss."

"My boss in name only. I ain't him or Needle Burnet."

"I know that, slick. I know you're a straight shooter trying to run an honest shop while saddled with a crooked boss and his attack dog. I wouldn't be talking to you otherwise."

"Thanks for the endorsement."

"Let me finish. Ol' Needle ain't just takin' Malo Garza's money. He's an equal opportunity scumbag with his hand out to anybody who will cross it with some long green. And I aim to find out which one of those anybodies sent a barnburner to Bart Hulett's place."

"What'll it be if you find out?"

"Used to be cuff 'em or blow 'em down back when I wore a badge. Depending on how they dealt the play. Not wearing one now."

"I am. You come to me if you get the goods on somebody that will stand up in court. That somebody includes Malo Garza and Blue Willingham."

Doggett pulled out one of his business cards and scrawled a number on the blank side with a pen.

"Here's my private line and a number for Guerrero's. Ask for Javier. He knows how to find me when I don't want to be found. Office number's on the front."

The big man took the card and flicked it with his thumbnail.

"Odds are long I'll call, but you never know."

"I'm betting you're still a cop at heart."

The big man raised his head and bored a hole in Doggett's skull with a stare that had scared its share of Dallas punks and badasses. Doggett knew he'd better meet those eyes head-on or fold his hand.

No words were spoken as the seconds ticked off, but a deal was cut. Doggett knew he would get a call if the big man hooked something that could be gutted in open court. The big man smiled — a dull gleam of stained ivory framed by a beard and cigarette smoke.

"Don't tell nobody."

The two men watched a sheriff's office cruiser pull up to the curb. Blue Willingham unfolded himself from behind the wheel, placed a Stetson straw on his head and walked toward the front entrance of the funeral chapel.

"Garza must be gone. Time to head inside. Give me a minute or two before you follow."

The big man nodded. Doggett stepped through the side door and into the buttery glow from the lights inside.

Showtime. Complete with crocodile tears.

Burch slipped back into the chapel just in time to see Willingham march up the center aisle toward the casket, slowing as the line of mourners parted, then sweeping his hat off and bowing his head in prayer with one hand on the pecan box that held Bart Hulett's body.

The sheriff turned to Hulett's daughter and son, back on station at the head of their father's casket. He bent down to hug Stella Rae then cupped her chin in a massive hand while looking into her eyes as he murmured the expected condolences. Jimmy Carl was next, managing to stifle the junkie sniffles and fake a stern and manly look as he shook the sheriff's hand.

Willingham gave a curt nod to Gyp Hulett then faced the filled pews and hard-bottomed chairs, stepping to the head of the center aisle.

"Friends, I apologize for barging in like this and cutting in line, but my time with you is short because I'm driving to Austin tonight to meet with state and federal investigators looking into the death of our great friend Bart Hulett."

A whispered buzz rose from the crowd. Willingham raised his hand for quiet.

"Now, we don't know that Bart Hulett's death was anything but a tragic accident, but we're sifting through everything with a fine-toothed comb and I've asked for help from both the state and the feds. We'll leave no stone unturned because we owe that to Bart and his family. He was a great man, a war hero, a civic leader, a cattleman of the old breed and a friend to us all. He was my mentor. And I was proud to call him my friend."

Willingham's voice broke on those last words and he bowed his head, looking like a man fighting to control his emotions. Burch couldn't tell if the sheriff was really having a moment or acting, but knew that a con worked best when served up with true conviction and emotion. Ask any pol or grifter.

The sheriff's timing was perfect. Too perfect. Almost as good as his teary-eyed moment on *The Larry King Show*. And the good citizens of Faver were lapping it up. When he raised his head to speak again, his blue eyes flashed in anger, his face a dark and frozen stone mask. His voice sounded like thunder echoing from the depths of a stone canyon.

"Our friend Bart Hulett died a hero's death, trying to save the horses he loved so much from the fire that claimed his own life. Let us hope it was just a horrible and tragic accident. But if it was not, then I swear to you that I will by God bring hellfire and vengeance on whoever had a hand in his death."

No one spoke. A scattered sob or two broke the silence. All eyes were on the sheriff. Even those of a cynical Dallas shamus who wasn't fooled by the performance.

No wonder people love this guy — he's scary good. Hell, if I didn't know he was taking Malo Garza's money, I just might vote for him.

Maybe that's why the first clue Burch had that Stella Rae Hulett had left her station and was standing right beside him was her fist socking him in the jaw. His second clue was the fingernails from that same unbandaged hand raking his left cheek and knocking his glasses askew.

Gyp Hulett stepped up behind her and pinned her arms in a bear hug, dragging her away from Burch. That didn't stop her from trying to stomp on the old outlaw's feet while screaming at Burch, her face red with a fury that contorted her features, her full lips pulled back over bared teeth, her dark blonde hair flying as she shook her head like a horse fighting the bit.

"You get the hell out of here right now, you cockbite sumbitch! Goddam asshole keyhole peeper! Here for more pictures of me? Want me to strip down nekkid and do a dance on my daddy's casket for you?"

Burch rubbed his jaw and straightened his glasses. He could feel every eye in the chapel on him and Stella Rae. When he spoke, it was loud and clear enough to hit every ear in the room.

"I owed you that shot, Stella Rae, and now we're square on our old business. But there's new business between me and you that means I got to ask you this question — how'd you burn that hand, missy? You burn it grabbin' on a hot rafter or a hot chain lockin' your daddy in that barn?"

Stella Rae's eyes widened, then narrowed again in pure hatred aimed at Burch. So did the gunsight glare of Gyp Hulett. Burch didn't care. He slid open the right side of his jacket, waiting for Gyp to reach for his Browning. The older man didn't. Stella Rae's hoarse scream broke the moment.

"You miserable piece of shit — you best get your worthless ass out of here right now or I'll kill you!"

Jason Powell stepped around Stella Rae and Gyp Hulett, striding toward Burch like somebody who wanted to do the man dance. Burch stepped up and stopped the guitar picker with a finger to the face and a street cop's command in his voice.

"You I don't owe a goddam thing so I'm happy to stomp your sorry ass till you puke blood, you *sabe*? You got a good hunk of Nita's money and the freedom to spend it on Stella Rae without slippin' around no more. Best leave it at that and not start writin' checks your body can't cash."

A steel vise gripped his right elbow. Burch glanced down at Sudden Doggett's left hand. He relaxed and let himself be led away. He looked back at Gyp Hulett. The old outlaw nodded his head once with a slight trace of the wolf smile on his face. Friends who wouldn't kill each other. For now.

Doggett's loud voice, speaking to the crowd: "Show's over, folks. I'm going to take our unwanted guest out of here."

A whisper to Burch: "Jesus Christ, son — the folks came here to pay their respects and listen to some words from the Good Book that gave them some comfort. Damn if you didn't preach a sermon they didn't want to hear."

"Where we goin'?"

"You get one guess."

"Don't need one. Graybar motel."

"That's to be determined by the sheriff of Cuervo County."

"Thought that was you."

"Not after the stunt you pulled. You get the man who holds the office instead of the one doin' his job. He's mightily pissed off at you —

mainly for takin' a shit all over his stage show. Signaled me to grab you then stomped on out of here."

"Guess I did steal his curtain call. I want Boelcke there. And Burnet best not show his face. That sumbitch has sucker-punched me for the last time."

"Lawyer's already on the way. Can't predict the outcome when it comes to you and Needle Burnet, but I surely believe your paths will cross again. Now hand me that Colt. Nice and easy with your right hand. You'll get it back after your chat with the sheriff."

Burch did as he was told. He liked Doggett.

Blue Willingham leaned into Burch's face, his breath soured by a day's worth of cigarettes and bad cop coffee.

"Just who the fuck do you think you are, barging into Bart Hulett's funeral and accusing his daughter of having something to do with her daddy's death?"

"It was a question, not an accusation."

"Don't give me none of your smartass, Burch. What the hell were you doin' there in the first place?"

"You know the answer to that one, Sheriff — your job. The one you're too chickenshit to do yourself."

Willingham's face turned a deeper and fuller shade of red — impotent anger tinged with shame. Spittle formed at the corners of his mouth. He said nothing.

Different dynamic for this little heart-to-heart. Behind a closed door in Blue Willingham's office. No cuffs. No interrogation room. No bolted-down metal chair. No chain to a D-ring in the floor. No Burnet. Boelcke standing next to Burch. Sudden Doggett standing next to Willingham.

"Cards on the table, Sheriff. You don't like me. I don't like you. But you need a cutout to take a hard look at Bart Hulett's death. I've been hired to be that guy. You know that. I can ask questions you can't or won't and get answers you may or may not want to hear. And I don't have to play by the rules. If I catch a bullet ... well, it's not like I'm somebody anyone 'round here gives a shit about."

Burch met Willingham's stare and knew the sheriff wanted to cold cock him, but was checking that impulse. At a cost. He wondered if the man was about to stroke out standing in front of him.

"You go on to Austin, Sheriff, and do your dog-and-pony show with the state boys and the feds. I'll keep doin' your dirty work while you keep climbin' the political ladder and tellin' folks how Texas tough you are on drug dealers, killers and other scumbags. Every low-life but Malo Garza."

Willingham gave him a murderous glare, flexing the huge hands that hung at his sides. Burch knew he should quit while he was ahead, but was having too much fun.

"You got only one thing to worry about — me finding out your buddy Malo had Bart killed. I know he wanted Bart dead, but it doesn't look like it played out that way. It's early, though, and I've been wrong before. Oh, you got one other worry. Your boy, Needle Burnet, might be involved. But I'll let Chief Deputy Doggett brief you on that."

That drew a nasty glare from Doggett. *Fuck it. Time for Sudden to get his ass off the fence, pick a side and be the real sheriff. Or keep being the prim-and-proper lackey for a fraud and a crook.* The three men stood their ground and stared at each other in hard silence until Boelcke spoke.

"Do you have any further questions for my client, Sheriff?"

"Get him the fuck out of here."

"I'll leave when you give me my gun."

Willingham nodded. Doggett handed him the Colt.

"Stella Rae was right. You're a cockbite, Burch."

"That true love talkin', Deputy?"

Boelcke drove him from the sheriff's office to Sartell's, pulling up next to Ol' Blue, ending the truck's lonely vigil as the lone vehicle left in the funeral parlor's gravel lot. He handed Burch the keys to his office and a slip of paper with the keypad code to the burglar alarm.

Lodgings for the lonely shamus. A leather office couch for a bed. A pistol for his pillow. A chair braced under each doorknob. Just a pinch of redneck engineering in case somebody tricked out the alarm system.

The lawyer waited while Burch opened the driver's side door and snaked his hand under the floorboard mat to fish out his key ring, the one with the bottle opener embossed with Louie's logo. Burch stood up and jangled the keys at the lawyer, giving him a silent nod.

"Try not to get killed."

Burch grunted an answer then climbed into Ol' Blue and fired up the big straight six. He drove the seven blocks to the Cattlemen's Hotel, winding around the courthouse square before parking on a side street and strolling through the front entrance.

He started climbing the three flights of stairs, pausing on the second-floor landing to pull the Colt and a penlight. He topped the third floor and moved slowly down the dimly lit hallway, the gun leading the way. He stopped four times to check his backtrail before easing up to the door to his room and pausing for a long listen.

Nada.

Burch clicked on the penlight and flashed the beam across the door latch. The wooden match he'd wedged there was gone. He flashed the sand on the threshold. The light caught the missing match and small footprints. He stepped over to the window. No wooden match in the sash. Another set of footprints in the sand on the floor.

Each footprint looked like a cloven hoof.

Twenty

A lawyer's office in Alpine. Two phone calls. One inbound, chilly and long-winded. The other outbound, nervous and very short.

"New player on the board, Counselor. Pokin' his snout into something you don't want him to."

"Goddamit, fuck. What the hell do you mean by new player? Who?"

"Guy named Burch. Dallas peeper. Used to be a homicide dick. Looks like Gyp Hulett hired him. Him and that round-heeled rich bitch, the one who lives in your town. Know who I mean?"

"Oh, hell yes. Don't tell me she was fuckin' him, too."

"Word 'round town was she was right sweet on our late, great friend."

The lawyer felt a bright band of pain tighten around his forehead — overture of a migraine. He opened the bottom right drawer of his honey-hued oak desk and pulled out the bottle of The Macallan 12 and a rocks glass. He poured himself four fingers and took a quick snort.

"Knowin' her, she was the primary source of that word 'round town. She always did like to brag about her latest conquest. Damn woman needs a chastity belt locked over that cunt and fat ass of hers."

"Oh, I don't know, Counselor. Like a woman with a little meat on her bones, myself. Wouldn't mind tearin' me off a hunk or two of that ass."

"She fuckin' Gyp, too?"

"I kindly doubt it. One Hulett was enough for her. The dead one."

The lawyer reached toward the front of his desk and dragged the frame of his Newton's Cradle desk toy toward him. The movement caused the suspended row of silver ball bearings to swing and clack.

He stilled the random motion and drew one of the end balls back to its apogee before letting go, watching the ball slam into the first of five stationary silver spheres, the energy passing through each and causing the one at the other end to swing into a high arc.

Clack, clack. Clack, clack. Clack, clack. The noise calmed him and the single-malt dulled the pain. He almost forgot the caller on the other end of the line.

"You playin' with your balls again, Counselor?"

"Jesus. Can you be a little less high school? I don't need your wisecracks. I sure as hell don't need to hear more shit about that woman's sex life. And I damn sure don't need no peeper lookin' into Bart Hulett's death. He wasn't supposed to die in that fire. It was just supposed to smack him on the snout and make him realize he was in a far more serious game than he bargained for."

"And yet the man got dead. What's that line about mice and men, Counselor?"

"Something about best laid plans turning into a total clusterfuck. What can you tell me about this peeper?"

"He don't look long smart, but don't let that fool you. And he don't mind shootin' somebody. You heard about them two Mex gunmen killed at that car lot Malo Garza's cousin owns?"

"Saw it on TV and read about it in the paper. Shit, don't tell me ..."

"'Fraid so, Counselor. Burch was the star of that little show. Took both them shooters down."

"Fuck. You sound like you like the guy."

"Me? No, cain't stand his ass. Call it hate at first sight."

"Then why is he still walkin' around?"

"Don't go there, Counselor. One, you'd have to pay me some serious money — enough to get gone for good. Two, my boss don't want me to. Not yet, anyways."

"Why the hell not?"

"I think the sheriff likes the idea of Burch stirrin' up some shit on this deal. Keeps his hands clean and his options open until something floats up he cain't ignore. See, Ol' Blue don't know what you and I do and he'd like Burch to do his findin' out for him. If Burch gets dead in the process? Well, that's his goddam problem, not the sheriff's."

"You're no goddam help."

"That's where you're wrong, Counselor. See, I know exactly where that peeper is right now and where he's going to be later and I got a good guess who he's going to meet. Got a pen?"

The lawyer snatched a jet-black Pelikan fountain pen with silver clip and accent bands from the green desk blotter and slid a steno pad underneath the nib. He scribbled as the voice on the other end of the line gave him the time and place Burch would be that afternoon.

"I figure your outfit's got some nasty boys on retainer who'll know how to deal with this peeper. You best dial them up right now."

"I got time."

"Not really."

"What the hell do you mean by that?"

"I mean that Burch fella is on his way to see you and will be there soon. That's why you need to quit whinin' to me and make some hasty arrangements. Fucker already smacked around that used car salesman he rescued. Bounced his head off the wall like he was playin' vertical basketball. Ol' Bustamante was so shook up and bloody, he had to be put out of his misery. 'Bout ten minutes after Burch left his office."

"I bet you enjoyed that. Regular angel of mercy you are. Bet you even made it look like Burch did it."

"Now, now, Counselor — you know I don't kiss and tell. You best make that call."

The line clicked dead. The lawyer pressed the "talk" button with his index finger and got a dial tone. He punched up a very familiar number.

His heart rate was spiking. The head pain returned.

"Deke? This is Lucius. We got trouble and it's headed my way."

"Already know and already on it, Counselor. You just sit tight and

play it cool. Help is on the way."

"Easy for you to say."

"Easy for you to do since you don't know a damn thing about the particulars. Stall the guy and remember — you're one of us and we take care of our own."

"That's cold comfort."

Click. Dial tone. With a shaky hand, he took another snort of single-malt and hoped the dark cavalry he summoned would get there in time.

Twenty-One

Burch punched Ol' Blue as fast as a faded red Ford pickup with a straight six-banger would go, testing the fresh top-end overhaul on U.S. 67, headed northeast toward Marfa, where he'd make the turn east on U.S. 90 for the climb up to Alpine.

The truck rocked and swayed as Burch coaxed the speed up to seventy-five and held it there. About the best he could hope for from the big engine, which had enough bottom to pull a horse trailer out of the mud, but wasn't much for eating up the blacktop miles with straight-ahead speed.

Both door windows were rolled down, blasting him with warm air that barely kept him cool. The Ray-Bans cut the glare and kept the road grit from blowing into his eyes. He was wearing the windbreaker to keep the Colt and shoulder rig covered. Wearing his own shirt and jeans, too, stiff and scented with detergent from the *lavandería* where he traded his clean duds for the sleep-wrinkled clothes of a dead man.

Eyes on the road, he rolled and rubbed his neck, cricked from a restless night on Boelcke's couch. He couldn't light a Lucky in the cross breeze and the tin of Copenhagen he used while staking out the lovebirds was long gone. To stave off the nicotine withdrawal, he fished in the glove box for a pouch of stale Red Man and made do, slowly working the dried tobacco into a moist chaw.

He spit the juice into an empty Dixie cup with a paper napkin stuffed in the bottom and watched the stark desert mountains roll by, blue-gray in the hazy distance, dead and dull shades of brown up close.

At his ten o'clock loomed the Davis Mountains, a V-shaped wedge of volcanic rock that was part of the Eastern Rockies that barreled from northwest to southeast across the Trans-Pecos. With the point of the V resting near Fort Davis, this range was dominated by Mount Livermore, an 8,378-foot peak. These mountains were tall enough to force moist air upward, creating a micro-climate blessed by more rain than the sun-blasted rocks that cut jagged lines against the sky to the south, southeast and southwest.

Over the far horizon to the northwest, Burch knew the Franklin Mountains dominated the El Paso skyline. He once spent a warm evening waiting in the rocks above an overlook parking lot high on the mountain grade, gazing at the bright lights of El Paso below, the dark patch of the Fort Bliss reservation and the lesser glow from Ciudad Juarez further south, wolfing two brisket sandwiches washed down with twin longnecks of Tecate.

On that night, an H&K MP-5 submachine gun rested in a duffle bag at his feet and his 1911 was stuffed behind his back, digging into the flesh above his left kidney. It was a comfortable pain and Burch felt intensely alive even though he was on the run from cops who wanted him for a murder he didn't commit and gunsels sent to kill him by the drug lord he blamed for his partner's death — T-Roy, *El Rojo Loco*.

His sunburned scalp was covered by a cocked Resistol straw with sweat stains, a cattleman crease and a rancher dip as he enjoyed the view and the cool air whistling through the mountain pass, welcome relief from the day's blast furnace heat. He was waiting on a suave and oily flesh smuggler named Silva Huerta to seal the deal for a night flight over the border with that crazy Tennessee blonde, Carla Sue Cantrell.

It was a turbulent midnight run, threading the needle between jagged peaks lit by lightning to land at a dirt strip and hunt T-Roy down to avenge his partner's death and the murder of Carla Sue's uncle.

Their luck soured. Hunters became prey. Burch wound up hogtied on a stone altar, seconds away from having his heart carved from his chest, when Carla Sue stepped up and blew out T-Roy's lights with eight shots from her own 1911.

Still alive, but just barely. Left with some permanent souvenirs — a busted jaw that still popped and cracked when he chewed, a partial plate to replace broken teeth, a white scar across his forehead from a pistol whipping. And nightmares that had him grabbing for the Percodan and guzzling Maker's straight from the bottle.

But not right now. Right now, he felt just as alive and full of the jazzy electric jolt of the hunt as he did that night waiting for Huerta on the slopes of the Franklin Mountains.

He almost died in this stark and primal country and he still had those demons lurking in their rocky holes. But as he drove north, he was a hunter unafraid, a cop working his bloody trade and drawn to the grim beauty of these unforgiving mountains and the way they clashed and collided — the Rockies slicing in from the northwest, vestiges of the Ozarks creeping in from the northeast and the Sierra del Carmens knifing out of the southwest and Mexico.

It was as if the gods, ancient, angry and always thirsty for blood, had ripped open the flesh of the earth and exposed its bones. It was savage country, inhabited by spirits more terrible than the demons of his nightmares.

It was a place where those demons couldn't hide. If they arose, they'd be out and exposed in the burning sun where Burch could see them — in the blinding light, their hold on him broken by the harsh glare of the land itself. If he lived here, he wouldn't need the whiskey salvation and the half-a-Percodan sacrament.

His mind snapped back to reality and the road ahead. Didn't keep him from chewing on what he was told by men who got themselves dead — Bustamante and Lopez. Burch hadn't learned much from Bustamante he didn't already know, but the fat hustler did give him Lopez.

Paydirt with Lopez. He milked pure gold out of that treacherous little bastard before Gyp Hulett snuffed out his candle with a 9mm slug. Gave him Needle Burnet and tied the deputy to the barnburner. Left him with a riddle, too. *Hamburguesa.* A name, a nickname or nonsense? Burch didn't know, but couldn't ignore it.

Burch never got the chance to ask about this riddle. Or anything else. Like who hired the pyro. And whether Burnet was acting with the High Sheriff's knowledge when he gave Lopez that guide dog job or was just another bent tin star acting on his own nickel.

Questions for later. Right now, he had his sights set on Alpine and a lawyer named Lucius Schoenfeldt, front man for the Bryte Brothers' assault on the Bar Double H ranch. The next scumbag with a day that needed to be ruined. The next turd to shake loose from the shit tree.

Burch checked his back-trail every five minutes or so as he rolled along, studying the wide rearview mirror in the cab for a car or truck he'd noticed before. Traffic was light on this stretch of highway, which made it easier for him to spot a tail and harder for the tail to stay hidden.

As he left Faver, he spotted a dark green car trailing him. Looked like GM iron. Something long, big and heavy. But lurking just out of range. Too far away to tell if it was a Ninety-Eight, a Caddy, an Electra or Impala. Didn't have the telltale shark snout of a Catalina or Bonneville.

Once he hit the highway headed north, Burch didn't spot the car again. Didn't mean it wasn't back there. Nothing much between Faver and Marfa. Easy for a tail to drop back and wait until he got near the town that gave those mysterious lights their name, then close up. He could feel somebody back there, but needed to be sure.

He was ten miles out of Marfa when he spotted a lonely Shamrock convenience store with two pumps and a cinderblock building covered by a tin roof.

Perfect.

He didn't need gas but pulled in anyway. He rolled up to the pumps and stepped out of Ol' Blue, stretching his back like a road-weary traveler then turning toward the highway to brace his palms against the rail of the stepside bed to flex his legs in a runner's stretch.

The big dark green car ripped past the station. An Olds two-door. Knew it was GM iron. Bigger than a Cutlass. Maybe a Delta Eighty-Eight. Driven by a fat Mexican with a moon pie face looking right at his red pickup in surprise as Burch turned toward the screen door of the store.

Nobody riding shotgun. Nobody in the back seat. Time for a little *mano-a-mano* between him and that Chuy fucker.

Burch banged through the screen door, peeling off his Ray-Bans to see the gloomy interior. A short, plump Mexican woman with gray hair pulled back in a bun sat behind the counter, eyes glued to a *telenovela* glaring from a small black-and-white portable.

"*Los baños?*"

The woman slapped a key on the counter, dull brass tethered to a weathered wooden stick with a leather shoelace. She pointed to the rear of the store. Burch grabbed the key and lumbered down the center aisle toward the restrooms, ducking under *ristras* of dried red chiles hanging from the rafters.

Make that restroom, singular — and at a right angle to the open back door. Burch gagged on the mixed smell of piss, shit and disinfectant penetrating the closed door as he rattled the key into the lock. Holding his breath, he unlocked the door, which opened toward the front of the store, pulled the key out of the lock and used the door to hide his side step to the back exit. He eased over the threshold and into the sun, slamming the restroom door closed with a flick of the wrist.

Flattening himself against the back of the building, he checked both directions while putting his Ray-Bans on against the cloudless glare, tucking the cable temples behind his ears. To his right, he spotted the edge of a dumpster with rust stains and flaking brown paint, its lid propped up by the pungent garbage overflow baking in the sun.

He rushed to the corner of the building as fast as bulk and bad knees would let him, boots shuffling through the sandy soil, then peeked around and saw only the snout of his pickup. In a crouch, he covered the ten yards of open ground between the building and the dumpster in what only seemed to be a semi-eternity, then kneeled behind this smelly hideaway, eyeing the highway and the entrance to the store's gravel lot.

Burch breathed through his mouth to keep from gagging, the Colt dangling from his left hand. Sweat matted his shirt and windbreaker. He didn't have to wait long for the big green Olds to slowly turn off the highway and glide into the gravel lot. A Delta '88. Cleared up that mystery.

Nice car. Dusty but well-waxed and meticulously cared for. Sunlight exploded off the polished chrome like diamonds spilled from a rich girl's hand. The driver was eyeing Ol' Blue and the store's front door as he angled the car across the lot. He turned into the far left corner at the front of the lot. Burch saw the Olds' backup lights blink on as the driver slipped the big, two-door coupe into the slot between the building and the dumpster.

Pig-blind luck. Better than no luck at all. A gift from a dumbass. He'd have to speak to Garza about the piss-poor skills of his hired guns. The driver was watching the front door, his head angled toward Burch's pickup, leaning back against the door in his plush bucket seat, colored a lighter green than the body.

Burch saw he could break for the driver's side door along the front of the dumpster without his image appearing in a rearview mirror. He switched the Colt to his right hand, rushed up to the car and yanked open the door with his left. The driver spilled out, his hands grabbing air. Burch grabbed him by the front of his shirt and yanked hard, pivoting his body to add speed and momentum to the fall.

The driver hit the gravel with a thud, air whooshing out of his lungs. Before he could catch his breath, Burch slammed his bulk down, straddling the driver's chest, his ruined knees pinning down both arms. He jammed the barrel of the Colt into the driver's mouth and heard a front tooth break off. The driver tried to scream, but was muffled by gunmetal now rimmed with blood from his mouth.

"This is gonna be a very short conversation, motherfucker, so you best lie quiet, suck on my gun and listen close. *Comprende?*"

The driver tried to nod his head, but winced in pain.

"I'll take that as a 'yes,' Chuy. And yes, I know who the fuck you are and who you work for and how much of a badass killer you are. I should just blow your skull apart right now and dump you out back for the vultures and coyotes to pick clean."

Chuy's eyes were dull and black. No fear there. Not even with a Colt jammed between his teeth. Man might not be able to run a tail worth a fuck, but he had balls. He'd need 'em after the trick Burch had in mind.

"I'm not going to kill you now, Chuy, because I need you to be a messenger boy. You tell your boss he needs to talk to me. Not send somebody like you to kill me. You tell him I know he wanted Bart Hulett dead, but somebody beat you boys to the punch. You tell him I'm after that somebody, not him."

Burch yanked the Colt from Chuy's mouth, taking out another tooth. Chuy started to scream, but Burch muffled the noise by jamming a dirty blue bandana between the gun hand's bloody lips.

"You understand the message, Chuy?"

Chuy's eyes flashed in anger. He was trying to cuss Burch out despite the gag. Burch shoved the balled-up bandana a little deeper. Chuy gagged.

"Tell Malo what I said, word for word, motherfucker. And Chuy — if I ever see you again, I'll just shoot you dead on the spot."

Burch punched Chuy twice in the face, putting all his weight behind the left-handed shots. Then he clubbed him twice on the side of the head with the butt of the Colt. Once more for good measure. He pulled the bandana out of the bloody mouth, wiped his Colt clean and felt inside with his fingers to make sure Chuy hadn't swallowed his tongue.

He raised Chuy's eyelids, then pressed his fingers into the man's neck and felt a pulse. Lights were out but somebody was still home. Asleep. Bet the dreams wouldn't be sweet.

Damn, sport model. You put a hurtin' on that greaser. Did my heart good to see that. You know he woulda blasted you as soon as you came out that front door. Might as well ice him now and let somebody else deliver that message.

See your point, Wynn, but it needs to be him deliverin' that message. Besides, I'm not done playin' with our pal Chuy.

Whatchu got in mind, sport model?

Watch and see, Wynn. One of the tricks I learned from you. Pupil tippin' his hat to the master.

Damn, but don't you know I love tricks. Long as the shitasses are on the butt end.

Oh, I promise you, this shitass will be.

Burch grunted as he lifted Chuy into a sitting position. He patted him down then rolled him, finding the Colt Python parked over the gunsel's right kidney and tucking it behind his own belt at the small of his back. He also found a switchblade in the back pocket of Chuy's baggy jeans and a stiletto tucked in a sheath clipped inside the top of his right boot.

Man likes his blades, likes to get up close and personal for wet work. Burch slipped both into the pocket of his windbreaker, then used his legs and arms to lift Chuy into the driver's seat.

He reached over Chuy and opened the glove box. Inside was a full pint bottle of tequila. Nice. He cracked open the pint and splashed some of the cheap *blanco* into Chuy's mouth, then poured the rest down his shirt front and crotch, tossing the empty bottle and cap into the passenger's seat.

Fingers to Chuy's neck. Still a pulse. Eyelids raised. Lights still out. Burch stood up straight, then walked to the back of the building, easing his hand around the corner of the open back door to rattle the restroom door knob, swinging it into the hallway and stepping behind it to enter the store again.

Holding his breath, he reached into the restroom to flush the toilet. It gurgled weakly and caused the pipes to bang. He stepped from behind the door and closed it, making a show of securing the lock and testing it.

Whistling a bar or two of "Tulsa Time," hearing the J.J. Cale version on his own private radio tuner while hitching up his jeans, Burch ducked under the *ristras* again to place the key on the counter. He reached inside a cooler and fished out an icy bottle of Jarritos orange soda, snapping off the metal cap with the opener built into the box. He put $15 on the counter.

"Sorry to take so long back there — ate something for breakfast that disagreed with me. This should cover the soda and gas."

The woman tore herself away from her *telenovela* long enough to swipe the key and money off the table.

"Stop the pump at fourteen, *hombre.*"

"*Gracias.*"

Opening the door of his pickup, Burch plunked the soda bottle into a wire cup holder hanging from the dash, then ducked his head under the steering wheel to reach up past the column and feel for a baggie taped to the lip of metal right behind the speedometer and dash instruments.

The baggie held four fat joints Carol Ann gave him to calm his nerves on this road trip. Deep Ellum Torpedos. Once there were five, but he smoked one in the parking lot of a Super 8 in Big Spring on his way to Faver. It helped some, but when the nightmares rolled, he preferred whiskey, with or without an 'e.' To wash down the Percodan that made those dark-thirty terrors seem cartoonish and friendly.

Burch pocketed the baggie in his windbreaker, then popped the latch of the bench seat and reached under the Model 12 pump for a quart of 10W30 Havoline, Texaco's finest, and a funnel. He popped the hood, unscrewed the oil cap to the engine then set up the funnel and quart to pour down the pipe.

When he reached the driver's side of Chuy's car, he pulled the Colt again and kept it centered on the man's skull until he was satisfied the lights were still out.

He pulled out one of the torpedos and fired it up with his Zippo, letting the flame get a strong grip on the dried weed and paper before blowing it down to a bright red ember and letting the smoke fill the car, pulled across Chuy's body and into his clothes by the open driver's window that served as a convenient chimney.

Burch opened the ashtray in the dash and put the burning joint inside. He opened the glove box again and dumped the other three joints inside, loose. He pocketed the baggie to throw away later. He fished through the glove box until he found a matchbook from a Presidio bar — *El Lobo Azul*.

He flipped open the cover and used a Bic to print three lines on the inside:

Hulett

Bar Double H

Midnight

Burch closed the cover, then tossed the matchbook back into the glove box and closed it. He tucked the Python back in Chuy's belt slide and replaced both blades.

Damn, sport model. You've triple fucked our ugly brown friend. And I'm so proud I could just shit. Let me guess your next move. Up the road a piece, you'll pull over again and drop dime on our friend here. Sheriff or Rangers?

Maybe both, Wynn. Maybe both.

Burch buttoned up his pickup, pumped his gas, then headed for Alpine. Two more sets of eyes were tracking Burch. These he didn't see or feel. They were waiting for him dead ahead.

Twenty-Two

Let's go to the videotape!

Warner Wolf's signature line. Hyperkinetic blowhard with the bad dye job on a fluffed-up mane. Still made Charley Burghardt gnash his teeth every time he heard it. That and Wolf's other catchphrase — *BOOM!*

Burghardt couldn't stand the guy but got a bellyful of his gassy patter growing up in Chantilly, Virginia, watching WTOP with his dad to get the latest scoop on the Redskins and Senators. No escaping the gas and bombast back then. His dad loved the guy almost as much as Sonny Jurgensen and Frank Howard.

Let's go to the videotape!

Burghardt still hated Wolf, but the tagline was perfect for the images running through his mind as he drove a dusty gray '72 Dodge crew cab pickup with Hooker Drilling & Well Service painted in red on the two front doors.

Drill bits, collars, spanners and hoisting chains rattled around the scarred-up bed. Coveralls, hard hats, map cases and boots were scattered over the back seat and floorboard. A rust-streaked toolbox behind the rear window rounded out the perfect cover for two guys running a tail in this part of the Trans-Pecos, stark and parched country where oil and gas were scarce, but water was also a rare commodity.

A 360 V-8 with a four-barreled carb gave the truck enough giddyup to stay in the hunt, but stealth and camouflage were its strong suits — like a moonshiner's slip-by car. Nobody noticed two well diggers headed to another thirsty rancher's spread.

Riding shotgun was an ex-cop from Houston, a gun hand with a helmet of thick, blond, layer-cut hair and an even thicker moustache, carefully trimmed and waxed. A weightlifter's build. Thick shoulders, flared lats and bulging biceps stretched the fabric of the slate-gray shirt with the fake company name embroidered over the left chest pocket. Blue-gray eyes hidden by mirrored, wrap-around shades and a long jaw pocked by acne scars.

Bartel. No first name given or asked for. Sent down to join him and find out what the hell went wrong when word broke that Bart Hulett was dead instead of badly shaken and ready to cut a deal with the Bryte Brothers. Packed a Smith & Wesson Model 27 .357 in a behind-the-back leather holster, the four-inch barrel threaded for a silencer. Had a .308 FN FAL with a folding stock in an oiled canvas bag buried underneath all that backseat junk.

One for close work, the other to reach out and touch somebody.

A deal gone south was why the videotape was playing in Burghardt's head. The setup had been perfect. Lots of hay in the barn. Dry, warm weather that had baked out a winter of heavy rain. A tractor parked inside, close to stacked bales and loose straw, positioned just right to serve as centerpiece for an artfully set blaze that left no telltales for an arson investigator.

But his clients also wanted to send a clear message to Hulett. That's why he secured the barn's double doors with a ten-foot length of rusty chain and a padlock. *This wasn't an accident. This was us. We can reach out and touch you anytime we want. Right where you live. Be smart and cut a deal. Don't keep us waiting. Don't make us come calling again.*

Leaving a message rankled Burghardt. It queered the perfection of a sweet setup for his flawless performance. It ruffled his professional pride. Burghardt was a barn fire virtuoso who learned his skills working at thoroughbred stables and racetracks, first in Virginia and Maryland, then in Kentucky, New York and South Carolina.

Short and wiry, with a shock of unruly, reddish-brown hair and a pug-nosed face that looked far younger than his years, he had a natural hand with horses and started out as a hot walker and exercise rider. Not much of a future in that because he wasn't skilled enough or small enough to become a jockey.

An old-timer named Punky Barnes turned him on to the darker trade of a barnburner for hire. Punky also taught him the terrible art of killing horses with a hot shot, electrodes clipped to the ear and anus, then plugged into a wall socket — a sudden death that resembled a lethal colic. For a less dramatic death, he used a terminal cocktail of painkillers and barbiturates. Had to find a bent vet to okay a cocktail death, but that was easy to do for a couple or three centuries.

When a show horse or racer didn't perform as expected, Burhardt got a call and a $10,000 fee. The owner pocketed the insurance money. When a stable faced bankruptcy or an owner had a sudden reversal of fortune in the stock market, they needed cash quick. That's when Burghardt got a call for his undetectable hand as a barnburner. And a $30,000 fee.

He could fray electrical cables and wires to make it look like rats had gnawed away the insulation, using a small metal tool he made himself. He could open a junction box without leaving tool marks and was equally masterful when picking a lock. He could rig a short in an electric heater or a leak in one fired by kerosene or propane.

He rarely used accelerants, preferring the flammable liquids commonly found in a stable or barn, augmented by the most common combustible of all — hay and straw bedding. He had a sixth sense about hot spots in hay stacks and could coax crackling flame out of a slow smolder, using one of those cheap, hand-held mini-fans he could pick up at any Wal-Mart.

Burghardt got pinched in Kentucky after setting fire to a barn at a stable south of Lexington owned by a real estate wheel named

Bordelais Quarles, king of the speculative condo complex who got smacked hard in the savings-and-loan bust that flushed his primary source of easy money. He needed a quick injection of insurance gelt and was willing to kill ten thoroughbreds to get it.

Burghardt got the call and burned the barn down for the promise of his customary fee. Trouble was, Quarles had a twenty-something mistress, a coke whore who chattered nonstop on the phone about things she shouldn't have even known.

Trouble was, Quarles shared her lust for blow and told her everything. Bragging about how smart and slick he was. Naming names, including Burghardt's. Trouble was, her line was bugged by a PI working for an ex-wife who wanted to jack up her alimony payment. When Quarles told the ex to go to hell, she had the PI go to some cop buddies who didn't ask too many hard questions about whether the names and information came from an illegal wiretap.

That's how Burghardt took his only felony bounce. The cops couldn't quite pin a first-degree arson rap on him. Good thing because Kentucky had a fierce penalty for arson — up to thirty years in prison. They did hit him with a second-degree arson charge, but knocked it back to conspiracy when they couldn't stick him with any physical evidence.

Quarles. *Fuck him. Ratted me out by proxy to his chippie. Stiffed me on the $30,000 fee. Roll on that bastard and get yourself some easy time.* That was one of the voices in his head, urging him to drop dime on the condo king and lighten his own load. He listened to that voice long and hard.

But there was another voice and it sounded like Punky Barnes. *Don't be a rat. Keep your mouth shut. Do your time. Be a stand-up guy. The right people will remember. I'll make sure of that.* That was the voice he listened to.

He served two of a five-year jolt at Kentucky State Penitentiary. Tourists called it the Castle on the Cumberland for its baroque architecture and scenic vista overlooking Lake Barkley, a Corps of

Engineers reservoir named for U.S. Sen. Alben Barkley, who served as Harry Truman's vice president. Inmates called it something far less flattering — Shitbird Castle.

Inside those ancient stone walls, Burghardt stacked his time. He kept his mouth shut. He pumped iron and put some muscle on his wiry frame. He found a piece of metal in the prison laundry where he worked and made himself a shiv. He stuck it in the neck of a hulking redneck outlaw biker who caught him in the showers alone and tried to cornhole him. He ripped open the biker's carotid and let him bleed out on the cracked tile floor, ditching the shiv down a drainpipe.

After that, nobody bothered him. It helped that Barnes reached out to some old-line cons who put the word out that he was with them. Dixie Mafia types. Moonshiners, meth cookers and weed farmers. Guys with cousins and brothers and uncles on the inside. They let him know they had his back.

He was friendly to them, but kept his distance. He found another piece of metal, fashioned another shiv and kept it close. He spoke to no one about Quarles — on the inside or the outside. Walls have ears and every other inmate was a snitch looking to carve a hunk off their sentence.

He let his memory roll the tape without the Warner Wolf blather.

When he walked out of the prison gates, there was Barnes, a smiling fireplug of a guy with thinning red hair and the ruddy face of a lifelong saloon sport. They shook hands and walked to the older man's burgundy '75 Coupe de Ville, gleaming in the warm spring sun like it did rolling fresh off the showroom floor a decade ago.

Barnes kept an arm draped over his shoulder as he steered him to the passenger side of the two-door hardtop. He held the door open like a valet at a swank hotel as Burghardt slid his butt across the buttery leather seat and tucked his legs inside. He closed the door with a flourish, then opened the trunk to sling in Burghardt's duffle bag.

There was the solid thunk of well-made American iron, then Barnes slid his paunch behind the steering wheel and reached inside his tweed jacket to hand him a silver flask.

"Here, kid. Take a pull of Kentucky's other best-known export — the one that don't have four legs, a tail and a pea-sized brain."

Burghardt took a slow sip, letting the bourbon roll around his tongue, its sweet burn filling his mouth. He savored the liquor then swallowed, feeling the smooth, warm fire fill his stomach. He took another much longer sip, bubbling the flask before screwing the cap back on and handing it to Barnes.

"You look good, kid. Prison agreed with you. But I think we need to get a big porterhouse in your gullet and buy you a hooker for dessert. We'll overnight in Louisville and get you fed and fucked."

"What about Quarles?"

"I guess you ain't heard. They fished his body out of the Ohio River a few weeks ago. Somebody did the double tap, then parked one in his mouth for bein' a loudmouth rat."

"What the hell happened?"

"Short version? He got mixed up with some very nasty people to keep his condo empire from going under, got jammed up and tried to cut a deal with the feds to save himself. Got himself dead instead."

Burghardt chewed on this for a minute, then looked at Barnes.

"Good. Means I don't have to kill him myself."

"No. You can put Quarles in your rearview for good."

"Thanks for looking out for me in there, Punky. I'm alive, I'm free, but I'm broke. I need to line up some jobs."

"I know, kid. You're too hot for the horse industry right now. But have no fear, Punky's here. I know some guys in Houston who are looking for somebody with your skills and proven ability to keep his yap shut when the screws are put to him."

"Houston? Who the hell do you know down in Houston?"

"We'll talk about it later, kid. Lay back and take a snooze while I steer this magic carpet to the land of cowflesh, whiskey and pussy."

That's how he wound up working for the Bryte Brothers. That's how he wound up here in West Texas, following a Dallas peeper and a Mex tailing him in a big, green Olds.

227

Let's go to the videotape!

Burghardt re-ran the instant replay on his night mission to Hulett's ranch. Led there by a local named Lopez who posted up as a lookout. Waited until midnight. Cased the ranch house before entering the barn. Nobody home but Hulett.

Cased the bunkhouse and small cabin of the ranch foreman. Both empty. Both men wore disposable booties and latex gloves. After setting the blaze, he was careful to slide the barn doors closed and had Lopez help him thread the chain through the handles so it wouldn't rattle.

"Fucker shouldn't have died. That blaze was going good when I split the scene. Lock and chain shoulda kept him out of there. He didn't have the key."

"Shoulda, woulda, coulda. Quit your whining. The guy got dead. That makes it murder. And I guess you've never seen what a twelve-gauge can do to a lock and chain. Couple of rounds of double-ought. Bingo."

"How do you know that's how he got in?"

Bartel turned his head, tipped his shades forward and shot a stare across the cab that reminded Burghardt of a hungry wolf.

"I don't. But I never met a country boy yet who didn't have a twelve-gauge in the house. That ain't the big mystery, though."

"No? What is?"

"Our guy in the sheriff's office says no chain or lock was found at the scene. Doors were closed, which makes them suspicious, but no chain. Leaves you in the clear because they can't prove it was arson."

"Means somebody was there after I left and Hulett went in."

Bartel grinned, pushed his shades back in place and faced the windshield.

"Bingo, again. That's why I'm here. Find out who that motherfucker is and steer the heat their way. Keep tabs on this loose cannon from Dallas and all the other moving parts of this clusterfuck. Make sure everybody on our side keeps their mud packed tight."

"Or else?"

"Quit fretting. You did your job right and they know that. They also know you don't talk. It's this other guy they're worried about. And this fuckhead from Dallas. Keep your eyes on the road."

"What about that beaner tour guide?"

"Him? Our guy will take care of his sorry ass. Relax, you're ridin' with the pros now."

They were following the dark green Olds in a very loose tail. Had been since watching the big guy leave a lawyer's office in Faver while they sipped coffee and munched breakfast tacos and saw the Olds nose out of a side street to slipstream the peeper's pickup. South of Marfa, Bartel eyeballed a Shamrock convenience store on their right.

"Burch pulled in there."

Burghardt lifted his boot off the gas pedal.

"No, no — keep going. Hit it."

Two miles ahead, Burghardt saw the big Olds lurch across the median strip in a dusty U-turn. Bartel whipped a dark blue cap off his head and grabbed a hardhat from the floorboard, slapping it over his blond helmet with a forward tilt, slouching in the front seat to feign a nap.

Burghardt kept his eyes forward as the Olds passed, raising his two fingers from the steering wheel in an open-road highway greeting straight out of the Bubba handbook. Nothing to see here. Just two tired bubbas headed out to the next drill site.

"Do we follow?"

"Not only no, but hell, no."

"Why not?"

"Looks like a little herd thinning is about to go down. That's good for our side. Bad for one of these guys. But we don't give much of a shit about that. We know where the peeper's going so we'll head there. If he shows up, means he won. If he don't, one less problem for us."

"Who's this other guy?"

"No clue. A Mexican. Dough-faced bastard. If he wins, I doubt he'll show up."

"You takin' bets on this?"

Bartel sat up straight, tilted the hardhat back and grinned.

"My money's on the peeper."

"Why. Know him?"

"Know of him. Know a guy in Houston who hates him a lot. Blames him for getting his partner killed a couple of years back. Homicide dick named Cider Jones. Weird guy. Got some injun mystic thing he does to commune with his murder vics. Stares into their eyes."

"That's some morbid shit."

"You bet. Jones also says our peeper buddy is easy to underestimate and hard to kill."

"Sounds like grudging respect."

"Smells like more injun horseshit. Respect your vaunted enemy. Respect, my ass. Blow 'em down and make 'em yesterday's news, I say."

"I'll take the Mex."

"For a C-note?"

"Make it half a yard. Our masters haven't paid me yet."

"Done. When we get to Marfa, pull over someplace. I gotta take a piss and call in. Then we head to Alpine and see whether shithead shows up."

"Better get some gas. And some cold drinks, too. Already got my lunch."

Burghardt held up a Whataburger bag, good grease picked up in Faver.

"Jesus, you're addicted to those things. We do a quick stop then get gone. Whatever goes down back there ain't going to take long. I'll drive. You eat."

"Nah. I'll stay behind the wheel. Eat it when we get to Alpine."

"An addict with willpower. Didn't know you had it in you."

Whataburger. Hamburger. *Hamburguesa.* Burghardt.

Twenty-Three

Burch eased Ol' Blue off the main drag through Alpine just before it split into two one-way arteries, threading through oncoming traffic and entering Sul Ross Avenue about a dozen blocks west of the center of town. He banged the floor shifter into third and let the engine slow the truck to a glide on this east-west side street, which bore the same name as the state university on the northeast side of town.

He didn't pick this parallel path because it was named for the famous Texas Ranger, Indian fighter, governor and savior of Texas A&M University, although any Texan worth his salt knew who Sul Ross was. He took the scenic route with the historical name to buy time to slow down his mind and shift it into a more focused and watchful gear, free from the distractions of cars, trucks, fast-food joints, motels and used car lots out on the drag.

He also wanted to shake off the last, echoing jangles of the adrenalin rush he felt while bushwhacking Chuy Reynaldo. That had been fast and brutal. Needed to be with a killer like Chuy. But it had also been a violent free fall, a sudden release of the pent-up rage and fear Burch had been humping for more than a year.

Burch reined in that rage just in time, checking his plummet to keep himself from beating Chuy to death with his bare knuckles, feeling a loud snap in his brainpan as he broke free of the blood-red joy he felt pounding on the man's head.

Bad juju to blow your cool and kill off the messenger boy before he could deliver the message. And a sure way to earn a hot lead kissoff from Garza, one he might get anyway just for asking questions about Bart Hulett's death.

He needed Chuy to deliver that message. *I'm not gunning for you. I know you didn't kill Bart Hulett.* But he also needed Chuy to be out of action for a few days. He followed through and dropped dime with the Rangers and the Presidio County Sheriff's Office about a drunk Mexican, reeking of tequila and reefer, passed out in a dark green Olds parked at a Shamrock convenience store south of Marfa.

When he stopped at a gas station on the outskirts of Alpine to sic the lawdogs on Chuy, he dug out the address of Lucius Schoenfeldt's law office from the weathered Yellow Pages hanging on a chain underneath the phone. 203 W. Holland Avenue, the eastbound-only segment of the divided main drag through town.

He figured this put the lawyer's office a block south of the only courthouse Brewster County ever had or needed, a simple and stately wood-framed building constructed in 1877, with a brick façade and triangular dormer windows peeking from below a flat-topped tin roof painted white. He passed along the east side of the historic building and the mangy lawn shaded by tall but spindly pecan trees, slowing to a crawl like a man looking for a parking spot, keeping an eye open for somebody looking the wrong way at the wrong time.

It was a Monday and curbside spots were packed with cars and pickups, the sidewalks and courthouse steps alive with briefcase-toting lawyers in polyester suits leading seedier-looking clients to a hearing, sheriff's deputies in crisp khaki uniforms and steam-creased straw hats climbing the steps or heading out to their Crown Vic cruisers and Broncos, women in matching skirts and jackets lugging cased stenotype machines that marked them as court reporters.

Lunch hour was over and it looked like the afternoon court session was about to begin.

He slipped Ol' Blue into a gap in traffic, passing the front of the courthouse and the squat gazebo used for outdoor concerts and weddings. He turned again to close his loop around the courthouse square, eyeing the entrance to the low-slung annex where a different clientele was headed in or leaving.

Ranchers in sweat-stained chambray shirts and battered straw hats looking to file a well permit, title company operatives in wrinkled khakis and loud plaid shirts looking to pull land records, real estate clerks in tight jeans and floral cowgirl blouses bustling in with quit claim deeds.

Nada. Nobody who didn't belong. Nobody taking a wrong step or looking the wrong way. No hairs standing up on the back of his neck.

Time to scope out Schoenfeldt's office building. From knocking around Alpine while tailing the wayward guitar picker husband of Nita Rodriguez Wyatt, he knew Fifth Street was the dividing line between east and west addresses on Alpine's avenues. That meant the lawyer's Holland Avenue office was somewhere between Sixth and Seventh.

Burch had spent just enough idle hours to digest a glossy Chamber of Commerce nickel tour of Alpine history he found in his motel room and nose around town to get his bearings. He admired the fine old lines of the Holland Hotel, a white-faced two-story edifice named for cattleman John R. Holland and built by his son in the grand Spanish colonial style in 1928. It ate up most of the block where Burch figured the lawyer's office was located.

From the glossy, Burch also knew the eastern corner of the block was home to the more modest sandstone and tan brick building that was the original hotel old man Holland built in 1912 during the mercury mining boom along the border eighty miles south of town. It was built to house retail and office space on the first floor, which fronted Holland Avenue and Sixth Street, with guest rooms on the second floor. Had to be home to Schoenfeldt's office.

Both of Holland's namesakes had seen better days. There were sporadic attempts to bring back the glory days of the bigger hotel. They all sparked and sputtered before dying out. Some of the Austin ex-pats were making noise about another revival attempt. They ignored the older hotel.

These days, the only guests in Holland's first lodging were ghosts. The upstairs rooms were cobwebbed and filled with piles of dust, busted old furniture and the musty odor of mildew. But the ground floor was still a roost for cheap retail and office space, perfect for a lawyer serving as point man for a West Texas land grab by a bunch of hard-nosed developers from Houston with a nasty reputation for terminal payback.

Burch wanted to find a place to plant Ol' Blue and watch Schoenfeldt's office for some long, sun-baked minutes. He preferred to surprise the lawyer in his office and make him very uncomfortable with pointed questions, an air of menace and a light love tap or three to loosen the man's tongue.

If the Bryte Brothers' mouthpiece wasn't in, he'd jimmy a door lock and rummage through his files. An oiled canvas tool roll tucked between the springs of the passenger seat held lock picks, wire cutters, screwdrivers, slim jims, a small knuckle-buster wrench and a small hammer. Burch was handy with these tools and might have had a career as a burglar if he hadn't become a cop.

He jogged Ol' Blue east on Sul Ross, aiming for Fifth Street and the parking lot of the Amtrak depot, hoping to find a slot that gave him a good view of the two street-front sides of the corner office building where Schoenfeldt hung his shingle.

As his tires crunched across the gravel lot, he eyed the dozen or so vehicles already parked there, scattered around three double rows marked by concrete curbs. All but one was empty. The lone exception was a mud-streaked Dodge crew cab pickup parked in the shade at the northwest end of the lot, fronting Holland.

The stretched pickup was gray with red lettering on the passenger-side front door. Two guys in dark ball caps were lounging inside, windows rolled down. One blond-headed, the other brown. Both dragging on cigarettes and blowing smoke into the still, hot air.

Burch slow-rolled to the south side of the lot and backed into a space fronting the tracks where he could watch the building and the watchers in the gray Dodge, careful to stay out of the line of sight of the watchers' rearview mirrors. He dug out his old binoculars from the glove box — a pair of World War II surplus M3s made by Bausch & Lomb, weathered and dinged, but with glass that was still sharp.

Sharp enough to spot a flash of the orange Whataburger flying W on the wrapper the watcher on the driver's side let flutter to the gravel.

Hamburguesa?

Caused his old cop instincts to tingle, but Burch tucked it away. He scanned Schoenfeldt's building and the lettering on the watchers' Dodge — Hooker Drilling & Well Service.

The angry voice of Wynn Moore growled.

Well diggers my pimply white ass — that's hired muscle, sport model. Looking for you.

Don't you know it, Wynn. I doubt them boys are just babysittin' that lawyer. How'd they know I was comin'?

Appears you had more than one set of eyes ridin' in your six, son. You're startin' to draw a crowd. Shows you're makin' some progress and got some folks worried. That's a good thing. But it means you're going to have to stay sharp and alert. Lay off that damn Percodan.

Shit, haven't had to pop one today. Them demons are stayin' in their holes long as I'm workin'.

Glad to hear it. But you need to figure out who those hombres are, whose side they're on.

Well, they ain't on mine. Doubt they're Garza's people — they're Anglos. They're either Bryte Brothers muscle or belong to a player we don't know about.

What are you fixin' to do?

If you weren't a ghost, I'd say the two of us would just roust those sumbitches and find out what's what.

You handled that Mex pretty good all by your lonesome. Might be time for a little more herd thinnin'.

Maybe so, Wynn. Maybe so. Not here, though. Some place a little more lonesome.

Now you're thinkin', sport model. Now you're thinkin'.

"Where the hell's our boy?"

"Relax. He'll show. And if he don't, that means the Mex musta won and I owe you fifty bucks."

Burghardt sucked icy Dr. Pepper from a straw then belched as he scanned the northwest corner of Sixth and Holland, ignoring the passing traffic, keeping his eyes on the first floor of Schoenfeldt's building.

The lawyer's office fronted Holland with a double-door entrance in white wood trim. Gold-leaf script arched across the tinted plate glass window that tastefully told the walk-in trade that here was an attorney-at-law who specialized in real estate transactions, including title searches. There was also a first-floor entrance on Sixth you had to make part of your scan.

After wolfing down a Whataburger with cheese, extra onions and a side order of fries, Burghardt felt drowsy in the midday heat, sated like a junkie on the nod after a fresh spike of Mexican brown. He'd only been in Texas for two weeks but was seriously addicted to Whataburgers after hitting the one in Faver just a few hours after he arrived.

Had one before picking up Lopez and heading to Bart Hulett's place. Had a powerful jones for another so he bought the one he just ate before he and Bartel drove up from Faver. Wasn't sure Marfa or Alpine had a Whataburger and wasn't in the mood to accept a poor substitute.

Out of the corner of his eye, he saw Bartel pull out the cigarette lighter and replace it with a power cord to a metal box with a meter, a toggle switch and a numbered dial. He plugged a jack into the box then settled an earpiece into his left ear. He plugged in a second jack with a short cable that led to a pocket cassette recorder.

"That what I think it is?"

"Depends on what you think it is."

"Don't get cute. You bugged the guy's office, right?"

"That I did, buddy. Slipped into his office on my way to meet you and left a couple — one under his desk, the other in his bookcase. Thought they might come in handy and damn if they didn't."

Bartel fiddled with the dial and watched as the meter needle jumped, then settled at a level that satisfied him. He placed the box on the dash, then turned to grin at Burghardt, a thin, white braided wire running from the box to the earpiece.

A short, paunchy man with thinning sandy-brown hair and a round, ruddy face turned the corner from Sixth and walked toward the lawyer's office. He was wearing a blue blazer, an open-collared white dress shirt with no tie and khaki rancher's slacks with shiny dark-brown boots.

The uniform of a strictly in-town Texan.

Bartel nodded toward the man, now unlocking the office door.

"The mouthpiece. Musta ducked out for lunch."

"What's the play, here?"

"Watch and listen. See if Burch shows up. Make sure our guy keeps his mouth shut. See if we learn something we didn't already know."

"We're gonna let Burch just waltz in and talk to the guy?"

"Those are the marching orders. Hey, our guy is a lawyer for a legitimate development corporation. Doesn't know nothing about a rancher getting killed in a barn fire. Damn sorry it happened to a man he was doing business with. We're here to make sure our guy sticks to that line of talk."

"And if Burch gets rough like he did with that used-car guy in Faver?"

They had been watching when Burch did his little tap dance on the Bustamante's head and saw an unmarked cruiser follow the peeper when he pulled out of the lot. After Burch and his lawdog tail left, they eyeballed a short, skinny guy with ginger hair and a huge handlebar moustache ducking into the side door of Bustamante's office.

They heard two muffled pops followed by a third and saw Bustamante drop. The skinny guy slipped out the way he came in. None of their business.

Bartel chuckled.

"If the big man gets rough again, then we see if our guy can take a punch, bleed a little and still keep his yap shut."

"And if he can't?"

"Another thing you don't have to worry about. That's why I'm here."

Burch watched the watchers, sweating in his windbreaker and trying to coax a workable chaw out of that dried-up pouch of Red Man. He chuckled when he saw the blond guy on the passenger side fiddle with a metal box and an earpiece.

Bugged the lawyer's office. Must be worried the boy might babble. To the lawdogs. Or him. Muscle tailing him and eavesdropping on the Bryte Brothers' mouthpiece.

Told him a lot without having to ask a single question. Told him they had something to hide. Murder, maybe. Or something crooked they didn't want dredged up in a murder investigation and splashed on their shoes.

Also told him they were worried about an *hombre* who wasn't playing by the lawdog rules. Nice to know somebody was taking him seriously — been a few years since that happened, back in the days when he still carried a gold shield.

Burch dearly wanted to get these two assholes in a room with no windows and ask them some serious questions. Bounce them off the wall a time or two. Rattle their skulls a bit. Hook 'em up to a car battery and let the juice make 'em scream. Make 'em see Jesus with a cattle prod.

Damn, beating on Chuy's skull has made me all bloody minded. Gotta keep that in check.

Maybe not, sport model. I keep tellin' you there ain't no rules for the game you're playin'. You think those assholes are doing things by some kinda book? You don't got a badge no more so you can do your colorin' outside the lines.

You're right, Wynn. But I still gotta keep my shit in check and maintain control.

Yessir, but chuck that fuckin' rule book we had to follow right out the goddam window and fly the black flag.

He didn't need Wynn Moore's ghost to remind him there weren't any rules to the game he was playing. Sapping the shit out of Eduardo Lopez already proved he was flying the black flag.

Beating Chuy Reynaldo to a pulp and framing him for a weed bust showed he was willing to pull a nasty trick to get what he wanted. That gave him an idea about how to get those watchers in a room for a heart-to-heart talk. In his mind's eye, he saw an abandoned house with boarded-up windows just a few miles north of Faver.

Perfect place for a cattle-prod chat. He cranked up Ol' Blue and slipped out of the parking lot, looking for a gas station or convenience store with a phone booth to make two calls.

Once he did that, he'd come back to brace the lawyer — watchers be damned. One way or another, they would be.

Lucius Schoenfeldt heard the snick of the lock to the back door of his office suite and the soft rustle of the kickplate rubbing the thick green carpet. He wasn't surprised and knew to keep his hands on the top of his desk, flanking the open file he was reading for a land deal he wasn't sure he'd live long enough to close.

He looked up as a big, bearded man wearing a dark blue windbreaker and pointing a .45 semi-automatic at his face shambled into the room. The muzzle looked as big as the mouth of a trash can, freezing him in place.

The man was beefy, balding and wore dark aviator shades that hid his eyes, adding to the air of menace. He grabbed a ladder-back wooden chair with his right hand and spun it to rest backwards in front of the desk, straddling it while keeping the gun steady in his left hand, much closer now and leveled at the lawyer's face. The muzzle now looked as big as the top end of an oil drum.

Schoenfeldt played it cool and polite, his voice taking on a pleasant tone that ignored the gun.

"You're Mr. Burch, aren't you? The PI from Dallas. Been told to expect a visit from you."

"Nice to know you take walk-in traffic, Counselor. Glad somebody called to give you a heads-up."

"Thought you'd be here more than an hour ago. Hunger got the better of me, so I ducked out to grab a bite. Just got back. Would have missed you otherwise."

"I would have waited. Sorry I didn't meet your schedule, but I decided to meander around your little town, taking in the sights. Saw some things of interest."

"Such as?"

"The courthouse, for one. That's a fine old building. Glad to see you folks didn't knock it down to build some gutless hunk of concrete and glass. The Holland Hotel. That's a place worth restoring. Of course, this building right here was the original hotel old man Holland built. The other place was built by his pup after he died."

"Seems you're a bit of a history buff, Mr. Burch."

"I like to study on old things and the people who built them. 'Course, the most interesting thing I saw on my little tour wasn't that old."

"Oh, what was that?"

"Two guys sitting in a Dodge pickup in the Amtrak parking lot, pretending to be well diggers."

"How do you know they were pretending?"

"One guy was fiddling with an earpiece to a receiver sitting on top of the dash. Pretty damn obvious about it. Guy looked too pretty to be a well digger. Looked more like an actor in one of those TV cop shows. Or a bouncer at a fag bar. My bet is he's eavesdropping on our conversation right now."

Schoenfeldt kept his mouth shut, recalculating the odds of his survival. The dark cavalry he called could kill him just as easily as save him.

"If you're wondering why they're sitting out there and I'm sitting in here, you're asking yourself the right question, Counselor. If they were here to protect you, they'd be busting through your front door right now."

"I'm wondering why you think those two men are somehow connected to me. I'm a lawyer and represent clients who are aboveboard in every way. I specialize in real estate deals and represent developers, not drug dealers and street thugs."

"You're a mouthpiece for the Bryte Brothers, Counselor. They've got a nasty reputation and, to them, you're as disposable as a used tampon. You also fucked up in your dealings with Bart Hulett and he wound up dead."

"My dealings with Bart Hulett were strictly aboveboard. He was a difficult man to do business with, but I'm truly sorry he died what I understand to be a horrible death. I was hopeful we could successfully close a deal on his ranch despite the difficulties we had. I'm still hopeful about dealing with his heirs."

"That's a nice speech, but you must be nervous. You've said 'aboveboard' twice in twenty seconds. Kind of a verbal tic. A tell, in poker terms. You play poker, Counselor?"

Schoenfeldt didn't answer. Burch let the Colt drift away from the lawyer's face and dangle over the top rung of the ladder-back. He reached inside his windbreaker and pulled out his Luckies, shaking the pack to edge a nail onto his lip. He took his time tucking the pack into his shirt pocket, pulling out the Zippo to light up.

While Burch did this, the lawyer's eyes danced from the Colt to the Luckies then darted from the Zippo to the smoke he jetted from his nostrils. Burch took another drag then took the Lucky off his lip.

"Lemme lay some cards on the table, Lawyer Lucius. Mind if I call you that?"

No answer. Burch nodded as if the lawyer had said "yes."

"Here's the first one. It's no secret Bart Hulett had zero interest in selling his ranch to your clients. Also not a secret that he spent a lot of money buying up land adjacent to his ranch to keep you boys from fencing him in and sucking the water out from underneath him."

"As I said, negotiations with Mr. Hulett were difficult, but I remained optimistic."

"Is that another way of saying the Bryte Brothers don't take no for an answer? Rhetorical question. Let me play another card, Lawyer Lucius. There's about a dozen affidavits from bankers around West Texas that say you were the one bad-mouthing Bart Hulett's finances, trying to make it sound like the ranch and all his other business dealings were on shaky ground. Pretty stupid of you to do this yourself instead of using a cut-out man or two."

"That's a matter of rank conjecture."

Burch raised the Colt and wagged it back and forth like the conductor of a gunsmoke band. Schoenfeldt's eyes followed the pistol until he caught himself and stopped. A line of sweat appeared on his broad forehead, just below his thinning hair.

"That the way you're going to play it with the bank examiners who are looking into those loans to the Bryte Brothers for this deal? Those boys really don't have a sense of humor and don't like it when they hear about an officer of the court doing a hatchet job on a guy who is on the board of a couple of banks they oversee. Neither does the state bar association."

"That's a gross mischaracterization of what was said in those conversations. It was no secret that cattle prices had taken a hit and that several of the oil and gas deals Bart Hulett pursued were dusters."

Burch slid the Ray-Bans forward on his nose and gave Schoenfeldt a dead-eyed stare, the kind the scumbags used to dread in Dallas. Meant the hammer was about to be dropped.

"Time for my hole card, Lawyer Lucius. There's another affidavit you might not know about. From Bart Hulett, his ownsef. Filed with his local attorney and a couple of other law firms in Dallas and Austin. I've seen a copy of that. He says you threatened him with financial ruin and bodily harm if he didn't come to terms with the Bryte Brothers."

Color flushed up from Schoenfeldt's neck and flooded his face. The sweat line on his forehead started to run toward his darting eyes and down his fat cheeks.

"That's a goddam lie. I never threatened Bart Hulett."

Burch was bluffing. He knew it. So did Schoenfeldt. But the eavesdropping watchers didn't. He kept his true hole card tucked away — Lopez and the connection to Burnet. He played his bluff big.

"Oh, it gets worse, Counselor. Believe me. A whole helluva lot worse. Turns out Bart Hulett taped a phone call you made to him. Got you on tape blowing off steam about Bart siccing the bank examiners on y'all and reminding him the Bryte Brothers could hurt him and his family."

"That's another damned lie. I don't believe a word you say."

"Doesn't matter whether you do or don't, but that tape don't lie. Neither does the transcript. Copies of both are at those law firms I mentioned."

"If any of this were true, I'd be in jail right now. I'm not because it's not true."

"Oh, it's true, Counselor. Bet on it. The only reason you're not in jail or graveyard dead is the folks who hired me don't trust the High Sheriff of Cuervo County to do his righteous duty. Haven't turned the tape and transcript over to him yet. They sent me up here first to see what I could stir up."

"You're stirrin' up a washtub of horseshit."

"I'm preachin' the gospel to you, Counselor — God's own truth. And you keep forgetting something — Bart Hulett is dead. Got killed in that barn fire about three days after you threatened him on the phone. Makes you the perfect fit for a murder rap. It'll be circumstantial, but men have been sent to the chair on less."

"I didn't have a thing to do with Bart Hulett's death."

"No, but you know who did."

"I don't know a thing."

Burch stood, tipping the chair forward until the ladder-back banged into the edge of Schoenfeldt's desk. Still straddling the chair, he stepped forward and grabbed the lawyer by the shirt collar, jerking him off his padded leather perch and jamming the Colt into the side of his neck.

"You sure as hell do know something, you puzzle-gut shitbird. And if you don't tell me right now, I'm gonna blow a hole right through your carotid artery. Who killed Bart Hulett? Talk fast, asshole. You're a dead man if you don't."

Burch could see a dark stain grow across the crotch of the lawyer's creased khakis. He was shaking and whimpering. Burch tightened his grip and jammed the Colt deeper into flesh. The words tumbled out in a rush of fear fever.

"Bart Hulett wasn't supposed to die. They were just trying to scare him. Just trying to get him back to the table. Prove they could hurt him where he lived. Prove they could ruin him if he wouldn't play ball."

"Who? The Bryte Brothers?"

Schoenfeldt nodded, his eyes bulging in pure terror that Burch and his Colt didn't cause. Burch growled in the lawyer's ear.

"A name, shitbird. Who pulled the strings on this deal? Gimme a name."

The lawyer gave him two. Burch released his grip and Schoenfeldt staggered back, tumbling into his chair.

"I wouldn't give a dried cow chip for your chances, Counselor. You were circling the drain before I got here, but you flat flushed yourself just now. Better say your last words to Jesus and say 'em fast."

Burch slipped out the way he came in with the Colt still in his left hand. He heard the front door rattle as he locked and shut the back, then ambled up the dimly lit hallway that smelled like broken dreams, desert dust from decades past and cat piss.

Twenty-Four

The cup was halfway to Carla Sue's lips when she heard Garza's bellow echoing down the tiled hallway that ran from his office to the den where she was curled up on a leather couch, sipping coffee and reading the latest copy of *Texas Monthly*.

She knew just enough Spanish to get the gist of Garza's tirade. Chopping off a man's balls. Force feeding them one by one to the owner. Then killing him slow, piece by piece. Till he screamed for a mercy that would not be granted.

Jesus. So much for a quiet morning coffee. So much for finishing a Joe Nick Patoski profile on Joe Ely.

Love me some Joe Ely. Yessir, ol' Joe is in heavy rotation on my personal playlist. Got me "Cool Rockin' Loretta," "Cornbread Moon," "Hard Livin'" and that Jimmy Dale Gilmore classic, "Dallas," and it's opening line: "Did you ever see Dallas from a DC-9 at night?"

Well, Dallas is a woman who will walk on you when you're down
But when you are up, she's the kind you want to take around,
But Dallas ain't a woman to help you get your feet on the ground
Yes Dallas is a woman who will walk on you when you're down ...

Jimmy Dale nailed Dallas in his song. His Lubbock buddy Joe Ely sang it true, his edgy and plaintive cover waiting with his other tunes on a road mix cassette in her Cutlass convertible. The boulevard cruiser, sitting in the garage of a friend in San Antonio, waxed red steel waiting for her roundabout return.

Song reminded her of what Big 'Un used to say about his city, which he always called "The D," never its full name. Cold and mirthless. A place where the rich ate their young. No pity for losers on the downhill slide. That earned you a stiletto heel to the eyeball.

Big 'Un should know. He was living a dead-end life in The D. But at least he was semi-safe. Until he was stupid enough to come back to these border badlands.

She heard Garza's bootheels thunder down the hallway. She killed the soundtrack playing in her mind, put down the cup and magazine and waited for him to enter the den. She knew their conversation would be unpleasant and could take a lethal turn if she didn't play it just right.

Right on the edge. Hard-nosed and smart-assed. Backing down could earn her a bullet.

Garza rounded the corner and entered the den, his face red and the twin inverted Vs of his eyebrows and moustache knotted in anger. She pinned him with a blue laser stare and lit him up with some up-holler brass.

"Who the fuck thumped your balls and got you bellowin' like a boy calf on the cuttin' table? Can't even enjoy a quiet cup of coffee with all the yellin' you're doin'."

Garza stopped and looked startled. The inverted Vs relaxed. He laughed. It sounded like the sharp bark of a coyote calling the pack to a fresh kill. The image of a deer carcass in the moonlight flashed across Carla Sue's brain. She hoped it wasn't an omen.

"Who pissed in your Cheerios, lover boy? Flores again? Another probe or is he upping the ante?"

Garza's reply was clipped and cold: "It isn't Flores. It's your friend, the cop from Dallas."

"Ex-cop. And he's not my friend. What did he do that's got you so pissed off?"

Garza hooked a hassock for an overstuffed easy chair with his bootheel and slid it across the polished wooden floor. It stopped next to her perch on the couch. After four long strides, he was seated and facing her, gripping her wrists in each hand, his face close, his eyes locked on hers.

She didn't blink and kept the blue heat in her eyes. He told her what Burch did to Chuy Reynaldo — the bushwhack and beat-down at the convenience store, the *mota*-and-spilled tequila frame-up, the scrawled note on the inside of a matchbook cover, the anonymous call to the Rangers and the Presidio County sheriff's office.

Garza catalogued Chuy's injuries — a severe concussion, double vision, five teeth broken off at the gumline, a lacerated scalp, a swollen jaw, broken ribs and a busted nose. Bruised and bandaged, Garza's top *sicario* was cooling his heels in the Presidio County jail in Marfa, booked on charges that ranged from suspicion of murder and marijuana possession to public intoxication and driving without valid proof of insurance.

Carla Sue stifled a smile. Big 'Un had outfoxed Garza's best man, serving him up like a corny dog at the Texas State Fair with a dollop of mustard on top. The lawdogs were eyeing Chuy for Bart Hulett's death and the local district attorney got bail denied at the preliminary hearing.

She was proud of Big 'Un. Not sure why, but didn't let it show. She kept looking into Garza's eyes as he told her of the message Burch gave Chuy, a message meant for him. *Stop trying to kill me. I know you didn't have Bart Hulett killed. I know you wanted to, but somebody beat you to the punch. I'm after that somebody, not you. Let's have a sit-down.*

"*Coño*, this bastard has a big set of *cojones* on him. A pea-sized brain, but balls that clank."

"That's what they say about Mario Cuomo."

"*¿Cómo?* Oh, the governor of New York. His balls may clank, but he'll never be president of the United States and he knows it. He looks too much like a Mafia don. Or one of us. America will never elect a president who is black, brown, yellow or red. Or somebody who looks like he just came off the boat from Sicily."

"So Burch and Cuomo both have balls that clank. Did you send Chuy out to kill him?"

"*Sí.* How did you say it the other night — *plumo o plumo?*"

"Pretty goddam stupid if you ask me. And you didn't. You're damn lucky Burch didn't just kill him. This Hulett guy's death is a sideshow and a luxury you can't afford. You wanted the guy dead and he got dead. What the hell does it matter to you how he got dead or who did it? You let your vanity get in the way of logic. Now you got one of your top hands tied up at the very time you need all your muscle against Flores."

She was very close to overplaying her hand and she knew it. The Vs were knotted again. His eyes were frosty.

"Maybe now is the time for you to tell me more about how you and your friend met. Or should I call him your associate."

"More like partner in crime. We both wanted the same man dead. And we sent him to hell."

She told it straight. Told Malo about that old Dallas pimp and drug lord, Neville Ross, ordering T-Roy to set up the hit on her Uncle Harlan. T-Roy double-crossing Ross and disappearing into Mexico. Burch blaming T-Roy for the death of his partner. Ross framing Burch for the murder of T-Roy's mistress to strap him into a kill-or-be-killed straitjacket. The shoot-out at Ross's ranch where she pumped eight hollow-points into that silver-haired shitass, earning her equal billing with Burch on a wanted poster.

At some point, she stopped seeing Garza, his face replaced by the smells, sounds and images from the tale she told.

The stench of blood and burnt gunpowder. A Colt booming in a bat cave. The quivering flesh of a freshly excised heart. Burch, naked and hogtied on a stone altar. T-Roy's death mask, one eye cored by hollow-point from her gun, the other giving the look of a shark that could still kill.

She felt drained when she finished.

"Were you lovers?"

The question pissed her off. Her blue eyes blazed as they locked on Garza again.

"Hell, no. I did have to listen to him bang his ex-wife a couple of times while I was trying to sleep in her living room."

"No three-way?"

"No, asshole. I liked her, though. Strong woman. She was another one who got dead in this deal. Collateral damage. Killing T-Roy didn't make up for that. Didn't make up for Uncle Harlan or Burch's dead partner."

Garza's face softened. He looked at her without trying to stare a hole into her skull.

"You avenged your uncle's death. There's honor in that, but it doesn't erase the pain of losing someone so close. For you or Burch. I respect what the two of you did."

"Does that mean you're going to have a sit-down with Burch?"

"We'll see. Maybe I'll greet him at the door with a hot lead handshake."

"Jesus. *Plumo o plumo.* You're like a broken record. And it's really starting to piss me off."

"Not a hard thing to do, my little hillbilly lover."

"Listen to what I'm telling you, then do what you want. But listen, first. I learned one thing about Burch — he's a helluva lot smarter and tougher than he looks. And he makes people pay for underestimating him. Your man Chuy just found that out the hard way."

"I should kill him for that alone. It's going to cost me a lot of money to get Chuy out of jail."

"Money you've got plenty of. What you need is more muscle and more eyes and ears. Burch can be the latter. Who's he working for?"

"Gyp Hulett, Bart's cousin."

"That's the one you do business with, right? Hell, that means Burch is already working for you. At arm's length. He's already told you he's not coming after you. Sit him down and see what he has to say. Rough him up if you want to. But let him keep poking around that Hulett fella's killing."

"You've convinced me, but I'm tired of talking about this Burch. Something more interesting has caught my attention."

He leaned forward and kissed her, kneading a breast through silk fabric with his left hand. *Let Burch do his thing. Then let Chuy kill him.*

She tongued Garza's mouth and stroked his cock through his trousers. *I bought you a reprieve, Big 'Un. But I didn't buy you salvation.*

Twenty-Five

The high heat of mid-afternoon baked the bare rocks and dirt of the rise that gave a barren vista to an abandoned, adobe brick house with better days decades gone.

Strictly ghost town decor. The front door was missing, the window glass was busted out and the flat tin roof had gaping, lace-edged holes caused by rust cancer that left random skylights and a swaybacked sag to the ridge.

The strip of tin shielding the concrete block front porch was warped and dented, but cancer-free. Better grade of metal. Or newer. One edge was unmoored from the weathered *piñon* rafters, free to flap and bang in the hot wind.

Burch sat on a rusty metal chair under the thin strip of shade offered by the anchored end of the porch roof, his boots propped up on a plastic milk crate. The Winchester pump rested across his lap with six buckshot shells in the tube and one in the chamber. The Colt was cocked, locked and holstered. Extra shells and spare mags bulged the pockets of his windbreaker.

From where he sat, Burch could look down the long slope of the rutted gravel drive that led to the four-lane spur to Faver, roughly fifteen miles away. Ol' Blue was parked near the mouth of the drive, pointed toward town, hood jacked up, thin, bluish smoke rising from the engine.

The smoke was a juke — fresh Havoline poured on the hot block by his own hand — a small hunk of bait for the trap he set. The stench of fried 10W30 would linger long after the smoke was gone, selling Ol' Blue as a broke-down junker. All the smart gumshoes use Texaco for better trickery.

No motor oil slathered over the biggest hunk of bait — himself, sitting bigger than life on the porch of a house that looked like it was sliced from the gunfight finale of *Rio Bravo*. He pulled his flask from an inside pocket and took a short pull of Maker's.

Here's to hopin' I didn't set a trap for myself.

Whisky without the 'e' was his only company. No reinforcements from the phone calls he made in Alpine. None he could see or hear. Nobody in the house. No trucks or Jeeps rumbling up the goat trail in back. No Comanche bird whistles from the brush. Yet. He'd settle for toothless old Stumpy and his double-barreled scattergun. See how far the old man could still toss a stick of dynamite.

He figured those phony well-digger watchers were about thirty minutes behind him. Maybe a few ticks more if they let Lawyer Lucius plead for mercy before popping him. The mouthpiece was a dead man as soon as he coughed up those two names.

Deke Clayton and Benton Henderson. Bright boys for the Bryte Brothers. Burch scrawled them on three steno pad sheets, each with a short, terse note: *These are the fucks you want.* Folded and stuffed in his wallet, where anybody could find it. And two places that might be overlooked — his right boot sock and down his shorts, tucked under his balls. Just in case this little showdown went sideways on him.

The first name the mouthpiece gave him sounded like an *hombre* who didn't mind getting dirty at a distance. Put the play in motion and pay the grunts who did the wet work. Former muscle jockeying a desk, maybe. Second name sounded like a higher-up who never got grime under his fingernails, but gave the final okay to those who did.

Burch knew the watchers would be in a hurry to smoke him next. Before he could pass those names up the line. To a client. A lawyer. A lawdog. Contain the problem. Eliminate the risk. Do it quick. Do it now. Shut it down so the big boys can relax over a bourbon-and-branch or three and a thick porterhouse at Pappas Brothers.

He was counting on them running in high gear. Favoring speed and violent action over caution. If they were pros, they wouldn't be totally reckless. But they would have — how would the suits say it? — ah, an overriding sense of urgency.

Got an urgent need to waste your ass, right, sport model? So urgent they trip over their own dicks. Leastwise, you hope they do.

Don't need much, Wynn. Just a slip will do. Anything that gives me an edge.

Why the pump? You shoot better with that Colt.

Insurance and intimidation. You taught me that, slick. Besides, who says I'm gonna use the scattergun on these assholes?

Pump for show, the Colt for go?

You catch on quick. For a dead guy.

Fuck you, sport model.

Love you, too, partner.

Burch needed to stay on the porch long enough for the watchers to see him and head his way. After that, it would get real Western, real fast.

He eyed the empty doorframe to his left. Across its threshold and into the striated light and dark of the dusty interior lived an illusion of solid cover that vanished as soon as Burch ran a hand over crumbling adobe brick. Anything north of a cap gun could blow holes through the front wall.

A better bet was a brush-choked drainage ditch to his right. It offered chest-high cover and a gravel bottom that felt firm under foot. He had already checked the ditch for snake dens — none of the overpowering stench of rattler musk — and chucked rocks into the biggest brush piles — no angry whir of rattles.

At the back end of the ditch was a brushy hidey-hole that covered the rear of the house and the front left corner. That would be where he'd take his last stand. At the front end, another clump of brush covered the porch and the last few yards of the rutted drive after it topped the rise.

He lit a Lucky and waited. *All set for the party. All that's missing is the guests — both the friendly and hostile kind. Hate that this is turning into a one-man Alamo kinda deal.*

Where the hell are your buddies, sport model?

Don't know, Wynn.

Well, this here kinda sucks the big wiener, them leavin' you hangin' like this.

Me and you faced longer odds.

Operative phrase bein' "me and you." Two of us. Only one of you at this goat ropin'.

Don't I know it.

Stay chilly, partner.

Only way to play it.

Tires crunched across gravel. Burch saw the gray Dodge pickup nose along the far flank of Ol' Blue, leaving only the snout and part of the right front tire exposed. Smart play, grabbing cover where there was little to be found. Bad news, though. Showed they weren't in a tactically reckless rush.

Upping the ante was the only play. Burch ditched the Lucky, stood up and raised the Model 12 to his shoulder.

Time for a little buckshot music.

Helmet Hair leaning over the far front fender of Ol' Blue. Shades flipped up across his forehead. Looking at the big six. Smelling the oil. Blond locks framed by the raised hood and the near fender. Fifty yards out. Too far for a riot pump.

Aim high. Three rounds rapid. Boom-boom-boom. Three mule kicks to the shoulder. Glassy pump action. The solid thwack of lead striking metal and the sound of shattered glass. Sorry, Blue.

Helmet Hair out of sight. Hunkering behind the far fender. Using the big six for cover. Maybe.

Three side steps to the left. Gun still up. Eyes searching. Duck behind the near side of the doorframe. New angle. Rear of the Dodge crew cab in sight.

Aim high. Three more rounds rapid. Three more mule kicks. More metal thwacks and shattered glass. On Ol' Blue and the Dodge. Two steps to the right. Crouch to reload. Knees popping in protest.

Quick look around the doorframe. Helmet Hair braced against the rear of Ol' Blue's cab. Long, wicked rifle barrel dipping down to center on his head.

Nose-dive to his right, spawling across the dirt floor. Six fast shots from Helmet Hair. Deep-throated cracks. Splintered wood and jets of pulverized adobe spurting where Burch's head was a nanosecond ago.

High-velocity reminder — no cover here. None at all. Move. Move. Move your fat ass, old man. A skittering crawl toward the back door. Knees and elbows screaming. Shotgun in the dirt. Dirt in the mouth, beard and nose. Dirt dusting his glasses.

Four more cracks. The zipping buzz of lethal bees.

What the hell is he shootin'? Big caliber with a deep magazine. Man wants to reach out and touch me. Make me dead. Right now. Move, old man, move. Tumble out the back door.

More rounds thrown his way, turning the front wall into powder and thudding into the back. But not through. Good to know.

Crouching run to the drainage ditch. Jump to the bottom. Pain shooting from his knees to the roof of his mouth. Can't see the trucks from here. Sweat fogging the glasses. Hobble to the front of the ditch, head down.

Shuck the windbreaker. Hang it on the backside branches of the first brushy hidey-hole. Grab the extra mags. Leave the buckshot shells. Prop the shotgun in the crook of a stout brush branch. Poke the barrel out front. Hobble back to the last stand station.

Spit on the grimy glasses. Scrub the lenses clear with a bandana. Swipe that dirty rag across the face.

Skin the Colt. Spit. Wait. Spit. And sweat some more.

The faint murmur of an engine. Grinding gears. Behind him. An echo against the rocks? Shit, they're leaving. Stay chilly. Wait. Silence. Shit, they're gone.

Wrong. Four more deep-throated cracks. Followed by five. A little recon by fire. To keep his head down. Bad guys still here. So am I, motherfuckers.

Minutes and more sweat. The long gun was silent. Boots scuffling across gravel. Closer. Colt in his left hand. Eyes on the front corner of the house. Closer.

Helmet Hair at the corner. Eyes running the ditch. Pivots left and raises the long gun — an FN FAL with a folding stock. NATO favorite. Stuttering rip of a mag emptied on full auto. Shredded windbreaker. Dust and flying branches. Metal sparks. Ruined shotgun.

Wait. Wait. Helmet Hair drops the empty mag. Burch steps from cover.

No cop's warning. No "freeze, asshole!" Let the Colt do the talking. Under the black flag. Deep booms. Eight Flying Ashtrays downrange. All center mass.

Helmet Hair twists and shudders. Gun spinning to the dirt. Body follows. Got you, motherfucker. Drop the Colt's empty mag. Slam a fresh one home. Ears ringing. Eyes to the front corner. One more bad guy out there. One more to get. Bust 'em or blow 'em down.

Maybe not. Deep, booming voice punching through his deafness. Gyp Hulett.

"Put that gun down NOW, son. Do it or die. Your choice."

Burch clambered out of the ditch like a gut-shot bear and staggered to his feet. Gun up, he kept his eyes on Helmet Hair's still body as he lumbered toward the front of the house.

Helmet Hair was on his back, his shirtfront shredded and bloody, his mouth open in silent protest of sudden death, his blue eyes staring at a high sky he could no longer see, his face frozen in an angry grimace.

His shades were still perched on top of his forehead. Burch toed the body with a boot, then bent down and slipped the shades over the dead man's glower.

"Here you go, slick. Got your cool back with them shades on. You can't believe you got gunned by a second-rater like me. Look pissed about it. You ain't the first one to make that mistake."

Using his sweat-soaked bandana, Burch pulled a big wheelgun from a belt slide holster riding the dead man's left hip. A Smith & Wesson Model 27 .357 with a dark blue finish and a threaded barrel.

Southpaw. Like me. Toting an old-school revolver rigged to take a silencer. Handy for quietly whacking Lawyer Lucius in his Alpine office.

He stuffed the Smith behind his back, picked up the FN with his right hand and straightened up.

Be back later, slick, to get your particulars. Rifle through your wallet. See who you were before some pill-popping drunk from The D stopped your clock. Shades make you look like David Soul playing the killer cop in Magnum Force. *Before* Starsky & Hutch. *Before Huggy Bear.*

Dead looks good on you.

Burch barked a sharp laugh at his own little joke then took a deep breath to stifle the post-gunfight giggles and steady himself. He glanced over at the brush where his shredded windbreaker was hanging, twisted and tangled by high-velocity lead. The stock to his Model 12 was shattered into bright splinters.

"Gyp Hulett — that you out there?"

"You bet, son. Me and the other scumbag. Saved him so you could have a chat with the boy."

"Comin' out."

Burch rounded the corner. Hulett was standing near the front porch, his Hi-Power leveled at the other watcher, a nervous-looking dude with unruly brown hair stuffed under a blue ballcap. He didn't look happy, shifting his eye from Hulett's gun to the Colt in Burch's hand.

Burch ignored him and growled at Hulett.

"Glad you could finally make it, old man."

"You did awright."

"No thanks to you, slick."

"You gonna get all pissy on me like a schoolgirl?"

"Believe I can do better than that."

"Oh, I seen you work out on a man with a sap. Mighty impressive. But me and the boys were curious to see how a big-city detective handled himself going up against somebody who wasn't tied up to a chair with the shit kicked out of him already."

Two of Hulett's crew stepped from the brush, cradling shotguns and smiling. Burch placed the FN on the porch, setting it down carefully so it wouldn't be scarred by the rough concrete blocks. He dug out his Luckies and hung a bent nail on his lip, then looked at Hulett and his crew and grinned.

"How'd I do, boys?"

"Pleasure to watch you work, son. Suckered them right on in here and nailed the gun hand. Noticed you emptied your gun on him. Why was that?"

"He wasn't going down fast enough."

Burch growling. Hulett chuckling and shaking his head.

"He'd of done the same to you. Neat trick you pulled with that windbreaker. Fooled him."

"He got stupid and got in a hurry. Thought having more gun made him bulletproof."

"His mistake. Now, what do you want to do with this shitbird?"

"Bring that cattle prod?"

"You bet."

The bushy-haired watcher looked pale and shaky — like a man

having a hard time putting up a tough front. Burch lit the Lucky then ambled over to get in the man's face.

"What's your name, slick?"

"Lawyer."

"Wrong answer, asshole. Ain't no law here. Not a badge among us. Sure as hell ain't no lawyers. We're playing by a whole different set of rules. Truth be told, we threw the rule book right out the window, so you can take that hardass con game and stuff it straight up your ass."

"Lawyer."

Burch sighed, then locked the safety on the Colt and handed it to Hulett. He grabbed the man's shirt with his left hand and belted him three times with his right fist. With a fourth punch, he knocked the man to the ground.

"Best answer the man's question, boy. Seen him beat a man half to death with a sap for being a smart mouth."

The watcher looked up at Hulett, then at Burch, blood streaming from his nose.

"Let's try it again, slick. What's your name?"

"Burghardt. Charley Burghardt."

A jolt ran through Burch's brain. Lopez's puzzling last word. A yellow wrapper with a flying W fluttering to the ground.

Hamburguesa. Hamburger. Whataburger. Burghardt.

He looked at Hulett. The wolf smile flashed as the old outlaw handed back the Colt and holstered his Hi-Power. A deal remembered.

"You a barnburner, Charley?"

They were in a flat about a half mile down the goat trail that ran from the back of the house, shielded by creosote, yucca and cholla. A jacked-up Chevy four-by with a short box, knobby and oversized backcountry tires and a roll bar with poacher's lights clamped on top sat on the trail, dust covering its dark blue paint. A rig only a bubba or *tejano* would love.

Hulett handled the high-voltage prod, a crude-looking wooden baton with a Bakelite handle and an on-off button on one end and a tip made from the same kind of plastic with two naked copper electrodes poking through. He called it The Persuader and it was clear this wasn't the first time he had used it on a human target.

Burch handled the questions, looming over Burghardt, who was tied to the rusty metal chair from the front porch, shirtless, with his jeans around his ankles, blood from his busted nose dripping down his chest and belly. Boxers instead of briefs.

"Listen here, Charley — when I asked if you were a barnburner, that was an entirely rhetorical question. We already know you are. We had a chat with the *hombre* that was your guide dog and lookout. Gave us your name and told us you burned down Bart Hulett's barn. Called you *El Incendiario.*"

Burghardt said nothing and bled some more. Burch nodded. With a faint wolf smile, Hulett dipped in with the grace of a *matador* and delivered the first zap to an armpit, causing the target's left arm and shoulder muscles to spasm. Burhardt bellowed an epithet that always got a baseball player tossed when he hurled it at an umpire.

"Did you just call my friend a motherfucker, Charley? He's many things, most of them bad, but I don't think that's one of them. I do think he likes to use that cattle prod, so maybe you're right."

Burch nodded. Hulett ducked in again. Another zap to the other armpit. More bellowing, incoherent and strangled. A dark stain spread across the front of Burghardt's boxers. The stench rose from the chair.

"You're a man who likes to yell, Charley. That's good. Exercises the lungs. Nobody to hear you out here. Just us. Your blond buddy's a hunk of dog meat that'll be feeding the coyotes soon. Nobody's comin' to rescue you. But you keep up the yellin' if it makes you feel better."

Burch leaned in close, aiming a hoarse whisper at Burghardt's left ear.

"You stink to high heaven, Charley. Pissed and shit your drawers. Let me tell you, though — those first two hits were just love taps. Just a taste of what's next."

Burch paused and cupped Burghardt's chin in his hand, tilting his head up to stare into his eyes.

"Do yourself a favor, Charley. Give us the name of the guy who hired you. We already know you were working for the Bryte Brothers, but we need a name. More than one, truth be told. Need the name of your contact here, the guy who set you up with the guide dog. Need the names of the guys who hired you."

Burghardt's head hung low. He took a deep, ragged breath and shook his head. Alamo city — Burch could tell the man was at the end of his tether, feeling shame because he wasn't nearly as tough as he thought he was but trying to make a last stand.

Burch held up two fingers and nodded at Hulett. Two zaps to the *cojones*. Screams instead of bellows.

"Enough. Enough. Jesus Christ, enough. I'll talk."

The scorecard: Four zaps from a cattle prod — two under the armpits, two to the *cojones* — were all it took to flush the dregs of Burghardt's ex-con act.

Burhardt told them everything and named the names he knew. Lucius Schoenfeldt, Deke Clayton and Needle Burnet. He only knew Lopez's last name. Same with the gun hand, Bartel.

Didn't know Benton Henderson. Never met Blue Willingham. Thought Burnet was acting on his own nickel, taking money from the Bryte Brothers to set up the burn. Talked about Bartel popping Lawyer Lucius in his office with the big, silenced Smith. Didn't let him beg for mercy.

Burghardt cast a nervous eye at Hulett and the cattle prod as he told his story. Hulett occasionally slapped the wooden barrel into his palm. Two or three times were enough to keep the pot boiling and the beans spilling. Burghardt told them about the perfect conditions for a barn burning and how he was irked about leaving the chain and padlock as a grisly warning.

"Nobody was supposed to die. Just the horses. It was supposed to scare the shit out of that rancher. Send him a message to play ball. Not kill him."

Burch could feel the rising heat of Gyp Hulett's anger. He put a hand on the old outlaw's arm and asked another question.

"Did you and Lopez pitch that chain and padlock in the brush after you found Bart dead?"

"Hell, no. We stayed long enough to make sure the fire was rolling, locked the door down with the chain and got the hell gone from there. That rancher was still sawin' z's in the big house when we left. And that chain was tight and locked."

Genuine surprise. Question caught the firebug flatfooted. Burch stepped in front of Hulett.

"Before you waste this shitbird, step over here and let me show you something."

"You gonna try to talk me out of somethin' that needs doin' again?"

Burch didn't answer Hulett. He called out to his crew.

"Get him cleaned up and ready to travel. Don't throw those boxers into the brush where the law can find them. Pitch 'em in the back of the truck."

The boys looked at Hulett and got a single nod. Burch kept leading the old outlaw until they were close to the goat track and the jacked-up Chevy, then pulled a slip of paper out of his wallet.

"Take a look at this — names I got from Schoenfeldt, that lawyer up in Alpine putting together the Bryte Brothers' deal."

Hulett reached inside his vest and pulled out a pair of reading glasses to perch on the end of his nose. Specs on a killer almost made Burch laugh. Hulett looked like the ghost of John Wesley Hardin trying to be a lawyer.

"What's this mean? 'These are the fucks you want.'"

"Message to you and Doggett in case I bought the farm. Got two more just like it tucked down a sock and my boxers. This is the one I meant for the bad guys to find so they wouldn't look for the others."

"These are Bryte Brothers guys, right?"

"Right. Burghardt just pegged Clayton as the paymaster who lined up the job. The other guy is probably upper management who greenlights getting nasty but stays clear of the details. The unseen hand. Schoenfeldt named both of them so they're a matched set on killing Bart. I got a guy who can help flesh out the details on both of them."

"Still runnin' down leads and diggin' up proof. You weren't so particular when you wrote this note."

"That was insurance in case I got snuffed. Dead man's revenge."

"But since you ain't dirt nappin' with Elvis, you want me to stick by our deal. Why keep this guy alive? We've pumped him dry and he's the guy who set the fire that killed Bart."

"I want to use him as bait. Let Doggett arrest him on suspicion of murder and arson — anything he can dream up. Cause alarm bells to start ringing in Houston. Get Burnet to jump. Maybe Blue and that third party we don't know about, too."

"Jesus Christ, no way in hell. The little shit will get sprung by some big city lawyer just as soon as those Houston bastards can fly one down here."

"I kindly doubt it. They won't want to let their names get within a thousand miles of our firebug friend. No, once they find out Burghardt's in the jug and ol' Helmet Hair is dead, they'll call Burnet. And I'm betting he is too proud to farm this one out."

"Too greedy, more like."

Burch grinned and lit a Lucky.

"I'll take either one. Or both. Just so long as he makes a move."

"And if you're wrong and a big-city lawyer shows up to spring the firebug?"

"If that happens and you can't get somebody to slip into the High Sheriff's jail and sink a shiv into that little bastard, you ain't half the outlaw you think you are. Be time to take up the rockin' chair, old man."

"You know what, our friend over there called the wrong man a motherfucker."

Burch blew smoke at the gunsight eyes and the full wolf smile.

"You're right about that."

Twenty-Six

They took the back way to Guerrero's, bouncing down ranch roads with washboard ruts that rattled the teeth and shook the rust loose from Ol' Blue's frame, running gravel tracks named for families long dead and gone and crossing the rocky beds of dry creeks that challenged the torque of the overhauled six.

Gyp Hulett, riding shotgun in the jacked-up Chevy driven by one of his crew, was in the lead. That meant Burch, with Burghardt cuffed and chained to a pop-up D-ring bolted through the passenger side floorboard, had to either eat dust or roll up the windows and get parboiled.

Burch split the difference, keeping his window rolled down after tying the bandana around his face, covering his nose and mouth. Burghardt's window, cracked from gunfight buckshot, was rolled up. *Fuck him — let him broil.* Ray-Bans covered Burch's eyes, complementing his improvised *narco* look. His shoulder holster was empty, the Colt stuffed under his belt, riding over his left kidney, the butt digging into his back.

Cop reflexes, cautious muscle memory from his days dragging perps to holding cells at George Allen. Not that the perp riding next to him was much of a threat to make a grab for his gun. Burghardt broiled, too busy trying to brace himself for the bone-jarring bumps to talk or be much trouble. Dried blood from the nose Burch busted caked the firebug's two-day stubble.

Caution was also the reason they were riding the outback trail. High-balling straight into town was too damn obvious and might spook Burnet. Better to meet Doggett at Guerrero's to hand over Burghardt. Make Burnet work to find out what was going on. Drop him a bread crumb or two, but make him guess and worry. Make the bait more tempting by making it harder to get.

Bartel's wheelgun was jammed behind the back seat, slugs dumped, wedged against the canvas case that held his ruined Winchester pump. The Smith & Wesson's serial numbers were gone, roweled off with a grinding wheel. Maybe the forensic wizards could raise them from the dead. Maybe not.

Maybe Burghardt would spill the same beans he fed Burch and Hulett. Maybe not. Didn't matter to Burch. He'd tell the chief deputy a sanitized version of his story, leaving out the cattle prod and Gyp Hulett. Then turn over the firebug, Bartel's revolver and the silencer he found in the glove box of the Dodge and let Doggett and whoever caught Schoenfeldt's murder up in Alpine worry about it. He'd even pinpoint the location of Bartel's body on a map.

What he wouldn't do was give up the cassette tape riding in the left snap pocket of his sweat-stained shirt. He found the tape and the surveillance gear in the Dodge. After listening to himself grill Schoenfeldt, he thought it would be too tempting for a Ranger or sheriff's investigator to use it to tie the lawyer's murder around his neck. Especially a lazy ass looking for a shortcut to close a case or a bent tin star with a hand out for Bryte Brothers money.

He wouldn't toss the tape. He'd stash it somewhere safe in case he did get jammed. Mail it to Boelcke, first chance he got. At the end of the recording, you could hear heavy footsteps — his boots on the hardwood floor — and the sound of a door being opened and the snick of a latch — him going through the back door.

Sobs and whimpers from a man who knew he was truly fucked. But no new voices. No pleas for mercy. No pops from a silenced pistol. Just the electronic screech of a bug getting ripped from its hiding place and squashed.

In the hands of a studhoss defense attorney, the tape would be an ace in the hole. *Hell, Racehorse Haynes got T. Cullen Davis off the hook for murdering his wife with a helluva lot less.*

Back when he wore a gold shield and believed he was on the side of the avenging angels, he hated guys like The Racehorse — and all those other high-dollar courthouse vultures with their dark, hand-tailored suits, hundred-watt smiles and forked-tongued sincerity.

More than once, he'd been sucker-punched on the witness stand by a well-coiffed hyena-for-hire, forced to watch helplessly as a murderer, a child molester or a drug dealer fandangoed their way to freedom. All because they had the gelt to hire the best mouthpiece in Satan's stable.

Now that he was a semi-outlaw his ownsef, he had a greater appreciation of the Sixth Amendment and his constitutional right to the best counsel money could buy from that plush hell known as the criminal bar. *If I get pinched, I'll be squeezing cash from you, Gyp Hulett, and you, Nita Rodriguez Wyatt. Or we'll all be bunking in the stony lonesome.*

Burch didn't like thinking about the shield he lost. Being a detective in The D had made him proud. He had the juice to make the bad guys quiver and shake. Cuff 'em or smoke 'em. Didn't matter to him. Just as long as the streets got swept clean of maggots and scumbags so Joe Bob and Janie June Citizen could sleep soundly at night.

It was righteous stuff. A constant high that fed his soul and self esteem. Better than top-shelf bourbon or a huff from an opium pipe. Better than slamming a defender pancake flat to spring a tailback to six-point paydirt.

When he still had his shield, he was as haughty and self-righteous as a deacon who saw sin in everybody but himself.

A true believer, blinded by faith. He didn't much care for the candy-ass clichés — brotherhood in blue, the thin blue line. But he had enough leftover Baptist reflexes to believe his was a higher calling.

Then he lost his shield. Nobody's fault but his. And his free-fall from grace slapped the preachy self-confidence clean out of his soul like sledgehammer strikes to a plaster wall.

No blind faith. No higher calling. No more.

Nothing but the threadbare knowledge that he still had a street cop's savvy. Still knew how to cut sign on a badass thug and hunt him down. With or without a badge.

What few beliefs he held were small and simple, scattered like broken knickknacks in the ruins of his past life. The lethal knockdown power of hollow-points from his Colt. The heft of a woman's breasts and the taste and feel of her pussy.

Making a man pay for his wicked ways. That was still big with Burch. So was the numbing grace of Percodan and ninety-proof whisky without the 'e.'

Road dust masked a deep divot that battered the springs and shocks, blurred the vision and rattled the bones and teeth. Burghardt lost his balance and slammed into Burch. Burch fought to keep Ol' Blue on the gravel track while using a forearm shiver to smack the firebug into his corner.

"Jesus, where the hell are we going?"

"Nowhere good. Now shut the fuck up, slick. Stick a cork in it and bleed quiet — *sabe?*"

They skittered and fishtailed down a steep set of switchback curves carved into a mesa overlooking Guerrero's and the narrow ribbon of asphalt that snaked past the store and crossed a sand and gravel track to form a crude four corners.

Lit by the low-angle light of a late afternoon sun, the blacktop looked like a four-lane superhighway to Burch, holding the promise of smooth, civilized driving that didn't batter the brain or butt. Not much promise offered by Guerrero's, despite a tin roof silvered by a semi-fresh paint job.

The adobe bricks of the original store were crumbling. Cracks fissured the bare concrete blocks of a back-end addition. Rust streaked the twin gas pumps out front and a lonely tin sign tacked near the door that hawked cold Tecate *cervezas.* Odds were long the sign was telling the truth.

Burch curled Ol' Blue close to the northern side of the store, blocking exit from the passenger's door. He checked the firebug's cuffs and chain before stepping out, holstering the Colt. He peeled the bandana from his face and blew dirt-laced snot into the rag, shaking his head at the buckshot holes in the hood of his truck.

The jacked-up Chevy pulled up next to the pumps. A thin, hard-looking hand named Juanito stepped from the driver's side and started pumping gas into the rig. A guzzler, not a sipper. Gyp Hulett eased out of the passenger's side, yawning and stretching the kinks out of his back as Burch walked up.

"Hey, Juanito — watch our boy over there, *por favor*, while I talk to *El Patrón.* I'll finish pumping gas into this hog."

Juanito shot Burch a glare that telegraphed hate and lethal intent, then spat out the same carnal epithet Eduardo Lopez used before shame and a leather sap broke him down and Hulett blew out his candle.

"*Chúpame la reata.*"

Burch met the glare with the flatline street cop's stare, tempered by a grin. He eased the sap out of his back pocket.

"Heard that one before. In that shed at Bart Hulett's place. You were there in the shadows, weren't you, slick?"

Juanito didn't answer.

"Tell me this, Juanito — why does every *pendejo* I've ever rousted go right to telling me to suck their cock for the ultimate insult? Pretty damn lame and predictable, if you ask me. Makes me study on the thought that you'd rather have a man suck your cock than a woman. And return the favor."

Juanito hissed a string of choice profanity at Burch and started to rush around the Chevy's tailgate. Hulett pulled his Hi-Power and cut him off in a commanding voice that carried death's cold certainty. Juanito froze.

"Back the fuck down, Juanito. Do it now or I'll kill you myself."

They watched Juanito sulk his way over to Ol' Blue, shooting dark glances at Burch before leaning against the rail on the driver's side and turning his attention to Burghardt. Hulett holstered his pistol. Burch slid the sap into his back pocket.

"Jesus. Bad enough we got to watch out for Needle Burnet, now I have to worry about this asshole?"

"Benny's his cousin. And you're the man who scrambled his eggs so hard he might never ride a horse again. Don't know that for a certain, but it's gonna be touch and go with ol' Benny for quite a while."

"Shit. Why'd you bring him?"

"To keep an eye on him. The other boys are rock solid and really don't give much of a shit about Benny. Didn't like him very much. Blood kin is a different animal."

Burch shucked a Lucky and lit it. Hulett flashed his wolf smile.

"What's the play here?"

"Dead simple. Get Javier Guerrero to call Doggett and tell him his package is here. All wrapped up with ribbons and bows. Wait on Doggett. Takes him about forty minutes to get here."

Hulett shook his head and pinned Burch with the gunsight stare.

"That all there is to it? Thought we were using this asshole as bait."

"We are."

"Don't see how."

"You weren't the only one I called when I was up in Alpine. Called Doggett, too. Got him on his private line and let him know who I was after and what I was up to. Told him he'd either get a call from Javier to come pick up a package or have to start looking for my corpse stuffed down a hole out in the desert."

"Still don't see how that sets a trap for Burnet."

"Have a little faith. Doggett said he'd let the word leak out so Burnet would hear it. Javier will call Doggett on his office line, the one he's pretty sure Burnet has tapped. Private line gets swept every day."

Hulett slow rolled a wolf smile at Burch.

"I was wrong before. You're not just a motherfucker, you're a devious motherfucker."

"That's exactly right."

As he banged through the screen door of his store, Javier Guerrero looked like a sawed-off version of Doggett — same sad eyes and drooping moustache, same dark *moreno* skin, same deep chest and bow-legged limp.

Two inches shorter, maybe, and a decade or two older. With a tight cap of black curls frosted by gray instead of Doggett's military cut. The hat he slapped on his head was greasy gray and sweat-stained instead of a Stetson straw with the crisp crease favored by Texas lawmen.

The differences weren't enough to hide being blood kin to the deputy. Cousins, most likely, and not that distant. Tall black boots with riding heels and a polished gleam marked Guerrero as a horseman. So did the buckskin gelding tied to a hitching post on the southern side of the store, opposite of where Burch parked Ol' Blue. Another trait shared with Doggett, but hardly one that marked a blood tie. Not in West Texas.

"You're Burch? Where's the package?"

The voice was gravelly, clipped and flat-toned, lacking the sing-song lilt that marked a Mexican speaking Spanish or English. Meant Guerrero spent some years away from here — long enough to rasp away the border accent and speech pattern.

Burch nodded to answer the first question, then jerked his thumb toward Ol' Blue to answer the second.

"Better to bring him inside, I think."

"You bet. You make the call?"

"Soon as I saw you coming down off the mesa. On his office line. Fella that answered said he was already on the way. Said for you boys to sit tight with the package."

"Shit. You didn't talk to Doggett? Something's up. I'll bring the package indoors. Got something to cut all this trail dust I've swallowed?"

Guerrero smiled and jerked his own thumb toward the battered tin Tecate sign.

"Cold?"

"Like your ex-wife's heart."

Said over the shoulder as he gave them his back and sauntered into his store, letting the screen door bang closed. Hulett laughed. So did Burch. *I'll be goddam. The man believes in truth in advertising.* Burch turned his head to look back at Hulett.

"Best gather up Juanito and scoot, old man. Something's got Doggett's panties in a knot and already headed this way. If Burnet does show, I don't want him spooked. I want him to see my rig and Doggett's cruiser. That's it."

"Your call. We'll grab us a couple of *cervezas* and get gone. Won't be too far away. Know where he's going to hit you from?"

Burch turned and squinted into the sun, shielding his shades from the harshest light with a cupped hand. A tall mound of rocks marked the edge of a mesa rising west of the store, jutting into the sky like the prow of a battlecruiser.

"That's where I'd be."

Thhhhhhh-wack.

High velocity lead punching a spider-web hole through the windshield of Ol' Blue. Burghardt's head jerking on impact. Small black hole over the dead man's left eye. Red mist halo rising from the crater punched through the back of the skull. Sharp crack of the shot echoing a one-Mississippi later from the mesa rocks backlit by the setting sun.

Hulett, legs braced, pulling his Hi-Power, angling it high, firing rapid rounds toward the rocks above. Burch spinning on his boot heels. Rushing Hulett. Choppy steps. Shoulder planted in the old man's hard belly, driving him to dust and gravel. Sprawling on top.

Thhhhhh-wack. Slug kicking dirt inches from Burch's face. One-Mississippi. Crack.

"Get the fuck offa me."

'Move your ass, old man. Gotta grab some cover."

Scrambling over sharp gravel and powdery dirt. All arms, hands and knees. Up on the feet, crouching low. Bobbing and weaving. Knees screaming. Dodging around the gas pumps. Diving behind the jacked-up Chevy. Crawling to put engine block iron between supersonic lead in full-metal jackets and flesh, blood and bone.

Thhhhhhh-wack. Slug punching through sheet metal. One-Mississippi. Crack.

"So much for all your bait bullshit. Burnet knew we were coming and got here first."

"You got a talent for stating the over-fucking-obvious, old man. Either Doggett got careless or somebody else on your crew is taking money from Burnet."

"Not fuckin' likely."

"Guess you forgot about our buddy Eduardo Lopez. Must be nice to erase somebody from the memory bank once you smoke 'em."

Four barking blasts — sharp and deep. Very close. Burch tracking the sound with his Colt. Guerrero in his sights, tucked behind the far corner of the store, firing an old M-1 Garand. In the American caliber — .30-06. Four more blasts toward the rocks above and the telltale "ping" of the spent clip flying free.

Kerrrrr-wow. Kerrrrr-wow. Two more blasts to their left and rear — less bass, more baritone. Juanito in a slow walk from the side of Ol' Blue, firing a Smith & Wesson Model 29 .44 magnum with a two-handed grip, barrel angled high.

A Dirty Harry moment. Juanito playing Clint. A private screening for his mind only. For two more blasts from Harry's favorite hand cannon. Kerrrrr-wow. Kerrrrr-wow.

Thhhhhhh-wack. Juanito staggering, splay-legged. Mouth open in a wide oval. Wheelgun still pointing at the rocks. A look of shock and betrayal on his face. Dark blood blooming across the chest of his pale yellow shirt.

One-Mississippi. Crack. Juanito falling away, bouncing once on his back, boots rattling the dust and gravel, pistol spinning from his hands. Stillness.

"Motherfucker thought it was High Noon *and he was Gary Cooper."*

"Wrong movie, wrong actor, old man. Every swingin' dick that carries that gun thinks he's Clint Eastwood. Even the bad hombres."

"This ain't no Hollywood movie."

"Nope. This here is your basic clusterfuck."

Four more blasts from Guerrero's M-1. The sudden crackling of automatic weapons on bush-time rock 'n' roll, echoing from the rocks above. No incoming rounds. No more thhhhhhh-wack, one-Mississippi, crack.

"Cavalry?"

"F-Troop, more likely."

A roar from the road headed north. Screeching tires. Squealing brakes. A '78 Ford Bronco with a light bar and Cuervo County markings sliding sideways into the store's dirt-and-gravel lot, raising a cloud of dust and spraying stone shards, striking the jacked-up Chevy and gas pumps like birdshot.

The Bronco stops sliding, rocking on its springs and shocks. The driver's door opens. Sudden Doggett, one boot in the dirt, the rest of him still in the cab, speaking into a radio mic, then listening to the static-filled answer.

"Got the jump on him. Thought we had him. He shot his way past us and slipped away. Had that damn AK with him. Need dogs and a tracker up here. And a meat wagon. Brewer got hit in the leg. Ricochet. Not too bad."

"Roger. I'll call this in. You boys stay sharp. He may try to circle back around now that it's gettin' dark. Check in every ten minutes. Stay off the air otherwise unless something pops."

"You'll hear if it does."

Doggett tosses the mic on the dash and steps out of the Bronco. He shakes his head as he walks their way, his eyes sad and his jaw set.

"We sure fucked this one up, boys. All to hell and back. Burnet knew what we were up to and lit a shuck for here. Slipped a tail. Got my thumb out of my ass and got here soon as I could."

"What about your boys up in the rocks up there?"

Doggett frowns.

"Sent them on ahead as insurance. Before Burnet slipped that tail. Didn't send them soon enough."

Twenty-Seven

Needle Burnet was bleeding as night fell, below the high rocks, hidden in a thicket of creosote, mesquite, Texas madrone and hackberry. He could hear voices above and the skittering sound of stones kicked loose by their movement.

Full dark was ten or fifteen minutes away. Safe to move, then. Time enough to tend to his wounds.

A long furrow plowed the length of his right forearm by a bullet. Superficial, but painful. A slug lodged in his right shoulder — a ricochet. He could feel it grind against bone whenever he moved, causing pain that shot along his neck and jaw. A deep cut grooved his cheek just an inch below his right eye, carved by a rock shard chipped loose by flying lead.

Burnet peeled back the right side of his camouflaged hunting shirt, easing his arm out of the sleeve, wincing as the fabric brushed across the forearm furrow. He wrapped that wound with an Ace bandage, tight, tucking the loose end into the last loop of the stretchy fabric.

He ripped open the pouch of a battle dressing, pressing the bandage against the jagged hole in his shoulder, using his fingers and teeth to tie it down. He eased back into his shirt, rolling the sleeve down so the Ace bandage wouldn't show in the dark, then buttoning the shirt clear to the collar to help hold the battle dressing in place.

Not bad. Have to do until he got to Lupe's across the river. He flexed the arm and felt the slug in his shoulder grate against bone. Pain he could tolerate. At least he wasn't losing a lot of blood. Just some slow seepage. Staunched by the bandages. What had leaked through his shirt was drying quickly in the desert air, leaving the fabric stiff and sticky.

Shit, ain't no thing. Got hurt worse in 'Nam, bleeding like a stuck pig with the gooks chasin' my ass. Thick as fleas on a blue-tick hound. Still slipped away to fight another day. Fuck it and drive on. Don't mean nothin'.

Dark now. Dark enough to move.

Around his neck, he draped the light netting he used to create his hide up in the rocks, then slung his rifle over his left shoulder — a bolt-action Remington 700 little different from the M-40 he carried in 'Nam.

This one had the Unertl 10X fixed-power scope, an upgrade for later generations of jarheads, instead of the piece of shit Redfield 3-9X Accu-Range scope he was stuck with while killing NVA regulars up on the DMZ. Shot .308s through a heavy Hart barrel.

A goddam tack-driver. Took down many a muley at 1,000 yards or slightly less. And the occasional two-legged quarry for Blue Willingham and others who crossed his palm with the right amount of cash. Fifty Ben Franklins would do it. Thirty, if he was in a charitable mood. He rarely was.

He hefted his AK-47 in his right hand, bought in Saigon's Bring Cash Alley and smuggled stateside under the false bottom of his footlocker. Staying in a low crouch, he slipped out of the thicket, careful to keep his face turned away from the rocks above, tugging his boonie hat low across his brow.

He followed the faint outline of a game trail through a maze of creosote brush, sotol and ocotillo, keeping an eye out for cat's claw, white-thorn acacia and other desert vegetation with the nasty habit of slashing and cutting the unwary. Ears fine-tuned for the warning rattle of a Western diamondback, king of the desert pit vipers.

He was two miles away from his brush-covered Jeep, a '65 CJ-5 painted in a mottled pattern of dull grays and browns, parked in a thicket on the near bank of a dry wash. Easy stroll, even with the spent slug grinding in his shoulder. Water and venison jerky were waiting in the Jeep, a vehicle he kept stashed in a shed behind his house, used only for hunting and never driven to town.

Water. He needed it. Drained his canteen while waiting in his hide up in the rocks. Piss poor discipline. Type of thing that could have been fatal up on the DMZ. But that was twenty years ago. Not so fatal with a gallon of water in the Jeep.

Voices from the high rocks faded as he walked. They were still looking for him up there. Dumbasses. They showed up about ten minutes before that cocksucker Burch arrived at Guerrero's with the barnburner in tow.

He stayed put, watching through the scope, working a chaw of Red Man, waiting for his chance to nail the last link between Bart Hulett's death and his Houston paymasters. They were paying him a half million for this kill, wired to a bank in Monterrey.

Nervous money for them. Deke Clayton nearly shit a brick when he dialed in with the latest intel on the plan cooked up by Burch and Doggett to grab the barnburner and his bodyguard.

Burch and Doggett. Another pair of dumbasses. Doggett thought he didn't know about that private line. Didn't think the guy who swept that line could be bought. Stupid, sad-eyed piece of shit. He was listening when Burch made that call from Alpine. Knew Schoenfeldt was dead meat, too.

That left Burghardt. Deke met his asking price. Easy money for him, large enough to take this risk and disappear from Faver for good.

Not much to leave behind. An old ranch house he rented twenty miles east of town. A roan gelding he rarely rode and a slick-forked Wade saddle. Mex kid he paid to feed and water the horse could have those.

A few whores and grass widows he favored. The whores would

only miss his money — the grass widows would find other men to fuck. His dealer — an ex-con named Luis who lived in Presidio. Not a problem. Plenty of Mexican brown floating around. Plenty of dealers.

What little he valued was in a duffle bag stuffed in the back of the Jeep, including ten thousand in walkaround money and a passport in another man's name.

The game trail became wider and the walking easier. Eyes and ears still on alert, he let his mind tally a flashback scorecard.

Semi-sweet kill shot on the barnburner. Four hundred yards. Quartering wind. Target lit up by sunlight. Hold point a tick or two low for downhill shooting and the windshield glass. Point of impact above the left eye and the red mist rising from the back of the skull. Magnified by the scope's sharp glass.

Second shot. Not so sweet. Burch moving faster than a big man should. Tackling that piece of shit, Gyp Hulett. Aiming for another head shot. Missed by a cunt hair.

Flat-out stupid pride. Wanted to nail that cocksucker. Bad. Hated that Dallas peeper. Clouded his cool. Should have aimed for center mass.

Third shot. A head-down warning. Fourth shot. A gimme. Dead easy. Just let the fool walk into the right mil-dot and gently squeeze. Like a practice shot on the range at Lejeune.

Incoming rounds from below, whanging the rocks near his hide. Movement close in — his unwelcome guests. Time to di di. Most riki-tik. Stuttering chatter and muzzle flashes to his left and right. Lead buzzing, pissed off and looking to kill. Sling the rifle. Unlimber the AK. Let fly at the flashes.

Move, move, move. Burn line along the forearm. High whine of a ricochet, spent slug smacking his shoulder. Short bursts from his AK. A muffled curse. A body biting the dust. Hope you die, motherfucker. Move, move, move.

The warning burr of a rattler. Loud and close. He froze. Flashback gone. Mind focused on the present danger. Ears sucking in the sound. Head turning to dial in the direction. At his ten o'clock. Real close.

Burnet backed away. Slowly. Five feet, ten, then thirty. The burring rose, then fell. He eyed some open ground to the right of the trail and took a detour around Brother Diamondback. Professional courtesy. *Calm down, friend. Trail's all yours. Happy hunting. Nail yourself a fat antelope squirrel.*

He was sweating and had the gunsmoke shakes. Not good. Breathe deep. Keep walking. It'll pass. Always did. Another ten minutes. Easy stroll. Keep your shit packed tight.

He hit the bank of the dry wash about fifty yards north of where he stashed the Jeep. He backtracked, then angled south through the brush, unwilling to walk along the open ground on the lip of the wash. Too risky. Too stupid.

There it was, square and dark against the surrounding thicket. He stopped to listen and watch, sliding the netting over his head and covering his face, ready with the AK. Five minutes. Make it ten. Make it twenty. No sound.

He moved quickly to the near side of the Jeep and slid the AK through some covering branches to rest the gun on the passenger seat. He shucked the brush hiding the Jeep from sight.

He unslung the rifle, snicked off the safety then slid open the bolt to clear the chamber and empty the magazine. Lake City M118 National Match rounds. None finer. He slipped the rifle into a silicone gun sock then slid that bundle into a canvas case he wedged against his duffle bag.

Water. And jerky, double-bagged in plastic and stuffed in a coffee can caked with dried axle grease and horse dung to discourage nosy critters, the lid secured by duct tape. He tossed the can up front. He winced in pain when he tried to lift the water jug with his right arm, switching to his left.

Burnet eased into the driver's seat, then took a long pull from the water jug. And another. He sighed then looked for the coffee can. It was somewhere on the floorboard, hidden by the dash. Fuck it. He settled for a fresh chaw of Red Man, working a string of tobacco into his jaw and leaning back to look at the stars and do a little after-action inventory.

Primary target taken out. Secondary targets — one miss, one kill. Two bullet wounds, none that serious. A cool half million in that Monterrey bank. Whipped cream with a cherry on top of all that long green he slowly piled up, grease for years of wet work.

Kiss that killer-for-hire bullshit goodbye. All he had to do was get to Lupe's. Get patched up and get gone. Dead easy. He fired up the Jeep and chuckled. *Beat all of you sorry bastards. Every last one.*

"Semper Fi, motherfuckers. And *adios.*"

Needle Burnet let out the clutch, reared back his head and howled like a wolf. A lone wolf who had no need of his own kind.

The tin star carnival came to Guerrero's, a law enforcement spectacle complete with yellow crime scene tape, sawhorse barriers and rotating beacons of red and blue from a dozen cruisers bouncing off the store and turning the rocks above into a garish lair for gargoyles and griffins.

The blinding white strobe and short siren blips from a meat wagon rolling into the lot added a frantic note to the grim festivities.

Deputies, state troopers and a couple of Rangers milled about in their snappy Stetson straws, each trying to look tough, essential and important while two harried crime scene investigators snapped their photos of the dead, guess-timated trajectory angles of the incoming rounds and collected spent shell casings and other evidence.

Blue Willingham, Sudden Doggett and a tall, beefy Ranger with a long, weathered face stood apart from the badge pack. The Ranger had sharp eyes that missed very little and the air of a man in charge. He listened as the High Sheriff of Cuervo County filled him in while his chief deputy toed the dirt and kept his eyes down and his mouth shut.

Burch eyed the trio but was too far away to hear their conversation.

Didn't matter. He could make a pretty educated guess at the half-truths and omissions of Willingham's spiel and how they'd track the white lies and blank spaces of the story he told Doggett while handing over Bartel's revolver and silencer about a half hour before the sheriff rolled up on the scene.

No matter how the High Sheriff told the tale, it didn't look good for his reputation or his political ambitions — having one of his top deputies turn out to be a gun for hire, killing a prime suspect in the murder of a prominent citizen, then slipping away like a ghost.

There was a tarnished silver lining to that cloud — Willingham couldn't afford to throw Burch or Doggett to the wolves. That would make the High Sheriff look too dumb to know there was a killer in his ranks. Or too scared and crooked to do anything about it.

Willingham's only play was to claim Burch and his wrecking-ball methods as his own — sell himself as the grand puppet-master pulling the strings on some regrettably rough, old-timey and messy Western justice, with Doggett as his whip hand. Even Gyp Hulett would get a free ride as a necessary evil — takes an outlaw to catch an outlaw.

A bitter cup of gall for the High Sheriff, but fuck him, he had to gulp it right down and smile like he loved it. The man was perfectly happy to let Burch do his dirty work while still taking Malo Garza's money. Perfectly happy to let Burch eat lead, too. Too damn bad if shit got slopped on his shiny boots and sullied the pure lust of his precious pursuit of power.

Burch would still spend some time in the box with that sharp-eyed Ranger. So would Doggett and Hulett. But that was strictly for show — the crossed T's and dotted I's of the Ranger's report. They all wanted this to end with Burnet in a box.

Burch closed his eyes against the harsh lights of the crime scene carnival. He sat on an overturned blue plastic bucket, boots planted in the dirt and gravel, knees throbbing, leaning his back against the warm adobe bricks of Guerrero's storefront. He was nursing a half-full bottle of Tecate that was still a cold balm to his dust-clogged throat and jangled nerves.

Javier Guerrero passed by at a dogtrot, carrying his M-1 Garand loose and low by his side. He caught Burch's eye and hefted the rifle over his head.

"Korea — Clash of '52."

Four empty bottles lined the wall next to Burch — quick-guzzled victims of a man short on whiskey and long on need of a half-pill Percodan hit. Cold Mex beer as a stand-in chaser for his pharmaceutical sacrament.

It would remain one of the mysteries of God's own universe why Javier Guerrero had Tecate in his icebox. It was the only beer Burch halfway liked, the brand his Uncle Jack favored and used to teach him how to drink when he was twelve.

Sure as hell wasn't God granting him a small favor at the end of a hellish day — unless the Good Lord was a sadist. Six to five and pick 'em on that.

An unfamiliar voice ended his spiritual odds-making. It was parade-ground loud and the owner was headed his way.

"You best get a damn tourniquet on this mess, Sheriff. Pronto. If you don't, we will."

Boots crunched the gravel with a heavy step. Burch opened his eyes and looked at the Ranger staring down at him.

"I'm Dub McKee. Need a word with you, son."

"You bet."

Burch knew the name and the reputation. A no-nonsense straight shooter. He placed the fifth Tecate, now empty, next to the other dead soldiers and stood up. Both knees popped in protest. He staggered a step. McKee blinked as Burch shook his hand.

"I got one question for you, son — you think Blue Willingham is behind all this?"

"Nope. I think he's compromised and too chickenshit to do what needs to be done. Somewhere along the way he lost his balls. That's why you got a guy like me doin' the heavy liftin' with Doggett riding shotgun."

"That ain't how Blue is telling it. To hear him tell it, you're just a piece of his master plan."

"Sad thing is he's probably got himself convinced that's true. You haulin' me in?"

"Hell no. You seem to be the only sumbitch getting anything done around here. Can't afford to put you on ice. Sober up, son. Your day ain't done. We'll talk again. Real soon."

Doggett, in his face and on the prod.

"You ride with me. Your truck is headed for the impound lot as evidence. Got anything in there you don't want found, best get it out now."

Burch hobbled over to Ol' Blue and opened the driver's door. Glass shards littered the front seat, flashing blue and red reflections from the cruiser lights. The harsh rays also lit up the blood, hair and brain matter speckling the rear window. Burghardt's corpse had been removed, slipped into a body bag and strapped to a meat wagon gurney for a final ride to the county morgue.

He flipped the seat back forward and pulled out the go-bag that held his reserve of Flying Ashtrays. From under the seat, he fished out his burglar tools, evidence of the least of his crimes. He slipped the tools and his sap into the bag and hobbled back to Doggett's Bronco.

"Where to — graybar motel again?"

"You're not that lucky. We're headed over the river to get Burnet. Snitch told me where he might hole up. Found blood up in the rocks. Means he's hurt. Got men covering some of his other hidey holes, but you and me will take this one."

"How solid is this snitch?"

"You should know — he's your lawyer."

"Boelcke? That means the info comes from Malo Garza."

"That'd be my bet."

"When did you talk to him?"

"Just now. Dialed up Javier and asked for me, not you. You were sittin' on your ass, loadin' up on Tecates. Thought you were a whiskey man."

Burch ignored the insult and eyed the timing of Boelcke's call. Way too tidy. Way too soon.

"Why the hell does Malo Garza give a shit about catchin' Needle Burnet?"

"You said it yourself, remember? He wanted Bart Hulett dead, but somebody beat him to it. Malo doesn't like being upstaged and wants to send a message. He's also got a turf war on his hands and don't need no loose cannons rolling around."

Doggett punched Burch in the chest with an index finger.

"Malo don't want him caught. He wants him dead. And Needle Burnet ain't the only loose cannon in this deal. I'd study on that if I were you."

"You ain't. Might be better if me and Gyp handled this. We got you into this mess. We ought to clean it up."

"Not a chance in hell of that happening. And this is your damn mess — Gyp Hulett was just along for the ride. Just like me."

"Don't poor-mouth like a pussy. You want Burnet dead as bad as I do. We meeting the *federales* over there or doin' this under the radar?"

"By our lonesome."

"Like I said. Flyin' the black flag. Better take off that badge. You're going to enjoy being an outlaw."

"Shut the fuck up."

Twenty-Eight

A gibbous moon rose above a thin deck of clouds, casting light over the flat river surface as they eased down a steep, sandy grade to the old smuggler's crossing. Doggett braked the Bronco to a halt at the river's edge, popped out of the cab to lock the hubs, then jumped back in and downshifted into low-range and first gear, the same granny creeper he had in Ol' Blue.

"Get ready to get your boots wet. Water will be over the floorboards when we cross."

"Just peachy. Good thing I don't give a damn about these Justins."

"Shit kickers like those? Gettin' 'em wet will add character. Hope you got an extra pair of socks in that bag. You'll need a dry pair for the hike we got to make."

Doggett looked at him and grinned. Burch hoped it meant a thaw in their private little cold war. Didn't need to be walking into a gunfight with a man who was pissed at him.

The Bronco waddled into the water like a pregnant cow, with Doggett keeping steady feet on the clutch and gas pedal for a smooth flow of power to all four wheels. His head was up as he eyed a spire of rocks on the far bank to keep the Bronco in the groove of smooth, flat stones smugglers had plunked to the river bottom since the Spanish claimed this land.

Water rose above the floorboards. Burch wedged his boots high under the dash to help keep them dry. A foolish gesture. He relaxed, lit a Lucky and blew smoke through the open passenger window into the cool night air.

The half-hit of Percodan he popped at Guerrero's kept his circuits chilly. The beer buzz was long gone. His belly rumbled, churning through a microwaved burrito, a bag of Fritos and two large black coffees he scored at the store. He popped and chewed two Tums tablets, washing them down with warm water from a G.I. canteen. Sleep was just a distant memory, something dead men do.

They reached the other side, clearing the river and climbing a steep, graded switchback cut into a bluff that rose from the sandy banks. At the top, Doggett shifted into high range, keeping power to all four wheels for the rutted road ahead.

"Where we headed?"

"Little village called Ascensión. About an hour southeast of here."

"Know it?"

"You bet. Got a lot of cousins there. My great-grandmother's people. Some like me. Others don't."

"The badge?"

"That and my great-grandfather was black."

"Didn't know that."

"No reason you would. Kind of makes me an exile in my own country. Claimed by nobody. Means I've had to work on folks to gain their trust. No hall pass for me."

"You've done okay. I see the way people look at you. How your men treat you. You ain't no outcast. Only fly in your ointment is the High Sheriff."

Doggett nodded. The conversation died out. Burch could tell it cost the chief deputy to reveal even a small nugget of himself. He might regret showing Burch anything. And with regret might come recrimination — a snarling reversal of the thaw. Instead, there was silence without tension.

Man don't much like talkin' about himself, does he, sport model?

Nope, Wynn — he sure don't. Surprised he said this much.

You kindly like the boy, doncha?

Yup. He's the one good apple in a rotten barrel.

Seems straight up and solid.

He better be, partner.

The going was second-gear slow. Sometimes granny-gear first. Rough road and a steady climb into the foothills of the Sierra del Carmen. The minutes dragged by. Burch was bored, but alert. To give his hands something to do, he pulled out the magazines for the Colt and topped them off with Flying Ashtrays.

Five Wilson Combat mags — one for the Colt, two for the pouch under his left armpit, two extras for his back pockets. Forty bucket-mouthed fat boys in the only caliber a man could count on — .45 ACP.

He could shoot well with a shotgun and was fair-to-middlin' with a rifle, enough to make Marksman with an M-14 during basic training. But when his life was on the line, he preferred to rely on the genius of John Browning and those lumbering, Mack truck hollow-points. No such thing as too many.

"Got enough dynamite there, Butch?"

It took Burch a second or two to realize Doggett was shooting a line from *Butch Cassidy and The Sundance Kid.* Doggett was almost on target with the Kid's dialogue, but not quite. Burch decided not to be a prick and call him on it. Instead, he threw out a favorite line from Butch.

"Boy, I got vision and the rest of the world wears bifocals."

Doggett snorted a laugh, then shot another line from Butch: "Who are those guys?"

"Joe Lefors, Lord Baltimore and Mr. E.H. Harriman of the Union Pacific Railroad."

"You're good."

"Damn good movie, slick. One of my favorites. Doesn't hold a candle to *She Wore a Yellow Ribbon* or *The Searchers*, but I'll watch it every time it's on the furniture what talks. So, what's the play when we get where we're going?"

"We'll get as close as we can to Ascensión, park the rig and go see one of my cousins. *Hombre* named Jose Matos. He owes me for getting his son off the hook for a little fracas on our side of the river. They're *coyotes.* Only in the skin game, though. Give the *narcos* a wide berth."

"Hard to do. Guys like Malo like to control all the action on their turf. Like to use illegals to mule dope."

"These guys are small time. If they're not on a run, we'll get the lay of the land from them. Find out if Burnet's been spotted, see if any of Malo's people are lurking and get a line on a fella named Lupe Villaneuva."

"That the fella hiding our friend Needle?"

"You catch on quick. Lupe lives at the end of a box canyon a couple of miles south of the village. Interesting guy. Ex-con. Did a bit in Huntsville for running a chop shop in Brownsville about a decade back. Rumored to be the muscle part of a forgery ring. Fake driver's licenses, Social Security cards, even passports. Burnet was a Brownsville cop at the time. Don't know what their connection is beyond that or what type of hold Needle has on Lupe."

"You've been doing your homework on this guy."

"I've been building file on Needle Burnet for a long time. Like to keep tabs on what he's up to, who he knows, who he's seen with. We'll ask my cousin, but I doubt Burnet has ever been up here before — Anglo like him would stick out like a nun at a whorehouse. He and Lupe have been spotted together at a bar in Ojinaga a time or two."

"Lemme guess. Another cousin owns the bar."

"Nah — guy I used to rodeo with when I was a young buck."

"All this homework you done on Burnet — any of it tie the High Sheriff to this deal?"

"No. My take is pretty much the same as yours — Burnet does Blue's dirty work, but he's also a free agent gun for hire. Works for the highest bidder. And Blue has turned a blind eye to that just like he has Malo Garza."

"For a kickback?"

"No. Other way 'round. Blue pays Needle a piece of what he gets from Garza to keep his damn mouth shut. Got no proof of money changing hands, but that's the play."

"What brought Lupe here?"

"Don't know. Sure wasn't family. He showed up a few years back and built himself a place back in that canyon. Comes and goes. Keeps to himself, mostly, except when he's called on. My cousins say he's a *curandero*. A folk healer. Got the gift from God, they say. People come to him for herbs and prayer and chants to ward off evil and counter *brujeria*. Witchcraft."

"I know what *brujeria* means."

Said in a terse, icy growl, matched by the sudden frost that shot through Burch's blood at the mention of witchcraft. Quick flashes of *La Madrina,* T-Roy, a stone altar, a dark knife and a winged serpent raced through his mind. Then disappeared like windblown gunsmoke.

"You okay?"

"You bet. Are we there yet, dad?"

"As a matter of fact, we are."

Doggett eased the Bronco off the rocky track and nosed the rig next to a small stand of mesquite. Burch watched him take off his straw hat and carefully place it on the dash, crown-side down to spare the crease. He unpinned his badge and tossed it on the dash with a clatter that sounded like a rattlesnake's warning.

"Like you said — the black flag. Grab that shotgun above your head. You're gonna need it."

"Will do. But right now, I gotta take a piss."

They were high up in the rocks that capped the box canyon walls rising above Lupe Villeneuva's house, following a goat track that ran just below the western rim.

Felipe Matos, Jose's son, led them in the moonlight, an old Stevens twelve-gauge pump with the double-hump receiver strapped across his back on a rope sling. Strips of leather bound the cracked stock.

The elder Matos was on a run, leading a string of illegals toward the promised land. Felipe was the son Doggett got off the hook, knew he owed his distant cousin a debt of honor and didn't balk at serving as guide for a lawman from *El Norte*. Blood ties and duty to family trumped traditional hostility between the desperado and the badge, the Texan and the Mexican.

Doggett looked like he was on a Sunday stroll, cradling a CAR-15 with two twenty-round mags taped together jungle style. Burch brought up the rear, huffing like a steam engine pulling freight cars up a steep grade and sweating like a mule.

He felt like an overgrown hunk of sausage, stuffed into a Kevlar vest Doggett made him wear, topped by his shoulder holster and a black windbreaker he wore inside out to hide the big-lettered white logo on the back — CCSO, for Cuervo County Sheriff's Office.

Burch carried a Mossberg riot pump in his right hand with a seven-round extended magazine tube and five extra buckshot shells tucked into loops of an elastic sleeve stretched over the butt end of the stock. Soot from a coal oil lantern in the Matos house blackened his face, forehead and bald crown.

Felipe told them Burnet arrived two hours after sunset — an hour before he and Doggett got there. The fugitive deputy drove in from the south, which meant he used a different river crossing known only to local *coyotes* like Matos.

He didn't pass through the village, but its people knew he arrived. Hard for a *gringo* to go unnoticed by naturally wary and watchful folks with an outlaw tradition. No sign of Malo's crew, but that didn't mean they weren't around. They weren't *gringos* and were far stealthier.

The trio had crossed the mouth of the box canyon to reach the goat track, which climbed sharply toward the canyon rim and made a steep drop at the far end. They would have to cross open ground to reach Villenueva's house. Bad juju if the moon was still up and Burnet was waiting behind a rifle scope. They'd wait until the moon set.

It was a few ticks before midnight when they started their descent. Burch's boots skittered rocks over the edge of the track. More than once, he plunked himself down on his butt to negotiate a tricky drop between the rocks, holding the shotgun out like a counterweight, hoping he didn't drop it.

The wind was picking up, whistling down the canyon like a wraith ghosting through a graveyard.

They took a breather at the bottom, crouching behind rocks, eyeing Villaneuva's house half a football field away. Burch bent over, his lungs heaving like a blacksmith's bellows, his heart pounding like John Henry's sledgehammer.

Felipe pointed out a fold in the ground, a crease that offered slight cover for a crouching approach. Doggett put a hand on his cousin's shoulder and leaned in close to whisper.

"Gracias primo. Nos tienes aquí y puedes irte ahora. Dile a tu padre que la deuda ha sido pagada."

"Me quedaré. Necesitas otra escopeta para este trabajo. La deuda no se paga hasta que esto termine."

Burch listened and watched. Doggett nodded and gave Felipe a pat on the back.

Burch approved. *Kid's got moxie and pride. Won't let Doggett send him home. Wants to see it through. Debt's not square until the deed is done. And we need a third gun on this deal. He'll do. All we got to do now is get Burnet and not get ourselves killed.*

Doggett leaned close to Burch.

"Your Spanish good enough to know what Felipe said?"

"Yup. The kid stays. He's a stand-up guy."

"Good thing. I'm thin on charm. Something else breaking our way — don't have to worry about no dogs sounding an alarm. Felipe says Lupe don't like them. Shoots any dog that gets near his house. Come to think of it, Burnet isn't much of a dog-lover either. Got in a fight with one of our trackers once for putting the boot to one of his bloodhounds."

"Reason enough to smoke both these bastards. Never did trust a man who don't like dogs."

The moon slid below the canyon rim. The ground ahead darkened. Time to move in.

Burch felt cold and clammy in the rising wind as he slowly worked his way to the back of Villaneuva's house. Doggett, with his short-barreled CAR-15, had the front door. Felipe was posted behind a pile of rocks and a clump of cacti that gave him good shooting angles on anybody who got past the older men.

He had ten minutes to slip into position and do a little scouting. The house was long and narrow, with a wood frame and stucco walls that were a pale contrast to the surrounding darkness. Looked like a shotgun layout with a front room and a long hallway aligned with both entrances, flanked by two bedrooms. Wouldn't know for sure until he got inside, but that's what years of kicking down doors told him.

The stench of an outhouse smacked Burch's nostrils as he rounded the back corner. Fighting off a gag reflex, he eased close to *la dependencia* and listened. He was rewarded with the loud gasps and moans of a man grunting through a massive shit.

"Madre de Dios, mis entrañas están en llamas."

Another loud grunt. A splash. A cry of pain.

"Oye, creo que acabo de abrir mi culo."

Burch wanted to laugh. *What's the matter, Lupe? Too many chile pequeños in your heuvos con chorizo? Been there. Makes a man worry he's going to shit out his eyeteeth. Hang tough. About to give you a different kind of pain in just a few seconds, pendejo. Take your mind clean off your digestive troubles. Better than Maalox. Guaranteed.*

Rustling from inside. The sound of crumpling paper. The quick zizz of a zipper. A contented sigh.

The door slowly opened, swinging away from Burch. Sweeping butt stroke with the shotgun, catching a fat, shaggy-haired man square on the chin and slamming him back into the outhouse.

Burch moving fast, crowding Villanueva, putting his weight behind four downward jabs with the shotgun butt. Followed by three straight shots with his right fist.

Lights out for Lupe. Wad of old newspaper jammed into his mouth. Door shut and latched. Rock wedged against the bottom edge of the outhouse door. Nice and tight. All he needed was a sign — *Ocupado. Go Away. Do Not Disturb. Out Of Order. Hazardous Waste.*

One down. One to go. Then the sound of a squeaky door hinge, causing Burch's heart to lurch and leap into his throat.

Twisting dive to the right. Belly flop of a land whale. Sharp stutter of an AK-47 on full-auto. Slugs thudding into the outhouse, shattering the midnight silence. Splintering the wood, slapping flesh, turning an unconscious man into chopped, dead meat.

Humming slugs, chasing Burch, barely missing. Two rolls to the left, with all the grace of a tumbling concrete block. Flat on his back. Shotgun up. Four shaky blasts toward the back door and a jutting black gun barrel. Jagged holes in the door. Gun barrel gone.

Muffled thud-thud-thud echoing from the front of the house. Doggett kicking in the front door? Not sure. Stutter of the AK, answered by the sharper chatter of a CAR-15. Deeper boom of a shotgun. Pistol shots. Big caliber. Muzzle flashes strobing through the windows.

Right arm numb. Stabbing pain in the shoulder. Fuck the shotgun. Up on his feet, Colt skinned, limping toward the door. Left knee locked up. Cartilage chip. No time to work it out. Inside the door, eyes adjusting to the gloom.

He was right — a shotgun house. Long hallway running from the back door to the front room. Bedrooms on both sides. Bath and a galley kitchen bringing up the rear.

Eyes forward. A lone figure framed in the open front door, straddling something on the floor he couldn't quite see. Move silent, old man. Get your ass up that hallway.

"*Been waiting a long time to kill you, Doggett. Shoulda done it a long time ago but Blue Willingham wouldn't let me. Didn't fit his grand plan."*

"Blue Willingham don't have nothin' to do with the bad blood between us. Finish it."

"No. Gonna savor this a second more, send you to hell then finish off your asshole buddy out there. Think I nailed him pretty good already. Give him the double tap and get gone."

Colt centered on the dark figure. Deep, loud growl filling the house.

"You ain't goin' nowhere, asshole."

Muzzle flashes both blinding and illuminating. Eight Flying Ashtrays rapid fire. Quick-frozen images of Needle Burnet, turning to fire a big revolver once.

Flame tongue reaching toward Burch. Big slug zizzing his ear. Burnet spinning, body jerking, arms flailing, falling as those bucket-mouth hollow-points hit.

Burch thumbing the release to let the spent mag drop, struggling to pull a fresh mag and slam it home with his weakened right hand, wincing from the white-hot pain that knifed from his shoulder and down his arm.

Colt cocked, eyes on target, limping into the front room to kick Burnet's revolver into a skittering slide across the floor.

"Paid in full, motherfucker."

Doggett, back to Burch, wheezing like a man with broken ribs, facing the door, looking at a dark, sprawling lump in the dirt.

"The kid didn't stay put. Wanted to pull his weight. We got him killed."

"Not hardly. Needle Burnet did that. And we squared the deal. For Felipe and Bart Hulett."

Burch didn't believe a single word he said.

Spent brass inventory, butts in the doorway dirt, leaning back against rough concrete blocks, breathing in the cool night air to chase the acrid stench of gunsmoke from their nostrils. Burch lit two Luckies and handed one to Doggett.

"Haven't smoked in years."

"Resume the habit. It's therapeutic."

Doggett chuckled, then hissed in pain.

"Don't make me laugh. Hurts too goddam much."

"You hit?"

"He caught me with that pistol while I was swappin' mags. Knocked me on my ass. Vest stopped the slugs. Busted a couple of ribs. You?"

"Jammed hell out of my right shoulder hittin' the dirt. Believe the man was tryin' to kill me."

"Thought he had us both. You sounded like the voice of God comin' down that hallway to nail him. Many thanks."

"*Por nada*, slick. Couldn't let him kill you — you're my ride home and my 'get-out-of-jail-free' card."

Another hiss of pain.

"Told you not to make me laugh."

"Sorry. Won't happen again."

Burch felt a twinge of sorrow as he looked at Felipe's body, sprawled face up in the front yard dirt, his old Stevens pump still in the death grip of his right hand. *Doggett was right — wasn't the boy's fight, but he signed up and we got him killed. Add another name to the scorecard of guilt.*

He shook his head then looked back at Burnet's scrawny body — a ripped camouflage rag doll staining the linoleum floor with blood. Anger burned away the sorrow. *A hunnert of this cocksucker's kind ain't worth one Felipe, let alone one Bart Hulett. Smokin' him don't square the deal. Not by a long shot. Not until I burn down those Bryte Brothers fucks.*

"C'mon. We got some bodies to move. How we gonna play this?"

"We'll take Felipe to his house. Find some of my cousins and tell them something pretty close to the truth. I'll have to come back and look his father in the eye. Don't look forward to that."

"Don't imagine you do. What about Burnet? A hole in the desert?"

"Burnet goes with us. We caught him at the crossing. The rest of the story's the same — you killed him savin' my ass. But it happened there. No Felipe. We'll scatter some brass, fire some rounds into the brush. Take his Jeep up there and shoot it up some. What about Lupe?"

"He's dogmeat. Got chopped up in the outhouse when Needle tried to nail me with that goddam AK. Missed me but killed the shit out of his buddy."

"Damn. I was hoping you sapped the shit out of him and he'd just wake up with a headache. Bad enough we got Felipe killed. Folks are gonna be pissed about their *curandero* getting iced. Hell, we ought to dial up Malo Garza and get him to clean up this mess."

A voice from the dark, sounding cultured, self-confident and amused.

"I can save you the trouble of making that call, gentlemen. I'm right here and would be glad to be of assistance. It's the least I can do since you've done me the great favor of killing this interloper."

Burch and Doggett froze, smart enough not to reach for their guns. Malo Garza stepped up where they could see him. He was flanked by four *sicarios*, guns leveled, two on each side of the *patrón* of *Los Tres Picos*.

"My men will clean up your mess and make sure the chief deputy of Cuervo County gets safely across the river with the interloper's body, back to *El Norte*, where the badge he isn't wearing means something. We'll take care of the family of this unfortunate boy who got killed and extend condolences from the two of you as well as ourselves. They'll be compensated for their loss."

"Burch rides with me."

"No, Deputy. I've been waiting to meet the famous Mister Burch for quite some time. By all accounts, he's quite the *pistolero* and I wish him to be my guest for a little while."

"Do I have a choice?"

"You do, but you wouldn't like it. Very toxic. Very permanent. I'm offering you a far more pleasant option."

Twenty-Nine

The first shot was a gloved right fist buried deep in his gut, forcing the air out of his lungs in an involuntary rush as his body automatically folded up as far as the big goon pinning his arms back from behind would allow.

The second was a left-handed sidewinder that cracked bone on the right side of his ribcage, halting his ragged recovery breath with a sharp injection of pain. The third was an overhand right to the face, busting his lower lip and filling his mouth with blood.

The glasses flying off his head were a bonus, fuzzing his view of the sow-bellied punch-out artist with the concrete fists, black beard and slick-backed hair. *Tres Flores* again. Floral-scented pomade of choice for Mex thugs like this one. And the late Eduardo Lopez.

His tormentor made the mistake of stepping in close to admire his handiwork, sneering and ready to deliver a choice insult. Burch spat mucous-laced blood into the man's face.

"Best you can do, Pancho? My granny hit harder than you, *pendejo.*"

Burch didn't see the fourth shot coming. It sent him straight into a swirling black fade out.

The water was ice cold and hit his body like an electric shock, snapping him from punchy dreamland to instant, sputtering consciousness.

His right eye was swollen shut. His lips looked like bruised and overripe plums. Every breath brought stabbing pain to his right side. He was drooling blood into his beard and the front of his shirt. Someone had shucked his Kevlar vest. The Colt and shoulder holster were also missing. So was his partial plate, probably fished out of his mouth to keep him from strangling after the knockout shot.

Burch tested the boundaries of his confined universe. He was tied to a metal folding chair, his arms bound behind him, rough rope gnawing his thighs and wrists. He scanned the darkened room with his good eye, his vision sharpened by the unseen hand of whoever had slapped his glasses back in place while he was out. A low ceiling with ancient wood rafters, guttering candles in iron wall sconces and racks of dusty bottles were all he could see.

He could hear rather than see others in the room, watching him from dark corners. A shuffled foot. The sickening sweet floral smell of pomade. A stifled cough. The strong odor of a good cigar cut through the *Tres Flores* stench and hit his nostrils, triggering a nicotine hunger.

A voice from the gloom: "Happy you could rejoin us, Mister Burch. Welcome to *Los Tres Picos*, my humble ancestral home. How do you like my wine cellar?"

Burch spat more blood on the floor. A thin blade of pain stuck his ribs.

"Make mine whiskey. Wine is just old grape juice gone sour."

Malo Garza chuckled and stepped into the light. Another dramatic entrance. A long, fat cigar with a dark wrapper jutted from his mouth like the bowsprit on a full-rigged frigate.

"Exactly what I thought a gunslinger like you would say."

"I ain't Bill Hickok." Without his teeth, Burch sounded more like Walter Brennan gumming his dialogue in *Rio Bravo*. Stumpy without the dynamite or the Duke.

"No, you're still alive, although why that is so is beyond me. You've only been in our midst a short time but have managed to attract an astounding number of enemies who want you dead."

"Including one of yours."

"Yes, which is why you're my guest tonight. Your little stunt with Chuy is costing me quite a bit of money to undo. Crooked judges and DAs don't come cheap. I'm also going to have to buy him some dentures for those teeth you knocked out."

"Tell him 'Welcome to the Poligrip club.' He's lucky I didn't just get it over with and kill him."

"That would have been an unfortunate and fatal move on your part. That you didn't I choose to view as a courtesy to me. I did get the message you gave Chuy, although he had to write it on a piece of paper. That's one of the reasons you're still alive."

"The other being I tracked down the assholes who killed Bart Hulett, doing everybody's dirty work — yours, Gyp Hulett's and Blue Willingham's."

"Yes, we all owe you for that. I can't speak for those other gentlemen, but I'm a man who pays his debts. Always. You tracked down these interlopers and saved me the trouble of killing them myself. You did me a great service, but you also left me with a dilemma. I had to pay you back for the damage you did to one of my most trusted lieutenants. That's why I had my men rough you up a little. Not as bad as what you did to Chuy, but enough to balance the ledger."

"I ain't done yet. The paymaster and the suit who greenlighted this deal are still above ground."

"True, but I've already addressed that. I've had some intermediaries contact the Bryte Brothers and let them know they're no longer welcome to play in my backyard. In truth, they never were. They'll be selling their holdings in Cuervo County to me at a deep discount and moving on to greener and less dangerous pastures. When they have done that, I'll consider the matter fully closed. I urge you to do the same."

"Gyp Hulett might have something to say about that. Blood is thicker than business."

"You let me worry about our mutual friend Gyp. I believe I can convince him of the folly of any further pursuit of vengeance that could only draw more attention to our business here. I suggest you concentrate on licking your wounds and getting ready to return to Dallas as soon as you can."

"If you say so."

"I'm afraid I do. I also strongly advise against you ever returning to Cuervo County. My decision to let you live is a limited guarantee. Voiding that would greatly upset the person who gave me another reason not to kill you."

"Who would that be?"

"I believe you know her — the lovely Carla Sue Cantrell. She was quite the staunch advocate on your behalf. I was moved by her story of your mutual pursuit of the man behind the death of her uncle and your partner. There is great honor in that."

"I'll be goddam."

"Come back here and you will be."

"You look the same — old, ugly and beat to shit."

"Nice to see you, too, slick. You couldn't stand it if I was in my Sunday best. Wouldn't be able to keep your hands off me."

"Don't flatter yourself, Big 'Un. You're a mistake I've always been able to avoid."

"Mistake is just another word for temptation. Step over to my good side so I can see you, slick. Malo's boys left me with only one eye that will open."

"Kinda like you better with a busted jaw. Less backtalk."

Carla Sue Cantrell stepped into his line of sight, a slight smile on her thin lips, her blue eyes still icy clear and permanently startled, her hair a little longer than he remembered and a lighter shade of dirty blonde. She was wearing a black leather jacket with a dark blouse, jeans and boots that blended into the deep shadows of the single digit hours before dawn.

He had to rely on his memory to fill in the details — the small, crescent-shaped scar on her cheek; the taut, horsewoman's body, hard muscles softened by full curves. He also remembered the .45 in her purse and how those blue eyes flashed when she shot somebody.

She stood next to the passenger door of a Ford F-250 four-by, a well-worn ranch vehicle that smelled of old sweat, stale cigarette smoke, oiled leather and dried dung. He was slouching on the bench seat just inside that door, plunked there by two Garza thugs who carried him from the wine cellar through the front doors of the big house, trying to find a way to sit that didn't cause his shoulder and ribs to fire off flares of pain.

"Here's your iron and your fake teeth." She handed him the Colt, tucked into his shoulder holster, and a small paper towel packet wrapped in a rubber band that he assumed held his partial plate.

She clunked an ice bag on the dash — an old-fashioned fabric oval with the plastic neck and screw-on top. "You'll want to ice down that eye. Your flak vest and canvas bag's in back."

"Right thoughtful of Malo's crew to tote my luggage before beatin' the shit out of me. You one of Malo's go-fers these days? A maid or a house mouse?"

"Movin' up in the organization. Done so well I just got a promotion to chauffeur. Got to haul your sorry ass across the river and get you cleaned up and doctored up. You stink to high heaven and need those ribs looked at. Think you can hang tough for a couple of hours without dyin' or passin' out on me?"

"I'm too damn ornery to die, slick, but I can't guarantee I won't pass out or fall asleep. Bring me that go-bag. Got some mother's little helpers that will ease my pain."

They bumped along in the deepest dark before dawn, headed for a different river crossing, a shallow ford south of Las Vibras built up by

Garza's men to keep the law and rival *narcos* guessing. Carla Sue knew the way, which told Burch she knew deep details about the man's organization and the rugged terrain surrounding *rancho Los Tres Picos.*

Didn't surprise Burch. She was a double-tough, sharp and dangerous woman who used her brains and body to gull and outwit two *narcos* he watched her kill with her own big Colt. She thrived on the lethal voltage of a high-wire double-cross.

Garza better watch his pompous ass. Check that — keep letting her run her game, Malo. I'll get a fifty-yard-line seat, a hot dog and a cold Tecate, then lean back and watch. Bet she's playin' footsie with the hombre muscling in on your turf and got you thinking she's spying for you. Bet she's playin' the both of you hombres.

The truck lurched into a deep rut, bouncing them both hard and drawing a sharp and single "Fuck!" from Carla Sue, spat from the side of her mouth in an up-holler twang as she fought the wheel. Burch dropped the ice bag he had pressed against his eye and was conscious of the pain flares shooting from his shoulder and ribs. But with two tabs of Percodan under his belt, he was floating in a state of pharmaceutical grace that made it feel like another man's agony.

"Sorry, Big 'Un. That one slipped up on me."

"Don't worry about it, slick. Long as I got my narcotic Jesus, I'm fine. Puts the pain in another area code and keeps the demons in their holes."

"What the hell do you mean by demons?"

"You oughta know. You were there. Got nightmares about T-Roy, that stone altar and that knife he was fixing to cut my heart out with before you blew him down. Except he's still alive. All shot to hell, one eye just a jagged hole, smellin' like the grave. Ready to finish the job."

He could feel Carla Sue's eyes on him but stared straight into the dark where the demons were out of their holes. Waiting.

"And you — you just give me the kiss-off and walk away. That winged serpent and those other demons he was always raving about are there, hovering in the dark. I wake up screaming, but not before T-Roy brings that knife down and starts sawing into my chest."

"Jesus, Big 'Un. You live with that shit?"

"Every damn day since that deal went down. It was bad for a good long while. Until I figured out how to hose those demons down with bourbon and these little jewels."

He fished out his bottle of Percodans and gave it a rattle that sounded like beans shaken in a hollowed-out gourd.

"Funny thing. When I work, I'm semi-okay. Downtime and I get the shakes. Since I landed in the middle of all this shit, I been right as rain. Or as right as I figure I'm ever gonna be. Just enough Maker's and pills to maintain. Feels like the old days. Back when I had a shield. A gen-u-wine, by-gawd murder cop. Except I ain't playin' by those rules. Been flyin' the black flag on this one. Everybody dies."

A soft, low chuckle from Carla Sue.

"Everybody but you, right, Big 'Un? You were flyin' that blag flag last time I saw you. We both were. You were a badass then. You still are no matter how much whiskey and mother's little helpers it takes to get you down the road."

"Maybe so. But I'm deep in Indian country on this one, ridin' solo. Everybody's got an angle. More than a few want me dead."

"I know. That's why I'm driving you across this river and making sure we get you somewheres safe. Nobody hurts you long as I'm here. Not Malo and not nobody else. And I'm not going to give you a kiss-off and walk away."

"Malo said you told him about our little revenge run. Said there was honor in it that touched his coal-black heart."

That drew another low, soft chuckle.

"If I'd left it up to Malo, you'd already be dirt nappin' in a desert hole somewheres. And I just bought you a temporary hall pass."

"How'd you change his mind?"

"Told him if he didn't let me take you across that river, I'd take a walk from our little deal and he'd never get to fuck me again."

"What is your little deal, slick?"

"You oughta know. You were there for my last floor show."

"Yeah, I know. Playin' both ends against the middle, takin' their money and leavin' 'em dead with that Colt. One of these days, somebody's going to yank you off that high wire you like to walk."

"You sound like my Uncle Harlan. I was his shinin' pride, so he always worried about me."

"Don't know about that. Never had the pleasure. Damn shame. Think I would have enjoyed spendin' time with him."

"Believe you're right. He liked bubbas and good ol' boys who could hold their liquor, handle a gun and knew how to act right."

"One thing I do know — I don't have to worry about you shootin' me."

"What makes you so sure?"

"I ain't got no money."

A sudden, thunderous snort drew Carla Sue's attention from the gravel track in the headlight beams to the snoring hulk slumping in the corner of the truck cab, the go-bag wedged behind his head, serving as a half-assed pillow.

She was tempted to smack him in the shoulder to stop the chainsaw sounds Burch had been making since sliding into dreamland, but couldn't remember which one was jammed up. Let him sleep. She could always stuff cotton in her ears. Or two of his Lucky Strikes.

Big 'Un. In about the same sorry shape he was when *La Madrina's* crew took him across the river at Los Ebanos a little more than a year ago. A little less bloody, maybe. And his jaw wasn't broken. But beat to hell all the same and giving off the jangled vibes of a guy with frayed wiring and blown fuses.

Sure didn't look like the guy who smoked two Flores *sicarios* and whipped the ass of Malo's best gunhand, leaving him soaked in tequila and framed for a marijuana and murder bounce.

Nice touch with the weed. In Texas, you could murder a man and get off light, particularly if he was a shitass what needed killin'. But get caught with a baggie of home-rolled doobies and you'd wind up under the jail. For decades. What was the saying of that blowhard sheriff? Oh, yeah — We're Texas Tough On Drugs.

She almost laughed when Malo told her the part about the planted joints. Fit Big 'Un to a T. A badass with a sense of humor and an eye for drama. But she fretted about his nightmares. She had witnessed the same madness — not as up close and personal, but near enough. Hadn't left her screaming in her sleep and shaky when awake. Might mean there was something broken in Big 'Un that couldn't be fixed.

She hoped not. She would never admit it to him, but she was fond of the slumbering wreck in the corner of the truck cab. They both came from hillbilly stock — East Tennessee by way of North Dallas for her; North Carolina via North Texas for him. They each recognized the up-holler grit in the other and fell into an easy, rednecky and smartass banter that shouldered aside the more formal speech patterns they saved for polite company.

But the bond between them was darker and deeper than that, seared by that bloody revenge run to kill T-Roy and settle the score for her Uncle Harlan's murder and the killing of Big 'Un's partner. Code of the mountains and the tough Scots-Irish people who lived there.

They were north of the river, about another hour out with three hours before dawn. The gravel track was a private ranch road that ended at a locked gate and cattle guard that fronted two-lane, farm-to-market blacktop thirty miles southwest of Faver.

Before he nodded off, Big 'Un gave her a key hooked to a rectangular blue plastic fob etched with a motel name and address.

The Cactus Blossom. Good deal. She knew the place. They wouldn't have to parade through town to get there. They'd hole up until she got him showered, bedded down and doctored up, then figure out a safer hidey hole where he could heal up and get gone.

Savin' Big 'Un's ass again. Getting to be a goddam habit. Carla Sue grinned, her teeth flashing in the low dashboard glow. Followed by another low, soft chuckle.

Big Un snored.

Thirty

In his dreams, Burch was on the gridiron again, pulling out to lead a back around the corner on a toss play — Southern Cal's Student Body Right, copied by every team that ran the Power-I — the smell of sweat, fear and torn turf in his nostrils, the taste of blood in his mouth.

The wide-eyed look on the linebacker's face as Burch smacked him with forearm and shoulder pads, driving him into the dirt. The grunts and roar of the cleated herd rushing past. The back barreling into daylight. In his Percodan dreams, it was 1965 and he was a fast, svelte and brutal beast who would never grow fat, bald and old.

The image died a sudden death, gone like a TV snapped off by a grouchy pensioner finally bound for bed. Burch's eyes popped open, an adrenaline spike kicking his heart into high gear as he searched for his Colt and felt the weight of something move behind him.

"Easy, Big 'Un. It's just me."

Carla Sue's body felt cool against his back as she slid into bed, flipping the sheet to cover them both, her heavy breasts pressing into his shoulder blades.

"Thought I was a mistake you didn't want to make."

"I changed my mind. Most women do that, you know."

"You ain't most women."

"Shut up, dumbass."

Her breath felt hot as she nibbled his ear, then gently turned him onto his back. Her nipples dragged across his chest as her mouth found his, tongue stabbing deep and dancing with his. He cupped her ass with his hands and pulled, wincing as pain knifed his ribs and shoulder.

"Relax, Big 'Un. I know what you want."

She straddled his chest, then grabbed the headboard, sliding forward to lower her cunt to his mouth and tongue. Slow, rocking motion with her hips. His tongue probing deep, tasting her sweet saltiness. She threw her head back, the dirty blonde hair falling away from her face, moaning softly at first, followed by a low growl as his tongue found her clit.

Carla Sue reached back to stroke his cock. Then she spun around, taking it in her mouth as she ground her cunt against his face. Burch felt the cum rising in his balls. She grabbed the base of his cock and gave the head a thump with her finger.

"Not yet. We're just gettin' started."

She pivoted to lower herself onto his cock. She looked down at him, her hair falling forward, a smile on her lips.

"Glad to see you live up to your name."

"Ed Earl?"

"I never call you that, Big 'Un."

Burch rose from the deep well of drugged and sex-induced sleep with the snot-nosed reluctance of a fourth-grader. He wanted to stay in its depths and resented the hell out of the tiny warning bell in his brain that wouldn't stop ringing.

He slowly opened his only good eye, keeping the lid half closed, peeking through the lashes, the room a blur without his glasses. He could see a faint shaft of gray angling through a gap in the drapes. Dawn's early light, but that was about it. He was wide awake, but kept still, feeling Carla Sue's warm body against him, her arm draped across his chest, her head tucked in the hollow of his neck and undamaged shoulder.

She was sleeping soundly, her slow breath tickling his chest hairs. Must be the cause of that warning bell. He smiled to himself, enjoying a carnal playback. After riding his cock to a mutual climax, she sucked and stroked him until he took her from behind, shoulder and ribs be damned, thrusting hard enough for the headboard to bang against the wall as their cries filled the room, the pain making him last longer.

He drifted back down into the well, but the warning bell started ringing again. *Wake the fuck up, asshole. Somebody else in the room. How'd they get in without that cockeyed door screeching across the concrete? Fuckin' motel finally fixed the goddam door. Too doped up to notice when we came in.*

Wake the fuck up.

He opened the good eye wide — no sense playin' possum — and reached for the Colt on the nightstand with his left hand. Carla Sue murmured in sleepy protest and burrowed closer.

"You won't need that, *señor*. I'm here to talk. I've got a gun on you both, but I'm here to talk."

Carla Sue bolted upright in bed, jerking the Colt from underneath his outstretched hand and spinning to point it at the intruder with a buck naked, two-hand grip. *Good form, slick. Bouncing breasts a bonus.*

"Who the fuck are you? You got two seconds before I blow you straight to hell."

"Easy, slick. Man said he's here to talk. Let him talk."

"*Sí*, like I said. I'm here to talk. And listen. I'll put down my gun if you do the same."

"You first or we all go to hell."

Burch could make out the shape of a man seated in one of the room's ladder-back chairs, reaching toward the coffee table. He heard the sound of metal clattering on wood. Carla Sue lowered the Colt but it didn't leave her hands.

Burch clicked on the bed table lamp and slipped on his glasses. The room snapped into focus. There sat the gaunt Mexican in the black suit he caught watching him at Bart Hulett's funeral, a faint smile on his lips. A Walther PPK was on the coffee table in front of him.

"Who the hell are you, mister?"

"Best answer her, slick. Before she changes her mind and shoots you."

"My name is Vicente Roca and I believe we have a matter of mutual interest to discuss."

"You gave me the slip at the funeral parlor. Thought you were a ghost."

"I'm very much flesh and blood, *señor*. I'm very sorry to disturb your sleep, but I thought it best to slip inside before the sun came up. To avoid prying eyes."

"How long have you been sittin' there?"

"About an hour, *más o menos*."

"Do us a favor. Turn around so the lady can get dressed, then we'll talk."

Roca spun his chair around to face the opposite wall. Carla Sue handed him the Colt.

"You blast his ass, Big 'Un, if he twitches funny."

"Yes, ma'am."

Carla Sue bounded across the bed to clothes piled on the other side. Burch took in the show — the muscular ass, the swinging breasts — and sounded a low whistle. She shot him a smile and a middle digit. She shimmied into black jeans and slipped into a speed-snap shirt of the same color, leaving the tails out. Bra and panties stayed on the floor.

"You can turn around now, slick. I've got a pretty good idea who you are. You're the mechanic Malo Garza hired to kill Bart Hulett. Word is you're a specialist who can make it look like an accident."

Roca didn't bother to spin the chair around. He straddled it, facing Burch and Carla Sue with his hands hanging loose over the top of the ladder-back.

"I can do better than that, *señor.* I can make a murder look like a natural death." Roca held up the index and middle finger of his right hand, pumping his thumb three times.

"With a hypo?"

"*Sí,* loaded with something potassium based that leaves just what a medical examiner would expect to find with a natural death. There are other options as well."

Burch kept his eye on Roca as he found his shirt on the floor and dug out his Luckies and Zippo. Five smokes left. Need to get the motel owner to do a run for whiskey, food and cigs. He lit a bent nail, taking care not to deeply inhale, ignoring the shirt and his jeans, wrapping the top sheet around his gut.

"If things had gone like Malo planned it, I would've been goin' after you. But these other guys beat you to the punch. Beat Malo, too."

"That is correct. And I now know that having you pursuing me is not a very pleasant prospect. But that's not what happened."

"No, it ain't. So what kind of mutual interest do you think we have?"

"I'll get to that in a moment, but let me explain myself a bit. When I agree to take on a client, his problem becomes my problem. I tend to get very possessive and won't rest until I eliminate that problem. It is as if the client ceases to exist and I cannot rest until the problem that has become mine no longer exists."

"Not sure I follow."

"I lost far more than money when Bart Hulett died by the hands of others. I take a great deal of pride in what I do. And when it gets taken away from me like this, it's like a piece of me has been carved away and lost."

"Why were you tailing me?"

Roca laughed then reached into the inside pocket of his coat. The Colt came up.

"Permit me to join you in a smoke."

Burch nodded and Roca pulled out a thin cigar, firing it up with a slender silver butane lighter.

"I started tailing you because my initial information was that you were the man who killed Bart Hulett. At least, that was the conjecture after you killed those two gunmen — you were a gun for hire, just arrived in town to do work for parties unknown."

"Yeah, the High Sheriff had people believing I was the second coming of the Black Death and John Wesley Hardin. Had every dead body in the county hung around my neck."

"I quickly learned this was a fiction created by people who weren't interested in the truth. I also learned that you were the only person interested in finding out the truth and doing something about it. That changed the reason for me following you."

"I felt eyes on me the whole time."

"Yes, but mine weren't the only ones watching. You attracted a lot of attention from some very bad men. That you're still alive and have brought the ultimate justice to those who deserve it is impressive."

"Maybe so, but I was still hornin' in on something you felt you owned."

"Yes, but for some reason, that didn't bother me as long I was there to witness it — or see your handiwork afterwards."

"The job still isn't done, but I've taken this as far as I can."

"I know. That's why I am here. To finish the work you started and restore the natural order. My natural order."

Burch took a shallow drag to give himself time to think. Getting to those Bryte Brothers honchos by the book was a dead end. Didn't have a lick of evidence tying them to Bart Hulett's death. All the living links were dead. Nothing else to work with. Nothing to hand to Doggett or that Ranger, Dub McKee.

Getting them under the black flag wasn't in the cards. He was banged up, running out of whiskey and pills and his nerves were scorched and flayed. Besides, Houston was the home of a homicide dick who bore him a terminal grudge and would love to see him hang. Hell, Cider Jones would bring his own rope. Blamed Burch for getting his partner killed and burned with a hatred he knew only too well, the kind that uses guilt and self-loathing as primary fuels.

Even if Burch got lucky then sidestepped Jones, Malo Garza would send some of his boys to park him in a desert hole. Or a landfill near DFW. Whatever was handy. Wouldn't matter to Burch where his body wound up.

Fuck the book, sport model. Fuck Malo. Fuck Cider Jones. Keep flyin' the black flag as best you can. By proxy, if need be.

He gave Roca the two names he wanted — Deke Clayton and Benton Henderson.

"Hope you like Houston."

"One of my favorite cities in all of Texas. I am in your debt, *señor.* And now, if you'll permit me to pick up my gun, I'll take my leave."

Roca pocketed his pistol, took a quick peek through the drapes, then cracked open the door and slipped through like liquid smoke.

Burch stubbed out his Lucky, put the Colt on the nightstand and eased back into bed.

"Lock that door and jam that chair under the knob."

"That man is bat-shit crazy and spooky as hell."

"A mite on the obsessive side. Reminds me a little bit of T-Roy. Why don't you shuck those clothes and get back in bed?"

"Why would I want to do that?"

"You'll think of something."

Thirty-One

Night fell hard and fast, opening the overhead vault of glittering stars and a waning moon still bright enough to outshine the lone, flickering streetlamp at the far end of the motel parking lot. Made it easy to see movement if a man stood still while looking through a gap in the drapes with the room lights off.

Burch did that for a thirty-minute stint, careful to stay back four or five feet so his pale face wouldn't show. Carla Sue took another thirty-minute turn, standing in the same place, covering her blonde hair with that black leather jacket. Rinse and repeat.

Nada. Didn't mean there wasn't anybody out there. Just that they didn't show.

Time to go. Back across the river for Carla Sue. A safer hidey hole for him — Gyp Hulett's place.

The old outlaw was already on the way with a few of his crew, the trusted ones who didn't have cousins working for Malo Garza. They'd gather up Burch, stop by the home of an old horse doctor who patched up gunshot wounds and other two-legged maladies on the sly, then head for the lawless side of the Devil's Backbone.

For a one-eyed fat man with a banged-up shoulder and cracked ribs, Burch felt semi-normal. He had a fresh bottle — Evan Williams instead of Maker's — and a carton of Lucky Strikes. His belly was full of good grease — burgers and burritos. His carnal itch had been well scratched. And his blessed rite of mixing bourbon and Percodan kept the pain and the demons at bay — a blasphemous Eucharist perfect for unrepentant desperados and ex-cops. A redundancy in his case.

He wasn't coughing up blood, so reckoned his ribs were cracked but not busted into bone spears and piercing the lungs or other innards. The horse doc would make sure. Carla Sue had his right shoulder wrapped tight with an Ace bandage, which came in the same box as the food, whiskey and cigarettes, fetched by the motel owner, a bald and bandy-legged retired oil and gas tool salesman named Roland Sparks.

Sparks had an enormous handlebar moustache, its gray hairs waxed into place, and the tight-lipped discretion of a man whose business depended on people who wanted to fuck someone who was not their wife or husband. Burch called him to the room while Carla Sue was in the shower, slipped him a fifty lifted from her wallet and sent him on a run.

"Sure do appreciate your doin' this for us, Mister Sparks. We don't get to see each other that often and need to keep it on the QT because her and me ain't, well, uh, because..." Burch let his voice trail off.

"Say no more, son. Say no more. Glad to do it. I understand your need for privacy and hope you and your lady have a nice stay here. Got just one thing to ask — could you keep it down a little bit? Y'all got a little loud and rowdy last night and the couple next door complained. Course, they was here for the same reason as y'all so really don't have no call to gripe."

"You bet."

"Don't mind me askin' — how'd you get that eye?"

"Bar fight. Fella put his paws on Sally Ann — whoops, I shouldn't of said her name. She's got kin around here."

"Understand. Your secret's safe with me. I'll be right back."

As soon as Sparks closed the door, Carla Sue stepped out of the bathroom, a thin towel wrapped around her body, drying her dark blonde hair with another.

"Sweet Jesus, Big 'Un — could you have laid it on the man any thicker? And I sure as hell ain't no Sally Ann."

"Thought I played the bashful cheater pretty good. Just enough 'aw shucks' to sell it."

"Think he bought it?"

"Believe he did. Never can tell, though."

So far, their luck was holding. Needed to for one more slow-motion hour. Burch took another turn at the window, replaying the conversation again — his hustle, Sparks' response — listening for false notes. Prudent thing to do since he was betting on the sleazy honor of a no-tell motel owner who catered to cheating spouses and was supposed to keep his mouth zippered.

A sharp gambler would call it a sucker's bet, but Burch was going with his gut — fine-tuned by years of reading killers, thieves, con artists, whores and pimps at a glance. The street cop's take: Sparks was a stand-up guy working a dingy trade. Repeat cheaters looking for a regular matinee of mattress rodeo kept him in the black. Random overnighters with the same randy itch were gravy he'd like to lap up more regularly. A loose tongue would wreck his chances.

Burch knew he still had to do the lawdog dance with Doggett, the High Sheriff and Ranger McKee. That didn't worry him much. He'd have Boelcke at his side and the lawyer would have the tape of him grilling Schoenfeldt in his safe.

But he wasn't ready to meet them yet. He wanted the horse doc to check him out, then hole up at Gyp's a day or two to rest and think without people barging in, trying to kill him.

Let the tin stars sweat a little. Let 'em think Malo snuffed out my candle. When I'm good and ready, I'll stroll in and do the dance. Then get the hell back to The D and disappear into a deep whiskey fog for a while.

Get a big dose of that carnal medicine from Carol Ann. "I got all the cure you can stand." I'll need it after this goat ropin'.

To keep the demons at bay. And dull the heartache he knew he'd feel just as soon as Carla Sue walked out that motel room door.

She'd be a bittersweet memory. One he'd eventually savor. For a long time.

There was another reason for stalling the tin stars. He wanted to have a serious talk with Gyp about Bart Hulett's daughter, the wild and reckless Stella Rae.

They both knew she played a role in her father's death. She may not have set the barn on fire, but she sure as hell ran that chain back through the door handles after Bart blasted his way in with a shotgun, burning her hand and arm on the hot metal links.

Burch couldn't prove it, but that's what his gut told him. Stella Rae wanted her daddy dead, closing off the only way out of that flaming death trap, then tossing the chain into the brush when those rafters collapsed and crushed him, leaving only a shrunken corpse — shriveled, blackened and almost anonymous.

The reasons why didn't matter to Burch. He knew her motives were rooted in some twisted family dynamic he didn't give a damn to hear. What mattered was Stella Rae slamming that barn door shut on her father and the final rattle of those seared chain links.

He wanted Gyp to see that ugly truth and suck it down. Stare down the gunsight glare and force the old outlaw to shoulder the dark weight of another in a long line of Hulett family sins. He also wanted to go eyeball-to-eyeball one more time with Stella Rae, nail her again with his harsh gospel and watch her soul flinch.

He owed that much to Bart Hulett, a man he never met. After that, he was done, his debt paid. She was Gyp's problem, her perfidy a matter for blood kin to settle. Or ignore.

"They're here, Big 'Un."

Burch stepped behind Carla Sue and trained his one eye on the gap in the drapes. He saw the jacked-up Chevy roll past with two of Gyp's crew perched on the side rails of the pickup bed, hefting long guns he couldn't quite make out. Then came Gyp's dark green C-20 and a dusty blue, four-door Suburban four-by-four he didn't recognize, gun muzzles poking from the rolled down windows.

The three vehicles wheeled around to form a shallow horseshoe, the hollow centered on Carla Sue's pickup, parked nose-first one floor below their motel room door. Men spilled from the idling trucks, spreading out along the metal flanks, guns covering a wide arc of the rocky moonlit ground beyond the gravel lot.

Burch wrapped his arms around Carla Sue and pulled her close, leaning down to nibble on her ear. She leaned against him, then turned to hug him hard. He winced, but didn't flinch. She slipped a hand behind his head to guide him toward her lips, searing him with a kiss that was all tongue and heated breath.

"Still think I'm a mistake?"

She rested her head on his chest and gave a low chuckle.

"Not a mistake. Not even a temptation. You're a bad habit a woman could get used to."

He cupped her chin in his hand and tilted her head up so he could look her in the eye.

"Let's not kid ourselves, slick. You love that high wire way too much to ever change. And I'm just smart enough to never ask you to. Besides, after the fire died down, we'd probably shoot each other."

She grinned and shook her head.

"I'd never shoot you, Big 'Un. You ain't got no money."

Burch laughed then kissed her again. Long and hard. Like it was for the last time. She broke the kiss then whispered in his ear.

"*Adios,* Big 'Un. Get your ass back to The D and don't come back. I'll wait here till you're gone, then slip back across the river."

"Not sure that's the smart play. You stuck your neck out for me with Malo. He might want to take an axe to it."

"You let me study on Malo. Now get yourself gone. And Big 'Un? Think about me every once in a while."

"Count on it, slick. But only for the rest of my life."

"Did you get that bastard?"

"Graveyard dead."

Gyp Hulett smiled his wolf smile and shook Burch's hand. They were standing on the concrete walkway of the motel's first floor, leaning on the hood of Carla Sue's pickup, using the engine block and thin sheet metal as a flimsy shield against any high-velocity trouble.

In the rising morning light, Burch could see the Ford was dust-covered and dull brown, about the color of something plopped from the south end of a northbound cow. Still gave him slight comfort to have a quarter-ton of steel as cover, no matter the ugly hue. Better than the bare-ass walk he made from Room 35 to the steel stairway halfway down the second-floor balcony, his scalp twitching like spiders were running across it as he imaged cross-hairs centered on his skull.

"You look beat to shit. Malo's boys put the boots to you?"

Burch dug a Lucky out of a half-finished pack, fired it up and nodded.

"Payback for what I did to one of his gun hands, but he decided to let me live for services rendered. For now. Long as I get the hell out of Dodge and never come back."

"That sorry-ass greaser wanted Bart dead. He's damn lucky we ain't gunnin' for him."

"The man's a fuckin' control freak who sees himself as a man of honor. He wanted Bart killed his way. By his lights, nailin' the shitasses who beat him to the punch squares the books and earns me the right to stay vertical for a while."

"The books ain't squared with me. Not by a long shot. That greaser is going to pay a price for wanting a Hulett dead."

"That's between him and you. Burnet's dead and I'm out. I've taken this deal as far as I can. I can't touch the Houston boys who made this happen, but I have put something in play with someone who can."

Burch told Gyp about Roca's visit, his way with a needle and his lethal obsession with anyone who horned in on a job he considered his own. He ground out the Lucky with his boot heel, then stared straight into those gunsight eyes.

"You and me got one more thing to settle. Stella Rae."

"What about her?"

"She had a hand in Bart's death. She didn't set that barn on fire, but she made sure he couldn't get out."

"You think I don't know that? I'm the one who showed you that chain and that busted padlock, remember? Or is your brain too scrambled by all them pills you wash down with whiskey?"

"My memory's fine, old man, but we never talked about what that chain meant. I didn't know for sure until I saw that bandage on her hand and arm at Bart's funeral. I can't prove a damn thing, but you and I both know what she did. And you need to stare that truth dead in the eye and own it. I can't touch her and wouldn't if I could. That's between blood kin."

The gunsight eyes broke away. The old outlaw shook his head. When he spoke, his voice sounded tired and ancient, like an old-time preacher wrapping up a reading from Leviticus.

"Awright, then. Blood kin it is. A family matter between her and me."

Burch felt like a half ton of pig iron had been lifted off his chest. All he had to do was have a hard talk with Stella Rae, stay alive and return to the mirthless charms of The D.

Gyp told him to stay put, then trotted over to the green C-20 and swung it around so the passenger door was just a few feet from where Burch stood. He stepped into the cab, wincing from twin flares of pain, dropping the go-bag on the floorboard.

Burch badly wanted a long pull from the bottle in that bag, but left it zipped up and resting between his boots. He made his mind blank and pulled the Colt from his shoulder holster, checking to make sure a live round was in the pipe, then snicking off the safety.

"Expecting trouble?"

"Always."

A quick scramble of armed men swinging aboard the Suburban and jacked-up Chevy. A three-truck convoy spewing gravel, roaring and fishtailing out of the motel lot — Suburban in the lead, Gyp following, the outback Chevy rig bringing up the rear.

Cussing from Gyp. Gears grinding, three-on-the-tree shifter sticking between first and second. Suburban leaping ahead by forty yards. Chevy jamming on the brakes, smacking the rear bumper of Gyp's truck.

Whiplash and familiar pain flares. Hard head thunk into the windshield. Gear unstuck, dropping firmly into second. Gyp mashing the accelerator to close the gap.

Burch, eyes ahead, spotting the sudden flash of three automatic weapons from roadside rocks, hearing the deadly stutter a split-second later.

Bright sparks rippling along the passenger side of the Suburban. Jacketed lead chopping up men closest to the incoming rounds. Suburban slewing sideways, skidding to a stop. Survivors spilling out the driver's side, returning fire.

Gyp jamming on the brakes. Burch rolling down the window, firing the Colt with his damaged right hand, trying to line up the sights with his left eye, teeth grinding against the pain.

Dark car, big and fast, leaping from the backside of the abandoned gas station.

Blinding high beams. Bone-jarring boom of a T-bone hit. Squeal of shearing metal. High harmony of shattering glass. Both vehicles in a spinning death grip. Blinding pain as Burch's bad shoulder and skull smack the door post. Colt spilling out of his hand, into the darkness.

Gyp stepping from the cab, hatless and reaching for his Hi-Power. Boots on the pavement, pistol rising toward the rocks. Slugs smacking metal and flesh, jerking Gyp's body on impact. Dead before he hits the ground.

Burch helpless. No gun. Door jammed. The round moon face of Chuy Reynaldo, bloody and sporting a gap-toothed smile, rising in the door window frame.

"Got you now, pendejo."

"Get it done, you cockbite motherfucker."

"Killing you is gonna be a pleasure. Wish I could do it twice."

"You talk too goddam much. Sound like a goddam whore on the make."

Angry scowl wiping away the smile. A step back. Burch staring down the barrel of a Colt Python at Chuy's blood-streaked face. Smile returns.

"See you in hell, cabron."

Bracing for the farewell blast. Chuy's eyes pop wide open, his mouth an 'o' of surprise and broken teeth. Solid slap of rounds hitting flesh. Chuy's face falls away.

Burch leans out the window. Dumpy body crumpled on the blacktop. Python still filling a dead man's hand. Burch looks up. Carla Sue standing on the motel balcony, slapping a fresh mag into her Colt. She spots him.

"You okay, Big 'Un? Savin' your sorry ass is gettin' to be a bad habit."

Burch slumps against the door post and smiles. Gyp's men rush past him from the jacked-up Chevy. Mop up. The whiskey bottle calls. Burch answers it, bubbling the bottle until his throat burns.

Thirty-Two

The sun was sliding behind the sharp spires of the Devil's Backbone, pushing the ridgeline's long shadow toward three ragged rows of tombstones boxed by rusty wrought iron.

A young woman with a freshly bandaged right hand stood on the outside of a gate filigreed with *fleur-de-lis,* her left hand on the latch, her body frozen in hesitation, her eyes fixed on dust spinning from the turned earth of two new graves.

One belonged to her father, Bart Hulett, and flanked the grave of her mother, Mary Nell, marked by a shared tombstone. The other belonged to her much older cousin, Gyp Hulett, and stood apart from the other graves, which held the decayed remains of the generations of good Huletts who had lived on the Seco Creek side of the Bar Double H.

To Stella Rae Hulett's eye, Gyp's tombstone looked lonely and out of place, like a sinner who stepped into a Sunday school class instead of a saloon. He was the last of the bad Huletts and by ironbound family tradition, he should have been buried with his own outlaw kind on the other side of the ridgeline.

A month ago, she had decided the age-old fiction of good and bad Huletts needed to be buried with the newly dead and had ordered the ranch hands to dig her cousin's grave near her father's. The hypocrisy that killed them both had to end. Now she had her doubts.

Goddam it, stick to your guns, girl. The flare of anger thawed her frozen hesitation. Her bitter resolve to set things right returned. She flipped the latch and pushed the gate open, ignoring the screeching protest of rusty hinges. There were no good Huletts or bad Huletts, just a family that lied to themselves and the outside world for more than a century, tainted by the same bad blood.

It was the blood that ran through her veins, pumping the evil urge to see her father dead and driving her to make sure he wouldn't get out of that burning barn alive. Her right hand bore the mark of the flame-seared chain she double wrapped through the handles of the barn door she shut, her mind the guilty scar of that last glimpse of her father, crawling through the flames and smoke.

She couldn't shake that final image. It flashed again and again in the nightmares that caused her to wake up screaming for her dead daddy. To save her. To forgive her. To end her agony. To give her peace.

She couldn't stand to stay in the ranch house that was her childhood home. Too many ghosts. Too much dread. Too many memories. Her brother, Jimmy Carl, moved in. She stayed at The Cactus Blossom, Room 35. Alone. Jason Powell was long gone. He took his ex-wife's kiss-off money and slinked back to Austin.

At daybreak, she would head for the ranch to help the hands run the cattle and plow through the paperwork of her father's estate. Big surprise there. She and her brother wouldn't inherit the ranch. They could live there as long as they liked, but her father had signed the land she loved over to a tree-hugging conservation trust. The last family tie severed.

At sunset, she would drive back to Faver and Room 35, stopping for a bottle of tequila to help her sleep. She had only one companion on these daily runs. Her great-grandfather's Colt Peacemaker, the pistol her daddy liked to carry while riding and hunting the outback.

At night, she would drink straight from the bottle and pull the pistol from its double-loop Mexican holster. She'd run the cool, ancient metal of the barrel along her cheek and under her chin. She'd cock the hammer or spin the cylinder with the loading gate open, watching the primers and bright shell bases click past.

Soothing. Peaceful. Final.

Soon, she thought. Very soon.

Thirty-Three

Burch took a sip from his double Maker's served neat, watching the blue smoke rise from a peppery H. Upmann Churchill perched on a cut-glass ashtray and thinking about nothing other than the porterhouse he planned to order for a late supper at the Hoffbrau.

He was back in The D, parked on a stool at the short end of the bar at Louie's, waiting on his buddy, Krukovitch, the cranky and contrarian columnist for the *Dallas Observer*. The place was packed with a Friday happy-hour mix of regulars, slumming coeds and frat rats from SMU and tourists from North Dallas daring to rub elbows with the great unwashed.

Loud laughter and clashing conversations drowned the jukebox favorites. A thick haze of tobacco smoke hung in the air. Whitey and Little Hutch patrolled the duckboards. Karen and Deb worked the tables.

Burch was happy to be home. He felt clean and rested. The demons were staying in their holes and he didn't have to hose them down with Percodan and whiskey. Just half a tab and three fingers to make sure they stayed put. As needed. Maybe once or twice a week.

He was financially flush and felt somewhat raffish, sporting a tailor-made brown herringbone jacket with Western piping and slash pockets, an off-white oxford shirt with pearl speed snaps, tan gabardine rancher slacks and new Lucchese boots with lizard skin vamps the color of cognac.

The threads were guilt-free gifts to himself, courtesy of blood money from a dead man and a rich woman with a wandering eye. Even though Gyp got killed, Nita Rodriguez Wyatt made good on the old outlaw's promise to wipe out his debts to his shyster, Fat Willie Nofzinger.

Pumped another fifty grand into his bank account to boot. Only one string was tied to that bounty — come see her the next time he was in Alpine. Which would be never, thanks to Malo Garza's lethal warning to stay away from West Texas.

Lookin' good, sport model.

Just followin' one of your rules of life, Wynn — a man's gotta maintain his affectations.

A black patch over his right eye was the topper. Made him look like a corporate pirate, maybe one of T. Boone Pickens' oil-patch raiders, hunting for takeover plunder.

He liked the look. Kept him from thinking about the real purpose of the patch — dressy cover for the padded gauze protecting an eye healing up from surgery for a detached retina. A late-blooming gift from Malo Garza's big-bellied punch-out artist, the one with the concrete fists and the *Tres Flores* stench.

On his second day back in The D, he woke up to find the top half of his vision in that eye gone, like someone had pulled down a window shade while he slept. Scared the shit out of him. A panicked call to Carol Ann, whose cousin was an ophthalmologist. A high-speed referral to one of the top retinal specialists in Dallas, Dr. Sachin Mudvari, a Texas transplant from Nepal.

Surgery two hours later. Doc Mudvari told him if he'd waited until lunch, he'd have been blind in that eye. That was a month ago, four weeks cooped up in his apartment, healing up under strict orders to lift nothing heavier than a whiskey glass and not bend over. Cabin fever set in, broken only by carnal nursing from Carol Ann and a call from Boelcke to tell him Nita was paying to patch up Ol' Blue. Again.

Burch took another sip of Maker's, a silent toast to the doc who saved half his sight and a dead partner whose ghost kept him semi-sane and somewhat honest. A gift box nestled in his inside jacket pocket held his thanks to Carol Ann — a silver oval pendant with a tiger's eye stone, strung with a matching silver chain. He'd give it to her over dinner at the Hoffbrau.

A long puff from the Upmann. A glance at his watch. Krukovitch was thirty minutes late. Which annoyed Burch, but meant the scribe who pissed off The D's conservative establishment and liberal martyrs in equal measure was right on time. By his lights. Burch had been putting up with his friend's habitual tardiness for more than a decade.

He loved to needle Krukovitch, a short, nervous guy who compensated by being a fiend for free weights, forties vintage suits and jackets with padded shoulders, wide and loud hand-printed ties and wing-tipped shoes with lifts. He was born in Fargo and unnerved by the worst atrocities Texas had to offer but also thought the New Deal was the origin of a cancerous socialism eating America's soul.

To Krukovich, an Anglophile who revered Churchill and the royals, FDR was America's original anti-Christ. JFK and LBJ were his hellspawn, tattooed with the mark of The Beast. He also hated Ross Perot, but loved Lincoln, Frederick Douglass and Western swing.

Burch often accused him of being a hip monarchist who wouldn't mind seeing a crowned despot rule America. Long as they could quote Proust and groove to the Ramones, the Sex Pistols and Bob Wills. And made lynching a capital crime.

Krukovitch was also a paranoid who loved a juicy conspiracy theory. He dialed Burch up three hours ago, claiming to have urgent information best told face-to-face. Probably an inside scoop on something Burch already knew — like Malo Garza still wanting him dead. More fat in his future wasn't the only reason Burch had the tailor give the jacket a generous cut — needed to be full enough to button across his gut and conceal his Colt.

Burch spotted a gray snap-brim fedora with a thick black ribbon band bobbing just below the wavy layers of smoke. Krukovitch pushed through the crowd, putting the padded shoulders of a charcoal jacket to good use, spotting Burch with a nod that caused the thick lenses of his wire-framed bifocals to flash and the Carlton stuck on his lower lip to tilt upward.

Just like FDR and his jutting cigarette holder. Perfect. A fresh needle for Burch to use. Burch slid his barstool a few inches to give Krukovitch enough room to hang an elbow on the bar, drawing a squawk of protest from a flush-faced SMUster wearing a white golf shirt with a Kappa Sig logo.

Burch growled at the frat rat: "Fuck off, kid." He flagged Whitey with a raised finger: "Need a quiet spot."

"Boss's office is empty. He won't be in till nine."

"You sure?"

"Hey, I won't tell Louie if you don't. And if he figures it out, I'll blame you."

Burch pointed at his empty glass: "Another double Maker's, neat. Get the scribe a double Very Old Barton on the rocks and a black coffee. My tab."

"I'll bring 'em back."

Burch nodded, then picked up his cigar and led Krukovitch to the inner sanctum of Louie Canelakes, the gravel-throated Greek who owned the best bar in The D. They took opposite ends of a couch with cracked leather and sagging springs. Two crates of empty Old Style longnecks served as a coffee table.

Krukovitch opened his coat to sit down, giving Burch a first look at his tie — as wide as a Love Field runway and electric blue, with parrots, pineapples and bananas haphazardly scattered like a half load of clothes spinning in the glass of a front-load dryer.

"Carmen Miranda called. She wants her headdress back."

"I'd say you look like Rooster Cogburn with that eye patch, but those threads are way too sharp to be true grit. Perfect for a funeral, though. Yours, of course."

"I've always said you're the dumbest smart guy I know. Told you a long time ago there's a codicil in my will that says I'm to be buried in a black suit, a black shirt and black boots. Man in black — just like Johnny Cash."

"We'll keep the eye patch, then. It blends. We'll sell those threads you're wearing to help pay down your bar tab. Louie will have to write off the rest as a substantial loss."

They kept up the banter till Whitey came in with their drinks and an open bottle of Maker's with the pour spout corked in the neck. Burch slipped him two fifties.

"Thanks, Whitey. Keep it. I may slip out the back when I leave. Close the door on your way out."

Whitey palmed the fifties then shot Burch a deadpan look: "An aristocrat, eh?"

"Dead uncle with some oil wells."

"Right." The door snicked shut.

"You shouldn't lie to your bartender. That's worse than telling lies to a priest."

"Is the Krukovitch confessional open?"

Krukovitch made the sign of the cross then took a long sip of whiskey, chasing it with a coffee.

"Tell me of your sins, my son. Spare no detail, for Christ's love covers all."

Burch made his confession, winding his way from Bart Hulett's death to the final shootout at The Cactus Blossom where Gyp Hulett and Chuy Reynaldo were killed.

No apologies for his actions. Very little remorse. He told the story flat and straight, without gaudy flourish or cheap rationalization, like an old soldier recalling the details of battles and fallen comrades for their own sake, capturing the details before they fully faded away. He left out only three names — Carla Sue, Stella Rae and Vicente Roca.

Never did get to take another run at Stella Rae, a debt he still owed her father, a guilt she would carry to her grave, early or late. After the gunfight at The Cactus Blossom, Carla Sue split before the tin stars arrived. Doggett and the Rangers hustled him out of town, stashing him in an Odessa motel for a session that was one part third-degree grilling about Garza and the blonde in his motel room and two parts making it clear the death of Bart Hulett was a closed case, officially marked as a tragic accidental death.

They gave him a one-way ticket to Love Field and told him to stay the hell out of West Texas. Dub McKee pulled him aside, shook his hand and gave him a card embossed with the Rangers' star-in-a-wheel badge.

"Weren't for you, these hombres would have gotten away with it. We'll remember what you did. We'll also remember what some other folks did or didn't do and make sure they're held accountable. That includes Blue Willingham. Unofficially, of course. You call me the next time you get in trouble."

Doggett clapped him on his good shoulder and kept it short: "Thanks for savin' my ass."

Krukovitch listened, sipping whiskey and coffee, chain-smoking Carltons, refilling both of their glasses with a practiced hand. He only spoke once, when Burch told of killing Bartel then slipping the dead man's sunglasses over his sightless eyes.

"Good of you to do that, old sport. Kept the buzzards from pecking them out."

After detailing his own sins, he told Krukovitch of the rekindled fire of a murder cop and how good it felt to again be on the trail of killers, looking to avenge the murder of a deeply flawed but decent man instead of tracking down a wayward spouse or a cheap savings-and-loan chiseler. Then he connected the dots between Malo Garza, Blue Willingham, Bart and Gyp Hulett and the Bryte Brothers.

When he was done, he felt better than he had in a very long time, his bruised and battered soul unburdened and sandblasted. He took a long sip of Maker's, re-flamed the cigar and leaned back in the crook of the couch.

"How much of that you can use in the public prints without getting me killed or you thrown in jail, I don't know."

"Not a damn bit of your avenging angel act. As for the Bryte Brothers, Garza and all that, depends on how much of this gets in the public record — lawsuits, indictments, hearings and the like. Some stuff is already coming to the surface. Your buddy, Blue Willingham, was in line for a plum post on the Public Safety Commission, but word is the governor has put that one in the deep freeze. Lots of rumors floating around Austin about Sheriff Blue — none of them good. Bet you'll soon stop seeing his mug on all those Texas Tough On Drugs ads."

"Good. The High Sheriff is crooked as a snake and needs to take a fall, but whether he does or doesn't don't help me a damn bit with Garza. And those Bryte Brothers boys — they don't play nice and already know I'm the one who tied them to Bart Hulett's death. Them Houston boys will want payback."

"You worry too much. Like I said, the more of this that comes to light from other quarters, the less that light shines on you. There's a reason I called you. A little bird sang to me of some interesting developments that might put your mind at ease."

Krukovitch smiled and made Burch wait, refilling their glasses with whiskey and fiddling with his Bic lighter and a fresh Carlton. Why he bothered with those filtered low-nicotine paper tubes was a mystery to Burch.

"First off, let me tell you about your boy Garza. Got blown up by a car bomb two days ago in Monterrey. Word is, he and another *narco* named Flores were both taken out by a rival who has taken over their turf."

Burch started laughing and couldn't stop. *Goddam. He was right. Carla Sue suckered both those hombres. Played them against each other and got them dead. With a fat payoff from the third party, no doubt. Hope it was enough to get her long gone forever. Some place warm. With an ocean view.*

"What's so goddam funny?"

"A joke with a punch line I cain't never tell nobody."

Krukovitch stared at him with an annoyed look on his face.

"Don't pout. Malo gettin' blown to bits is good news. Might mean I can go back there and get my truck without getting smoked. What else you got?"

"Just this. The same little bird told me that over the past month, three Bryte Brothers execs have died. Two from heart attacks in their sleep. A third from a cerebral hemorrhage while on vacation in Costa Rica. That's on top of state auditors and bank examiners crawling up their ass about their little Cuervo County venture. The timing makes the cops suspicious, but they can't find any evidence of foul play."

"Got any names?"

"Deke Clayton and Benton Henderson. Clayton was head of operations. Henderson was a senior veep for new acquisitions and development. Third guy was royalty — Franklin Bryte Amato, in line to be the next CEO."

"Jesus."

"What do you know?"

"I'll tell you what I told the Rangers and the chief deputy of Cuervo County. That barnburner and the lawyer, Schoenfeldt, both fingered Clayton and Henderson. Clayton was the paymaster, Henderson greenlighted going after Bart Hulett's barn. But I didn't have a lick of evidence proving what those two songbirds said and they both got clipped. Amato's name never came up."

"He's family. Killing him sends a powerful message, if that's what happened."

"Yeah, stay the fuck out of Cuervo County."

"Same message you got. Think they'll lean on you about this?"

"I kindly doubt it. The Rangers weren't too keen about going after Clayton and Henderson on the word of an ex-cop and two dead men. There's a homicide detective down there who hates my guts, though."

"Cider Jones? He's that half-breed mystic who stares into the eyes of murder vics, right?"

"That's the one. If he gets hold of this, he could try to make my life difficult enough to hire a lawyer. But it won't get him nowhere. I've been sitting on my ass up here, healing up from a detached retina. Got medical records, doctor visits and Carol Ann stayin' over most every night to vouch for me. Got every bartender and waitress in this joint, too."

"But you know something, right?"

"Leave it alone, my friend. Natural causes can kill a man."

Burch drained his glass and glanced at his watch.

"Shit, I'm late. Gotta meet Carol Ann at the Hoffbrau. Thanks for the info and the confessional, your grace."

"Go with God and sin no more, my son. You and Carol Ann getting serious?"

"About as serious as I ever get."

"Ah, no worries, then. You'll fuck it up."

"A near certainty, old friend. Like drought in the summer and the Cowboys missing the playoffs."

Dinner with Carol Ann was great and the pendant was a big hit. She dragged him back to her place and fucked him to a frazzle, letting that silver and tiger's eye dangle between her breasts while she rode his cock.

When he limped into the foyer of his Marquita Street apartment building the next afternoon, he found a postcard tucked among the bills and grocery store ads stuffed in his mailbox. Once inside his apartment, he poured himself a short whiskey and flipped the card back and forth.

On the front was a beach scene — white sands, clear turquoise water and "'Come To Belize" scripted in red across the blue sky.

On the back was a Honduran stamp and postmark, his name and address and a single sentence with no signature. "Think of me every once in a while."

He stared at the card for a long time before killing off the whiskey and torching the thick paper stock with his Zippo.

"You bet, slick. But only for the rest of my life."

ABOUT THE AUTHOR

Jim Nesbitt is the author of three hard-boiled Texas crime thrillers that feature battered but dogged Dallas PI Ed Earl Burch — *The Last Second Chance*, a Silver Falchion finalist; *The Right Wrong Number*, an Underground Book Reviews "Top Pick"; and now, *The Best Lousy Choice*. Nesbitt was a journalist for more than 30 years, serving as an editor and roving correspondent for newspapers and wire services in Alabama, Florida, Texas, Georgia, North Carolina, South Carolina and Washington, D.C. He chased hurricanes, earthquakes, plane wrecks, presidential candidates, wildfires, rodeo cowboys, migrant field hands, neo-Nazis and nuns with an eye for the telling detail and an ear for the voice of the people who give life to a story. He is a lapsed horseman, pilot, hunter and saloon sport with a keen appreciation for old guns, vintage cars and trucks, good cigars, aged whiskey and a well-told story. He now lives in Athens, Alabama. Visit his Web site at: https://jimnesbittbooks.com.

Made in the USA
Las Vegas, NV
24 October 2021